LOVE'S TENDER MELODY

BOOK ONE OF THE 1N7 SERIES

GRETCHEN REDD

Pages Promotions, LLC
1221 Bowers Street, Unit 31
Birmingham, Michigan 48012-9998
www.PagesPromotions.com

© 2025 Gretchen Redd
© 2025 Cover Design By Gretchen Redd
Edited by Heather Ashlee; HB Ink, LLC
Published by Pages Promotions, LLC
Paperback ISBN: **978-1628283372**
E-Book ISBN: **978-1628283389**
Library of Congress Control Number: On File

ACKNOWLEDGEMENTS

Thanks to my wonderful husband, who has kept his eye-roll to a minimum as I've begun a new adventure in writing. You have been very supportive and stood beside me. It means a lot.

Also, I am grateful for my two wonderful children. My son, who helped me figure out tricky parts of my story; and my daughter, who should have been studying for her biology final, reviewed dozens of my book cover attempts. You two have gone on this ride with me.

Thank you to all my friends who have supported me and didn't laugh when I started writing again. You have all heard me drone on and on about my stories and have given me so much strength. Without you, I probably would have quit years ago.

To Mr. C, you have been a good friend and teacher. Any mistakes I've made concerning Seoul, Korean tradition, and the language are purely because I didn't listen to you! I hope to meet you in person one day and travel across Korea with you.

Mandy Jo, thanks for your encouragement and for hooking me up with the two best editors ever; Diana Kathryn and Heather! I couldn't have done this without the three of you.

사랑의 부드러운 멜로디

배빈의 이야기

Kim Baebin pulled a large suitcase to the elevator, utterly exhausted and thrilled to finally be alone. It had been a long, punishing week. Physically, it had been rough, but mentally, he was overwhelmed with demands that pushed him to the limit. *I would* kill *for one brief moment to breathe and hear myself think!* But his brain was stretched so thin, he didn't know if he could muster one coherent thought. This was one of those weeks when he definitely hated being team leader.

Not only did he have to worry about his own part in their K-pop group, Insatiable 7, or IN7 as they were generally known, but as the de facto "dad," it was his responsibility to take care of the other six members and make sure they stayed in line. He also acted as the go-between for his teammates, with their manager, and their recording label, South Korean Entertainment Corporation.

They were in a "transitional period" since winning the MAMA Artist of the Year Award. No longer newbies, they had to evolve and grow to keep their tenuous grip at the top. *Echos*, their fan group, wanted something different from their usual hip-hop style, and they needed to produce now or lose out on the next award cycle.

Bending to their fans' requests, last week, the group scrapped the entire routine for "Summer Crush" that they had been working on for a month in favor of a new, edgier dance. They also finished two recordings for the next album, which was due out in a few months.

He could tell their choreographer, Mr. Shu, and their teammate, Ko Kyong, the best dancer in the group, who also helped create their dances, were struggling to make the new changes. Everyone's frustration levels were rising between learning the new routine and maintaining their usual schedule of meetings, fan shows, and publicity sessions. They all needed a break.

This was supposed to be their downtime, the slowest part of the year. But the reality was, there was no downtime. *Ever.*

Baebin wished he could sleep for a month straight.

His mother was clamoring for a visit. It had been too long since her baby was home, but with the noisy, chaotic week he'd had, he couldn't stand any more togetherness. He needed to be alone in his new place.

"New" wasn't the right word. He bought the place six months ago, but had only been there a handful of times. It was safe to say the new apartment wasn't home. Yet. But he had high hopes. If only he had time to spend there with his crazy, busy, insane schedule, he could turn it into his oasis.

If only.

It was rare for someone in their early twenties to own an apartment in Seoul—particularly one this size and in this location. Four years of being a trainee—then a shooting superstar in the music industry—afforded Baebin this little luxury.

The overly long slog to make it onto the charts surprised everyone: the group, their families, and their fans. It should never have taken this long. Why they didn't quit—or SKEC didn't let them go years ago—still baffled him. He knew they were good. Very good. But every time they had their chance to debut, the door ultimately slammed in their faces. Year after year, time after time, destiny was denied. Until, *finally*, they got their chance.

Now they were "overnight stars," and everyone wondered where they were all this time. As if they had intentionally gone unnoticed, living in the shadows, loving the misery of nothingness.

Long days and millions of headaches later, he managed to buy his dream home. Baebin loved his friends and teammates. They were the next best thing to his family. But living in such close quarters for so long while being their team leader and *hyung*, the eldest in the group, was draining and exhausting. He needed space and, finally, at twenty-four, he got it.

The eighteenth-floor apartment filled the entire southeast side of a skyrise building just northwest of the Han River, overlooking city central. He was high enough that cars seemed like ants, and the noise wasn't noticeable. The views were amazing, day or night—mountains in the distance, tall buildings, shimmery pools of light from the bridges across the river, and the moving stream of taillights on the busy roads that weaved everywhere in Seoul. It's hard to have privacy in such a big city, but from his perch above it all, the hum of busyness faded away like stars in the sky.

He waved and dipped his head to the middle-aged man who stood sentry at the lobby desk, protecting the doctors, CEOs, and other minor celebrities who lived in the building. Baebin wasn't sure what the diminutive, sweet man could do in the face of rabid fans, but he appreciated the kindness and dedication of all the building staff.

Minor gatekeepers though they were, the security was still a major selling feature and one of the reasons he bought the apartment. Baebin encountered this particular man maybe five times in six months, but the sharp-eyed elder recognized him instantly and waved him past with a welcoming smile as if he were a regular fixture in the building.

Punching in his door code, he let himself into the *hyeongwan*. The entryway of the apartment was supposed to be where you shucked off outside life and changed your shoes—the gateway to the peace and privacy of home.

His was empty.

Crap. My slippers. I took them to the dorm. Images of his bandmates flashed across his mind's eye. *A sinbaljang would provide enough cubbies for everyone else to have slippers, too. And if it was low, it could be a shelf for keys....* He smiled. *I'll need one pair of slippers big enough for Yejoon's freakishly large feet.*

Baebin moved three steps inside, and already, he had a growing mental list of what he needed to buy. *Slippers,* sinbaljang, *umbrella stand....*

Kicking his shoes off into the corner, he stepped up into the open space. The massive living area with its tall ceilings, chandeliers, and plain white walls stared back at him. Bright afternoon spring sunlight streamed through the large bank of unprotected balcony windows, glinting off the weeks-old dust motes floating from the cardboard boxes in the empty space. The stale air reeked of mildew and the previous owner's grandma-esque perfume that still hadn't dissipated after all this time.

His happiness to finally be home was quickly replaced with a familiar, unpleasant weight again. The overwhelming task of turning this empty monster into something that suited him made his stomach churn. He really wanted a place of his own to escape work and the constant, never-ending swirl of activity. But he had neither the time, inclination, nor knowledge of how to do it.

Baebin didn't feel the warmth and carefree love of his parents' place. Or the serviceable mess of the dorm at the SKEC Campus, where he'd lived and trained with everyone since their days as trainees.

There was a stark difference here. His new personal life off-campus boiled down to a beautiful apartment, a ridiculously large pile of boxes, a few pieces of donated, mismatched furniture, and a piano.

He paid the previous owners nearly twice the instrument's worth to keep it, but the piano belonged in the space. Currently, dust covered its glossy black surface, and piles of boxes surrounded it. The piano sat unreachable and unused.

The boxes were an excellent goal for the long holiday weekend. It would be enough to keep his mind and body busy with something other than the group's latest mini album and production problems. He was reasonably sure his missing clothes and rice cooker were somewhere in the pile.

It was warm for May, and hazy remnants of the spring pollen still clung to the city, but Baebin opened the large sliding balcony doors and let in the fresh air. A stiff breeze gusted across the city and river, swooshing up the building to blow the dust inside his apartment into little tornados.

Even in stocking feet, his footsteps echoed as he passed the mess. Dragging his suitcase through the hall, he paused along the way to toss his backpack, overflowing with sheet music, into the locked room guarding a new, state-of-the-art sound studio.

The studio was his only requirement, and a major renovation was needed before moving in. It took weeks to convert the interior bedroom with its ensuite bathroom into his dream. He'd fully stocked the newly soundproofed space with microphones, computers, and all the recording equipment he would ever need. Anything he could do at the Campus, he could do here.

It was both a work in progress and the most complete room in the apartment. He was still missing storage compartments for office supplies and kitchenette equipment. His personal IN7 memorabilia, which he wanted to display in the room, hid somewhere in the boxes.

Laying his suitcase on the ground in his bedroom where the dresser should be, Baebin returned to the living room. He turned on the TV for company and opened a box. Several hours later, he found a few necessary items but no rice cooker. The sun was getting low, and he wanted air that didn't include decades-old dust.

And he needed food. There was nothing in the fridge. He had a few bags of instant ramen in the pantry, but other than that, it was empty, too. Food and drinks expanded his mental shopping list. *I should have stopped before coming here.*

Slippers, sinbaljang, umbrella stand, food, laundry soap, desk organizers, a coffee pot for the studio, hangers…. What else was I—oh! Patio chairs…

The same older man was still at the lobby desk. As Baebin approached, he read the nametag pinned to his jacket. Bak U-Jin. Bowing slightly at the waist, he begged for directions. Mildly surprised at the man's ability to expertly work Google Maps on his phone, Baebin was soon out the door, following the path to his destination.

Timing himself, he ran slowly up the steep hill, away from the river, keeping an eye on his phone to follow the twisting, winding streets of his sliver of the Dongbinggo-dong neighborhood that was a part of Seoul. Almost to his destination, he passed MinGo, the restaurant Mr. Bak recommended. It looked busy, and the delicious, spicy smells wafting through the open door made his stomach growl. Both were indications of a great meal.

The steep hill was different from the Campus's treadmills and the flat downtown streets he was used to. By the time he arrived, he was gasping for breath, and the backs of his thighs were burning.

Mr. Bak was right. The small outdoor fitness center was secluded, quiet, and perfect. Somewhat-new equipment sat scattered around, and the elevated view of the Han River and downtown were terrific. City windows shimmered orange and pink in the setting sun, and lights across the bridges flickered on. The weights at the *sansjang* were lower than he was used to, so Baebin quickly cycled through each piece three times with minimal breaks.

An hour later, the sun disappeared. Taking a moment to cool down, he sat on a secluded bench farthest from the only streetlight in the area. It was a perfect spot to unwind from the long week. The city that shimmered with the warm glow of sunset now sparkled like Christmas lights against the inky sky. Unwittingly, his mind drifted, and he contemplated his uncertain future while admiring the view below and all the people moving about in their own worlds.

Baebin wallowed in confusion and doubt. *I have to keep going. I have to do better. Be better. We won't get another chance like this. But all I've done is focus on today—what about tomorrow?*

His future should be easy. He kind of knew what he wanted. He wished for an entire life just like this last year with his teammates, but he knew it wouldn't happen. They had waited so long to get to the top. The MAMA award was great, but still, he felt unsettled. Already, the life ahead without IN7 weighed on him.

He had five years before mandatory enlistment. Less than five years left with the group as they stood now. Then what? *What will I do without the guys when this is all over? What can I possibly do alone?*

After everyone else cycled through their two-year military service after him, would IN7 still be together? *Will we disband then? Or will we already be has-beens?* Every cycle of albums, tours, and award seasons brought him closer to happiness... and *finality*.

Shaking off the depressing thoughts that sprinted circles in his head, Baebin started back down the hill, stretching his shaking muscles. He was pleased with the discovery of the *sansjang* overlook. His stomach rumbled, responding to the pungent, fermented smell of *kimchi* stew and spicy *buldak* from MinGo. Better than any neon sign, the savory, delicious aroma drew him inside.

The homey restaurant was as wide as it was deep, with a long counter separating the tables from large steaming vats of rice and soups and a window to the kitchen beyond. Even at this late hour, MinGo still buzzed with the conversations between families and friends from the many occupied tables in the small space.

Baebin planned on takeout until he noticed Bak U-Jin sitting alone at an empty table closest to the counter.

Hesitantly, he approached the older man, not wanting to disrupt his private dinner. "May I join you, Sir?"

Mr. Bak looked up, taken aback by the tall, younger man, but he graciously stood and offered the chair across from him.

The building staff knew Baebin "worked in music," but the finer details were left out. Intentionally. It didn't matter who lived there; their job was to guard the building, not keep scorecards on which residents had more interesting lives... even though several had dreadful, eye-rolling reputations. But this young boy was polite, rarely there, and when he was, no one ever heard a sound from him. He had friends over a few times, and they were all just as large and kind as he was.

Mr. Bak chattered nervously with his unexpected company. "I'm glad you are giving this restaurant a try. You won't be disappointed. MinGo is special. The owner is, too. She has her own recipe for *buldak*. It's called 'fire chicken' for a reason! She's owned the place for years, since before her husband passed away, and now runs it with her two children. We have been friends for more years than I can count."

Baebin sensed his close bond with the family in Mr. Bak's gentle smile but also noticed his pink cheeks and wondered if he felt something more for the owner. "The equipment and view at the *sansjang* were perfect, and if the food here is half as good as it smells, I'm sure I'll love it."

They ordered from the boy who worked alone in the busy restaurant and continued chatting. "I'm new to the neighborhood, so if you have any other recommendations, I would be grateful," Baebin said.

Mr. Bak nodded, instinctively knowing what the young man needed. "I'll prepare a map for you—help you avoid the busier areas around here. There are some nice, quiet places you can visit." He noticed the boy's shoulders relax, even as he continually checked and adjusted the hat that covered his bright-red hair and avoided eye contact with the rest of the room.

Suddenly, the door crashed open, banging off the moss-green wall behind it. Baebin whipped around at the heart-stopping commotion, and his throat spasmed when he saw her.

She was too much to take in all at once. Overly tall, she was thin but well-rounded in all the right places. She had long, stick-straight hair that flew out behind her like a satin cape, an instrument case in her hand, and a reed in her mouth. It was overwhelming.

Spitting fire, she found who she was looking for and made a beeline for him, screaming and pulling the reed from between her lips to wave it like a baton. "Min-Jun! Hey! You brat!"

Mr. Bak chuckled quietly and whispered over the table to Baebin, "That's Choi Go-Ri. The older sister. MinGo was named after those two. They love each other, but *oi!* Can they fight!" Mr. Bak's thin face squished in a grimace of pure delight, watching over his shoulder as the two combatants squared off at the counter.

Min-Jun fiercely spouted back at his sister, "Wha—! Get out! Leave me alone!" Flicking the dripping soup ladle still in his hand, bits of pork, cabbage, and onion arched through the air, halting his sister's forward charge as she tried to avoid the flying *kimchi* stew. "Why couldn't you work last night? I had a study session!" Throwing the ladle back into the vat, he pointed to two bowls he had dished up and jerked his head to Baebin and Mr. Bak.

Go-Ri stuck the reed back in her mouth and stalked over to them. Her flowered skirt flowed around her calves, and her heaving chest fascinated Baebin. He couldn't take his eyes off her. She thunked down their bowls, sloshing stew onto the table. When she got a whiff of Baebin, she wrinkled her nose and barely even acknowledged the family friend, who grinned at the young man's bewildered face.

Spinning back to her brother, she chased him around the counter, yelling, as he tried to retreat to the kitchen. "Study session, my butt! Don't lie to me—you skipped and stole my computer to play video games *again!* Do you know how much Omma pays for those extra classes?!"

"Oh, and you're not playing, too?" Min-Jun pointed to the case she dropped beside the counter. "You always leave Omma and me here so you can play at that stupid club! If you tell Omma I skipped class, I'll tell her you had students in here again this morning! You know she hates it when you teach in her office!"

"Aiech! You—! That's not the same! Where else am I going to teach right now? But you need those classes to get into University! Don't you *dare* skip again!" As quickly as she blew in, Go-Ri finished her tantrum, slammed her way out the door, and walked down the hill in a huff. None of the other patrons seemed shocked at the siblings' confrontation. They continued eating as if this were a common, everyday occurrence.

Min-Jun peeked through the kitchen window to look for his sister. With a long-suffering growl, he brought over rice, chicken, and beer to Mr. Bak and Baebin, slapping them on the table with as much force as his sister had.

"I skipped *one* study session, and it was like I caused the North to invade again! Mr. Bak, it's not fair! She's always off doing something, but I can't take a break? Why am I always the bad one?!" Not giving the elder a chance to answer, he huffed away to clean the soup splatters before they could leave red chili paste stains on the counter and floor.

Mr. Bak grinned at Baebin. "I don't know why he's surprised. Go-Ri lives for music. Everyone knows it. You should hear her play. I've never heard someone as talented as her." He nodded to himself in amazement and dug into his dinner.

"What does she play?"

"I think the shorter list is what she *can't* play; seems like she's mastered every instrument in Korea—maybe the world. She must be heading to *The Jazz House* for a gig tonight."

Baebin would never tell his mother, but MinGo was better than one of her home-cooked meals. Chili peppers lit sparks in his mouth, but the unique blend of garlic, ginger, and rice syrup tempered the heat of the chicken. Baebin polished off the stew next, sopping up the remaining liquid with spoons of rice. After their meal and another beer, the two men companionably parted ways at the door.

The mini mart down the street was still open, and Baebin reviewed his shopping list. *Food… laundry soap (or was it dish soap?)…. She's pretty. I wonder if Mr. Bak was just bragging about how well she could play….* Twenty minutes later, his hands full of shopping bags, Baebin pulled out his phone and texted his favorite bodyguard, Chu Kwan.

B: U BORED?
CK: OF COURSE

Chu Kwan chimed back instantly. He was young, single, and hated sitting still.

Within an hour, Baebin returned home to shower and change into his favorite comfortable jeans, a sock hat over his hair, and oversized black-framed glasses. Kwan picked him up outside the apartment, and they headed to *The Jazz House.*

Nervous energy rolled in his stomach, mixing with the undigested stew, as they drove the short distance to the tiny bar sandwiched in the middle of a busy block. *Good grief, what am I doing?* he thought. *I have better things to do. Like sleep.*

The owner of the small, unassuming club met them at the back door. He bowed low several times, holding out his business card with two hands. He had never received a call from the Campus before and was anxious to learn about the two men coming to his club.

If he played this visit right, he could make a big profit. South Korean Entertainment Corporation was one of the largest entertainment companies in Korea, and visitors from SKEC meant he was finally getting noticed.

Mr. Shin walked them over to their table. It was tucked out of the way but had a clear view of the stage.

The second set had already started, and Choi Go-Ri sat perched on the edge of a tall stool, playing the sax. One long leg stuck straight out, while the heel of the other shoe hooked on the top rung of the stool, hiking up her skirt enough to give Baebin a glimpse of toned calf. Eyes closed, foot twitching in time with the offbeat, her fingers seemed to melt over the keys. She pulled, drew, and urged each note effortlessly from the liquid melody.

The piece intrigued and tugged at Baebin's music-loving soul. He didn't know much about jazz but knew enough to recognize her talent immediately. The drummer and bass guitarist on stage with her were capable, but she earned the spotlight.

She was good. Better than the Kim Sisters from the '50s; better than BTS' first hit. He just couldn't seem to stop looking at her. She was even prettier now than she was at the restaurant.

Chu Kwan knew even less about jazz, but always got a kick out of the strange trips Baebin took him on. The two men dropped their designated protector/protectee roles almost as soon as they met two years ago. As Baebin's popularity grew, along with the need for Chu Kwan's protection, so did their friendship. Clandestine excursions while on tours and at home became their escape from the reality of working in entertainment.

They were the same size and could pass as twins, but that is where the similarity ended. Unlike Baebin, Chu Kwan could swing a guy over his shoulder in an instant, but couldn't even sing in the shower. Their easy camaraderie, which allowed their appreciation for each other to blossom without demanding requirements or expectations, made them fast friends.

Both loved quirky, unique adventures and were always up for trying new things. As long as it was under the radar, it was a green light to them. From an art museum in France to a tuk-tuk ride in Thailand to a disco club in Berlin—which got a little hairy—of all the nighttime trips he had been on with Baebin, *The Jazz House* was a new one for his diary.

The music was good, and the room filled fast. Chu Kwan kept busy for a while, judging and meticulously inspecting the crowd. It was an easy Friday night. The place was packed mostly with ladies drinking wine and a few guys puffing their chests with no hope for a hook-up—all out celebrating the end of a work week.

Baebin was left alone to ogle the long-legged, long-haired beauty rotating instruments on stage. She was just as talented on the keyboard and oboe as she effortlessly switched back and forth between songs and sometimes played more than one in the same piece.

After a final look around, Kwan sat back and turned to Baebin. Following the direction of his stare, Kwan snorted in amusement. *Mmm, that explains this trip.* The girl was the closest thing to his friend's type he'd seen in a while. Hot, tall, unpretentious, and a fabulous musician… even if it was jazz. He hid his smile and hollered over the din, "She's not bad."

Baebin made a throaty grunt, grabbed his cola, and sat back. The flush on his neck had nothing to do with the warmth of the room.

While watching the crowd around them, Kwan also kept an eye on his friend, as his friend kept an eye on the girl. Deciding to play nice, he withheld the male ribbing and left Baebin to drool in private. *This is going to be interesting,* he thought, grinning to himself.

Before the third set ended, Baebin and Chu Kwan slipped out the back door, unnoticed by anyone except the owner. Mr. Shin, disappointed at the cheap tab, hoped this wouldn't be the only visit to his club from the men.

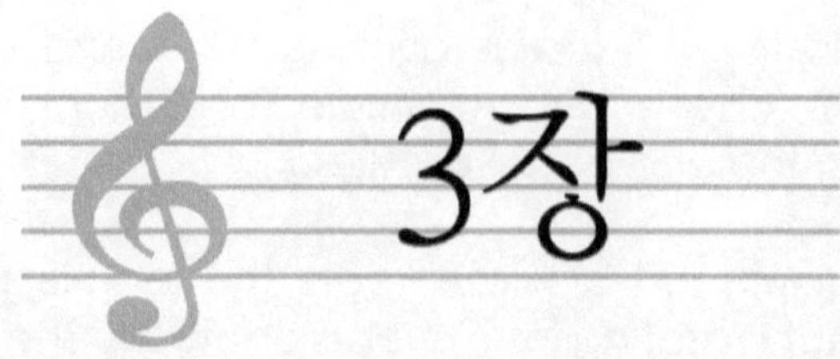

Baebin woke to blinding sunlight punching holes into his brain. He didn't even drink at the bar last night. Either he needed to move to a new place that didn't face the rising sun or buy blackout curtains. The pillow he crammed over his face only made him stuffy, sweaty, and annoyed.

Giving up on sweet extra sleep, he changed his focus to his rumbling stomach.

There was food in the fridge now, but he only had one pot. This was also annoying. He had a lot of work to do today if he was going to stay here another night. On the verge of surrendering to his mother's whims, full meals, and his childhood room with more than a mattress on the floor, he took the new box of cereal and his bowl from yesterday to the living room floor to eat.

Baebin ran through his shopping list again in his mind until he felt his eyes cross. *Slippers... ~~food~~ got some—not enough... ~~dish~~ laundry soap—wrong one... desk organizers & coffee pot for studio... broom... hangers... umbrella stand...* It was too long. *It really doesn't matter,* he thought ruefully. He needed at least two of everything in the store, anyway. He dug out a notebook from his work bag and began writing.

Lists and notes always helped clear his mind. The guys laughed at him for writing down the smallest details, but having things on paper gave him a screwy sense of controlled freedom. The cereal box was half gone before he finally felt full and had enough energy to move.

He started going through more boxes. Three hours later, he found clothes in a box labeled "books" and in another one from Mom, his favorite old blanket. Everything smelled musty, like old wet cardboard. He unpacked some small kitchen items and left them next to the sink with his breakfast bowl, ready to be cleaned.

He desperately wanted a nap, but with only a few days off, he didn't want to waste his free time sleeping. His two options were to continue unpacking or go shopping again. He needed to buy laundry soap if he wanted to use the blanket tonight, and he really wanted to cook dinner.

Shopping midday on a weekend at the giant box store wasn't his best idea. Several fans recognized him, and it was difficult to concentrate on his list. Still, he gave everyone who approached him his personal time and gentle, carefree, trademark smile.

In the open, Kim Baebin was Yong-ee. Initially, he created the stage name to insulate his family from his work, but as IN7's popularity grew, he appreciated the separation for himself. His second name was a light switch that kept his private and public lives separate.

Fans were his livelihood—the reason he worked so hard. The better he did for the fans, the more they appreciated him, and the more confident he felt in his ability to weather the hard times. It was a symbiotic relationship that he enjoyed. *Most of the time.* It came with the job.

He knew pictures of him pushing his overflowing cart— unwieldy with everything he could find in the kitchen aisle, pillows, soap, cleaning supplies, and more food—would be posted on the *Echos* fan group webpage before he even left the store. An idol shopping for a broom guaranteed a week's worth of comments. *As if stars didn't need a broom.*

After multiple trips with his apartment building's luggage cart, Baebin was finally able to unpack his new toys. Music blared and echoed through the rooms, energizing him again for the work ahead. He crammed everything he could in the dishwasher, loaded the washing machine, and returned to the pile.

The large, thin crates standing in the corner turned out to be, as expected, the pictures and paintings he collected over the last few years while on tour. Ripping the foreign shipping labels off, he tucked them into their frames and scattered them around the apartment, ready to be hung.

Having the pictures out cheered him up. The wild, eclectic array of colors and prints brightened the rooms and made him feel like he was finally getting somewhere. He added a hammer and nails to the ever-evolving list.

Progress slowed when he unearthed four heavy boxes from the Campus. Unlocking the studio door, Baebin slowly unpacked his treasures along the wall. The stack of photos and album covers grew next to multiplying rows of trophies and awards. The pile of gifts and mementos from his friends and fans overflowed in the corner.

Baebin felt an almost disembodied interest in seeing what he'd mindlessly kept for no reason. *Turns out, something stuffed in a drawer years ago because you were too busy to throw it away can make you cry six years later.*

The dance card and bib number for his SKEC tryout and Chinmae's first notes to him before they became best friends in the group, along with a huge pile of IN7 concert tickets that Manager Kim saved for each of them over the years, moved Baebin to tears.

Tears turned to groans when a simple blue fabric strip peeked out from under a ratty rabbit headband caked in old makeup and hair gel. What they not-so-affectionately called the "Five Step Hell" almost tore the group apart. It was a rollercoaster night of stress, exhaustion, pain, and emotions.

Almost a year of training had dissolved into bickering attitudes of superiority. Their lead choreographer and dance trainer, finally out of patience, turned into the worst drill sergeant this side of the DMZ.

Baebin had intentionally forgotten that traumatic night.

With ribbons tied to their legs and arms, their choreographer ordered them to spend hours repeating the same five steps over and over *and over* again, without a break, until seven talented individuals became one singular unit.

The bond to murder their choreographer transformed them into the most in-sync, well-matched, fluid group in the K-pop industry. But all that was second to the respect and admiration they learned for each other by surviving the breakdown together.

IN7 made it through that night, and before they crashed in their beds, they were forever bonded as friends.

If it weren't for the blue ribbon, they would never have won MAMA. Draping the strip of fabric over the large gold trophy, Baebin gave up unpacking and ran to the *sansjang*.

Beating yesterday's time, he skipped the equipment and sat on his favorite bench overlooking the city.

He looked out over Seoul. Thinking about the memorabilia he'd unearthed, his thoughts shifted from days gone by to what lay ahead. Each of the city lights below seemed to embody an idea, a suggestion, or a path toward his future. Ribbon. Ribbon and trophy. Ribbon, trophy, and his studio. Ribbon, trophy, and his *future*. As the string of lights stretched into the distance, he couldn't tell which was the brightest—the *right* light.

Just like last night, his thoughts spiraled. *What am I going to do next? What am I going to do without my friends? I know they look up to me, but I'm nothing without them. I don't want all this to end.*

Growling at himself, Baebin threw his hat down and yanked at his hair. *STOP with this pity-party! Wallowing doesn't get you anywhere! Just focus and think!* Snatching up the hat, he stalked down the hill.

The battle inside his skull fizzled as he slowed to a halt outside of MinGo. He really wanted to cook for himself tonight, but he couldn't get over the tantalizing, mouth-watering smell. *It's all about the food,* he told himself.

He knew it wasn't.

What would she be like today? Was she working? Just one peek to feed his curiosity. MinGo was crowded again, but he only saw Min-Jun clearing tables while an older lady, who must have been his mom, cooked in the kitchen. Not only did they have the same cheeky personality and physical build, but they shared the same almond eyes.

Did Choi Go-Ri have the same eyes as well? He had seen her twice, but he didn't know the shape of her eyes. She hadn't looked at him. Disappointed, Baebin hid in the corner, quietly looking around as Min-Jun packed his order to go.

Passing the convenience store next door, his heart skipped. *She works here, too? How many jobs does she have? The restaurant, the store, and playing at the club— does she make any time for herself?*

He stood gawking at her through the windows, watching Go-Ri stock a shelf while listening to her earbuds. Multiple pencils stuck out from her twisted knot of hair, exposing a long, slender neck that he itched to touch.

He sniffed his shirt, praying he didn't smell as bad as yesterday, before slipping inside the store. She bagged his drinks, took his money, and returned to stocking, never looking at him.

Long after his heart rate returned to normal, he continued to think about Go-Ri.

The rest of the holiday flew by in a blur of monotony. Whittling away at the boxes was his priority, but Baebin made time every day to visit the *sansjang* and often stopped for food on the way home. He tried other places, but nothing so far measured up to MinGo.

After begging Mom for her recipes, he officially used his new kitchen for the first time. His tablet sat propped up on the counter, covered in fingerprints of caked chili powder, soybean paste, and oil splatters. His first meal needed improvement, but was pleasantly edible.

Celebrating with a cheap bottle of convenience-store red wine, he polished off the whole meal in front of the TV.

Go-Ri worked every night, either at the restaurant or the store, and he always saw her with earbuds in or reading a book. He grew more intrigued every time he saw her. It wasn't just her gorgeous hair, curvy body hidden under flowing skirts and loose tops, or her musical talent that sucked him in; there was something strange about her. Tantalizing. Interesting. Fascinating. She was getting under his skin.

Watching, almost to the point of stalking, he noted she appeared friendly and even feisty with her brother at times, but her energy coiled tightly under strict control. Her lips never fully widened or relaxed. The palpable barrier around her shouted, "Stay away!" But just once, he wished to see Choi Go-Ri truly smile. He desperately wondered what color her eyes were.

He wasn't bothered by the fact that she didn't know who he was. He didn't expect everyone in Korea to fall on their knees before him. But she never even *noticed* him, even as a normal man. They never had a conversation beyond, "Will that be all?" Her attention never strayed further north than his shoulders. *Hello…! Just look at me. Just once!*

Baebin was so flustered, he didn't know what to do. *Good god. I'm twenty-four! This is worse than puberty! If I can talk to the girls in UNI and SugarCube at work, I can say hi to Choi Go-Ri!*

He spent the last morning of his vacation working out at the *sansjang* as the sun rose over the city. Sitting on the stone wall to cool off, Baebin let his thoughts wander. It would be a while before he could return here.

It surprised him that he was already sad to go. Just last week, he was ambivalent about being at the apartment and almost left it to escape to his parents' home. With IN7's upcoming schedule, it would be at least a week before he could come back.

And see Go-Ri again.

Most of the guys would be coming by tonight to reconnect before work started again in the sound studio and on the dance routine for "Summer Crush."

Only two of them had their own places so far, and his was the newest and closest to the Campus. The apartment was far from finished, but a week's worth of work made a huge difference. The cold, boring apartment was coming to life.

The lights were still off at MinGo, but the door was open, and Baebin could see Go-Ri working inside.

Horrible screeching that no one could *ever* confuse with music, but possibly emanating from a clarinet, sounded from the back room, and she reprimanded the player as she started up the grill.

Noticing him in the doorway, she gave a slight bow before waving him in and calling a halt to the ear-piercing noise. Baebin grinned to himself. *She snuck her student in for a music lesson again. I wonder if her brother knows.*

Baebin's large delivery order for the evening received a raised eyebrow, and it was only after he paid that he remembered to buy water for the walk home.

She gestured to the cooler and took off to the back room, grimacing and yelling at her student as he started honking once more.

Yet again, she didn't notice me, he thought. *If I can perform for thousands at concerts, I should have the guts to say hello without sounding like an idiot.* Go-Ri had already forgotten about him as the lesson continued; there was nothing left to do but take the free water and go. He missed his chance. *Again.*

After cleaning the best he could, he was ready with drinks and snacks when he heard his door code beep. Han Tae-Si, Ko Kyong, Chun Daeho, and Yoo Chinmae came in, and shoes and bags quickly littered the floor of the *hyeongwan*. Kwon Yejoon was coming later after his radio show, and Paek Jaemin stayed behind one extra day with his family in Busan. *Crap. I forgot to get slippers.*

Tae-Si made a beeline for the gaming system and commandeered one of the few spots on the couch. Others sat sprawled on pillows on the living room floor or at the counter, inhaling the food Baebin set out. The rooms that just hours ago were lonely now rang with music and shouts of laughter.

Time sped by as the latest updates on family life and tales of greatly exaggerated home dramas swirled from one friend to another. All seven of them had close, loving families except for Chinmae, the *maknae*, or baby, of the group.

His friend was tight-lipped, and what little he'd shared of his childhood over the last six years was dreadful. His life was the classic melodramatic child-actor abuse story that was too crazy to be believed. But Baebin had seen the scars to prove it. Chinmae escaped when he got the chance to become a SKEC trainee. He was one of the few who actually liked the seclusion of the dorms.

Alcohol fueled their stories, weaving new ones with long-ago events from their trainee days until their cheeks and sides hurt. Daeho's comedy show recount of his two sisters fighting over a shirt before their dates had them rolling on the floor, while Kyong and Tae-Si took turns arguing over who was at fault for losing the video game. Chinmae, for the most part, sat on the counter, laughing at everyone else while hoarding an entire tray of apple slices.

Rarely did the guys spend so much time apart, so the mini reunion off-campus, just hanging out and not working, was refreshing.

The intercom rang over the din, and Baebin had to shush his friends to hear. Mr. Bak's voice came through the speaker. "Your order from MinGo is here. I'm sending her up now."

About time! He glanced over at the kitchen, where he could hear Daeho rifling through his pantry. *I'm already out of snacks, and Daeho's going to find my ramen.*

Wait, her? *Choi Go-Ri is here?* Instantly, Baebin had a terrible idea.

Dumping a trash can full of empty bottles and cans on the piano, he begged Kyong and Tae-Si to play along with his practical joke. Kyong lay sprawled on top like a cabaret singer with Tae-Si ready to start one of their popular old songs just in time for the doorbell to ring.

Baebin's heart raced, and he chewed on the corner of his lip when he answered the door. She was so pretty. Her salmon-colored top brought out the tiny pink flowers scattered among the large blue ones on the skirt she wore the first night at the club. Half her hair was twisted in a tight up-knot, sharply defining her features while highlighting its glossy length.

"Come in. It will be easier to put it all in the kitchen." Stepping through the doorway, he reached out to help carry the heavy metal delivery container, but Choi Go-Ri pulled away sharply out of reach, her blank gaze never leaving his Adam's apple.

Agonizing seconds passed as she debated what to do. Grudgingly, she followed him into the kitchen to unload the cartons and rice boxes just as Tae-Si started pounding away at the piano. Go-Ri recoiled from the sudden raucous music and sucked in a breath.

Her whole body shivered and clenched tightly as she searched frantically for the source of the painful noise. Baebin could see her visceral reaction, as if an invisible monster had suddenly appeared in the room, tracing evil tentacles up her spine.

Instantly, he realized his stupid idea was worse than he thought. This wasn't what he planned. She was supposed to be amused, not disgusted and enraged.

The music was beyond awful. Already afraid of being inside the strange apartment, and then the banging combined with the disrespect for the gorgeous Steinway, covered in trash, and the two clowns treating it like a toy, infuriated her beyond all sane reasoning. She snapped. Anger overruled all coherent thought. Her pale nervousness turned pink and then fire-red with fury, her voice rising with every word and ending in a screech as she laid into them. "Stop! Stop it! Get off! Don't do that! How dare you treat an instrument like that! Why would you—"

Daeho poked his head out of the pantry, and the noise from the piano halted as five men gaped at her. She slapped a hand over her mouth, cutting off the tantrum that now echoed in the space.

In the deafening silence that followed, Go-Ri's eyes traveled to each man before locking onto Baebin.

For the first time, she *really* looked at him. Black pupils replaced the warm chocolate eyes, and tears threatened to form before she managed to grab the last sliver of herself and yank it back behind her top-secret shutters.

"I-I'm sorry. I shouldn't have—please don't tell!" Choi Go-Ri unceremoniously dumped the food onto the counter and, hugging the metal container tightly, she retreated with a last peek at the men around her and the piano.

Go-Ri ran to the *hyeongwan* and barreled headlong into a hard body.

A whoosh of air escaped Yejoon as he lunged out to stabilize both her and the container.

Flinching, she shrieked in fright, snatched the container back, tripped over shoes and bags, and ran out the door.

Everyone stayed frozen, staring at their *hyung* and the doorway where the girl disappeared. Yejoon stood in the entry, rubbing his bruised belly, his jaw hanging to his knees.

"What did I miss?" he finally managed to ask as he walked into the room.

"Who's the weirdo?" Daeho quizzed as he abandoned his search for ramen in the pantry and joined the group.

"Takes one to know one. And don't call her that," Baebin retorted sharply, grabbing a rag and the trash can. He cleaned the piano in two wide swipes, pushing Kyong onto the floor, his backside narrowly missing boxes. "She's from the restaurant nearby. I've seen her around a few times." Baebin flopped onto the bench next to Tae-Si, smacking the keys with his forehead in a painfully dissonant chord.

"I don't think she liked Kyong's singing!" Tae-Si laughed as he rubbed *hyung's* head, sending it banging against the keys.

"Dude, stuff it! She couldn't hear me over your lousy playing!" Kyong countered as he picked himself up off the floor before turning to *hyung*. "So, what was up with the joke? It was for her right, not Yejoon?"

Everyone gathered around the piano, eyeballing him expectantly for more details, except Chinmae. He stood alone, resting a hip on the bookcase, arms crossed and eerily silent as he watched his friend. The glower that shimmered in his icy stare made Baebin regret the entire event more than Choi Go-Ri's outburst.

Yeah, why did I do that? That was the stupidest thing he had ever done. He wasn't in elementary school anymore, but he'd just pulled a girl's pigtails. *I just wanted her to notice me, to look at me.* Well, she looked at him, all right. *God, I'm an idiot.* "I don't know. I thought she would laugh. I haven't seen her laugh." *I even sound like an idiot!*

"She doesn't laugh? She really is a weirdo!" Daeho held up his hands, swiftly retreating from *hyung's* warning glare. "Sorry, not a weirdo. I meant to say… unique."

That wasn't any better, but Baebin let it go.

"Annnd? What else? She's hot. You like her?" Kyong wiggled his eyebrows, making kissy faces that sent the others cackling.

Baebin knew they wouldn't let it go, no matter how he answered. The bloom of embarrassment spread up Baebin's neck. "Mmm. Yeah. I like her."

"Sooo? You gonna ask her out?" Tae-Si grinned. "You know, we need to vet your dates. We can't let just anyone take you away from us."

"Maybe. I'd like to. I gotta get her to look at me first." His friends howled with laughter, making his ears turn red. *Ugh. Think before you open your mouth, you moron!* Chinmae was still glowering at him, the rest were teasing him, and he was regretting everything.

"I don't think she knows who we are," Yejoon mused, once he was able to settle down and stop laughing. "That's a good sign. She didn't seem like a wacko fan faking it to get close."

"Mmm. Yeah. She's not. But it's more than that. I can't explain it. She's different. It's not just her looks or her personality that interests me. I also found out she's a crazy talented musician. I mean, award-winning great. She teaches in the mornings at the restaurant, and I've seen her play at a Jazz House over in the next neighborhood. She's unbelievable."

"Whoa, seriously!?" Those around the piano talked over each other, giving him dating advice.

As if they even knew how to date. The few high school crushes or the clandestine outings several of them had since they'd debuted didn't count. Even so, their advice was freely given and widely discussed.

As everyone headed to the kitchen and started cleaning up the pile of spilled food, Chinmae detoured and stuffed his feet back in his shoes. "I'm tired. I'll head out now."

Name-calling and whines ensued, but Chinmae only spared one last cool glance at Baebin before the door shut behind him. *This isn't over.*

Go-Ri flew past the desk and Mr. Bak, leaving him calling after her in confusion. The sudden burst of anger had receded, leaving her shaking and nauseous. Yelling at her brother was one thing, but for a moment, she had forgotten her carefully constructed wall.

Not only could she have been hurt, but now the reputation of her mom's restaurant could be, as well.

The metal container clattered to the ground next to the scooter as she crouched down, hugging her knees and trying to fill her shriveled lungs with air to clear away the dark spots that floated in her vision.

How could I have been so stupid? Never on deliveries do I go inside! No talking. Keep a safe distance... That man who kept coming around this week made her forget her rules. He was so big and quiet; he made her shiver. *I didn't even see the others until that horrid music played! How could I have done that?! Don't I know better? Stupid. Stupid. Stupid!*

Never again. Stay away from him! Remember... don't let him—oh, I hate deliveries! She needed to strengthen her defenses. She needed to remember who she was now. She needed... needed. Scrubbing the heels of her palms into her eye sockets. *Breathe Choi Go-Ri. You're okay. Breathe. In and out...* She didn't stand until the buzzing in her ears dropped to nothing more than a hum.

Swiping away the mascara she'd smeared everywhere and squeezing the helmet on over her topknot, Go-Ri lashed the container to the scooter, just behind her sax, and eased into traffic. She was going to be late for the gig at *The Jazz House*.

Chinmae watched as she pulled away before climbing into his taxi. She had left long before he did, and he was surprised to see her still there, hunched over on the curb. He felt the shivers as they raced through her. He let out the breath he'd been holding when she stood and collected herself.

The moment he saw her in the doorway, Chinmae felt the delivery girl's anxiety and carefully studied her as she was drawn deeper into the apartment. When the girl turned into a banshee, it startled him as much as the rest, but he felt something else. It wasn't just anger. In that quick moment before she retreated, he saw through her window, and he recognized the familiar reflexive emotion that he'd experienced since childhood. The reaction born from pain and trauma. *Hyung, what were you thinking? That was a terrible mistake. You have no idea what you've done.*

The next morning, everyone sprawled on the dance floor at the Campus, trying their best to stretch and sober up. Chinmae looked at Baebin and jerked his head towards the door.

The hall hummed with people moving about, starting their morning training sessions. Each time a door opened, a burst of music echoed across the linoleum, only to be cut short with a *clack* as the door closed again.

Chinmae paced for a moment, his fists in the pockets of his joggers, pulling his baggy pants down. All night, he thought about how to confront his friend, but he was still afraid of crossing the line.

Baebin waited for the tongue-lashing that was coming. Rarely did Chinmae speak his mind. When he did, everyone knew it was only after deep consideration—and it was usually well deserved. Baebin huddled within himself, ashamed.

Chinmae stared at a dirt spot on the wall just over *hyung's* shoulder and stepped closer so his deep voice wouldn't carry in the busy space. "What were you thinking last night? It may have been funny to you, but obviously not to her."

Baebin whispered back, timbre low and shaking. "I don't know either. It was stupid. I just…" *Just what?* Wanted to see her react, see *something* from her? *Why did I do it?* "I just wondered what she would do." Baebin stared at his shoes and pulled his hoodie tighter over his head to protect his body heat from the cold drafts of the hall... and hide his face from his friend.

"You kidding me? Are you twelve? You brought a strange girl alone into the room with five of us to *test her*? Do you know how wrong that was—on so many levels?" Chinmae was slowly working himself into a lather. His glare flicked back and forth from the wall to his friend. "Not just for us and our reputation if she cries fowl, but for her own safety and protection. We wouldn't do anything, but how was she supposed to know that?"

Chinmae continued to stare at the spot on the wall— presumably a dead bug that had been squished decades ago—trying to hold back his anger. "She wasn't just upset. She was scared. She was afraid before she even came in. Who knows what your stupid stunt did to her? You're an idiot. I don't know what your game is, but when, *not if*, it falls apart, it won't end well. For either of you. Don't make the rest of us clean up your mess." Chinmae glared at his *hyung*, poking a finger into his chest. "You need to apologize and fix it."

He left Baebin standing alone in the hall as he stomped back inside. For the rest of the week, Chinmae avoided him at all costs.

Baebin rushed back to the apartment the first chance he had. On the way, he called MinGo for delivery but was disappointed to see Min-Jun instead of Go-Ri with his order.

Glowering and shoving the food at Baebin, Min-Jun said, "I don't know what you did, but *noona* has refused to deliver here again. You don't know her, so I'm warning you: don't mess with my sister." He walked away without another word.

Baebin was already in a foul mood from getting reprimanded by Chinmae and had hoped to put an end to this mess tonight. The food sat untouched on the counter while Baebin changed into pajamas, pulled beers out of the fridge, and slept on the couch for two days, uncertain how to fix his mistake.

The upcoming Japan trip was the dress rehearsal for their long-awaited debut tour in the United States at the end of the following month.

If they weren't recording or dancing in preparation for it, they were promoting it through TV shows and fan events. Most of the time, they worked together as a unit, but sometimes, they split up for "surprise appearances" around Seoul and the surrounding towns.

Their latest mini album, *Insatiably More*, released a few months ago, and already has several songs on the music charts. It took endless meetings to arrange their new concert setlist. Their new show meant adjusting the routines, costumes, and stage design. It was a lot of behind-the-scenes work for everyone at the Campus—and in a short timeframe—but the puzzle was finally coming together.

All that remained now was running through everything until it became muscle memory. They were leaving for Japan in eight days.

Baebin had been home here and there for time alone, but he no longer had long weekends free. Forward progress at the apartment ground to a halt, and he hadn't touched the remaining boxes in weeks. The mid-summer heat baked the apartment and opening the sliding doors didn't help. At least the funky mildew cardboard smell was finally dissipating.

The trips were an excuse to see Go-Ri. The nights he found her at MinGo, she avoided him. At the convenience store, she wouldn't even ask, "Anything else?" Her barrier was even colder and higher than before.

She barely acknowledged him when he stopped by for water in the mornings. Baebin desperately wanted to talk to her and apologize, but every time he came in, she would just point to the cooler and retreat to her work, doing double duty opening the restaurant and teaching her students.

Her morning lessons intrigued him. Over the last two months, Baebin could pick out a few of the students and followed their progress as they improved. The eclectic mix of modern orchestra and traditional Korean instruments was as wide as the age and talent range of the students. *How many instruments can she play? Mr. Bak wasn't lying when he said the list was long.*

Gradually, Go-Ri stopped scowling at him; she was back to her usual, distant self. He was half-tempted to get a new tattoo on his neck, just for her—an arrow saying, "Look up."

Unsettled, Baebin still hadn't figured out what to do. *It should be so simple. Just apologize, introduce yourself formally, and get it over with.* The longer he waited, the harder it was.

Leaving a few *won* on the counter, he walked out each time without saying a word.

Mr. Bak sat at the desk well past his usual shift, and Baebin made a detour to chat with the elderly man. Since their first meal together, the two had formed a bond. It was their new habit to eat together when possible, and often

Baebin would walk the shy, lonely widower home afterward.

It was the only bright spot to his infrequent visits home. Chatting with Mr. Bak late into the night, after a grueling few days, gave him peace. Comfort. The elder had become a friend and confidant. He helped Baebin get his head on straight, like the feeling he got making lists and notes. Mr. Bak gave him a sense of controlling freedom.

"Go-Ri is playing solo tonight. She tells me it will be music that she wrote herself." Mr. Bak's quiet voice rang out through the empty lobby behind Baebin as he pushed the elevator button to go upstairs.

The doors opened. Then shut. Mr. Bak didn't bother hiding his grin as he watched the young man wrestle with himself outside the elevator. Baebin turned and huffed back past the desk, wrinkling his nose at Bak U-Jin, who just laughed and waved him away.

I'm being ridiculous. Why am I so fixated on this girl who doesn't even know I'm alive? This is infuriating. Baebin wanted to slap himself.

It was the middle of the week, and the bar was barely half full. The AC provided a refreshing change from the humid heat outside but did nothing to dispel the odor of spilled beer that always seemed to permeate bars and clubs. Businessmen on their second—or third—round of an after-work party formed the largest and rowdiest group. Bottles littered their tables as the drunk men shouted over each other and milled about in the small space. The whole atmosphere made Baebin's skin crawl.

He quietly wandered to the end of the bar closest to the stage and found a seat away from everyone else. Despite trying to remain a small, nonexistent, unremarkable, mouse, the bartender spotted the new regular right away and opened a bottle of cola.

After sliding it over, the young man in a vest and tie finished washing a few glasses and cleaned the workstation.

He knew who the customer was; his sister was a huge *Echos* groupie with IN7 posters plastered all over her walls. He was surprised that a pop idol had become a recent visitor to such a small, odd place like *The Jazz House*.

The loud, drunk men called out for more soju and whiskey, but the bartender only waved to them. "I've been slowing them down for the last hour. I can't wait for them to leave."

"Are they going to be a problem for you?" Baebin worried the group was too difficult for the bartender to handle alone.

"I hope not." He looked over Baebin's shoulder at the group, keeping an eye on them, especially the loudest table. "They won't recognize you, Yong-ee. Just keep your hat on and face away from them." The bartender winked at him and grinned. Pointing to Baebin's hair, he asked, "You changed the color. New show?"

Baebin's eyes widened briefly before he nodded, adjusting the hat. The chances of being recognized *and* treated like a human were one in a thousand. "Time for a change. And please, call me Kim Baebin."

The bartender dipped his head in acknowledgement. "No friend tonight?"

"Mmm. He's busy, and jazz isn't his thing. He just comes to keep me company." Chu Kwan accompanied him a few times for fun off the clock, but Baebin knew his friend was just being nice. The small club was too dull for him. The radio cut out, along with their talk, as music started onstage. Baebin turned to watch.

She sat alone, wearing jeans that hugged her round backside and slender legs. As usual, a heel of one shoe was caught in the top rung of the stool. The soulful, breathy sound of her sax wove around a prerecorded soundtrack that played over the speakers. Wispy fly-aways fell along her face and neck from the soft bun at the back of her head.

The way she swayed to the melody with her eyes closed bewitched him. Even if no one else in the room noticed her talent, he did. He *drowned* in it.

I could listen to her all day. She should have an album. Baebin innocently questioned Mr. Bak about Go-Ri's music during dinner one night, but the sharp man picked up on his interest, and he backed off. *She needed to be in a studio recording, not in a small club with no one but me paying attention.*

Between the incredible artistry of her music and watching Go-Ri get lost in her own world, Baebin only desired her more. Wrapped up with her inside the swell of the sound, she took him through skies of pink, waves of deep, glassy blue, and dark, soulful nights. Each song was a ride exposing a sometimes-playful, sometimes-painful emotion deep in his consciousness.

Baebin's music was based on beat and words. The notes and melody mattered, but listeners remembered the words and the emotion of the stories IN7 told. It was about grabbing attention and pushing an idea.

He'd always had an appreciation for jazz, but Choi Go-Ri made it come alive. The quirky rhythm, the offbeat that emphasized an unexpected feeling. There never seemed to be a repeating chorus, just a continuation of the story, one chapter to the next.

It was a refreshing change from what he lived with day-to-day. It reminded him of why he liked music to begin with.

It was the emotion, the complexity, and the thrill that one song can emit and change daily for each listener.

Go-Ri's music excited him.

The disturbing clatter of overturned chairs and angry shouts snapped his attention back to reality. As he feared, the noise level at the tables grew, and a fight broke out before the barman could stop it. Pushing and shoving, two angry drunks staggered about before drifting toward the stage—and Go-Ri.

She sat frozen in fear, her background music playing alone like an eerie soundtrack to a movie. Helpless, she watched as chairs tumbled and the growing group swirled her way, one table closer at a time.

Others worked to separate and calm the combatants, but Baebin's only concern was Go-Ri and her growing look of terror with each passing second.

Chu Kwan should've come tonight! What do I do? She's going to get hurt if she doesn't move…! At the last moment, Baebin leaped onstage, knocking her off the stool as he wrapped her in a bear hug and lifted her in his arms. The cord around her neck snapped, and the sax banged to the ground, forgotten under trampling feet.

Baebin ran, carrying her through the tiny, empty kitchen and out the back door.

Momentum hurled him through the parking lot to his car, and he pressed her against its side. His weight held her off the ground for a small eternity before he thought to loosen his grip. He spun around, keeping her in his arms, and leaned against the door, his head thrown back toward the car's roof in a daze from the sudden rush of adrenaline.

For a moment, Go-Ri leaned into him, panting. Then, she splintered. Turning into a furious wildcat, she fought his hold, struggling, pushing, and clawing against him. Finally, Go-Ri stumbled backward as she shoved Baebin away. A loud wail tore through her, and she jerked up her bare foot, almost catching him in the groin.

Snatching her up again, he tossed her onto the hood of the car while blocking her attack. Instinctively, he jumped out of reach and raised his palms in surrender. He only meant to help, but she was hyperventilating, clearly in the middle of a panic attack.

Staring blindly at him, she shielded herself and broke down in gut-wrenching sobs.

One shoe was missing, her shirt was in disarray, and the bun had come apart, sending hair flying in all directions down her back and in her face. Gently shushing her, he edged close enough to brush her hair off her wet cheeks and tuck it behind her ear. A large, bright-red welt from the saxophone strap marked her neck, the swelling visible in the dull streetlight.

Concern creased his brow as the back of his fingertips gently traced the swollen ridge. Go-Ri reared in terror. A fresh screech ripped out of her as she started flailing her knees and elbows, desperate to escape his touch.

Baebin yanked back, startled, and his hat, already askew, flew off, exposing his now purple-streaked white hair.

She scrambled across the hood of the car, her chocolate eyes wide and glassy with shock. Black spots blurred her swimming vision as flashes of faces swam in her mind. Unable to separate tonight from the memories of her past, her world folded in like paper origami, and Go-Ri slumped over.

Wh-what the hell? She wasn't moving. Her loud screams cut off the moment she fell over, and now his ears throbbed with only the sound of his heartbeat. Baebin crept close enough to confirm she was breathing before pacing about, trying to calm down and understand what had just happened.

She lay helpless and exposed on the hood of his car. *I can't leave her. What am I supposed to do now?*

Praying she didn't wake up and fight him again, he cradled her in his arms and carefully settled her in the front seat, covering her with a jacket he found in the back. Baebin knelt outside her open door for a long time, debating his next moves.

Baebin parked outside the gate of the tiny house behind the restaurant that Mr. Bak pointed out weeks ago and turned off the engine.

The dim streetlight reflected in the slight sheen of sweat on her forehead, and the dried rivers of old tears lacing her cheeks. Snuggled under his jacket, her breathing seemed regular, and her coloring finally returned to normal.

Baebin lowered his seat to match hers and gently held her hand. Just as he started to doze off, she stirred.

Holding perfectly still, her eyes flicked around the dark interior of the car, then settled on him, unblinking for several long moments. The warm, solid weight of the fabric around her didn't bind or restrict her; it protected her. Shielded her. Her fingers stroked the linen lining inside while her chin rubbed against the twill collar. "You?"

"Mmm."

"Your hair... not red?"

"No. I changed it."

"You were there? Why?"

"To hear you play. You're amazing."

Memories creased her forehead. "You've been there before."

"Mmm." He was surprised she knew. *Had she seen me?*

There was a long pause as she chewed her lip, trying to arrange the slivers in her mind. The incongruous mix of woodsy cologne and, maybe, lavender hand lotion blended with the scent of his own body and gently permeated the warmth of the material around her. It calmed her, re-structuring her disoriented nerves. "What's your name?"

"I'm Kim Baebin."

Dreading to leave the unfamiliar cocoon, she forced herself to push away the coat and reach for the door handle. "Thank you." She gave a soft, mewing cry when her bare foot touched the pavement, but she stepped out anyway, shutting the door quietly.

Go-Ri staggered inside the gate. She was sick the moment it shut behind her and barely made it to her room before passing out again.

Thus ends the longest conversation to date, Baebin thought as the gate clanked behind her. *A dozen, or maybe two dozen, words.*

He watched her leave before screwing his eyes shut and throwing a forearm over his head. What was supposed to be a simple, quick trip to the bar for some music and a smidge of ogling turned into a nightmare.

He hadn't the foggiest idea what caused her to react like that tonight, but it was insane. Worse than when she had exploded at his apartment weeks ago. Her instinctive, involuntary response drilled through him, hitting every nerve and twisting inside him. Nothing made sense, except that she was afraid. Of what, he did not know, but her fear bothered him.

Eventually, he sat up and called the Campus Help Desk. SKEC had one specific department to help its on-site residents. Their duties ranged from buying takeout, returning bras, and bringing home drunks at night to, apparently, picking up scooters (without keys) and finding broken instruments and missing shoes, purses, and hats.

They must have entertaining stories to tell at holiday parties. Baebin hated calling, but he needed help, and for the first time, he allowed his star rank to get it.

Two hours later, he waved goodbye to the guys dropping off Go-Ri's scooter and collected the oversized bags holding everything else.

Jaemin, Daeho, and Kyong walked into the gym at five in the morning, just as Baebin finished his last cycle. By seven o'clock, he met with someone in the music department to see if the instruments were salvageable and ordered brand-new ones to be picked up the next day. Baebin was working with his personal choreographer in the dance studio and was already in a high sweat before the rest of the group came in. They had a busy day: dance all morning, a quick business lunch during a planning meeting, and then the sound room in the afternoon.

Baebin and Jaemin had a duet for this album, and it was Baebin's turn in the booth. Take after take—trying different tones, pitches, and emotions—the recording session stretched well past the allotted time. Yet, he still wasn't satisfied with his part of the ballad.

The sound building was dark when he stopped by the main desk and picked up the pile of new music stuffed in his personal mailbox.

Baebin worked through the night until he was notified that the new instruments he ordered were ready.

Picking them up and skipping both the morning workout and the weekly group meeting with their manager, he drove to MinGo. He got to the restaurant before it opened. The grills and soup pots were cold. Go-Ri sat at a table in the empty restaurant, in the darkest corner, staring into space. She looked tired and ill.

The door chime startled her out of her quiet, numbing reverie. Go-Ri didn't need to look up to know who it was. That guy seemed to suck all the oxygen out of any room he stood in—or at least any room she was in. Even though he was quiet and unassuming, she felt him when he was near. *Why is he here? Go next door for your stupid water and stop bothering me.*

He did bring me home the other night, though. I should thank him. If I do, he'll never leave me alone. I swear he's stalking me. But he doesn't feel the same as... She cut off the thought. Strangely, she didn't feel creeped out or disgusted. She felt... *what?*

Why couldn't he go away? Her memory was still fuzzy, but she knew she had acted like a fool that night. It was mortifying. Stomach churning.

Closing the book in front of her, she fisted her hands on top before risking a glance at him. Her heart thudded as she did a double-take. *He's dressed up today. He looks nice. Different.* Not that he looked bad before. At all. His legs seemed longer in the torn jeans than his usual track pants, and his toned body gently stretched the fabric of his dark dress shirt, accentuating broad shoulders underneath. The beginning of a tattoo on his collarbone was barely visible in the gap above the top button.

Averting her eyes, she focused on her book and what she wanted to ask. *What happened that night?* The fragments floated in her mind, just out of reach. *I remember being on the hood of a car... screaming.... Then he took me home? What else did I do?*

Picking at a hangnail, she worked it free until she felt a weighty pause fill the empty room. She snapped back to attention. "Wha–? What did you say?"

"I asked if your neck is okay." He pointed to where he had seen the welt from her strap. "I hope it didn't bruise." He'd come all this way, but now that he was here, that was all he could think to say?

She fingered the small red line. "It'll go away." She cleared her throat. "Umm. That night... I don't rememb—"

"I don't want you going back there again," he interrupted sharply and then winced at his own harsh words. He sounded like a jerk.

"Excuse me? Who are you to order me around?!" Her sudden and cold, furious glare bore into him. Giving a mutinous huff, Go-Ri rubbed the ache in her forehead that was starting to grow larger. "It's none of your business, but... I don't have much choice. As you can guess, there aren't many Jazz Houses in the city, and that one is closest to home. That night was... unusual."

He bowed his head, deserving the reprimand. "You're right. I shouldn't have said that. But you are terrific. I'm sure you could sign on to a recording label with a studio—if you wanted to." She gave him a new piercing glare, and Baebin waved his hand in surrender... unsure what he was surrendering to.

"Absolutely not. They only protect their own, and I don't trust them. I refuse to be told what or how to play. My music is for me alone."

Go-Ri abandoned her book as she stood and turned to the counter. "I don't want to perform onstage like a trained monkey, and I won't be controlled by others. Especially by those horrible recording companies." Go-Ri snapped her mouth shut and bit her lip hard. She was getting too close to her edge. This was always what happened when she couldn't control herself. Even talking to him the slightest bit put her at risk.

"I'm confused." Baebin scrubbed the uncomfortable tingling sensation at the base of his neck and let the monkey comment pass. "You play on stage at the club."

Avoiding him, she moved from table to table, gathering the chopstick containers. *Go away! I can't breathe or think around you! My life is none of your business! I don't need to explain myself to you!*

He was still standing in the doorway, waiting for her to answer. With a huff, she caved. "Yes, I do. But I don't want to. And it's not the stage I don't like; it's people. There is a difference. I hate being around people I don't know. I don't trust them."

That set him back on his heels for a moment. *Chinmae was right.* She was afraid of something—not necessarily of him, but fearful in general. "You don't trust people or the recording companies? I get that it can be scary—"

"Both! Just. Stop. Talking!" She slammed the container in her hand on the counter. Following the same route, Go-Ri turned back and started gathering soy sauce bottles.

He blinked at her outburst, then cleared the table next to him that she had intentionally skipped and carried the things over to the counter. "Why do you play then? If you hate it so much, why put yourself through it?" He noted that she changed direction, keeping space between them.

"Why do we do anything? Money." she said. Baebin understood the irony in her bark of low, angry laughter. "I need money to open my own lesson studio. Doesn't Confucius say, 'Those who can't perform, teach'?"

His lips quirked. "It wasn't Confucius, and I'm not sure that's quite right, but I see your point." Crossing his arms over his broad chest, he stood his ground, in word and space. He watched for any sign that she would attempt to flee again.

"But, I've heard you. You *can* perform. You *can* play. You are outstanding."

"But I don't want to!"

"Okay," he conceded again. "If you want to teach—and you're great at that, too—then music will benefit from your skill either way." He helped himself to water, set a few *won* on the counter, and took a large gulp, using the time to rack his brains for a way to defuse the tension and keep her talking. He swallowed. "Do you play other music, too? What about classical or pop?"

"*Not* pop! K-pop is stupid and full of show-off scumbags who—" She whipped around and stopped herself just in time. *Who use fame for evil, to be superior to others. Who...*

The nausea grew, and she took several deep breaths to lower the bile. Her stomach rolled as she saw the bottle freeze halfway to his lips. The thin, pinched look on his face alarmed her. A niggling thought to end the conversation formed for the hundredth time. *Apologize and make him leave.* Rattled and shaking, she hid behind the counter.

Letting out a big groan, she pressed a thumb to her throbbing eye. "Thank you for bringing me home, and I'm sorry for yelling. My mouth gets ahead of my brain." She turned red, remembering the previous time she'd yelled at him. "I don't know why I always do it with you. I-I just don't like pop. It's the worst kind of music. It-it's just noise." The more she rambled, the quieter, darker, and more ominous he became until she finally stuttered to a stop.

The cold water in Baebin's stomach slid into his bloodstream, and the insult boiled the icy tingles into a low, simmering bubble. A muscle twitched in his jaw, and a metallic taste oozed inside his mouth.

Can she be any ruder or more insulting? She doesn't have to like me or be a fan of my work, but I'm getting tired of her insults. Squeezing the plastic bottle, trying to keep his temper in check, he bit out, "I don't know how you can be so against something you don't understand. Or how you love music but not the music industry."

She stiffened noticeably and looked directly at him. "Don't tell me what I don't understand. I know more than you do. You have no idea." Air whistled through her nose. "Thank you again for the other night. But please stop with the twenty questions. I don't like it. You don't know me, and I don't want to know you. Just… please leave."

Baebin's phone chirped, interrupting his response. He was late to the photo shoot, and Manager Kim must be furious. Checking his message, he knew he had no choice but to leave. "I do know, and you are totally wrong. And I did want to get to know you—but forget it. I'll leave."

He turned to go. Noticing the forgotten pile of bags and black cases he carried in, he called over his shoulder. "Your scooter is in my garage. And these are for you. I replaced your saxophone and guitar. Yours are at the repair shop, but the tech said they may not be salvageable." Spitefully, he added, "They came from SKEC. I work with one of those scumbag groups."

He stomped out of MinGo before she could respond.

Go-Ri sat down hard in the nearest chair, watching the door rattle as he slammed it behind him. *Did he just say he worked for SKEC? Isn't that Nam Song-Ye's company?* Her hands shook violently when she picked up her book and the empty, crushed bottle he left behind.

The photo shoot went poorly. Baebin won the prize for displeasing the most people in one day. It was difficult to focus. What Go-Ri said annoyed him. His pride had taken a hit at her rejection, but the way she talked about music and his career was... unexpected. Sad. Infuriating.

She was so talented and seemed to enjoy performing, but this morning threw him. *I can't believe I was so wrong about someone. She may have her reasons for her mistrust, but she was plain rude. I would have listened had she just talked to me and not insulted me or my work.*

Baebin pounded through the rest of the week, never leaving the Campus, except on IN7 business. He rarely slept and ate very little. He could feel his stamina dip, but he needed to keep his mind and body busy. He did everything possible to stop thinking about Choi Go-Ri.

The struggle to keep his private life separate and stay focused on work was grueling. No matter how hard he tried to fight it, they blended until the most minor details annoyed him. He had a bone to pick with everyone. The stage lights were wrong, his turn on the second verse was wrong, and his friends were breathing wrong.

Everyone but Chinmae brushed off his irritability as pre-tour jitters. But Baebin didn't get jitters. Ever since that stupid night weeks ago, his best friend had been avoiding him, and the rift was only growing, which irritated Baebin even more.

Hiding in the back corner of the cafeteria, facing away from the noisy diners, Baebin popped two more pain killers and massaged his temples. The smell from his tray turned his stomach. Pushing it aside, he lay his head down on his arms, only to jolt upright seconds later when Chinmae sat down across from him, slamming his tray on the table. Grinding his fists into his throbbing temples, Baebin growled. "What? Can't I just have five minutes? Please?"

Chinmae ignored him. "You're a jerk." His deep voice simmered low under the din of the cafeteria. Stuffing an apple slice in his mouth, he scowled at his friend. "You know, Mrs. Bae from costumes didn't deserve to be yelled at. And Yejoon and Jaemin were only teasing. We are sick of your attitude and trying to help you chill out."

Chinmae was right, and that made Baebin even angrier. He didn't need or want a lecture on how bad a person he was. Picking up his tray, Baebin stood to leave.

"Sit down. I'm not done with you." Wiping his fingers on a napkin, Chinmae leaned back as he swallowed the last of the apple and waited quietly, brows raised, daring Baebin to walk away.

Baebin sat but refused to cower. The daggers exchanged in their glares were steely sharp.

Chinmae studied his friend from cover to cover. "What is it? It's not work. This is the same bull we always have to deal with. So... it's home." He read his *hyung's* face. *I'm close, but...* "It's *not* home. It's the girl."

"I fixed it. It's over." Picking up his uneaten tray again, Baebin snapped, "Happy now?" He walked away, tossing the entire thing in the trash. Tray and all.

Chinmae watched his friend leave. *No, I'm not happy. I'm sorry, Hyung. I'm so sorry.*

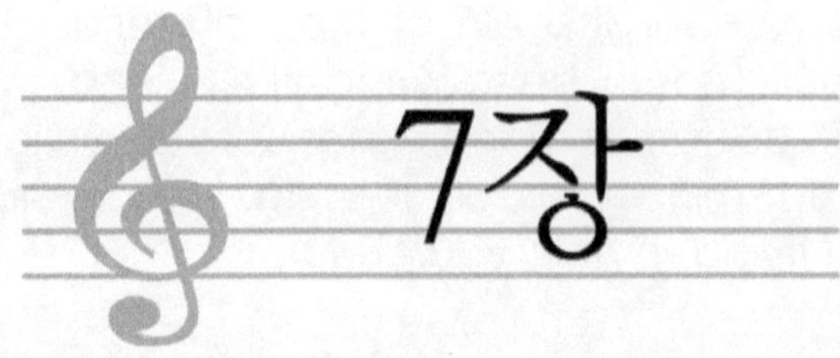

Two days before the Japan trip, Baebin had no choice but to return to the apartment for his suitcase. He planned a snatch-and-run, vowing to stay away from the restaurant and, more importantly, Go-Ri. He passed the desk without a glance and punched the elevator button.

It opened, and Go-Ri stood inside, holding the delivery case.

Well, that didn't work out so well.

They stared at each other until the doors started to close. Both reached out a hand and smacked them back open.

Before it could close again, Go-Ri stuck her foot out, blocking the doors. "I'm sorry!" she blurted. It was the only thing that came to mind. "I was tired, and upset, and... I'm sorry." The elevator started buzzing, angry that it couldn't continue with its job. "That's no excuse, but I'm sorry. You helped me, and I..." Her entire body collapsed inward. "You don't understand. I love music, but I can only have it my way."

The anger and frustration he had been carrying with him thawed into slivers of ice floating in a glass of cool water. How could he stay mad at her when she looked so dejected? He wanted to, but just couldn't. "No, you were being honest, and you shouldn't apologize for that. But I wish I understood better."

All week, he had been upset, but rewinding the argument for the hundredth time, he realized that the way she talked bothered him more than the actual words.

"Can we talk?" he asked. He seemed to be full of all kinds of idiotic ideas lately. "I know you don't want to see me, but will you come with me for just a moment?"

Wary and puzzled, Go-Ri chewed her lip.

Polite coughing nearby startled them, and their heads swiveled to the balding man waiting for his turn at the elevator. "I probably like romantic make-ups more than the average guy," he said, "but I haven't slept in three days. Could you two make a decision soon and let me on?"

The dark bags under his eyes and the hospital badge that hung on the man's bony chest supported his claim. Besides, their discussion was not meant for the elevator.

Robotically, Go-Ri took a step back, and Baebin joined her at the rear. The stranger stepped in, hit the ninth-floor button, and promptly fell asleep standing up against the wall. He reeked of hospital antiseptic overlaying a mild—but not *horribly* unpleasant—unwashed body scent with a light topping of... puke? Go-Ri politely switched to breathing through her mouth while mentally pinching her nose.

In unison, Baebin and Go-Ri peered over the man's shoulder, checking on him before shrugging at each other and suppressing their giggles.

She tried to distract herself with the memory of a pleasanter smell. *Kim Baebin's jacket smelled wonderful the other night.* Peeking over at him through her short lashes, she realized he was wearing it. Damp at the shoulder from the passing rainstorm, the deep-brown twill jacket she'd slept under hugged his arms, rode just at his hips, and... looked delicious. *If I move an inch closer, would I smell the same woodsy lavender scent? What man wears lavender?*

The elevator dinged and called out, "Ninth floor." The poor man shuffled out, unaware of his surroundings. Baebin stepped into the opening to watch him leave. Just before he was yelled at by the mechanical robot voice and alarm system, he stepped back inside. "He made it inside his apartment. No bodies lying in the hallway."

Go-Ri let out a small giggle, weirdly pleased at his concern for the stranger. "Do you think he'll make it to bed?"

Stroking his chin with a knuckle on his forefinger, Baebin scrunched up his face, giving comical life-altering consideration to the question. "I'm going to say... couch with shoes on."

"Pbht. You didn't leave me with many choices." Go-Ri rolled her eyes in mock disgust. "Fine. Then I'll go with bed, shoes off... but I'll raise you with face first, clothes on."

"Tie, too?"

"Obviously." Her grin of amusement faded when the elevator called out the eighteenth floor, and the door opened. Meekly, she followed him to the apartment she had vowed to stay away from. *I've lost my mind. What am I doing here?*

Setting the container down inside and removing her shoes, she automatically fished inside her bag for a second set of socks. "So..." the question burned on her tongue, "do you really work for SKEC?"

Baebin held up a finger while a voice came over the intercom, echoing in the hall. "Hello, this is Mr. Kim in 1802. I was really hoping you could do me a favor..."

Amazed, she listened as he placed a ridiculously large breakfast delivery order with the lobby desk for the man in 903. "Please have it delivered in..." he checked his watch and calculated the man's exhaustion, "ten hours. But if he doesn't answer, leave him alone. After twelve hours, just make sure he's still breathing."

Hanging up, he turned in time to catch her puzzled, fish-gaping expression. "Wha—? He probably only had ramen, coffee, and stuffed bread at the hospital. It's the least I could do for keeping him from his couch." She was going to argue the semantics of bed versus couch before he cut her off. "Sorry. I wanted to do that before I forgot."

She blinked, trying to get back on track. *Why am I here again?* "You really work for SKEC?"

"Mmm. Yep." He tossed his backpack on the empty floor of the dining room and shrugged out of his wet coat. *Ugh, I still don't have a coat tree.* He dropped it on the floor with his backpack.

"W-what do you do?"

Finding two glasses, he pulled out a cold liter water bottle from the fridge, refusing to look at her. "I work on shows and meet with people."

I'm a coward. It wasn't a total lie, but if he told her everything now, she would run. Chinmae would be furious at the omission, and he would be right. *Just give me some more time to explain everything,* he thought. *I just need time.*

"Mmm." She gnawed at her lip. *What does that mean? What shows?* Puzzling over his cryptic answer, she looked around. The last time she was here, the noise and his company distracted her, and she didn't get to truly see the space. *He has almost no furniture aside from the piano.*

Blushing, she remembered the beautiful, shiny baby grand. *What I wouldn't give to play it just once.* By her calculations, he had been here several months, but he was still living out of boxes. The large apartment was like a naked doll, just waiting to be dressed up.

Seeing the apartment through her eyes reminded him of how bare it still was, despite all his hard work. He saw the direction of her stare. "I'm sorry for the other night with my friends. I didn't mean to upset you." He had been wanting to apologize for weeks, and finally, he had a chance.

"Mmm. I overreacted. It was all my fault. It's your piano. You can do anything you want with it. That night was just… a lot all at once for me."

"It was supposed to be a joke. But I mishandled it. It was wrong of me. I almost lost a good friend because of it. Chinmae wouldn't talk to me for weeks."

Embarrassed, he cleared his throat. "Anyway, my work is sending me away on two trips very soon. One will be for two months. I know this place still isn't livable, but you can use it." Her mouth fell open, and she started to shake her head.

"No, let me finish. I'd like to hire you to clean, shop, and look after the apartment. You can also use the piano area for your lessons. I'm never here, and it's going to waste." He knew she should say no and run. He prayed she'd say yes.

She just stood there looking at him. "Wha–?! You… want me to be your maid? Why would I do that? You don't know me!"

"Maid is a bit extreme. And I know you well enough. You take good care of the store and the restaurant." Baebin paused for a beat, unsure how to explain further without inadvertently pushing her away.

"When I'm in Seoul, I usually stay in a room at work. I don't get to come here very much. You would have this place all to yourself. We could make this work for both of us. I know it isn't your own lesson studio, but it could be, temporarily."

Baebin had a lot of things he needed to apologize for. "You have your reasons to mistrust the studios, and that's okay. I don't understand, but you don't need to explain. If you need a place to play and your own space to teach, then come here. We both need help, so why not?"

Go-Ri blinked at him as he continued rambling. She plopped down on the piano bench, staring at him. Of course, "NO," should be her immediate answer. The last time they talked, she told him to stay away, and she absolutely, *one-hundred percent* meant it.

Go-Ri raised her hands to stop him and asked, "You aren't looking for anything more than cleaning and a house sitter? You swear?" When he nodded, she asked, "And you won't be here? We won't—this is just a business arrangement, right?" He agreed again. Before the rational side of her brain could get in the way, she blurted, "Okay. Yes."

Baebin froze, mouth open, ready to give more convincing reasons why she should agree. "Really?"

"Yes, but only when you aren't here. And this is only temporary." His wide grin lit his face. It was the same smile she saw him give Mr. Bak.

"One more thing." Baebin turned pink, scrubbing at his neck. "You any good at decorating?"

Alone in the elevator, Go-Ri banged her head against the wall several times, leaving a smudge on the shiny metal surface. *What just happened?* A piece of paper containing his phone number, door, and security codes burned in her pocket. Tomorrow, she had an appointment with him to pick out furniture. *How do I always get into these messes?*

It was getting harder and harder to remind herself that she didn't like him. Didn't want to be near him. Well, to be fair, he promised he wouldn't be in that giant apartment at the same time, so *technically,* they wouldn't be in the same space together.

Returning to the Campus with his suitcase, Baebin hunted down Manager Kim for help. The timing was awful, and he had some serious kissing-up and begging to do if tomorrow was going to work out.

Manager Kim almost burst a blood vessel at the request. "Furniture shopping? *Now?* You're kidding, right? We have a meeting in the morning and dress rehearsals all afternoon on the sound stage. Do it when we come back."

"I really want to go tomorrow. It'll only be for a few hours, and I'll be back in time. I swear."

Manager Kim scrutinized the youngster sitting in his cluttered office, wallpapered with multiple massive calendars and charts. *I've never seen Baebin in such a foul mood. If buying furniture, of all things, snaps him out of this nasty funk, then whatever.* He let out a pained sigh. All of his boys had him wrapped around their fingers. "Fine. Take a van and a few guards. But if you are one minute late, you're dead!"

"Aww. You love me. I'm your favorite." Baebin grinned and smacked a deafening kiss to his manager's cheek before running out.

Manager Kim groaned and tugged on his ringing ear.

Baebin and the guys finished packing and sent their main bags to the storage area for the vans to deliver to the airport. At eight o'clock in the morning, the entire two-hundred-plus crew that worked together for the concerts sat in the theater-style classroom with notepads, going over the trip with a fine-tooth comb. They did this before every trip, no matter how large or small, and it really did help everyone, from the makeup artist to the electricians.

Finally released from the meeting, Baebin and Chu Kwan sprinted to meet the driver. When Go-Ri pulled up to the furniture store, Baebin was waiting alone at the curb. Chu Kwan stood a polite distance away, and a few guards already scattered themselves inside, ready to create distance between him and any other shoppers on the slow weekday morning. The petite store manager, who had been called the night before, met them inside with a clipboard in hand.

The lightning-fast trip through the giant warehouse store was unlike anything Go-Ri had experienced. "What style do you like?"

"Style?" Both Go-Ri and the sales lady stood patiently, waiting for him to answer. "No idea. Not something ugly."

Ouf. This was not going to be easy. Go-Ri regretted agreeing to help. "Okay. Let's start with a table." One thing at a time. Small bites."

"That's easy. All wood and it's gotta fit at least a dozen people." Baebin looked around at the large selection crammed into one corner of the warehouse. Skipping over the metal and glass tables, he headed to three options at the far end for a closer look. "This one. What's next?"

A massive dark-oak table that could fit twelve to sixteen people with simple, no-fuss padded chairs, and a multi-sectioned sea-green couch—tested for cushiness, its fit for his long frame, and the capacity to hold all his friends—gave Go-Ri a sense of his personality and the feel he was going for.

Methodically, they hit every section, picking up speed as they settled on the style that best suited Kim Baebin and the empty apartment.

Go-Ri dragged him away from a unique collection of chairs. "No. I don't think ice cream cone shaped bar stools suits the apartment."

"Oh, come on! It's cool! What about the gold throne? Or that one—what is it supposed to be?" Baebin laughed and pointed beside the hideous eight-foot-tall plush throne to a weird chair shaped like a peeled banana or a starfish.

"Oi! Fine. Yes, we can put it in the bedroom next to your racecar bed." She rolled her eyes. "Pick one of these chairs instead." Go-Ri gestured to a more adult selection of seating, trying to hold back her laughter.

Baebin giggled, "I've always wanted a racecar bed! But my legs are too long now. It'll have to be custom-built." He loved watching her eyes roll.

Baebin's heart tripped madly at the sound of her laughter, and he worked to keep her small, snorty giggles going. She sounded like she was out of practice, unsure whether to unleash a full-on laughing fit or just a minor chuckle. When she wasn't so defensive and reserved, her smile lit her face like she was a different person. *What would it take to keep her smiling?*

"I want this lamp."

"No. You have awful taste." She had to admit the floor lamp, designed as a blue stick person with a lamp shade for a head, was funny.

"Fine. Then I'm getting that pink fur rug we saw back there, and you can't stop me."

As they walked behind the clerk in the row of beds, Go-Ri elbowed Baebin sharply, pushing him onto a mattress. "Hmm. You bounced. That one seems soft enough." She lost her poker face when he sat up, adjusting his glasses. The look of shock, quickly replaced by a playful, sexy gleam in his eye, immediately told her he was going to take it the wrong way.

Quirking a brow, he gave the bed a few good test bounces. "Aren't I supposed to be seeing if *you* bounce? Come here."

She stared at his outstretched arms, and her mind blanked, blocking any witty comeback. Risking a glance at the saleslady, Go-Ri prayed she didn't hear. *It's bad enough that we're shopping for furniture together like a married couple when we're just friends, but he had to make a comment like that?*

Wait. Not friends. Colleagues? No. Employee-employer? What are we? Gad. Go-Ri ran away to the next aisle, inspecting the tiny details of yet another dresser and slapping her burning cheeks.

The joke slipped out of his mouth before his brain could rein it back in. But the tomato-red color that flew up her neck at his sexual innuendo turned him on. *The bed* was *soft…. She'd look good in a pool of covers, propped against the headboard…* Before his jeans grew even tighter, he scrambled off and fled to a display of table lamps.

The sales lady looked back, espousing the fine quality of a makeup table to the couple, only to find herself talking to thin air. Helping families shop was often like herding cats.

Baebin questioned the mismatched armchairs, antique carved side tables, and modern deco-style coffee table Go-Ri recommended, but he agreed to try them out.

They ordered everything on their list—but for the long, padded bench he wanted to go along the wall in the piano room for storage and seating. Her attempts to rein in his reckless spending failed miserably. He never looked at prices and flipped the tag out of her hand if he caught her doing it.

He said he worked on shows, whatever that meant, but she was pretty sure he was spending more than what she thought a typical crew member could make in a year. Judging from the size of the apartment, as well, there was more to his work than he led her to believe. *Maybe it's family money,* she thought. This once, choosing to hide behind ignorance, she let it go. The day was too good to start an argument.

Time flew too quickly. Before he was ready, Chu Kwan walked past Baebin, tapping his watch. He forgot his friend was there, watching over them.

He left Go-Ri with his card and sole purchasing power for anything else she liked. An hour later, Go-Ri winced while signing the outrageous credit card receipt before arranging delivery.

Manager Kim walked into the dressing area thirty minutes early to find Baebin already sitting at a makeup table, waving his fingers and grinning. He raised an eyebrow and strode past, raiding the cabinets in the kitchenette for a bottle of pain killers. He was prepped and ready for a fight, but Baebin spoiled it. Emptying a water bottle in large gulps, he squinted at the boy playing on the phone.

Was the kid going through a second puberty? The smile was back, and things were right again in the world. He observed his young mentee for a long while. *Simply buying furniture couldn't cause such a dramatic shift in attitude.* This flip-flopping was giving him a headache.

It was all hands on deck for the season's first show, and it would be a long night.

Dress rehearsals reminded the guys of their early days as trainees, when debuting was a pipe-dream. Up before the sun to record, then schoolwork, then late nights dancing until the mirrors in the studio fogged up with steam. All their hard work was for times like this. To showcase how far they had come.

They ran through the show three times from start to finish. Several costumes required corrections, the crew adjusted stage air tubes to help cool the dancers, and Kyong repeatedly clashed with the lighting crew during several songs. The new mic system worked perfectly, and their vaguely scripted interview part of the show had the backstage crew cracking up as the guys worked through their Japanese lines.

The only thing they held back on was the vocals; instead, they mouthed along to the soundtrack, except for the four songs they would sing only in Japanese, not Korean. It was still mentally and physically exhausting, and by the end, all seven guys, their backup dancers, and the entire crew were utterly drained.

After midnight, the choreographers, managers, and Mr. Jong, the CEO of SKEC, who came to watch the last round, called it a night, pleased with the final product.

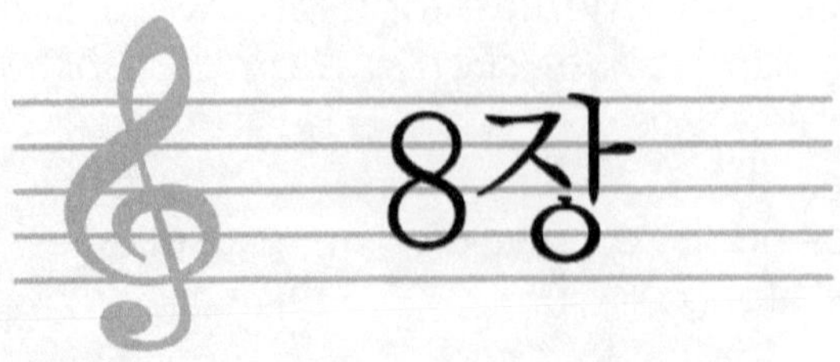

Touring overseas was a massive production.

The sun hadn't yet crested the southeast mountains of Seoul as several vans pulled out of the SKEC Campus, headed for the Incheon Airport. *Echo* fans and reporters claimed their spots along the rope lines long before the seven, tall, handsome K-pop idols pulled up to the terminal. After security and customs, they barely made their noon flight.

It was almost midnight before they got their room keys and collapsed on their hotel beds in Tokyo.

Most people looking at the members of IN7 would think they do nothing all day and just dance around onstage for fun. The reality was they were constantly on the move, with little sleep and always under the watchful eyes of fans and the media. Their work was physically and mentally challenging. They always needed to think three steps ahead.

When they weren't in public, they were in hotel gyms or a strange back room, working on vocals and choreography. They believed that if their team was working, they should be, too.

As grueling as the boys had it, being the face of the tour, they always pitied the stage crew, who worked tirelessly through the nights so that everything was ready when they arrived.

Three days later, Go-Ri walked to the building for her first day of lessons in the apartment. The staff, who received her teaching schedule from Baebin, welcomed her with a large bouquet of roses.

MinGo and Go-Ri were well known in the neighborhood, and all the desk clerks, not just Mr. Bak, had a soft spot for the girl. As she entered the elevator, Mr. Bak crossed his fingers and prayed that this would be the start of good things.

Go-Ri let out a long-held sigh when she made it inside the apartment without tripping the alarm. Police storming the apartment on her first day would be a bad omen. Being in his space alone was strange enough. The creepy feeling of invading someone else's home, even with permission, was unnerving.

The last two weeks confused her. *Bothered* her. Their argument after the night at *The Jazz House* should have put a stop to... whatever this was. She swore to herself not to be swayed by his looks and charms as they shopped for furniture together, but she'd failed miserably. Honestly... for some weird, crazy, inexplicable reason, she didn't care anymore. *He was... nice. Different. A book you didn't care to read at first, but couldn't put down until the end.*

Sitting on the step of the *hyeongwan*, she added her second layer of socks and shook off the tension in her shoulders. Settling on a pitcher for the flowers, she made a mental note to buy Kim Baebin a vase. Go-Ri made her way over to the piano. Her one solace. Her fingers tingled at her first chance of playing such a beautiful instrument.

The glossy Steinway was nothing like the old uprights or electric keyboards she normally played. Go-Ri needed a moment to breathe before she could accept this new shift in her life and her students arrived.

Closing her eyes, she played a few of her favorite Chopin nocturnes before switching to various Bill Evans and Keith Jerrett jazz compositions she always depended on during difficult times.

Four hours later, her last student left, and she was still sweeping the empty rooms when the delivery team arrived.

The apartment became a beehive of activity, with men coming and going up the service elevator under the watchful eye of Mr. Bak on the ground floor. They unwrapped everything, assembled it, and put it all into place. The men were an orchestra; she was the conductor. They weren't finished until each piece went exactly where she wanted it, even if it meant moving things a smidgen here or there or switching some pieces from room to room.

The last guy finally left, taking the huge bags filled with trash and bubble wrap with him. Wiped out but thrumming with pleasure, she fell onto the new couch. Go-Ri was thrilled with how the apartment had changed in just a few hours. She couldn't wait to show Kim Baebin.

Hitting send on a second batch of photos, she almost dropped the phone when it rang with an incoming video call. They'd agreed to texting, not videos. Her heart pounded in her chest as she hesitated a moment, unsure if she should take the call. Swiping away the mascara from under her eyes, she held the phone out and hit the green button.

Hiding in a backstage bathroom in Osaka, Japan, Baebin sat on a toilet, getting a tour of his apartment. "Wait. Go back," Baebin requested.

Puzzled, Go-Ri backtracked. "What? The table? Isn't it the right one?"

"The flowers." A twinge of jealousy cropped up.

Giggling, she zoomed in on the red roses in the pitcher. "The staff downstairs got them for me. You need a vase." She fingered one of the petals. "I've never gotten flowers before. Aren't they pretty?"

"Mmm. Yes." Baebin mumbled. *I should have gotten them for you. Why didn't I think of that?* He wanted to slap himself. Her happiness over the gift was unmistakable.

That night, Baebin pulled out his laptop and shopped online for a shoe cubby and dozens of slippers. Guessing at the measurements, he bought the biggest *sinbaljang* he could find that might fit in the entryway.

With his family, friends, and now Go-Ri's clients, he needed something to control the usual mess in the entry that could double as a hall-table landing zone.

Getting her flowers now would be lame. Still kicking himself for not thinking of a gift for her first day, he gnawed his thumbnail, wondering what to do. *Something musical would be more fitting.* Searching an online music store, he added blank score sheets and a wooden fountain pen engraved with *Love of Music* to the cart.

Baebin and Go-Ri struggled to keep their texts to a minimum while he was traveling. They both found themselves staring at their phones, inventing ways to contact each other and stay within the boundary she imposed. Heavily censoring themselves, each message was rewritten time and again.

B: ~~How are your lessons going?~~ Please check my
   mailbox
G: Ok
G: Electric bill ~~How's your trip?~~
B: ~~You working at the restaurant? Is it busy?~~
   I ordered a few things. You'll get boxes soon.
B: Put eggs on my shopping list please
G: Ok ~~We had rain today. Did you?~~
~~B: How are you today?~~
G: Can I buy furniture polish? And more floor cleaner?
   ~~I bet you can't wait to get home.~~
B: Of course. Get anything you need ~~I'm tired. Wish I was~~
   ~~home.~~

Distance was important for her sanity, but she found herself looking forward to his texts. By the end of the week, she didn't know if she was pleased or annoyed at his curt messages.

He was always quiet and polite, but on the shopping trip, he was fun and high-spirited. It was cute the way his large, almond-shaped eyes disappeared into curved slits when he laughed, matching the arch of his sculpted eyebrows. And she liked how his neck turned pink under his button-down shirt collar when she pushed him on the bed. She was surprised that she enjoyed herself with him, but now that he was back to strictly professional, business as usual, it felt strange.

Dang it. She was so confused.

G: ~~Are you insane!?~~ Received my pay. It was much
   more than we agreed on
B: It's for going shopping with me and being there to set
   everything up

That's just dumb. Besides, I actually had fun—doing both. She stewed over what to do with the money. The next day, she spent the extra portion on living room curtains, a large plant, and a rug for under the piano bench. Also, a vase.

Go-Ri dusted and finished his shopping list, checking and rechecking her phone for a reply. The two-inch tall rectangular box sat on the counter all afternoon, unopened. *Surely, it's meant for Kim Baebin and not me. This isn't my home; why would someone send me something here? Why isn't he answering about the box? He got the message. Was it for him, and I'm supposed to open it?*

Deciding to go for it, she grabbed the giant butcher knife and stabbed viciously at the package, refusing to let doubt stop her any longer. She could always try to tape it back together later if she was wrong.

Biting her lip in awe, she read the sweet gift note from Kim Baebin as she tested the new pen. Weighted perfectly, it glided over the music sheets with the classic scratching sound she loved.

The Japan trip went smoothly, and Baebin relaxed for the first time in months. They altered the old routine to include their new music and the fans loved the addition of new songs mixed in with their old favorites. Their reaction was what the guys thrived on.

Being away from home together, they used the opportunity to bond every night over a midnight meal in one of their hotel rooms. As if six years of living together wasn't enough, these trips helped them grow closer. They knew each other better than their own families did. They were more than brothers.

Maybe they were already married... to each other.

Even though SKEC provided translators for each overseas trip, they required their idols to speak several languages. Daeho, more proficient in Japanese than any of them, worked as the group's main translator during interviews and the "sit-down" segments that gave the guys a chance to catch their breath and cool off. His wacky antics on stage seemed effortless, hiding how hard he worked behind the scenes to ensure the fans stayed engaged.

The extra language lessons that began when they were trainees often overwhelmed them, but now, their unique ability to reach fans on a personal level outside Korea made them more marketable. It was a genius idea of SKEC that the boys hated to admit worked.

After five concerts, several interviews, TV shows, and live video chats, the crew loaded everything back onto planes, and they all headed home.

> B: BE HOME AROUND 7 TONIGHT. WANT TO COME OVER ~~FOR DINNER?~~ TO TALK ABOUT THE APARTMENT?

The ride back to the Campus in the private company van was blessedly quiet. Post-tour letdown settled in, and each of the guys huddled in their seats, desperately needing a few days off.

She's still not answering me. I shouldn't have asked. Baebin had no plausible excuse to invite Go-Ri over, other than he just wanted to see her again.

> G: OK. I'll come for a little bit around 8. Will bring dinner from MG.

Baebin couldn't believe it wasn't that long ago when he started working on the apartment, and his new life began in the hillside neighborhood. *I can't wait to see the changes!*

He couldn't wait to see Go-Ri.

He took a deep breath and let himself in. It was better than he hoped for. The setting sun filtered lightly through new curtains he knew he hadn't purchased that spanned the expansive living room windows, and a tall, symbolic Money Tree stood in the corner, soaking up the last of the sunlight.

The clean, modern lines against the strongly traditional elements suited him perfectly. The oversized, yet comfortable seating seemed out of joint at the store when paired with the inlaid, metal-bound, traditional wood pieces, but they flowed seamlessly in her arrangement here. The woods and soft neutrals let the accents of reds and yellows stand out without being too gaudy, and would be a perfect backdrop to his artwork when they were hung.

Even the chandeliers that filled the tall ceilings blended in with the design. He had debated changing them earlier, but they were works of art on their own that finally fit in with the décor. He tested every chair, turned on all the lamps, and ran his palms over the dining table, excited to have guests eat there one day.

I. Love. It! Absolutely perfect!

Carrying his bags to his room, he stopped and cocked his head, confused. Something else seemed different. *Nothing's missing. The boxes are still there. The furniture looks good—still need some things, but... something feels off.* What was it? Halfway down the hall, he realized the apartment didn't echo anymore. Baebin was used to any slight noise bouncing around the empty rooms.

His home wasn't empty anymore. It was warm and inviting—a place he was proud of. Smiling, he started a load of laundry from his dirty suitcase and headed for the shower.

He had just managed to store the music and recordings he had picked up from the sound department in his home studio when he heard the front door chime open. He grinned and raced to the entryway, sliding to a stop.

Casting a glance at him before kicking off her shoes, Go-Ri pointed behind her. "I stood out there forever. Wasn't sure if I should ring the bell or come in. This feels... weird."

Two weeks ago, she had insisted they not be at the apartment together. *Good grief, I'm a dope.* She had no willpower with this man, and even though she was still cautious, her curiosity was growing.

Long bangs and side tendrils that had fallen and curled from the heat in the kitchen of the restaurant softened her severe ponytail, and he watched as a blush spread around her neck and ears. The shade of pink made his lower half twitch in excitement. She must have been chewing on her lips the entire walk here. They looked kissable, all swollen and red. *Geeze. I'm an ogling monster.*

Sitting together for the first meal at the new table was awkward, but he couldn't imagine the inaugural event with anyone else. Needing to look anywhere but her exposed neck and pretty necklace, he gestured around the open space with his chopsticks. "The place looks amazing. I don't know how you did it."

Chatting to mask his nerves, he added meat to her rice bowl. *Japanese food is good, but I missed Korean food. Especially buldak.* The smell of chili pepper and ginger brought back the memory of his first visit to MinGo.

Before she was full, Go-Ri relaxed, and her smile brightened the room as much as his new lamps while she told stories of move-in day.

"I like the plant and the curtains." Teasing her was fun, but it upset him that she hadn't used the credit card he left behind. How did she pay for it all? He would have to increase her pay to make up for it. By the time he loaded the dishwasher while she packed away the leftovers, a new list of needs was growing, and she had forgotten to be embarrassed at being caught making unsanctioned purchases.

He had been traveling since before dawn but didn't want the night to end. She didn't either and offered to stay and help assemble the *sinbaljang*. Borrowing a tool kit from the lobby desk, they pushed the couch back to make room for the build. With music playing on the TV and a bottle of wine next to them, they spread out the parts and huddled around the confusing directions.

It took all evening—between laughing and squabbling over misplaced boards, and the screws that all looked the same, and mopping up spilled wine from a thrown pillow— but the unit slowly came together. Finally, they carried it to its new home in the *hyeongwan*. The light wood blended in with the flooring, and the cubbies were a perfect size. Storing the new slippers in each opening and choosing pairs for themselves, they tucked away their shoes that lay on the floor.

Draping his arm over Go-Ri's shoulder, Baebin pulled her to his side and marveled at their accomplishment.

With a sharp hiss, she recoiled and fled the *hyeongwan*.

Instantly, he regretted his impulsive act. It was something he had done with the guys a thousand times, but he had forgotten his place with her. *How could I have been so stupid?*

"I'm sorry. I didn't mean…" He waited until he could see her fists loosen and her breathing slow before taking a step into the room. "I wasn't thinking. I didn't mean to startle you."

Go-Ri commanded herself to calm down. *He did nothing wrong. It's not his fault I'm an idiot and overreacted.* Pasting on a huge, tight smile that went no higher than her lips, she began gathering the trash scattered about. "No, it's my fault. I was just surprised. I'm—umm—it's just a bad habit I've picked up recently."

Deep down, he had known all along that something, or someone, was the reason she was skittish and untrusting. "Choi Go-Ri, can you look at me?" Waiting patiently for her to turn around, he willed his body to relax, keeping his arms down and hands loose; if he was tense, she would be, too.

"There is nothing wrong with protecting yourself. I shouldn't have touched you without your permission. I am entirely at fault. Not you." He could tell Go-Ri was listening, watching her head tilt to the side. "You have no reason to believe me, but you are safe with me."

Still upset with herself, she regarded him for a long moment. It was strange and oddly touching to hear this man acknowledge her unspoken fears without knowing her past.

Would he still feel the same if he discovered why I can never trust others or—more importantly—myself any longer? Why I refuse to let anyone near me again? One mistake had left her broken in an alley, changing her life forever. She couldn't make that mistake again.

Instead of more excuses, Go-Ri only nodded her head in thanks.

Staying long enough to put the room back in order, Go-Ri picked up the toolbox, and Baebin walked her out. With the closed door separating them, both stood leaning their foreheads on the wood, just millimeters apart, sighing in pain, anguish, and misery.

I ruined everything, they both thought.

The following morning, Baebin ran to the hillside exercise center but mostly spent the time there watching the sunrise. The sky changed into varying shades of orange before the white ball finally crested the far mountain range, lighting up the summer haze.

He barely slept all night, thanks to his tumbling thoughts. She had said, "a recent habit." *What caused her to change?* His stomach churned with several possible reasons, every one of them horrible.

Early risers themselves, Mom and Dad answered his video call on the second ring. The three sat down for breakfast together over the phone, catching up on family drama and his trip. Making a huge pot of coffee in the studio, Baebin started weeding through the pile of music he had brought home, making notes for Tae-Si as he went. His friend was a great composer and sound mixer, who could untangle tricky phrases and tones to suit the group perfectly.

The apartment was dark by the time Baebin took off his glasses, scrubbed his dry eyes, and locked the studio door behind him. Skipping dinner, he landed face-first in bed and promptly fell asleep.

For his last day home, he decided to have a pajama day. As they'd prearranged, Baebin called Jaemin during his vlive show, surprising the fans who tuned in to the website to chat with their favorite singer. From day one, the boys understood each of them drew in a different crowd, and they never competed for recognition or fan time, but they would often 'mistakenly' call in or be a guest to help shake things up.

"Jaemin! Just checking in, seeing if you made it home okay."

"Hyung! Say hello! I'm talking to *Echos*."

"Oh. Sorry. I thought that was tomorrow. The tour confused my days. Hello, *Echos!*" Baebin spoke jovially to the listening fans.

Jaemin held up the phone to his camera, showing off a picture of Baebin he'd taken in Tokyo before replying. "I'm home. It was late last night, so traffic to Busan was light."

The two spoke casually for a few more minutes, then Baebin clicked off, leaving his friend to finish his personal chat with *Echos*.

 After folding his clean laundry, he sat on the couch for his own show. Still in pj's, he added his fluffy headband with cat ears that the *Echos* loved so much and oversized wire-framed glasses. Baebin talked about the recent trip and did a read-answer segment with his fans before signing off.

Darkness settled in, and Baebin turned on his new lamps before starting dinner. The rice cooker and his phone dinged simultaneously.

G: Want company? You can say no

Speechless, he danced in circles, gripping the phone tight. Just when he started to reply, he remembered his clothing. Before he could second-guess himself, he took a selfie and sent it to Go-Ri.

B: Do I have to change?

Twenty minutes later, she walked through his door and shed her raincoat to reveal her own pajamas and a dog headband with floppy ears.

Choosing the coffee table and a trivia game on TV, they ate before settling on a movie. Claiming separate corners of the couch and their own blankets, they sat in comfortable silence, enjoying the evening.

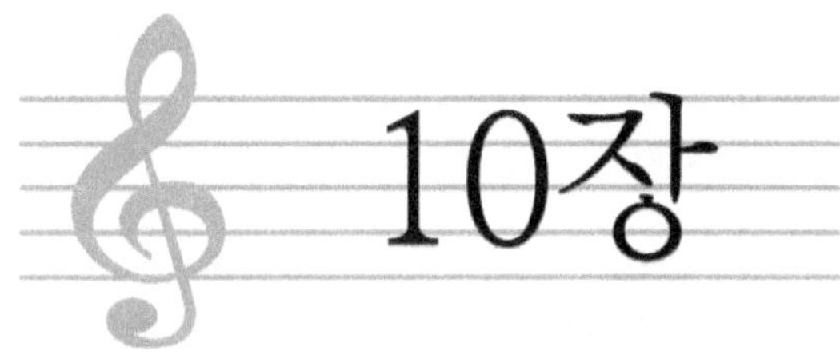

Even though Go-Ri was growing comfortable with the idea that Baebin worked for SKEC, she didn't want to be tangled with the company any more than she needed to be. But upon meeting the prospective students at a coffee shop, a safe public space, she instantly warmed up to them.

The quiet, young saxophonist—of whom she was initially most leery—impressed her. Mr. Lee was a new employee looking to earn more play time and a promotion by learning the oboe and bass clarinet. Gentle and a quick learner, he was laser-focused on his work.

The second student, Sun Woo-Ge, was her favorite addition by far. The adorable five-year-old couldn't reach the pedals or sit still at the piano for long, but his eyes glowed and he always came running in with a big hug, eager to learn. His dad sat on the couch as she taught Woo-Ge scales and worked him through his first music book.

Each lesson ended in a duet. As he learned a new song, Go-Ri accompanied him on another instrument, adding trills and flourishes to his simple melody.

The little chatterbox loved anything related to music, and Go-Ri started bringing more and more of her instruments, aside from the ones she used to teach other students, for him to see and hear. Baebin insisted he didn't mind the growing clutter, and it was easier to leave them at the apartment than cart them back and forth.

Since she was a child, Go-Ri had a knack for music. Everything she earned went to a new instrument, and she would teach herself how to play. She had most of the smaller traditional Korean woodwinds and strings. Her collection of orchestral instruments, like her favorite sax, was growing, too.

> G: I DON'T HAVE LESSONS TODAY, BUT CAN I GO OVER AND PLAY?
> B: OF COURSE. DON'T NEED TO ASK, HELP YOURSELF
> G: I'LL SWEEP WHEN I'M THERE
> B: DON'T. IT'S FINE. JUST HAVE FUN PLAYING

She began composing again—something she hadn't done in almost two years. Jazz, classical, and traditional music soothed her, and even though she was happier lately, her new emotions were jumbled up in knots. Composing helped re-order her brain and organize her thoughts.

Every time his apartment door opened, Baebin's phone beeped, indicating the security system was activated. He was happy that she was there.

> G: THEY ASKED ME TO PLAY AT THE CLUB TOMORROW. I SAID NO
> B: I'M HAPPY FOR YOU. CONGRATS.

Go-Ri and Baebin fell into an easy rhythm during the next month. Text messages became more casual and frequent, and they would leave notes tacked to the fridge or stuck in each other's slippers. He noticed the growing supply of socks in her cubby and loved the way her instruments filled the piano room.

She was there more than he was, and he continued to pay her weekly for her work. She always spent half of it on small things she could sneak into his apartment that weren't on the planned shopping list.

He saw everything but kept quiet. She never used his credit card for things other than food or cleaning supplies, and he always found it stuffed in a different kitchen drawer the next time he came home. It frustrated him, but he had to laugh at her persistence.

Small packages often waited for her at the lobby desk. He loved watching her on the security system as she shook each box, trying to guess the contents. When the large flute arrived, she texted him.

G: ARE YOU NUTS! YOU BOUGHT ME A DAEGEUM?! TOO EXPENSIVE. THANK YOU BUT TOO MUCH.

He recently found a CD in the stereo of a soloist playing the *daegeum*, and she didn't have one of those bamboo flutes in the apartment. *I thought she'd like it.* He flushed at the reprimand and, learning his lesson, Baebin dialed it back to smaller gifts.

The business arrangement evolved into friendship. He was nervous about going out in public with her—afraid of being recognized—and she said she didn't like crowds and people. So, mostly, they stayed in and listened to music while cooking together or watching a movie. It worked for them both. Sometimes, they would meet at the *sansjang* to watch the sunset when it wasn't too hot and sticky to be outside.

Always respectful of her personal space, Baebin took great care not to repeat the events of the night, building the *sinbaljang*. Each time they met, the tension in her shoulders and around her eyes seemed to fade little by little. As easy as she grew with him, he still noted her quirks outside the apartment or at MinGo. Always wary of her surroundings, she maintained a wall between her and others—not just physically but also emotionally. *I wish she didn't feel uncomfortable. Somehow, she's even more beautiful when she's relaxed and smiling.*

She never asked about his work, and he tried to convince himself that he wasn't lying to her. She knew he worked for SKEC and did something with music, and she had accepted that. Nothing else was said about her animosity toward the company or pop, but it was easy to see how much she avoided his music or anything concerning the K-pop industry. It was no wonder she still didn't connect him to IN7 and his stage name, Yong-ee.

More time. Next time I see her, I'll tell her who I am. But Baebin knew with every day that went by, he was digging a deeper hole.

Baebin's time at the Campus was busy and strenuous, and the days were long. The small hiccups from Japan were being ironed out for the American tour that would kick off in September. The longer set included two additional songs and three dances that they still needed to improve. The duet with Jaemin was finished, and the sound team was mixing the newest album already in production, *Galaxy*. Baebin's Chinese language lessons and never-ending music pile that he reviewed for future albums continued as usual.

As a rule, the group worked until ten o'clock at night, particularly if they had a TV show, a local concert, or a fan meeting session. Sleep was precious and never enough. Other days were heavenly short. Baebin started going home on those early days and would often move his morning fitness routine the following day, to lunchtime, so he could stay home longer. He continued working in his private studio, but if Go-Ri was free, they spent the evenings together.

It was crunch time for their eight-week America tour, and tempers started rising among the entire crew. In August, they celebrated Daeho and Yejoon's birthdays, which helped ease the tension—the guys had to apologize twice for the mess in the practice room after a cake fight—but it didn't take long for the brief respite to wear off.

The fires igniting from every direction required multiple weekly meetings. Emotions ran high, and even the guys started arguing more than usual. Three days in a row, Baebin had to jump in between Kyong and Yejoon, as they almost came to blows. *This is getting ridiculous! I want to strangle all of them! Something's gotta give.*

As another morning meeting with the production and stage crew spiraled out of control, Manager Kim exploded. Slamming his notebook on the podium, he threw up his hands and yelled at everyone in the room. "That's it! Go home. You're fired if you come back with a bad attitude." He looked at the seven guys and added, "This includes you, too." He grabbed his papers off the podium and stormed out the door.

Baebin burst into the apartment an hour later. Heedless of his surroundings, he hurled his duffel bag across the room, finally letting out the shrill scream he had been holding in for days. Go-Ri dropped to the floor, tossing the laundry basket and shattering the teacup she had been carrying. The bag sailed just over her head.

Bill Evans' unique rhythmic piano played over the speakers, masking the sounds of their spasmodic breaths.

She lay frozen. Baebin wasn't sure if he hit her, or if she passed out again. He collapsed on the floor next to her in a heap and stretched his hand to her as close as he dared, crying out over the music. "I'm so sorry! I'm sorry! I didn't know you were here! I forgot! Did I hurt you?! Go-Ri, answer me!"

Go-Ri lay curled in a ball, protecting her head and stomach from the pain she expected, as spots danced around the corners of her vision. The sound of his cries filtered in faintly through the blood rushing in her ears.

She stupidly let her guard down these last few months, and now, all the memories and the fears rushed back to hit her like a freight train. Her shoulder hurt from the fall, and her palm stung.

Where is he? What do I do?! How can I escape?!

Risking a glimpse, she saw a hand reaching toward her, which sent her reeling. *No, no, NO! Move! Run! Don't let him hit you! He's going to hit you!*

Go-Ri scrambled around Baebin, trying to put as much distance between them as she could, but her skirt tangled between her legs and hampered her movements. His hand followed, trying to reach her. Shrieking, Go-Ri lashed out with her foot, catching him in the ribs. Baebin let out a whoosh of air and clutched his middle. Using this chance to make it to the door, she was gone before he could breathe again.

Baebin lay huddled, pounding on the floor and crying out in his frustration, frightening the neighbor below. Annoyed with the problems around the important tour and all the fighting lately, he was angry, tired, and barely held himself together all week. In the privacy of his home, he'd shattered and let loose without thinking.

God, what did I just do?! I NEVER act like that! And she thinks I took it out on her! I didn't remember she was here! What did I do?!

Stumbling to his feet, he staggered to his bedroom where he dropped onto the bed fully dressed, his shoes still on.

> B: GO-RI I'M SORRY!
> B: I DIDN'T MEAN TO FRIGHTEN YOU! I'M SORRY!
> B: I WAS UPSET BUT NOT AT YOU. YOU DID NOTHING WRONG! IT IS ALL MY FAULT!
> B: TALK TO ME. YOU OK?
> B: GO-RI????? ANSWER ME.
> B: DID YOU MAKE IT HOME? WHERE ARE YOU? I'M WORRIED!
> B: GO-RI PLEASE! LET ME KNOW UR OK. I AM SO SORRY!

One text after another—everything he sent her remained unread and unanswered. Baebin fell asleep clutching his pillow, utterly wiped out.

Go-Ri got lost in the very neighborhood she grew up in. Nothing looked familiar—or safe. In panicked hysteria, she found an empty alley and huddled behind plastic crates and bags of stinking trash.

By nightfall, she came to and recognized the hardware store across the way. Her tea-soaked shirt had dried. Using the light from the phone she found in the pocket of her skirt, she inspected her stinging palm and freed the shard from the shattered teacup stuck in her flesh before sucking on the wound.

Finally home, she gently closed the gate, avoided the creaking porch step, and snuck into the bathroom without waking her mom or brother. After inspecting her bruised shoulder, she sat in the tub, letting the water splash over her. It ran cool long before she was able to move. Shivering with residual fear and bone-chilling cold, Go-Ri dragged herself out. Bandaging her hand and dressing in her warmest pajamas and two pairs of socks, she crawled into bed.

She massaged her numb toes roughly, warming them the best she could as she held off sleep for just one more moment. She needed to do something. Something she should have done from day one.

She stared at her phone, barely able to stop shaking long enough to turn it on. With a rending sob, she noticed his messages but refused to read them.

G: STAY AWAY FROM ME

Sliding her phone under the pillow, she pulled the blankets over her head, praying it would be enough to block out what she knew would come.

Her dreams were filled with nightmares again, but being awake was worse. She re-lived the night outside the club, what just happened at the apartment, and every moment from that horrible night two years ago. Her dreams blended them all together, switching around the faces and events, waking her up in a cold sweat. She didn't want to sleep; she didn't want to be awake.

Days later, she couldn't take it anymore. Go-Ri sat up in bed and turned on her phone. Kim Baebin had texted her non-stop. She could feel his pain in each message. The last two came this afternoon.

B: I'M SO SORRY. PLEASE TALK TO ME. I'M WORRIED.
B: I WON'T BOTHER YOU ANYMORE. GOODBYE GO-RI.

It sounded final. *It's what I want. Right?* So, why was she so confused? Why was she unhappy? *Why does it feel wrong?*

Scrunched tightly in a ball, she stewed in her thoughts. The acid in her empty stomach churned. *I took a risk and look where it got me. I can't do this. I can't handle this. I'll never be normal again. Why was I trying?!*

Would he think her an idiot if he knew how stupid she'd been a long time ago? Would he pity her? Would he even care? One horrible night changed her into this... crazy lunatic.

He said goodbye. Did he mean it? Will he show up at the restaurant? He won't bother me like Song-Ye did, right? Maybe if I told him what happened, he would go away for good. He will run when he finds out how much of a nut-case I am.

It was after midnight, but she punched in a message. She hit send before she could think better of it.

> G: IF YOU ARE HOME AND AWAKE, I'LL BE AT THE SANSJANG. I
>   NEED TO TALK.
> B: COMING.

Baebin found her huddled inside her brother's oversized sweatshirt, pale-faced and puffy-eyed, sitting on a hillside bench, staring at the city lights as they flickered against the Han River. It was a hot night, but he could see her shivering inside the thick material. His shoes crunched on the gravel, announcing his arrival.

Thank god she reached out to me. I wish she'd let me hold her and erase everything that happened. I want her to feel safe with me again.

Setting a bag with her purse and shoes next to her, he moved to the other bench, clenched his hands between his knees, and stared ahead, waiting.

Go-Ri's soft, gravelly voice hung in the dark air around them. "There was this guy I barely knew in high school."

He closed his eyes. No story that started that way was good. He wanted to cover his ears to block it out. Instead, he listened, not moving.

"I never liked Nam Song-Ye. Honestly, he gave me the creeps—always watching me, showing up when I wasn't expecting him. I was thrilled when he left school to join one of those companies to be a singer. It was nice not having to look over my shoulder all the time." She shuddered in revulsion. "Suddenly, he started coming back around and begging me for a date. I only went out with him in the hope that he would leave me alone when he found out I wasn't who he really wanted.

"Let's just say... the date didn't go well. He grew... upset. I didn't give him enough adoration, didn't worship his *stardom*." Go-Ri's fingers threw air quotes, and she grunted her derision. "At some point, I told him I was done—that I was uncomfortable and wanted to go home. I left the restaurant to go to the bathroom that was in the alley so I could think of a way to get back on my own. I needed to get away from him. I didn't know it, but he followed me."

Go-Ri could only stare at her hands and down at her damaged feet. She hadn't intended to cry. She didn't know when the tears started falling. "He hit me—so many times I lost count. I tried screaming, but the music from the theater across the street was loud, and no one heard me. He left me there in the alley on the other side of Seoul. I had no idea where I was... I just wanted to get home. So, I started walking. When I realized my coat and purse were still inside at our table, it was too late to go back. I couldn't get a taxi or the bus without my wallet, so I kept walking. I remember finally crossing the bridge and making it to my gate."

Swiping at the wet rivers running along her cheeks, she glanced at Baebin. *Is he laughing at me yet for being foolish?* His impassive, inscrutable expression gave away nothing. She wasn't even sure he heard her. "That was two years ago in January."

Her story shook him. He knew all along something was wrong, that something must have happened, but this was more than he'd expected. *Shit.* He needed to vomit.

He knew Nam Song-Ye, the leader of the band Xscape, and he already had reasons of his own to dislike him. But he hated himself more. *Didn't I basically stalk her, too? All the times I watched her work or looked for her. I'm a monster, too.*

"Did he... were you... raped?" He hated asking such a horrible question. *It's none of my business.*

She gave a strangled, harsh laugh. "No. That was the only good thing that night. I'm sure he was going to, but... he suddenly quit. He got off me and left. If I had been, would it bother you? Would it disgust you more? I'm a psycho freak."

"Disgust me?" It offended him that she asked, but he tried to soften his tone. "Some men may take issue with it, but not me. It *saddens* me. I would hate to think you might have experienced sex the wrong way. It should be a good thing between two people who care for each other. What you went through was bad enough. I'm glad that you have a nice family that helped you recover."

"My mom and brother don't know what happened." Go-Ri watched a boat navigate a turn on the river below. "I was too ashamed. Song-Ye and his friends and family come to the restaurant a lot, and I didn't want to cause any problems for MinGo. I didn't know if my brother would try to fight him. I hid for days at a friend's until I could cover the bruises. For months, I had to run away every time he showed up. But suddenly, *poof*, he was gone again. I haven't seen him in over a year. I don't know what happened, and I don't care."

Out of steam, and completely drained, Go-Ri wanted to go home. She wanted to hide until she had no more nightmares. "I tried to let it go. To start over and move on, but I can't. I can't forget. I can't stop... drowning. I can't *breathe*. I didn't mean to burden you, but... I just can't do this anymore. It's too much. I can't handle seeing you again." She stood to leave, fumbling with the handles of the bag he had brought her.

Baebin couldn't have known their past was tied to someone as loathsome as Nam Song-Ye. *Song-Ye was always a nasty prick, but I had no idea he was that bad.* He considered what to say next. *If she's truly leaving me, then I have no reason to tell her my secret. It wouldn't do her any* good. He scanned her face. *But what if she finds out later? Will she hate me more? Or hate other men because of my lies? If anything, I need to be honest. At least once.*

Resigned, Baebin spoke, stopping her before she turned to leave. "Have you heard of Insatiable 7, or IN7?" He stared at his clenched fists, refusing to look up.

She cocked her head to the side to think. "I don't think so." *What a strange question.*

"I am Kim Baebin, that's true. But most people know me as Yong-ee. I told you I work on shows, but really, I *am* the show. I'm a dancer, vocalist, and the leader of IN7. We are the highest-ranking K-pop group under the SKEC record label." He finished, gritting his teeth. "And I know Nam Song-Ye. We were trainees together before he and some others split off into their own group."

Go-Ri's knees buckled, and she sank hard onto the bench.

"I'm sorry I didn't tell you the truth earlier," he continued. "I figured since you didn't like K-pop, you wouldn't like me if you knew how involved with it I was. It was a stupid reason to lie and completely unfair to you. You have no reason to trust me, but I'm *nothing* like him. I *hate* that he hurt you. I couldn't help you then, but I want to be here for you now. I don't want you to go. Please don't run away from me."

Ghostly white, her eyes glittered dark in the gray pre-dawn light as she glared at Baebin on the next bench. *I could barely accept that he worked for SKEC, but he's just like Song-Ye? Of course, he is. The apartment... his schedule.... How could I have been so blind? So stupid? So trusting? So naïve?* Fighting against the weight in her chest and the thrumming in her ears, she forced herself back upright. Gripping the bag tightly, she staggered away, not looking back.

Baebin joined the design meeting already in progress several hours later, receiving a glare from Manager Kim. Baebin went through the daily motions on autopilot, doing what he had to, understanding nothing that happened around him. He had flatlined.

Fleeing to the dorm rooftop, Baebin watched as a tumble of gray storm clouds gathered over the city skyscrapers, hiding what few stars were visible over the bright city. Nowhere to turn, he texted his friend.

Chinmae stood at the railing ten minutes later, a jacket pulled tight around him to block out the wind. He was exhausted and utterly annoyed with Baebin. For almost four months, Baebin was different. They rarely talked anymore, and his friend was always running off alone. The entire group felt disjointed and out of sorts. It was all *hyung's* fault. "What do you want? Say it quick. I'm not in the mood, *Hyung*, and I'm too tired—"

"It's Go-Ri. I just need…." His eyes were already red and puffy, and his chest ached. Everything was a mess. He needed his *chingu*—his best friend. "I'm… I…" He sobbed, unable to go on.

"Who's Go-Ri?" Understanding slowly overtook Chinmae, and his hands itched to wrap around his friend's throat. "The girl. Before Japan." Anger boiled inside of him as he stood gripping the railing. Drawing in a deep breath to control his temper, he spoke quietly. "You told me you fixed it. I warned you not to allow anything to blow back on the group. What did you do?"

Baebin flinched under the painful truth. It wasn't what Chinmae expected, but yes, he screwed up.

As Chinmae turned away, Baebin grabbed his sleeve, unable to look at his *maknae*, his *chingu*. A sob loud enough to overpower the storm escaped him. "It's not like that. Please. I know you're mad, but I can't handle a lecture. You—you don't understand."

Chinmae was sixty-forty on whether to hit him, but it's cruel to kick a downed puppy. Taking in his friend's sorrowful expression, he relented. *Baebin has never been like this before.* Sitting on the bench, Chinmae looked over. "Okay. Then, make me understand."

Baebin held nothing back. Curled on the bench, half in Chinmae's lap, he lay broken. The stream of pitiful words became a flood, mirroring the steel-gray clouds bringing in rain. The fine mist evolved to a full-on storm, rolling over the two men on the bench.

After getting Baebin changed and into bed in his dorm room below, Chinmae texted the others.

IN7/C: Code 6. Now

Within five minutes of the emergency "man down" message, the rest of the teammates huddled together privately in Chinmae and Kyong's room, where Chinmae relayed what he just learned.

"WHAT?" Five voices shouted at once.

"Nam Song-ye? *That* ass?" Jaemin yanked on his hair in frustration, leaving it in spikes and sending dried flakes of hair gel floating through the air.

Tae-Si looked over at Kyong. "Remember way back in the beginning, when we had to share the big room with Song-Ye and Eun-woo? I hated living with them. They always snuck out when we weren't supposed to leave during training. Half of the time, they came back drunk. I was afraid they would get *me* in trouble by association."

"Yeah. And we always had extra dance practices because of them and their petty attitudes." Kyong grimaced. "I didn't trust them."

Yejoon held up his hand, shushing everyone as they all added their own reasons for hating Nam Song-Ye and his crew. "You're saying... *hyung* has a girl he likes that we didn't know about—well, except that she's the 'piano girl...' and she also happened to be attacked by that jerk *while* he was here at the Campus? You gotta be kidding me. Is this some screwed-up manga drama?"

The group heaved a collective groan and looked at each other. It was too unreal to be fake. Each of them thought about their friend, sleeping alone in the next room, and all that he had been through.

Chinmae hurt more than the rest. *I never even tried to learn or understand what was going on all summer. I left my best friend alone and accused him of hurting us, when I should have been supporting him.*

Daeho scrunched up his face, mentally sifting through the Campus rumors. "Wasn't Song-Ye part of the talent trade between Korea and Japan a few years ago? Isn't that why the Japanese guys, Asahi and Ren, are here? Xscapes's contract was supposed to be dropped next year, too, I think."

Everyone talked over one another again, piecing together the fact and fiction of the lackluster team they had all originally trained with.

The boys united and formed a bubble around Baebin. Daeho, his roommate, took care of him at night, while the others took turns during the day. They made sure Baebin was never alone and shielded him like six mothers with a cub. Supporting and protecting each other had become natural over the years, but during hard times like this, claws came out against any perceived threat.

Baebin loved his friends, but after a few days, he was suffocating. The constant watch kept him preoccupied, which he appreciated, but it grated on his nerves. They barely even left him alone to pee.

It should have hurt more to have his secret exposed to his friends. He was supposed to be stronger, smarter, and wiser as their *hyung* and leader. But he was tired. *I should have been focusing on the group, ensuring we stayed at number one on the charts. Or deliberating on what to do next. But no, I just had to be selfish. Unfocused.* If his stupid, reckless actions harmed IN7 and his friends, he wouldn't— *couldn't*—ever forgive himself.

He had met Go-Ri barely five months ago. In that time, his world turned upside down. IN7 sang about love being the center of your life, but he never thought it would be like this. It was supposed to be snuggles, romance, and tenderness. He realized this last week that he loved Go-Ri, and not once had they done any of those things.

Since the Japan trip, she had changed. Softened. Relaxed. Never once did she ask anything from him. She gave more than she received. She looked him in the eye now. She had the prettiest smile, and it melted him. They never touched, but he felt drawn to her, close to her.

He had met many men and women in the industry with the same drive as his to achieve their goal, but something about Go-Ri and her private determination to simply survive and continue the best she knew how, despite her pain and suffering, was more admirable. He liked her quiet grit.

I loved her. I lost her. Before I even had a chance.

Two complete sets of stages and crews left via plane and cargo ship, preparing for when the team members would arrive in America. They would be leapfrogging across the country, alternating venues, ensuring there would be no delay for each show.

Timing was crucial to pass through customs, and a specialized department worked for months behind the scenes, shifting pieces around and getting everything ready. IN7 had been overseas several times before, but the trips grew longer and more complicated every time.

The fan base was growing exponentially, the stages were bigger, and their productions were like nothing before. Who knew what would happen if things went well in the next two months?

Baebin felt the pressure to succeed. If he failed, then he let down everyone around him. When he started this dream years ago, he just wanted to sing on stage. Simple. Easy. He didn't realize how many thousands of people depended on IN7 for work; how intensive and demanding it would be, or what it would cost him personally—the long days, no privacy, no personal life, the compounding expectations. Sometimes, the responsibility weighed heavily on him.

It had been a week since the night at the hillside *sansjang*. Baebin couldn't stop thinking about the horrible events that happened the last time he was home. *Will I ever get over Go-Ri?*

He sent her a few texts, but they remained unread. His security system stayed quiet all week. *She meant it when she said she wasn't coming back.*

Nothing would ever be the same. He hated the apartment. It held too many memories. It used to be cold, empty, and lacking. Now, it was just lacking *her*. Baebin decided that the first call after the American trip would be to the realtor.

Since much of the crew was gone, the seven guys and the team members closest to them received the week off to decompress before the trip. They still had work to do independently, but they didn't have to be at the Campus. It felt like a full-blown vacation.

Dreading going back, Baebin had no choice but to return to the apartment. He already had several bags on the way to customs, but needed a few more things. Not only was this a long tour, but they would be taking planes and buses to thirty-eight cities in different climates. There was so much to consider and prepare for.

Baebin's friends worried about him being alone. What would happen if he ran into Go-Ri right now? He put his foot down when they offered to stay with him. *Gad, no.* He may still be miserable, but he didn't need babysitting any longer. Besides, they needed time with their own families, too. Baebin was going to pack his bags and hide at his parent's.

As he reached for the door that separated the lower garage from the lobby, it opened, and he stood face-to-face with Min-Jun.

The flush creeping up the younger boy's neck rose with each passing second. In a flash, Min-Jun's fist flew out, connecting solidly with Baebin's jaw.

Baebin's eyes rolled like marbles in his skull. No one had hit him since high school. Testing his lip with a thumb, it came back with a smear of blood, and he let his hands fall to his side. He was in no position to fight back.

"I told you to leave noona alone! Do you have any idea what she's been through?" Min-Jun pushed past him and strapped the delivery box to the back of the scooter.

"I do know, and I hate it."

"And you still toyed with her! You just couldn't leave her alone. Just like the other jerk who hurt her. Why do all of you assholes treat her like she's nothing? Just because you're famous, you think you can do anything you want."

"Wait, you know about that? She said you didn't know about Song-Ye." *Go-Ri said only her friend knew about the attack. When did Min-Jun find out?* The two fought like cats and dogs, but it would kill her if he knew her secret.

"*Phbt*. Of course, I do. You think I'm stupid?" Min-Jun rolled his eyes. "I've had to watch my sister die inside without saying a word! I'm scared to leave her alone. And when she goes out on deliveries or to that stupid jazz place, I'm terrified she won't come back!"

He stalked back to Baebin, thumping his scooter helmet against Baebin's chest. "Then you just *had* to show up and bother her. I wish she'd never gotten involved with you. I knew you would only hurt her."

"I never meant to. I didn't know until last week what had really happened. I like your sister a lot, but I don't want to cause her any more harm. I don't know what to do. I don't want to be a bad reminder for her. I thought I would just move. Maybe that would be the best." Baebin gestured weakly upstairs, unsure why he mentioned it to the teenager.

"Coward! Running away at the first sign of trouble. You stir the pot, then you can't handle what happens next. You've only dealt with this for a few weeks. You don't have a *right* to be upset. Fine. Run away. I'll clean up your mess." Min-Jun shot back as he climbed on his scooter and peeled out of the garage.

Spitting out a mouthful of blood and gently rinsing, Baebin inspected the damage in the bathroom mirror. There was a long gash inside his cheek and a cut on his bottom lip. The bruised jaw was already starting to swell. *Min-Jun really knows how to throw a punch! Any harder, and I'd be worried about the tour. This day is turning out to be* just *lovely.*

The boy was right, though. He'd stirred the pot, and his first thought was to run. *What else am I supposed to do? If I stay, she'll splinter. I want to be with her, but she won't even read my messages...* He felt lost and hopeless.

Holding a package of frozen vegetables to his face, he pulled out his two biggest suitcases from the closet and filled the first one. Storing his good IN7 "airport clothes" and makeup supplies from the studio and the connecting bathroom made packing quick and easy. *I need to buy those strange American outlet adapters. I should have ordered them weeks ago.* Closing the bag, he wheeled it to the *hyeongwan* and laid his sports coat with the rolled-up sleeves on top to wear the day they left.

The second bag was going to be more difficult. Tossing it on his bed, he began pulling things out of his personal drawers and closets. Fall in America: from Minnesota to Florida. He needed everything from sweaters to shorts, and Baebin couldn't remember what he had already packed at the dorm.

His fingers paused over his—oddly—*folded* underwear.

They were in the right place, but he was a *stuffer*, not a *folder*.

Go-Ri had done a few loads of laundry for him during the last few weeks, but it never occurred to him that she'd see his underwear. Or that she would fold all of them in the drawer—even the ones she hadn't washed. Blushing and hoping his more risqué no-show briefs were at the dorm, he grabbed a random handful before slamming the drawer shut and moving on to the next drawer. Pajamas were a much more neutral item of clothing.

Half-packed but mentally over it, he flopped on the bed next to the luggage, pressing the melting vegetables to his wound.

It was a nice bed. Soft. Big. I'll never get to try it out with my co-shopper. Depressed, he looked around. The warm wood and padded headboard with the matching nightstands and dresser blended nicely with the new burgundy bedspread she picked for him. It was peaceful and erotic at the same time. Masculine, but not overly so. *Months ago, I only had a mattress on the floor. Now, my first master bedroom is handsome. It's warm and inviting. Like the rest of the apartment, it's home. I don't want to leave... but I don't want to be alone here.*

A photo and a new side table he didn't recognize sat next to the comfortable but useless chair that was only good for holding yesterday's barely used clothes. Curious, he took the vegetables with him and sank into the thick cushion. Inside the black frame was a photo of him and his siblings. Judging by his hideous hair and swim trunks, he was, maybe, twelve or fourteen. *Definitely before my sister got braces.*

It was one of the last trips as a family to the beach before he joined the company. *Where did Go-Ri find it? She had it framed?* He burrowed deeper into the chair.

Baebin had just nodded off when the doorbell chimed. Swiping at the cold, wet spot on his groin from the dripping, defrosted vegetables, he shuffled to the monitor, guessing at which of his annoying friends was visiting.

Only a few people could pass the desk without him being notified first, and most of them knew his door code. He'd told his friends not to come, but of course, they wouldn't listen. He just wanted to finish packing and go to his parents'.

Flipping on the hall light, he checked the screen. "Wha—?" he gaped, bug-eyed and unbelieving. He was so stunned, he couldn't think to open the door until Go-Ri turned away to leave.

He yanked on the handle, and they both hesitated, staring at each other through the open frame. Baebin pulled out Go-Ri's new slippers before retreating to the kitchen to give her space to come in.

Silent, she rested her purse on the *sinbaljang*, fixating on it while automatically reaching for socks from her cubby. He watched as she put them on over the ones she already wore before sliding on the slippers. With palpable effort, Go-Ri stiffened and left the *hyeongwan*.

He said a quick prayer. Baebin never expected to see her again and was uncertain what to do. Go-Ri's light-blue ruffled blouse, which looked nice a few weeks ago, now matched her wan coloring and swam on her. She looked terrible. And so beautiful.

She was here.

Drumming her fingers on the table, she took in the dimly lit room and his suitcase—looking everywhere but at him.

"I'm only here for my suitcase. We're leaving soon for America, and I need some clothes. I wasn't going to bother you." Baebin pointed to the suitcase and the travel pack next to it with charging cords hanging out the sides.

She continued to look around as if she had never been there before, inspecting each item, one by one.

I'm going to have gray hair if she keeps this up any longer, he thought. Throwing the bag of vegetables back into the freezer, he yanked on the tail of his shirt to cover the wet spot on his pants. He hoped she didn't see it. There was no non-embarrassing way to explain dripping vegetables versus a wet dream. His neck flushed as pink as his striped shirt.

She kept drumming her fingers, her eyes still roaming before finally settling on him. Raising an eyebrow, she inspected his split lip. "Min-Jun said he hit you."

"Mmm," he answered ruefully, gingerly touching the cut. "I deserved it."

"Mmm." Go-Ri stared at him for so long, he started to itch. "You lied."

Baebin could do nothing but nod.

"From the beginning, I did not want to trust or be around you, but you kept dragging me in. I… wasn't ready, but you pushed me."

Her quiet accusation and direct honesty cut Baebin deeply.

Unable to look at his bruised, handsome face any longer, she paced to the large windows, hugging herself tightly as she stared out. Swiping at a tear sliding down her cheek, she asked, "Why? Why couldn't you leave me alone?"

That was the question he had been asking himself since starting this mess. The same question Chinmae and Min-Jun asked. *Everyone wanted me to leave her alone, but I didn't listen. I was selfish.*

"I don't know." He shrugged. "I know now that I stalked you, too. Like he did. But I didn't mean it. Not like that. I never meant to bother you. I was only... curious. I liked seeing you. I wanted to see what made you happy."

Baebin stood alone in the kitchen, afraid to continue but also welcoming the chance to explain. "When we got to know each other, when you started coming here... I don't know how, but you made me feel *normal*. I know I shouldn't have lied, but I couldn't figure out how to tell the truth. No matter when I told you, you would hate me, and I couldn't figure out how to avoid it."

Baebin flattened his hands on the counter to keep them from trembling. "I'm so sorry. I never wanted to hurt you. You can ask me anything, and I'll be honest. Promise. You deserve the truth."

She looked out the window for a long time, scrutinizing him behind her through the mirrored glass. There was no way to ensure he would be truthful with any question she wanted to ask. *I don't trust him.* She hadn't trusted *herself* in a long time. Her ability to recognize truth from fiction was shattered. She couldn't think straight. Her mind wandered, trying to decide what to do.

The apartment behind her, in its semi-darkness, seemed to mock her, like a reminder of their short time together. Empty at first, but now filled and beautiful. The lock on the hall door glinted in the faint glow of the hall light.

She wondered if the room beyond it was just storage, like she had thought, or a wild and crazy sex den. Whips and chains, or just more boxes? Stifling a giggle, she had to bite her cheek to return her mind to the present.

Mmm. Why not? If he promised honesty, then daring him to open this door seemed like a place to start. With a deep breath, she walked down the hallway and stopped at the locked door. "Open it," she ordered.

Baebin blinked at the unexpected request but stuffed his hands in his pockets and walked closer. He stopped where the hall met the open living area. "The code is the day I became a member of IN7—130310; it was a big day for me."

She nodded, understanding. Not only was Baebin letting her in, but he was also giving her the key.

Go-Ri raised her hand and flexed her fingers a bit, confirming if she genuinely wanted to do this. There was no going back. Quickly, she punched in the code, and the door swung open. She turned on the lights with a shaky hand and looked in.

He hadn't moved from his spot in the hall but said, "It's my private sound studio. Everything about my life in the industry is in there."

Looking around the room, Go-Ri was taken aback. While unsure what the room would hold, she hadn't expected all of this. She walked inside and let the feeling envelop her. The dark, padded walls and thin carpet suited the space well. The equipment was fantastic—better than the third-rate studio she had rented years ago to make the backup disk for her solo gigs.

A massive L-shaped desk divided the room into two sections. One side held video stands, recording sets, several computers, a highly technical soundboard, and a small kitchenette. The other side had multiple types of microphones, music stands, and headsets on their cradles.

Seeing the row of trophies on the floor and stacks of frames and pictures against the wall, she crouched down to get a better view.

"I want to display those here, but I fear they will distort the sound, so I'm stuck." Baebin propped himself against the doorframe and watched as she flipped through a stack of pictures. He told her about them and their importance— a trip to Rome, an album cover, their first show. He named all his teammates, telling her stories about each of them.

Go-Ri mostly looked for Baebin in the pictures, but was amazed at how they all changed through the years.

Go-Ri continued the tour, getting to know him for the first time. He seemed relaxed, leaning against the door, and she liked the smile in his voice as he talked about the things she was looking at. Moving to the closets, she gave him a questioning look.

He nodded, and she opened one. "That's all my old stage stuff—various outfits we used to wear. These either don't fit anymore, or we have changed the style since then. The seven of us have very different personalities and hate matching, so we may wear something similar, but our costumes are unique in small ways. The other closet holds clothes I need for trips or interview shows. This bathroom is only for the stuff I need for work. I keep my makeup, hair stuff, and a ridiculous amount of jewelry in here."

Embarrassed, he added. "I probably have more stuff than you do."

With a last look around, Go-Ri pointed to a computer, "I still haven't looked into your group, so help me understand. Can you play me your favorite song?"

It took him a minute to think. Powering up the monitor, he loaded one of their practice videos recorded in an old dance studio, and showed her where he started in the formation. Before he could sit down with her, she pointed to the large open space on the other side of the desk. "Nope, over there. I want a live show, too."

Tickled, he bowed low and went around, moving some equipment for more space. He couldn't even remember the last time he danced like this for his family. She hit play and sat back watching, her eyes flying back and forth between him and the person on the screen. By the end of the first chorus, she couldn't keep her foot from moving with the beat, and she constantly lost track of him in the quickly shifting formations on the screen.

When it was over, he took water from the mini fridge for them both, setting hers on the desk and drinking his in a few gulps. Wiping a bead of sweat on his cheek, he winced when he touched his jaw. He couldn't hold back anymore. "I know it's not your style, but..." his blush had nothing to do with the minor exertion of one song, "thanks for wanting to see it. You didn't have to."

Go-Ri just looked at him and gave him an unreadable *Umph*. But he caught a smile as she walked out of the room.

He played hoops with his empty bottle, watching as it dropped into the trash can without hitting the rim, and shut the door behind him.

So far, so good, he thought. Go-Ri wasn't running for the exit, and she didn't seem to be as tightly coiled as she was earlier.

She sat at the table, and after getting more water for them both, he sat down across from her.

She looked at him thoughtfully and asked in a tone that held no anger, worry, or fear, "Why? The room. I'm curious. Why do you hide something away that is so important to you? Because of me?"

He sat back and pulled one knee up to rest his arm on it. Smiling, he answered, "I built that room well before I met you. You are the first person who has seen it. Not even my teammates or my family have been in there. I've lived at the Campus with hundreds of other people since I was sixteen. I work very hard, and I'm constantly surrounded by my job. I wanted a place to escape to—that's why I bought the apartment. I love going home to my parents, but since being away for so long, it feels… awkward sometimes. I built the studio here so I can come home when I want to, but still do work if I must. I like shutting the door to that world."

"Mmm," she sighed, nodding. "That why you have a stage name, too?"

Baebin grinned, thinking back to the week he and his siblings spent picking out his name, when he was a nobody with dreams. "Kind of. I thought it would be something fun and cool to have. But I mostly wanted it to insulate my family, to let them be normal. Maybe a part of me wanted to protect myself, too. I love what I do, but I like being able to be just *me* sometimes. I get to choose who I let into my real world."

"Hmm." Go-Ri had to agree it all made sense. Baebin kept several intangible layers around him. They weren't impenetrable like hers, but they protected him all the same.

His carefully constructed cage gave him valuable freedom. Somehow, she had crossed inside the invisible barriers in his life without even knowing they were there.

Gnawing at her lip, she wondered again why he lied to her. *Did he do it for me or himself?* She wanted a better explanation, although she wasn't sure if it really mattered anymore. "What you did tell me about work was partially true—having shows and such—but you made me believe it was something else. Why?"

"Mmm." Baebin sighed and rested the cold glass against his bruised jaw. "I was going to tell you. I wanted to. But I was afraid you'd run if you knew the truth. I knew something about what I did for work upset you, and I didn't want you to feel the same way about me. What I do and who I really am are two different people."

He sighed and added softly, "After the bar… I knew something was wrong, and I only wanted to help, but what you said about the industry and pop, mmm… You called K-pop artists scumbags and monkeys." Baebin gestured to the studio weakly. "What was I supposed to say? You would have pushed me away right then. I got scared and lied." He shrugged his shoulders, as if settling an enormous weight.

Go-Ri blanched. *I don't remember saying that to him. I never meant… I never thought of* Baebin *that way.* It pained her to realize her easy, derogatory generalization could sweep up someone she knew didn't deserve the hurtful label.

She spent a long time digesting all he had said. She thought of the past before she met him, and every moment she could think of since he first walked into her mom's restaurant.

"What do you want from me?" she blurted out.

His ears turned tomato red. She wanted the truth, and if she hadn't already run away tonight, then he might as well lay all the cards on the table. *I have nothing else to lose,* Baebin thought.

"Okay… Honestly, I like you, and I want to get to know you better. I don't really want to talk about work, but I don't want to hide it either." He paused to put together more thoughts. "I want to see you walk in my door whenever you want and have us hang out and be together. I'd like us to meet our friends. I want to go on a real date and hold your hand."

He set his glass down gently and didn't look at her. He spoke so softly, she could barely hear. "I want to be with you, but if you want to stay only as we are now, then I'll accept that, too. I'll take anything that will let me be by your side."

The magnetic intensity in his voice, soft and raw, held her rooted to the chair. It sounded honest. She knew he was telling the truth, even though it was unbelievable. *He likes me? He could have anyone, but he wants to be with me? Even when I'm so screwed up?*

Finally, he had to ask, "My turn. What do *you* want?" Even though he confessed his feelings, any decision would be hers.

This past week, she was a trainwreck. Her world had flipped on its edge again, and she felt like she had lost what little mind she had left. First Song-Ye, then Baebin. Both men had destroyed her in different ways, making her distrust everything around her and, more importantly, *herself.*

Earlier, when her brother told her Baebin was back, she impulsively ran the entire way to the apartment. If she was truthful with herself, she was not sure what she wanted or why she was here. Was she going to push him away or pull him closer? Her life was comfortable inside her walls, but the thought of never seeing Baebin again disturbed her. *Deeply.* More deeply than she wanted it to.

She reflected again on the night at the bar and the last time she was here. Her eyes flicked over to the spot where she had fallen, reliving the fear like an outsider watching a movie. She instinctively knew all along, but couldn't piece it together until now: she wasn't scared of *him*, just of the situation.

He broke her trust, but he was the first person in a long time who didn't frighten her. Even before he knew about her past, Baebin always held back, giving her space and time. He was kind, caring, funny—she treasured everything about him. Go-Ri finally had to admit that she liked him.

"I need to work on forgiving you for lying," she said honestly. "But I understand why you did it. You're probably right, I would have gotten angry had you told me then who you were. But you still should have. You should have tried harder." Holding his gaze for a moment, she noted his quiet acceptance before she looked away.

It was easier to fixate on his long, thin hands that would never harm her. "I'm scared. I know you wouldn't hurt me intentionally. Physically. But I am scared of… my past… and the future. Of being hurt again… inside. I don't know how or when I'll break down next. Always living on the edge, not knowing what will set me off is… hard. I don't know if I can be normal again. If you think you can handle that, then… I'll try too. I'll try… with you."

After a minute, he let out a silent woosh of air, and blood started flowing to his extremities again. *She's giving me a chance.* She had opened the door a crack.

Go-Ri stood to leave. Everything was overwhelming; there was so much to process. She walked to the *hyeongwan* and changed into her shoes, stuffing the second pair of socks back in the cubby. Baebin moved to the end of the table to see her in the doorway. Pausing, she looked at his suitcase, then up at him. "What are your plans?"

A few hours ago, his plan was simple: pack, leave, and not come back. Now, he really didn't know. "I thought I would go to my parents' or back to the dorm. We have a few days off before the trip."

He debated whether he should really tell her the whole truth. But he didn't want to lie any longer. "Earlier, I thought about selling this place when I got back. If my being here upset you… I didn't want that."

Shocked, she could only gape at him, slack-jawed. *He would leave all of this because of me?* Go-Ri looked at his bag again and said softly, "If you stay, I'll come." She left before he could answer.

Baebin smiled. She didn't say when, how often, or for how long, but it was enough.

The next day, Baebin was ready. He set the scene and crossed his fingers. The locked door was open wide, and he took his music homework to the coffee table. Go-Ri would most likely work at MinGo in the morning, and he hoped she would come after her shift. If not today, he would do the same tomorrow… then the next and the next.

His skin tingled, and he looked at the clock every five minutes. With the TV on low, he sat on a pillow and went through the motions of reviewing the music.

The stack shrank and shifted from one pile to another when the door lock finally chimed. Squeezing his pen in a silent prayer of thanks, he watched her come inside. Go-Ri sat on the couch within reaching distance, and his body turned to gelatin. All his frayed nerves relaxed, and he couldn't be happier.

He grinned from ear to ear, drinking her in. Her straight black hair was in a tight braid down her back, and a purple V-neck blouse hugged her, displaying the delicate notch between her collarbones and the thin silver chain resting there. Last night, she looked gaunt and drawn, but less than twenty-four hours later, the tension around her eyes and shoulders had begun to disappear again. She was distractingly perfect.

Catching her inspecting the organized mess on the table, he patted himself on the back. Opening up about everything he did at work needed to be done in small, manageable bites. For both of them. Looking over music was step one.

Sheet music was all the same, no matter the style. Turning paper into sound was the difference. "Sorry, I was working. These are our potential songs. Each of us reviews the same music on our own, and then we get together and vote on what makes our next album. That one," he gestured to the one in her hand, "I'm rejecting."

"Let me try." Curious, Go-Ri scanned the page, reading the music more than the lyrics. She drummed to the beat, struggling with the unfamiliar tempo. Within a few lines, she got it and set the page aside with a *humph*, wrinkling her nose. She may not be a pro at pop, but the song was poorly written. "Mmm. Bad rhythm. What do you look for?"

"I thought that, too. I look more for overall flow and feeling. What suits our style. Kyong, our main dancer, also does flow, but he's good at picturing what our dance could be. Tae-Si and some of the others are more about rhythm and words."

He laid it in the reject pile. "Sometimes it seems like we have doubled our work doing this, but I think we're all happier that we get to choose our own music."

"I wouldn't want to be told what to play. Be forced to do music I didn't like." She sniffed slightly.

Baebin remembered she had said something like that before, but the animosity and hostility were gone. Now, she was making a simple statement.

Analyzing his career from her perspective, Baebin absentmindedly tapped his pen. "Starting out, yes, the company controlled our songs and performances with very little input from us. But... we also didn't know anything. We didn't know what our true style was or if anyone would even listen to us. They did the legwork while we did the learning. Now we know, and we have much more freedom to do our own thing."

Crisscrossing the piles, he gathered everything together and returned them to the studio. *I hope I didn't go overboard talking about work.* Winning her over wasn't today's goal. Acceptance was enough.

Go-Ri came prepared to be open-minded. His sly trick with the music didn't fool her, but it was a sweet touch. As he walked away, she considered what he told her. His observations shifted her preconceptions ever so slightly. *I still don't like the controlling nature of the industry, but what he said makes annoying sense.*

Go-Ri had planned a test for him and decided now was a good time. They needed a new, unfamiliar setting to start over. To reconnect. "I'm glad you showed me your music. It was interesting. My turn now. How about we take a walk? Would that be okay?" She hooked a thumb toward the door.

All night, she thought about what he said. The concept of officially dating gave her small tremors of panic, but it wasn't terribly different than what they had already been doing alone together in the apartment.

For anyone else, the list of dating activities could fill a page, but either she was afraid of them, or he probably couldn't do them. Amusement parks and crowded malls were definitely out. So, step one: a simple walk. This section of Dongbinggo-dong was older and a little quieter but full of quaint shops that he probably hadn't seen yet.

As they changed shoes, Baebin added glasses and donned a ball cap pulled low with most of his hair tucked inside. She was curious. "Do you always have to hide?"

"Not always," he answered. "Usually, when a few of us are together, we get spotted easily, but it tends to be harder to figure out who we are when we're alone. My hair color is usually a dead-giveaway. It's an occupational hazard. I'm used to it now. I hate to admit it, but it's kinda a blow to the ego when I don't cover up, and no one recognizes me."

Baebin held the door for Go-Ri, and they rode the elevator down together.

His self-deprecating humor and pink ears made her laugh. Grinning, she had to ask, "So, were you happy or upset that you didn't get noticed at the furniture store?"

His pink ears turned red, and he studiously read the posted sign about the elevator weight requirements.

Cocking an eyebrow, she looked at him. "What?" Her gaze narrowed in suspicion the longer he avoided her.

"Mmm. Well." He cleared his throat. His voice was so low, she had to lean closer. "I had some bodyguards come with me to keep everyone away."

She didn't hear that right. Her brows shot straight up. A snort turned into a giggle. By the time the doors opened, she was in a full-on rolling laugh, unable to contain herself.

At the desk, Mr. Bak spun around, flabbergasted at the sound. What he saw in the open elevator made him reach for his chair. Go-Ri stood, doubled over, clutching her sides, and Kim Baebin held the door, wearing a wonderful shade of embarrassment as he waited for her to stop.

Finally, just as the elevator started to beep in frustration, she managed to stand upright. Fanning herself, she snorted her way past the desk, trying to gather her composure. Baebin shrugged at the elderly man and wiggled his fingers in a wave as he passed.

Mr. Bak raised a prayer to his ancestors for the budding couple.

With a last, deep, gasping breath, Go-Ri reached the sidewalk and pointed in the direction she wanted to go. As she stepped off the curb, Baebin's light touch on her arm stopped her. "Go-Ri, if something happens, just do what I do and stay by me. Most of the time when I'm approached, it's easy, but sometimes it can get nutty. But I'll never let anyone hurt you. Okay?"

Cocking her head to the side, she gave him an easy smile. "Okay. I'll show you some nice places and you can protect me." With a nod, she set off again, looking back at him. "Together, it won't be bad. For either of us."

Choosing the less congested side streets that twisted and turned uphill, Go-Ri surreptitiously studied him as they walked the neighborhood. *His mannerisms are more reserved and distant than in the apartment. A little like the few times I've seen him at MinGo in the evenings. Or at the convenience store where I used to work.* He was still friendly and easy-going, but this was a different, quieter version of him than she was used to. *Is that how I look?* she wondered. *A split persona?* The thought niggled at her.

She was testing him, but she needed to test herself, as well. She took a risk and let her fingers brush his. *Would it be Okay? I think I can handle this much.* They hadn't touched since the night he came back from Japan. *Maybe now isn't the right time. Last night, he said he wanted to hold hands, but maybe he meant when no one could see.* He had to be careful with his public life. If he didn't accept it, she promised herself not to be hurt.

The brush of her fingers sent shockwaves up his arm. He couldn't keep the puppy-dog grin off his face or slow the rapid beating of his heart. Not letting her withdraw, he took her hand in his, linking fingers. Her thin, warm palm and long, bony fingers, with their tips calloused from playing string instruments, felt like heaven. *Perfection.*

Walking past small shops and through narrow side streets, they stumbled across a little studio with wood carvings and pottery. The storefront window, filled with dozens of art pieces, drew Baebin in. He admired the talent and patience it took to design each of the traditional sculptures and—unable to stop at just one—purchased three large carvings made from rare Ulleungdo hemlock.

Wooden bowls and an ample supply of chopsticks, along with several flowerpots and mugs created by the artist's friend, rapidly filled the counter. As the pile grew, the stooped store owner willingly agreed to deliver everything to the apartment.

How fast would she run away if I also bought wedding ducks? He snickered to himself as he peeked at the beautiful display of mating pairs, with threaded tassels wrapped around their beaks, symbolizing fidelity and respect in a marriage. *Probably faster than I could catch her,* he decided.

An image of her running away with spinning legs like a manga character made him bite his cheek to stifle the threatening snort. Oblivious to his thoughts, she knelt in the corner, admiring her favorite piece.

"I'd like to get that, too," Baebin whispered to the owner. Winking in agreement, the artist rang up the delicately carved, multi-tiered flute stand. Knowing all the Korean flutes of various sizes she had at the apartment— besides the European flutes and piccolos—he prepaid for two more stands of different sizes to be created later.

As the sun dropped closer to the western mountains and shadows lengthened, taking away the heat of the day, Baebin's confusion grew. She could tell he was lost. Trying not to laugh, she pointed up ahead to an elementary school. "Come on. There is a park up here with a fresh breeze. Let's go sit and pull up a map for you. I need a break." A few small kids darted around the aged playground equipment while the sounds of laughter drifted from a ball court around the corner.

Go-Ri perked up with a huge grin. Sneaking a peek at Baebin, she asked, "Mmm. You serious about meeting my friends?" When he nodded, she didn't give him a chance to back out. She stifled a laugh. "Okay. Get ready!"

Baebin cringed when she gave a deafening finger whistle and was surprised to hear it echoed seconds later from around the building. Two guys and a girl came hurtling toward them. The transformation in Go-Ri upon seeing her three childhood friends awed him. Her sudden sparkle and easy, light-hearted laughter made his heart skip.

Go-Ri felt a stab of uncertainty at drawing Baebin into their circle. *How should I introduce him?*

Leave it to her best girlfriend to do it for her.

Binna screeched. "You're Yong-ee!" Smashing a hand over her own mouth, her adoring gaze flipped back and forth from her blushing friend to the idol. "Sorry. That was excessive," Binna sputtered, blushing furiously at her own exuberance. Her pointed stare at her best friend warned of a thousand questions to come.

Waving off the girl's embarrassment, Baebin dipped his head in greeting. "Yes. But please call me Kim Baebin. Or just Baebin. I'd like that better."

The remaining two friends were much more composed. After smacking Binna on the head and elbowing her to hush, the guys greeted the newcomer. Their ready smiles betrayed hints of protectiveness. Lim Ji-U held out the basketball to Baebin. "We just got started. You play?"

Picking up on the subtle challenge and always up for a game, Baebin handed his glasses to Go-Ri and flipped his hat around; sprigs of white-and-purple hair poked out the front. While stretching, Baebin, Lim Ji-U, and Jim Kimh-so strategized a three-man game.

Go-Ri and Binna sat on the nearby swings holding hands, watching the testosterone-riddled battle. Fishing for details, Binna yanked her friend close. "How in the world did you meet him?! When did this happen? Spill it!"

"He moved into a building close to the restaurant." Binna wouldn't let go of her cheeks. Rolling her eyes in exasperation, Go-Ri added, "Umph. He is letting me use his place to teach. We are... friends." The growing flush made her friend grunt in disbelief.

With a sly grin, Binna asked. "So, does he kiss good?"

"I don't know!" Go-Ri pinked. She had been wondering that, too. She had only just now held his hand; working up to a kiss was going to take some time!

"Pbht. I'm tired of waiting for Ji-U. I'm friend-zoned forever. Now, your man... he's got a sweet butt, and I bet he's a stellar kisser." Binna held out her hands and scrunched up her face, mentally testing the depth and breadth of the rear in question as he made a basket.

"Binna! Don't you dare!"

"What! I can dream!"

"Keep my guy out of your dreams!"

Binna howled in a fit of squealing laughter as Go-Ri sputtered, trying to rewind what she just said. "So, you *aren't* just friends! I *knew* it!"

Ji-U froze mid-free throw, and all three guys watched as the two girls tussled before Go-Ri shoved Binna and sent her swing spinning. Go-Ri was flustered, Binna was hysterical, and the boys were baffled.

"You little sneak! But I'd be hiding that hunk away, too!" Binna continued swinging. She was thrilled her friend was finally inching out of her shell, but this was no easy matter. And it was Yong-ee—wait, Kim Baebin—no less. She hesitated, worried for her friend. "Does he know? And... are you okay with—"

"Yes." Go-Ri cut her short, brushing the hair out of her flushed face. Binna had helped her through the worst two years ago, keeping her secret and talking through the sleepless nights. "I kinda freaked out a while ago and had to tell him. He knows as much as I want him to. I didn't know who he was for a long time. He was just someone I was hanging out with. Sorry I didn't tell you sooner."

Watching the three guys shoot hoops together, Go-Ri spoke softly. "He's not like Nam Song-Ye." She gave her friend a reassuring smile and squeezed her hand. "I promise. I'm okay."

Thirty minutes later, the guys were sweating profusely and out of breath. Challenge over, peace reigned in the universe. Baebin stood near Go-Ri's swing as Ji-U and Kimh-so ran to squish Binna, wiping their sweaty shirts all over her, until she punched both in the stomach, while holding her nose. Go-Ri yelled her encouragement, as Binna chased them around the monkey bars.

On his third pass around the swings, Kimh-so snatched up Binna's discarded shoes and chucked them at her, nailing her in the back as the three continued to chase and scream at each other.

The clang of metal and the suddenly empty swing startled Baebin. Laughing only moments ago, Go-Ri crouched on the ground, white and wavering.

Alarmed, he knelt over her, and the ball he'd held rolled away, forgotten. He wanted to comfort and help in some way, but worried his touch would upset her more.

Binna came to his rescue. Snagging her shoes from where they had landed earlier and shoving them on, she ordered the boys to fetch the ball. Pushing Baebin away, she sat in front of Go-Ri, wiggling her feet and leaning in close to whisper. He could only hear snippets of her murmuring. "Fine... shoes... breathe... warm... not him... breathe..."

By the time Ji-U and Kimh-so crawled out from under the bushes with the ball that escaped down the hill, Go-Ri was gulping in air and sitting back on her heels. She was still pale, but her eyes were focused again. Before they could ask, Binna spoke up, shooting Baebin a warning glance. "Let's go eat. You know how she gets when she's hungry."

Dragging her friend to her feet and linking arms, she force-marched Go-Ri the long way out of the playground, giving the others no choice but to follow behind.

Baebin kept up with the steady chatter from the two guys beside him, but kept his eyes glued on the girls in front. Binna was a miracle worker. Before they were halfway down the block, Baebin could hear a small laugh coming from Go-Ri.

The chosen location for their dinner was based purely on the outdoor seating arrangement. Three foul-smelling men—one an idol—were guaranteed to cause a disruption. They chose a table at the far end, giving Baebin the seat facing away from other patrons. He noticed a group of girls a few tables over taking his picture, but let it go. If they approached, he would intervene. He had forgotten to warn the others that it might happen, but they'd seemed to anticipate it.

Go-Ri's friends welcomed the new addition to the group with fried chicken, beer, soju, and stories of Go-Ri's childhood, making sure to tell the juiciest, most embarrassing ones they could remember.

"Okay. Gotta ask." Kimh-so stopped everyone, waving a hand covered in spicy chicken juice in the direction of Baebin's jaw. "What happened to your face?" Everyone waited expectantly for a dramatic, hidden, K-pop fight story.

Baebin looked at Go-Ri for help. She smiled sweetly and said, "Min-Jun punched him. Let's just say… overprotective brother." The three friends knew Min-Jun well and almost fell out of their chairs, laughing, while Baebin turned tomato red.

A high-schooler punching a star. *Awesome.*

"You let him hit you?!" Ji-U cried out between breaths.

"I didn't want to!" Baebin stuffed food in his mouth. "It kinda just happened that way." Fresh peels rang out, and more customers turned their way at the disruption.

Sitting across from each other all night, Baebin and Go-Ri's knees touched under the table. Go-Ri often caught him looking at her. It made her skin tingle. She blinked and glanced his way when he shifted a foot to rest against hers.

She chattered on with more stories of the four of them growing up together as she and Baebin walked home under the streetlights.

He loved meeting her friends and seeing how she interacted with them. She was a different person. Bright and warm. How she probably was before the attack. *I want her to be like that again. All the time.*

"The swings..." He hated to bring up the upsetting incident. He didn't want to ruin the evening. "You don't have to tell me what happened, but I'd like to know what I could have done differently to help."

Something had triggered her, but Binna had managed to pull her back quickly. He wanted to be able to do the same.

Go-Ri had glossed over the part about her feet when she told Baebin what had happened with Nam Song-Ye. Being hit was bad enough, but a broken shoe had made the trip home a nightmare. The aftermath had given her a weird anxiety. She wasn't sure how to explain it.

They were back in the shadows before she answered. "When Binna got hit today, I panicked. That night... with Nam Song-Ye... I was trying to get away from him, and my shoe fell off. He used it to hit me and the heel broke. I ended up walking home barefoot."

"But you said that was in January! You didn't have a coat, *and* you were barefoot?!" Baebin asked in horror.

"Mmm." Go-Ri glanced down at her numb toes, as if to make sure they were still there. "So… now… I have a thing about my feet and shoes. I hate being cold. Today, Binna told me she wasn't hurt and reminded me to breathe."

"Mmm. Ji-U and Kimh-so don't know, do they?"

"No. I didn't want them to. I was afraid of what they would do to Song-Ye or how they would act around me. Binna is the one who helped me. I don't know what I'd have done without her."

He could feel her shudder and hear the pain in her soft voice. Gently squeezing her hand, Baebin hushed her growing tremors and any further memories. "Okay. I'll remember that. I'm glad Binna was there for you."

Letting his calm, soothing murmur wash over her, he talked quietly the rest of the way home. He held her hand and didn't let her go inside her gate until he heard her soft laughter in the cool air.

Back at his apartment, he put his shoes in the *sinbaljang* and stood staring at her cubby stuffed full of socks. Determined to be patient for the rest of the story, he pulled out his phone and texted Go-Ri.

> B: I HAD A GREAT DAY. SLEEP WELL. THANK YOU FOR GIVING ME A CHANCE.
> G: GOODNIGHT BAEBIN. THANK YOU FOR BEING PATIENT WITH ME.

The next morning, while Baebin waited in the car for Go-Ri, he texted the guys, inviting them for dinner the following day, before they all needed to return to the Campus.

Their time off flew by too quickly, and he figured everyone could use one last fun evening before they jumped into the jam-packed tour. Baebin wanted to be alone with Go-Ri, but he had a duty to his group to set the mood for the next two months. He'd failed these last few weeks as their leader and needed to redeem himself.

He hesitated, then added:

IN7/B: FYI, I MIGHT HAVE A GUEST. SO, PLEASE, BE NICE. BEHAVE AND DON'T BE CRAZY.

He hadn't even asked if Go-Ri would be willing to meet the guys yet. *Maybe it's too soon. I don't want to rush her.*

The dark gray clouds that hovered low over the Yellow Sea scared away all but the ardent beach goers, leaving Baebin and Go-Ri mostly alone at the calm shore with flocks of noisy seagulls. The gentle breeze that barely stirred the water was cooler than Seoul, and the briny salt air washed over them, erasing the smog and stress of the big city.

They spent the day walking on the beach hand-in-hand, meandering along the coastline. As the sea pulled out, exposing the tidal flats, Baebin found an unoccupied bench and emptied his shoes of sand.

Go-Ri desperately wanted to clean out her shoes as well, but the thought of taking them off made her stomach flip. Staring out at the water, she was taken aback when he pulled her next to him on the bench, drawing a foot onto his lap.

"Let me help. Okay?"

His calm, insistent demeanor didn't allow for rejection, yet she knew with a simple tug or shake of her head, he would willingly let go. First, one sneaker, then the next, was efficiently smacked clean of wet sand before being tied back into place.

He was concerned about her damp socks, but he didn't have any dry spares with him. Baebin made a mental note to keep a supply in the car from now on. The task finished, he pulled her closer, bringing her head to rest on his shoulder. They sat on the bench together until the pulse at her neck settled.

The quiet day at the coast stood in stark contrast to the turbulent drama of the last few weeks. *I wish he didn't have to leave. Not yet. We're just starting to figure things out, and now he's going for two whole months.* Go-Ri rested against him, unconsciously searching for his cologne over the salty air, one ear listening to his heartbeat, the other to the sounds of the sea.

Spicy *teokbokki* rice cakes and chicken skewers from the streetside *pojangmacha* food stall near the beach lulled her into a food coma for most of the ride home. After backing into his parking space, he lay across the wheel, gazing at his snoring passenger. He swiped gingerly at a line of drool edging down her chin. *I'd give anything not to go on tour right now.* He wished he could be a normal office worker. Be home every day. Be with Go-Ri every night.

The lack of motion from the car gently roused her, and she woke to find him staring.

"Didn't your mother teach you not to stare at someone?" She straightened up, rubbing the kink in her neck, discreetly checking her chin for wetness.

"She did. But I can't help it. You're too cute."

Go-Ri rolled her eyes and snorted. She climbed out quickly and fanned her reddened cheeks, waiting for him behind the car so they could walk to the elevator together.

Hiding in the spare bathroom, she stripped off her socks and soaked her feet in the tub. The frostbite damage was taking forever to dissipate. A few toenails were growing back, but the weird pasty colors still bothered her. Now the spaces between her toes were raw from being wet. Doing her best to warm up her feet, Go-Ri layered on fluffy socks before changing into clothing Baebin had gotten for her.

Already dressed in clean sweats and setting out a tray of fruit and a bottle of wine, he glanced up to see her walk into the living room. How could his old joggers and T-shirt be so sexy? His clothes were baggy on her curvy, thin frame, but she looked irresistible. The Eiffel Tower rested square in the middle of her chest, teasing him, highlighting the curves of both breasts.

He should have chosen a different shirt for her, for his sanity's sake. His groin tightened at the view, but more than that, he was just happy knowing she was here. It felt wonderful. Peaceful. *Right.*

Baebin settled in on his end of the couch, stretching his long legs under the table and hiding the small tent in his pants with a blanket. He waited for her to get situated on her usual end before starting the movie.

Baebin could feel her sudden anxiety as if it were a drumbeat growing closer. Gnawing at her lip, she sat stiff, drawn as tight as a bow string. Unsure of what caused the swift change, he slowly sat back up. "Did you want to go home instead? That's fine, too. I can walk you there."

Go-Ri shook her head. The feel of his arms around her earlier as they sat on the bench was abnormally thrilling. *Would he hold me again if I asked? I want him to, but he's leaving in two days, and this is too fast.* "No. A movie is good. But..." she pointed to the open spot next to him and whispered, "Can I sit there instead? Would it be all right?"

Baebin blinked, positive he heard wrong. "Of course. Come here." Settling back and pulling his blanket away to make space, he waved her closer.

Not giving herself a chance to rethink, she scooted over and nestled in under his arm, curling her body next to his.

He hit play on a movie that looked interesting twenty minutes ago. It wasn't half as good as how she felt next to him. With a light caressing kiss to her forehead, he nuzzled into her hair, keeping his eyes glued to the glow of the TV.

Two hours later, both felt numb in several places, the fruit and wine lay untouched on the table, and neither could remember anything about the movie they had just seen.

Rubbing his shoulder, Baebin hesitated and balled his other fist under the blanket. "I, um... I know you should go home, but I want to be greedy. I don't want you to leave. Would you stay the night? I'm not asking to do anything. I swear." He swallowed hard, his Adam's apple bobbing in his throat as he gestured vaguely around the apartment. "You can sleep anywhere. *Just* sleep."

His eyes were cautious and shy as they settled on her. "I promise I'm not asking for... anything. If it's too much, I understand. Since I'm leaving soon, I want to see you as much as I can." Picking at his thumbnail, his husky voice faltered. "I just... it's nice having you here. I don't want you to go yet."

Her mouth was dry. Her tongue felt like cotton. His boyish nerves were disarming. Deep inside her, she felt safe. Secure. Dizzy. Being next to Baebin was the most glorious feeling she had ever experienced, and she didn't want it to end. Instinct told her to go home. This was already too much. "I'll have to borrow more clothes."

Bringing a pair of his pajamas, a new toothbrush, and a hairbrush to the hall bath, Baebin waited until their eyes met, his wide, penetrating stare unwavering. "You can shower in here if you want. The door locks. I'm glad you are staying, but it's your decision where. I promise I'm okay with anything. I'll be in my room. Good night, Go-Ri. I'll see you in the morning." He pressed a light kiss on her palm before returning to his bedroom.

He spent an exorbitant amount of time in the master bath shower, debating if he should relieve himself. He was never going to make it through the night aroused like this, no matter where she slept. It felt perverted with her just down the hall in his spare bath. Thinking of her, possibly naked and wet in the other tub thirty feet away, was pure torture. He yanked the handle, and the steaming shower became a bucket of ice water. It didn't help much with his erection, but the sudden cold snapped him out of his thoughts.

After scrubbing himself warm with his towel, he slathered lotion on his dry elbows and hands and stared at his reflection in the foggy mirror. *What does she see when she looks at me?* His hair was weird, and, while he had good muscle, he wasn't as ripped as Daeho. His eyes were larger than most Koreans, and his nose was rounder at the tip. Hers was cute. Long and pointed.

Dabbing medication on a growing pimple, Baebin yanked on a shirt and snapped off the bathroom light. Straining to hear any sounds in the apartment, he lay back in bed, drawing his knees up, trying to relax his male parts. The night was going to be pure torture. It was his own fault—an inmate asking his jailer to abuse him.

There was no sound, but he knew she was there. He felt the air shift. Her body created a shadow in the open doorway. His heart flipped. He couldn't get enough oxygen.

Hesitating and fidgeting with the long cuffs covering her hands, she finally inched her way over and crawled under the covers. Afraid to move, he was glad the bedside lamp was too low to expose how hungry he was. Several ragged breaths later, she slipped closer, resting her head on his pillow at the edge of his shoulder.

"This okay? Just this? You promise?" she asked softly.

"Mmm. Perfect." He reached out to turn off the light and pressed a kiss to her temple. They lay quietly, for what seemed like decades, until they both finally fell asleep.

They shifted in the night, and he woke to find her back spooned against his chest. Glad he woke first, he took a moment of guilty pleasure, savoring the feeling. He buried his face in her hair, letting the strands tickle his nose. He should let go, but his left arm was her pillow... and he couldn't feel his fingers. *Crap. She'll be frightened if she wakes up right now.* Rolling carefully onto his back, he scooted his hips away to give her space.

She was already awake long before she felt him move away. His strong, warm body against hers felt like a soft steel cage surrounding her. The smothering hold didn't frighten her; it comforted her. Secured her. His unique smell that filled the room was stronger when he was folded around her. The instant he was gone, she felt cold and bereft.

She'd stayed awake half the night, afraid of waking up in a panic, but he was a buffer to her usual nightmares when she finally dozed off. It was the nicest sleep she'd had in ages. Her selfishness wanted just one more taste. Sitting up slowly, Go-Ri glanced over at him. One side of his hair poked out at strange angles, and his eyes were puffy with sleep. She probably didn't look much better. His warm, lazy smile erased the awkwardness of the morning.

Reaching up to adjust the collar of her shirt that had slipped and temptingly offered him an exposed shoulder, he pulled her back down to his chest. This position was uncomfortable, too, but he couldn't risk moving again. Now, her breasts squished against his side, and she faced his hard-on. He needed to say the alphabet or count sheep—or *something*—to control himself.

The steady rhythm of his heart under her cheek soothed her as she sank down, and he once again held her against his side. Like last night. Only better. She had to bite back a purr as his cool fingers smoothed and stroked her shoulder.

He needs curtains, she thought. The dawn was gray and dreary, but still, the straining sun invaded the room. She would buy them while he was gone. *I don't want him to go. I want to wake up next to him every day.*

Wait, wasn't this too much? Too fast? What am I thinking? She chewed her lip, arguing with herself. She needed to break free and escape, to regain some sense of control. Where was the security of her old defenses? But this felt safe, too. This felt *perfect.* Her head lay heavy on his solid, warm chest. *Stay... go... stay... go...* Each drumbeat of his heart pounded out the choices in her ear.

Go-Ri pushed herself onto her elbow and stared unflinchingly into Baebin's gorgeous, deeply slanted eyes. With the slightest hint of a tremor, she leaned into him, hovering for a moment before kissing him for the first time.

Someone, one of them, maybe both, whimpered when his hands drifted slowly up her back to cup her head, and he threaded his fingers through the tangles in her hair.

Hesitant at first, slowly sliding over one another, their lips explored the new sensation. She worried about rancid, obnoxious morning breath, but he tasted tangy. Acceptable. Pleasant. More than that, the dry, firm mouth that covered hers, slanting this way and that, fit flawlessly. The barest hint of a shadow on his upper lip tickled and scratched as he nibbled, before he slid his tongue in at the corner of her mouth for a taste.

Her soft chest pressed against his broad, hard one as she fisted his shirt. Breaking free, they both gulped in air and tried to calm their racing hearts. His warm breath tickled her cheek as his fingers tucked the fallen strands behind her ear.

She wasn't sorry for taking the risk, but before she did something she would regret, she eased out of bed.

"I really should go home for a bit. But I'll be back later. I'll bring lunch." She turned to leave but looked back one more time at the man she woke up with, still in bed. "Baebin, I'm… glad I stayed."

He watched as she fled before he could respond. He rolled painfully onto his stomach, gripping a pillow over his head. When he could finally move, he went to take a very long, very *cold* shower.

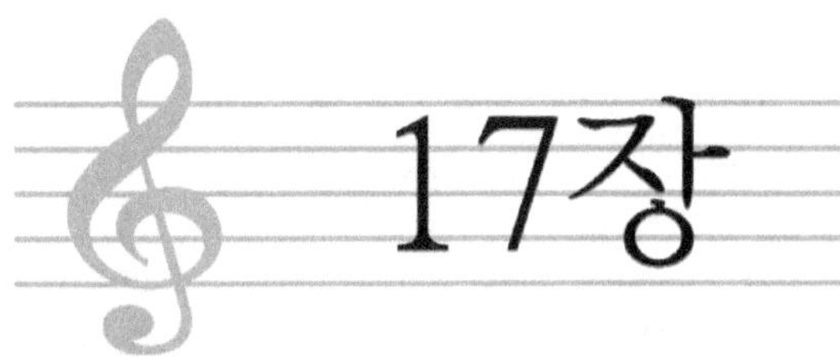

After putting on a touch of stage makeup to hide the bruise that was now turning an attractive purply blue color along his jaw, Baebin plugged his laptop into the TV for a video chat with his parents.

Eventually, his older brother and sister, and his little niece, joined to say goodbye. His family had given up their own privacy to support his dream. Instead of resentment for the loss of their freedom, they were his biggest cheerleaders.

Just as his niece, who sat on her mother's lap, wrapped up her long-winded story of her new favorite cartoon, Baebin's door lock chimed. Go-Ri promised to come for lunch, but she was early. Really early.

Calling out a greeting, Go-Ri walked into the dining room to drop food and her *haegeum* case on the table.

A woman's voice carried over the speaker. "Who's that?" A screen full of nosy, expectant people waited with baited breath. Even his niece was quiet.

Go-Ri froze, and Baebin grimaced in resignation. He answered, watching Go-Ri. "Mom, Dad. I want you to meet someone."

Her eyes grew even wider, and Go-Ri froze. Left with no alternative, she moved into camera view far away from him and gave the barest hint of a bow in greeting. Knowing his family wouldn't believe any excuses or wipe their silly grins off their faces, he signed off as fast as possible.

Go-Ri collapsed over the back of the couch and did her best not to groan in complete dismay. Baebin flopped over, stuffing his face in a pillow. His whining yell came out muffled. "I did not want you to meet my family that way. I am so sorry! I thought I could finish before you got here." He jerked up with a pout. "You're early!"

Go-Ri giggled. "I thought I would surprise you."

Baebin just groaned and fell over again.

They agreed yesterday that while she had her two lessons, he would catch up on work in the studio. After an early lunch, Baebin cleared space along the wall for the new case while she sat on the bench with the delicate two-stringed *haegeum* and its bow. Weeks ago, she wrote a song for Woo-Ge, and she needed to finish her part of the duet before getting a lecture from the five-year-old.

Baebin washed dishes and cleaned the kitchen while she finished composing. It was thrilling to watch her create a new song.

As a part of their training at SKEC, IN7 took lessons in composition for both music and vocals. Baebin never got the hang of the music side. He preferred writing lyrics, particularly rap, to a prearranged melody.

They decided to name Woo-Ge's song *Sunshine*, after the little boy who could light up a room.

Soon, the lobby called with the first of her students. Woo-Ge came racing in, shoes flying about, searching for Baebin, with his mother hot on his heels. Growing up with his mother's co-workers, they all were like family; his uncles—his *samchons*. Unfortunately, Woo-Ge's head had reached an uncomfortable height that, the last time he came to the studio, he'd reduced Baebin to a puddle on the floor, clutching himself, in tears. Baebin quickly scooped him up for a hug to avoid a repeated disaster.

Mrs. Sun spoke to Go-Ri as Baebin carried Woo-Ge upside down by the ankles over to the piano. The little boy squealed with joy, clinging to his *samchon's* knees as they traveled across the apartment. "I'm sorry I haven't been able to meet you sooner," she said. "If you know Kim Baebin's schedule, you know how difficult it is to get time off."

Mrs. Sun was another piece to Baebin's puzzle that should have been obvious to Go-Ri from the beginning. Baebin had said she was a co-worker, and Woo-Ge talked about her dancing. The lithe lady with a bright smile was one of IN7's backup dancers.

"Woo-Ge says you can play and teach everything," Mrs. Sun continued. "If you are accepting new students, I know of several people looking for lessons for various instruments. Most of them are children of my co-workers, but I have a few adult friends at the Campus looking for a teacher, too."

Go-Ri laughed at the praise from her youngest student. "I wouldn't say I can play everything," she pointed to the long row of instruments lined up against the wall, "but I guess, fairly close. I can write you a list. I'll accept the kids, but let me think about the others. I'm kind of choosy when it comes to adults."

Kim Baebin, Mrs. Sun, and Mr. Lee, her other SKEC student, were one thing, but being further embroiled in the company life was daunting. Last week, Mr. Lee also said he knew of others who wanted lessons. It was getting to be too much.

Worried about Go-Ri's rising unease, Baebin snagged Mrs. Sun for help on his vlive as Woo-Ge's session began. Sequestered in the studio, his co-worker inspected his memorabilia as he powered up his chat page.

After the usual slow start, waiting for fans to log in, the two began fielding questions posted to the feed. The entire episode centered on their daily life behind the scenes and what it was like, learning the routines and dancing on stage. The fans liked hearing Mrs. Sun's perspective.

Judging from the number of hearts and views, the spur-of-the-moment idea became his best show ever, and he was disappointed to hear the soft knock at the door, signaling Woo-Ge's lesson was over. Mrs. Sun waved goodbye and promised to give a secret hello sign to the fans at their next live show. Baebin continued to answer questions until the hour was up before he, too, waved off, promising that his next vlive would be from overseas.

He opened the door a crack to listen and could hear a guitar being played by her second student. Baebin slid quietly to his room to rest until the lesson was over. The book he was attempting to read was supremely dull, and twenty minutes later, he felt the bed dip on the far side. Cracking an eye open, he reached out his hand to her before falling back to sleep.

Go-Ri gently took the book off his chest, smoothed the wrinkled page, and marked his spot. The spacious, warm room was peaceful and luxurious. And he completed it. The smell of his usual soft, woodsy cologne mixed with hand lotion lingered in the air.

The description of an alpha's pheromones in her brother's strange Omegaverse manga books, which he tried to get her to read, came close to Baebin's scent. Arousing. Intoxicating. Calming. She didn't want to share his smell, his bed, or his apartment with anyone.

How dark would his hair be if he didn't dye it? she wondered. Long, straight strands lay across the bridge of his nose. She brushed them back and gave herself free rein to ogle him.

No wonder he was an idol, with his perfectly carved features wrapped in light-honey skin. The slight arch in his dark brows that dipped down at the ends, and the elegant bones in his cheek and jaw, were all softened by the pouty, defined lips created for smiling.

But she preferred the small, less noticeable quirks. His right eye had a double eyelid crease, and a cute, tiny mole rested just left of his nose, proving he was human after all. She watched his hand rise and fall with each steady, rhythmical breath as it rested on his chest, and the other stretched towards her.

Unlike her memory of the horrible day he had scared her, the smooth hand with long, thin fingers was now inviting. Beckoning.

Baebin's body registered his companion moments before his mind did. Before opening his eyes, he felt every millimeter of her from head to toe as she lay in his arms.

When she tilted her face up to look at him, he kissed the lips she offered. His mouth roamed over hers, sweet and unhurried. He tasted her—drank her in—before tucking her back against his chest.

He wished he could think of the best words to say for this moment. *Where's Tae-Si and his fancy words when I need him? He's better at writing—*

Crap. My friends. He winced as he remembered about tonight. Between the trip to the beach and... their night together, he forgot about the guys.

She felt him stiffen. "What is it?"

Breaking the news as gently as possible, he answered, "I completely forgot my friends are coming tonight. The last few weeks were rough at work, and I need to set things right with the group so we can get ready emotionally for the tour. I want you to be with me and meet them, but I absolutely will not force you. I wish I didn't have to do this right now." He could feel the terror wash over Go-Ri as she froze, unconsciously digging her nails into his bicep, where only moments ago, they lightly grazed his skin.

As quickly as her fear came, she shoved it away. Taking in a large, controlled breath, she looked calmly at him, her palm cupping his cheek. "You met my friends; it's only right I meet yours. It'll be fun."

It wasn't completely true, but she would do her best. *It would be just like they were coming to eat at the restaurant, and he will be there to help me,* she told herself. Six strange men. *Only six. Fewer people than on a busy night at MinGo.* She could—and would—do this for Baebin.

"I thought we agreed no more lies," he said gently, "but I appreciate you trying." The weight of her head on his shoulder eased his fears. "They may be slightly batty, but they are the nicest, most considerate guys I've ever known. You have nothing to fear from them. I'll always be right there. Okay? You're gonna blow them away."

She nodded, unconsciously burrowing into the gap of his collar.

They ran up the street to MinGo together, and as Baebin ordered food for the evening, Go-Ri changed clothes at her house behind the restaurant.

Mom knew her daughter had not come home last night and gave Baebin a sharp look. She wasn't stupid. But Go-Ri was a responsible adult.

The last few years had been an exhausting emotional rollercoaster. In the blink of an eye, her daughter flipped from being lively and outgoing to a total stranger. Any attempts to ask why were soundly rebuffed. She hadn't been that bad when she was twelve, maturing the same year she lost her father to a sudden heart attack.

Mom would see where things went with this man and put her foot down if needed. Right now, Go-Ri's dark cloud was disappearing, which was the only thing that mattered.

To take her mind off the upcoming evening, Go-Ri started cleaning. She left no surface untouched. Even the pillows were whacked free of invisible dust, all while piano jazz from Art Tatum and Keith Jarrett oozed from the stereo on repeat.

As Baebin dragged his last suitcase to its waiting partner by the door, the desk called. Both the wood carvings from the art studio and the new chairs he had found for the balcony arrived at the same time, creating a traffic jam in the service elevator and on Go-Ri's newly cleaned floors.

Once that flurry of activity was done, there was nothing to do but wait. Go-Ri's nerves began to climb. Her long hair, snagged in the warm breeze on the balcony, caught his attention as he searched for her. She sat huddled in a new chair with her skirt pulled tight over her knees, her face lifted to the falling sun.

Every day, every moment, Baebin loved seeing and feeling the minuscule changes in Go-Ri. Her calculating judgment, each time she so much as spied someone new, slowly faded. But when he told her about his friends coming, her defenses reappeared like lightning, her shoulders tightened, and the lines on her face returned.

She promised she would be fine tonight, but I'm not so sure. Is it because they're my friends? Or because they're men? Because of their job? Am I capable of helping her if she has another attack, like the one at the playground?

Through the glass, he watched her and prayed. Bringing Go-Ri a glass of wine, Baebin sat next to her, quietly holding her hand.

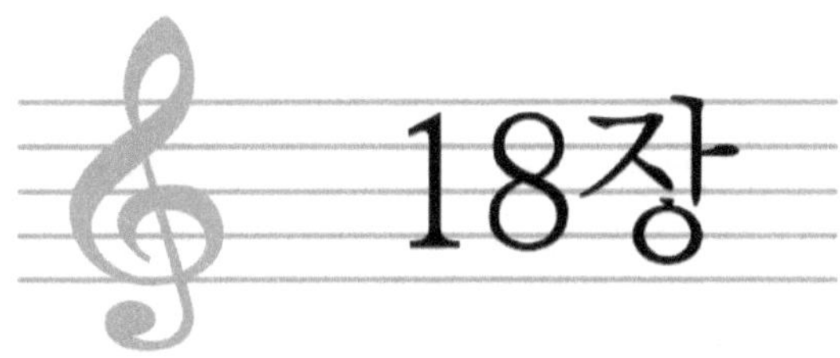

The sky was still pink when they heard the lock chime. Baebin looked at Go-Ri and raised her chin. "The second you tell me it's too much, I'll take you home. I swear. Don't overdo it." Forcing one of her fists to open, he linked fingers with her and drew her inside from the balcony.

Six noisy men tumbled through the door, kicking off shoes and dropping bags on the floor. The addition of the *sinbaljang* in the *hyeongwan* was impossible to miss, and from the door, they could immediately see other changes. He had *furniture*. "Whoa—! Hyung! You finally did something with the place!"

"Yeah! So, put your shoes away! I got the thing just for all you slobs, so quit leaving your stuff everywhere!" Baebin shouted at his friends from where he stood at the balcony door.

Mocking him and his anal-retentive habits, they followed orders and, one by one, as they left the *hyeongwan*, they stopped. Their crazy babble fizzled to a halt as they spotted the girl standing slightly behind *hyung*. His message yesterday about being nice to a guest ran through their collective minds.

Staring first at her with slackened jaws, they turned to Baebin with appreciative and bemused grins.

Of course, they were going to act like idiots, Baebin thought, wanting to smack each of them. Drawing her close, he never let go of her hand. "I'd like you to meet Choi Go-Ri. My girlfriend."

Jaws hit the ground—including hers. She and Baebin had talked about dating, but hearing the word for the first time shocked her. Her death grip on his hand tightened, but the pink flush in her cheeks looked prettier than the chalky white from a minute ago.

This was Choi Go-Ri that Chinmae had told them about during the Code 6? The guys broke into groups and approached slowly to introduce themselves. Some headed to the kitchen first to put their drinks in the fridge while waiting for their turn. Everyone was anxious to meet her, but she looked like a frightened rabbit ready to run.

She was pleased to have remembered most of their names from the stories he had told her of his friends when she had discovered the studio.

Baebin noticed the valiant effort she put into simply breathing. Even though her smile seemed relaxed, her eyes were dark, and the grip on his hand never let up.

Once the initial rush was over, Go-Ri sank into a chair in the living room to ease the shaking in her legs. Baebin stayed with her, perched on the side, his forearm casually thrown over the back. The imperceptible cocoon shielded her, allowing her a moment to unwind and acclimate to the boisterous group. Goosebumps shot over her as she felt his thumb stroke her nape under her hair, making her breath hitch. After a moment, she inhaled fully, and the faint whiff of his cologne calmed her nerves.

She risked a peek at him through her lashes. Keeping up with the stream of chatter, Baebin glanced at her and gave the slightest nod of encouragement, wordlessly assuring her. *You're doing great.*

"Hyung, when did you get all the instruments? You don't play these!" one of his friends hollered from the piano space.

Peering through the slats in the open bookcase, Go-Ri could see the thin, angular man with black spiky hair greased low on his forehead, kneeling by her long row of clarinets and saxophones. She arranged them in order of size, and he perched by her favorite—the dented sax in the middle. *That one's Han Tae-Si, right?*

Baebin called back, "Those aren't mine. They're Go-Ri's. She plays and teaches here."

"No way! You play all these?" The awe in his voice drew everyone else into the room.

Go-Ri joined them and stood at the curve of the Steinway with Baebin behind her, as everyone inspected her large collection. "Mmm. Yes. These are mine. I have more at home, but I'm already making a mess here, and I don't want them to be in the way. These are just the ones I teach or compose with."

I should have stored everything away. She watched, partially out of pride, but also out of concern, that they would fool with her babies, as they had in that prank several months ago with the piano.

Her worry was unnecessary. The care each of them took looking at instruments on stands or peeking in cases, but not touching the delicate, expensive strings or keys, pleased her.

As they rummaged through her large collection of Korean bamboo flutes, Jaemin spotted the bulky bag hiding deep under the piano. "What's that one? Don't tell me—it's a dead body!" He raised a horrified comedic eyebrow.

"It is. Wanna see it?" she quipped back. She crawled under the piano and pulled out her five-foot-long zither with its twelve strings. The *gayageum* was the largest and most expensive instrument she owned. It took forever to save enough money and find a decent used one.

Leaving it in the storage bag, she sat on the floor and rested the head of the instrument on her knee. Plucking its strings, Go-Ri played the opening verse of a song she was currently writing, before wiping the wooden soundboard free of unseen dust.

All eyes were on her. Suddenly aware of the attention, her skin felt hot as her heart rate pattered.

Baebin rifled through the music collection and found an old homemade CD of Go-Ri's. He discovered it mixed in with the pile shortly after returning from Japan. Soft jazz filled the air. "This is hers, too. She wrote and recorded everything on here. Until she is ready for another live performance, that is the only one you are getting."

Grateful for the distraction, she zipped the bag closed and shoved it back in place, away from trampling feet.

Tae-Si sat on the bench, looking at the meticulous care taken with the dozens of instruments. Out of all the friends, he was the only one who loved composing and production mixing. *Hyung*'s girl was better than he was.

"This is why you were so mad at us that night. It wasn't just our style of music. We disrespected the piano."

Tae-Si was horrible at reading the room, and Kyong and Jaemin both smacked him on the head. "What?! It's just that she plays every kind of music we don't, and it's obvious how much work she puts into taking care of all these," he defended himself, waving a hand around the room.

He looked at Go-Ri and absolved himself of all guilt. "It's his fault. It was supposed to be a joke." He pointed, unashamed of throwing his *hyung* under the bus. "I wouldn't have done it, but he made me."

Go-Ri's laugh filled the room. "It's okay. I know all about it. I admit, I kind of overacted that day. But you're right. Your music is nice, but I prefer... *other* kinds of music. I love instruments. Each creates a different sound, a different emotion... a different feeling. I like to write what I feel."

"Your instruments and music are beautiful. I'm sorry we hurt you that night," Tae-Si apologized, bowing his head with a hand over his heart. "I'd love to play and record with you someday. Any time you want to make another CD, let me know. I'm sure we can get you a booth at the Campus to record."

Guessing Tae-Si didn't know about the private studio here or her fears of SKEC, she only nodded in return. The guys continued to chatter around her and slowly drifted away to inspect the bedrooms and the rest of the apartment as the music continued.

A call from the desk alerted Baebin of the food delivery and, checking with Go-Ri first, he left to open the door.

Only Chinmae remained in the room. He definitely was, as Baebin mentioned several days ago, more reserved than the rest. At their base level, the two friends were the quietest and most meticulous, both with their words and actions. The eldest and the youngest were a matching pair.

"Can I...?" Go-Ri faltered. He barely spoke tonight, but she felt his brooding eyes on her more than the others. "Yoo Chinmae, I'm sorry for the rift I've caused between you and Baebin. I'm... not the easiest person to know, and I've given him a hard time. Please forgive him and continue to be his friend." She gnawed on her lips but refused to retreat.

The folder of handwritten sheet music Chinmae found on the bookcase was meticulous and fabulous. Baebin said she was a fantastic musician, and based on the pages and the music playing over the stereo, he had to agree. Pulling his gaze away from the folder, Chinmae regarded her with a cool, impenetrable stare as he dissected her.

He was watching the couple, studying their every move, their every private glance. Initially worried for his friend, it didn't take long for him to see what drew Baebin to her. There was something special about Choi Go-Ri. But what Chinmae liked even more—she truly cared for his friend.

"It was mostly my fault. I take responsibility, so don't worry; it's already forgotten." His eyes flitted over to his friend, talking to the delivery guy in the kitchen, before returning to appraise her. The shuttered expression slowly faded away. "I can see why he likes you. If he's good to you and you can tolerate him, then nothing else matters. Right?" He noted the minuscule release of her brows as her lips slid out from between her teeth.

Worried that he was overstepping his bounds, Chinmae chose his words carefully. "Baebin told me a little about you. I, umm, I understand what you are going through." He looked at the pages on the piano. "Tonight must not be easy for you, but we are happy you're here, and you're with our friend. Don't let us or anyone else stand in your way."

Go-Ri's eyes widened in shock, and she turned pink when Yoo Chinmae bowed slightly and swiftly walked away. *Baebin told his friend? About what? How much does Chinmae know? What did he mean by 'he understood'?*

Min-Jun stood, seething. He was surprised to see *noona* in a room of men, and he looked for any sign of distress from her. She stood alone with one, deep in conversation, and while she appeared stiff, she didn't look afraid. Turning back to Baebin, he snapped. "Do you have any idea—"

"Yes, I do." Baebin stopped the younger brother, laying a reassuring hand on his arm. "I swear, she is safe. Would you feel more comfortable if you stayed and helped me care for her? I don't mind. As her brother, you would be very welcome."

Min-Jun hesitated, looking over at his sister again while he unloaded the two full containers of food onto the kitchen island. Noona *looks okay. The men are rowdy, but they seem polite.* Min-Jun grudgingly relented. "No. Just be careful. I'm warning you: if anything happens, I'll do more than punch you. I don't care who you are." He stalked out before Go-Ri realized he was there.

Food filled the counters beside Go-Ri's platters of appetizers, and everyone loaded their plates as she reclaimed her position in the chair with Baebin at her feet.

Daeho dramatically tossed a towel over his arm and, bowing low to Go-Ri, held out a heaping plate for her. "Here, Princess. The fi-fi-finest dishes I have to offer."

She couldn't help but giggle at his cross-eyed, silly smile as he set the plate next to her on the table. Not to be outdone, everyone else joined in, and soon, she was surrounded by plates and drinks.

"Hey! What about me! I'm your elder! You should be serving me, too!" Baebin shouted in protest.

A chorus rang out. "Get your own!"

Daeho added, still cross-eyed, "She's our gongjunim. Only a princess gets such fi-fi-fi-fine treatment!"

"I hope your face freezes like that. I bought the damn food." Baebin muttered loudly with not an ounce of irritation. Leaning back on her lap, he opened his mouth like an expectant guppy. "Feed me, Gongjunim."

Unable to hold a straight face, she smacked him regally on the lips with her chopsticks. "No. They gave me this delicate offering, and I will not dishonor them by serving a peasant. Like. You." Cheers rang out in approval as everyone vied for seats around the coffee table.

As predicted, they were loud and crazy all night.

There wasn't an exact moment when Go-Ri realized she would be okay. But over the course of the evening, she relaxed. Her smile softened, the tightness in her forehead eased, and she willingly participated in conversations instead of being dragged into them. Soon, her sides hurt from laughing. It had been a long time since that had happened.

When had she forgotten most men were not bad people? Nam Song-Ye wasn't the only bad person in the world, but most were like the guys she met tonight. Sweet and honorable. Without realizing it, the tall, vibrant, imposing men, who terrified her and lived and breathed everything she hated, drew her out, and Go-Ri had... *fun.*

Baebin never left her. The heat from his body next to her leg encouraged her. When his head rested on her knee or his fingers brushed her ankle under her skirt, her skin tingled. She had gotten a sense of his extraverted, exuberant personality when they had dinner with her friends, but tonight, it was thrilling to watch him interact with his friends. Personable and outgoing, he never commanded attention or respect but received it anyway because he was genuinely a nice guy.

Every one of the guys remembered what Chinmae had relayed to them about Choi Go-Ri and Nam Song-Ye. In the beginning, as she sat huddled in her chair, her watchful, wary manner saddened them. The way she opened up and smiled was heartwarming. She became a different person as the night wore on.

It was painful to watch Baebin suffer the last few weeks; the private emotional whirlwind had almost ripped him apart. Meeting Go-Ri tonight, they saw now what it was all for. She was truly special, and no one could have found anyone better suited for their friend and teammate. Beautiful and smart, she was talented in her own right without any pretentious airs.

It was obvious she liked their *hyung* in a quiet, caring way, not like a fawning, simpering fan. They hoped and prayed for the new couple's continued happiness.

Well past midnight, Baebin and Chinmae walked Go-Ri home. Talking quietly as they walked up the hill, Baebin told Chinmae about the potential new clients she still hadn't decided whether to accept.

Tonight, meeting everyone gave her strength, but Baebin had been with her, and she felt safe with the group. She wasn't sure if she was ready for more adult SKEC students.

Chinmae considered her fears before commenting, his deep, soft voice tempering his directness. "You won't know until you get more information. I think you're trying to decide without knowing them or giving them a fair chance. I don't personally know them, but the ones I do know from the sound building are all great people. They care about music like you do."

His words stung. She was embarrassed that he could read her so quickly and find her faults. She used to be good at getting facts and making logical decisions from them. But she had stopped trusting herself, stopped trusting information.

Walking on alone around the corner, Chinmae gave the couple a chance to say goodbye. Twenty minutes later, he found Baebin leaning back against the wall with Go-Ri leaning against him, their heads bowed together, resting comfortably.

No better than a Peeping Tom, he watched. He knew his *hyung* inside and out, up and down. He knew Baebin almost better than he knew himself. *Hyung* was in his element on stage and at work. He loved everything about the group, probably more than anyone. But Chinmae had gotten it wrong. This girl was the true love of his life. He had never seen his friend so happy. So calm. So peaceful.

No one on the planet was better suited for his friend than Choi Go-Ri. He should have said more, been more supportive and comforting when he talked to Go-Ri earlier. He would do anything to ensure the couple stayed happily together.

As the friends walked back to the apartment, the two created a plan that was sure to terrify and infuriate Go-Ri. Chinmae detested lies and tricks, but sometimes, necessity overruled. Sometimes, you needed a mild push to make an informed decision. Sometimes, in order to make a life choice, you needed to go at it head-long and stop thinking about it from a hundred miles away.

It would still be Go-Ri's decision. She just needed to be dragged to the point of deciding—most likely kicking and screaming—and the two of them would be with her along the way.

Locking Baebin in a choke hold, Chinmae promised, "If she brings out her carving knives, just remember, I always outrun you!" He sprinted the rest of the way to the lobby door, leaving Baebin behind.

When Baebin and Chinmae pulled up to the curb the next day, Go-Ri was dressed in Baebin's favorite outfit—the one she used to wear while performing at *The Jazz House*. "Your message surprised me. I thought you were leaving today."

Ducking into the car, she was startled to find Chinmae in the back seat. The atmosphere crackled in the confined space; the two men looked suspicious. Defensive alarm bells clanged loudly in her skull as she looked between the two. "Good morning, Chinmae…. What's going on?"

Baebin started the car and took off before answering, ensuring the doors were locked. "We're taking you to Campus to meet the students."

As they expected, Go-Ri froze and then scrambled madly for the door, yanking on the locked handle. Throwing her weight against the frame, she desperately tried to jump out of the moving car. She turned back to glare daggers at Chinmae, who smiled and gave her a thumbs-up. *You're lucky I can't reach you. You better run when I get out of this car!*

Two corners later, Baebin reached for her hand. "Breathe, Go-Ri. I've got you. We both do. It'll be okay—just breathe."

White as a sheet and visibly trembling, Go-Ri slapped him away but did manage to draw in a shaky gulp of air.

She took his hand the next time he tried and held on tightly—enough to leave bruises. *Breathe in… breathe out.*

Locking eyes in the rearview mirror, Baebin and Chinmae prayed.

She barely registered crossing the Han River and easing into downtown traffic. The uneven seams of the pavement bumped along with her heart. Each beat drawing her closer to the lion's den. She focused on his hand in hers.

After picking up her temporary ID at the gate, Baebin pulled into his parking spot. Opening her door, he knelt to meet her eyes. His low, soft voice filtered in to her. "One or both of us will be with you the entire time. We will never leave you alone. Then tomorrow, you make your decision and be done with it. Either way, we won't be disappointed in you. You are doing this. That is enough for me. For us." They gave her space as she sat motionless.

Go-Ri climbed out and stood between the two men, feeling their solid presence around her. Clutching the fabric of her skirt, she asked, "Okay, which way do we go?"

The U-shaped, three-story sound building sat at the far end of the complex, and the grassy courtyard in the middle was littered with picnic tables. The boys had always worked in the "B" side recording artist studios and were unfamiliar with the instrument and composition "A" side which was arranged differently. The little group started roaming the halls, peeking into rooms.

Big or small, each room was full of activity and sound. Band studios and larger orchestra halls filled the main floor. All were in use and packed with people on both sides of the glass walls. Dozens of chairs facing a conductor's podium, microphones, video screens, sound boards, and computers filled every available space. Name tags on the doors indicated what was being recorded inside.

Works ranging from orchestral movie soundtracks to the instrumentals for The Boyz's next pop album filled the hall whenever a door opened. People everywhere carried instruments and music files. The noise and activity of the building set Go-Ri on edge… yet it strangely thrilled her, too.

The smaller practice rooms, where musicians spent the bulk of their days rehearsing, were on the second floor. Mr. Lee, her sax-oboe student, ushered the trio into a room and introduced them to the waiting group who sat in a circle, working on a new piece.

Over a dozen artists squished in together to make room to accommodate them. Baebin and Chinmae sat on either side of Go-Ri, quietly strengthening her. Go-Ri focused on the instruments, noting each one in turn before following the trail of fingers, hands, and arms up to the musicians' eager faces.

As the young musicians shared their roles in the company, even Baebin and Chinmae were impressed. After all this time, they never knew the complexity of the work that happened on the "A" side. The sheer number of songs the musicians had to learn, play, and record in one year was staggering. They not only recorded for singers, like IN7, but also for the TV and movie industry, both at home and abroad. They prepared some songs specifically for something already in production, while others were recorded and put into a vault for future use.

It was clear the artists all loved working behind the scenes rather than being onstage. Their passion to continually improve in their field warmed her. She felt their excitement.

After answering their endless questions and playing short pieces from the various instruments around the room, Go-Ri had six more potential students.

Leaving the building and weaving their way through the empty picnic tables, Baebin and Chinmae strutted like proud parents. Go-Ri, on the other hand, looked like an animal caught in the headlights. She stubbornly wanted to drag her feet and say no, but she was too stunned and overwhelmed. The group they talked to—actually everyone in the entire building—focused solely on the craft. The buzz of creativity vibrated deep within her.

Chinmae finally spoke up. "Well?"

Belligerently, Go-Ri wrinkled her nose at him. "You're mean." She reflexively punched his arm when he gave a bark of laughter but she couldn't keep her smile hidden away.

Thrilled at the successful morning so far, Baebin spoke up. "We have a little time before your next surprise, so let me give you a tour." Taking his cue, Chinmae headed off. Go-Ri grimaced at the word "surprise" but followed Baebin's lead.

The Campus was a mini city inside Seoul, and there were people everywhere. He took her through the dining halls, gym rooms, and the video department. He pointed out the dorms, medical facility, and commissary. One entire building was designated for makeup, hair, and costume design. There was a storage warehouse and a massive building for stage production and setup. This was where groups did final prep work before going on tour or recorded parts of their music videos.

They ended in the dance studio building, where he walked her past several practice rooms of various sizes lined with mirrors. Some were already in use, and Go-Ri could see groups working hard with choreographers.

Finally, they came to a door with an "IN7" tag stuck in the interchangeable nameplate and a room half-filled with an eclectic group of people. A video crew was setting up in a corner. Most of the guys she met last night were lying on the floor, stretching, and they all waved in greeting. A small, graying man separated from a row of monitors to meet them.

"So, *you're* the one." The blunt statement from Manager Kim made Go-Ri blink, unsure how to take it. "My boys haven't stopped talking about you all morning." Manager Kim waved Baebin off without a glance, sending him to change and stretch.

Go-Ri swore privately at Baebin's retreating back. *He promised never to leave me alone.*

Refocusing on the man in front of her, she couldn't decide if she was being interrogated by her school principal or interviewed by a prospective father-in-law. She was relieved when he finally shooed her away. He was more terrifying than the entire sound building.

Kyong scooted over to make room for her on the floor and whispered, "That went well. Trust me. Manager Kim likes to pretend to be all mean, but he's really a teddy bear."

Everyone else nodded in agreement as they stretched their hips and shoulders. All of them had a story to share of the torment they put the manager through and proudly claimed each of the man's gray hairs.

Baebin and Chinmae reappeared, having changed their clothes. Chinmae looked good in a new plaid shirt, partially open in the front, with jeans so low that you could read his brand of boxers. But it was Baebin that made Go-Ri's heart skip. His tight T-shirt and sleeveless sweatshirt clung to his chest and arms, while the jeans... *yummy*. Sun Woo-Ge, who rode on his back, wiggled down and ran over to the group, squealing with joy to see his other *samchons*. After getting hugs from all his uncles and then his teacher, he sat with Daeho, playing thumb war.

Everything was ready, and Manager Kim clapped the room to order. Go-Ri followed Mrs. Sun and Woo-Ge to a spot on the mirrored wall to watch.

The guys got into place with one final stretch, and the room went quiet. A hum of excitement filled her as the music started, and IN7 began recording the new practice video. Finally researching the group this last week, she saw some of these videos online. *I can't believe I'm seeing one being recorded in person.*

Mrs. Sun leaned over to her and whispered, "This is "SuperStars." It's the cover song for the next full album, *Galaxy*. They've been working on this dance for over two months. It has several other versions, too, for the stage and the music video. I have a part in some of those, but this is the most important one."

Go-Ri's eyes widened, and she realized she had no idea what it took for Baebin to do his job. Even this sliver of it.

After the song was over and the video director yelled "cut," crews dashed over to the guys to cool them off and restore order to their clothes, faces, and hair. They were at it again within five minutes, making a second attempt. They recorded a third and fourth take, and by then, the boys were gasping, leaning over with their palms braced on their knees. After watching the replay, Manager Kim called it a wrap.

Everyone in the room cheered as the guys groaned in relief. Woo-Ge tried to wiggle out of his mom's arms, but she held firm. They still needed time to collect themselves before being attacked by the five-year-old.

Go-Ri sat in awe looking around the whole room. *This was nuts. Insane. It's so different than what I expected.*

Manager Kim called for a food break and ordered everyone to return in thirty minutes for a meeting before they were done for the day. He looked at Baebin and gestured to Go-Ri. Her time was up.

The room cleared, and Baebin collapsed against the mirror beside her. Flushed, he drained his water before pulling off his hat, causing his hair to stick up all over. She wiped his face with a tissue and tried to flatten his hair back down. "I didn't know."

He gave a weary grin and said, "Most people don't. I guess if we make it look easy, we are doing our job right. Did you like it?"

"Mmm. Amazing."

Their last few moments together weren't long enough as he helped her to her feet. Hand in hand, they left the room and headed to the car.

She welcomed his warm embrace eagerly and held tight as they rested against the door in the busy parking lot. Cradling her cheek, he gazed at her before settling in for a long, tender kiss. She reveled in the small tremors that ran through his body under her fingers, knowing he could feel hers, too.

"I'm glad you came today. I know it was hard, but you did great." Baebin said, after he broke the kiss.

Go-Ri couldn't respond. It *was* hard. Yet... Surprisingly *exhilarating*. She held him tighter, not wanting it to end. Finally, she took a step back and, with a long last look, took his keys and drove away. He stayed briefly, watching as she disappeared through the gate. Then, collecting himself, he went to join everyone else.

Turning the last corner before the meeting room, Baebin screeched in surprise. Six men leaned against the walls on either side of the narrow hallway, doing their best to glare at him.

Unable to hide his grin, Yejoon chirped out, "You done, Romeo? Can we go now?"

Baebin punched him in the stomach as he walked through the gauntlet of idiots and opened the meeting room door.

The guys cracked up, making kissy faces and laughing behind him as his ears turned pink.

The members of IN7 loved their fans and didn't mind the public scrutiny. But a simple trip that would take an average person two hours to get from their car to their gate at the airport took the group twice as long, even for an early morning flight without luggage. It made for a long, grueling day.

After security, the crowds lessened, but they knew there was always a camera somewhere, so they would be "on duty" until they reached the privacy of their hotel room, hopefully within thirty hours.

The public didn't know that, aside from the *very* obvious ring of bodyguards and management surrounding them, a loose circle of staff walked nearby as they made their way through the giant Incheon airport to help keep the most rabid fans at a safer distance.

Go-Ri opened the restaurant, then turned on the TV and her laptop, looking for any information on the group's departure. When any artist left for a tour, these trips were always a hot topic in South Korea, and news flooded the media. She always avoided the hype in the past, but now, she hunted for anything she could find.

She had a lot of making up to do with Min-Jun and her mom for missing work this last week, so for several days, Go-Ri worked from open to close. She needed this time to think about what she had experienced lately and what to do while counting down the days until Baebin's return.

Two weeks ago, she was in complete misery; her world had collapsed again. But this last week had been the best of her life. Her stomach almost hurt with the change, and her head swam.

She admitted that Chinmae was right; she could take on the new Campus students and be okay. She relived each moment of her visit and still shook her head at what she'd witnessed, both in the music hall and the dance studio.

Mostly, her thoughts were of Baebin. He was still the same man she'd met months ago, but now, she saw a new and incredible side of him.

No, she corrected. Not a side of him; she saw all of him. His drive and commitment to his art impressed her. She loved his personality and the kindness he showed to everyone around him, both with his friends and the people at the Campus. How he treated strangers—like the doctor downstairs, the shop owner, fans, and even her friends—meant a lot to her.

She thought of all the times he held back, waiting for her to be comfortable, and she was humbled that he had always treated her gently and slowly, even from the beginning.

She would never forget this week for the rest of her life. When she had confronted him that night, he laid his cards on the table. This week, he followed through. He gave her every opportunity to back out by showing his hand, but as the days flew past, she was more drawn in. Entranced. *Committed.*

Running away again was no longer a possibility.

The six musicians she met during her visit to the Campus would be coming for lessons in pairs or late in the evening, due to their difficult schedules. She also had three new kids, each related to the IN7 crew, along with her original students. Go-Ri was thrilled to see that her plan of opening her own lesson studio was shaping up sooner than expected.

Waiting backstage for their first concert in Boston, Baebin hollered for Chinmae to come hear about her new students. It was difficult for Go-Ri to match their enthusiasm at five o'clock in the morning, her time, and she wasn't thrilled to be on a video call with Chinmae when she was un-showered and in pajamas. But the two made her glow inside. She was nervous and scared but their encouragement, half a world away, meant everything.

She thought they'd settled the details until the day before lessons were supposed to start. Unhappy that a large group of employees requested weekly time off during work hours, the company offered her a spare room in the "A" wing to conduct her lessons.

Arguing with the Sound Department over the phone went nowhere. Now, she would be going to her students instead of them coming to her.

That night, she tossed and turned, unable to sleep. Baebin and company were on a flight and unreachable for emotional support. She had chewed a hole in her cheek by the time the morning restaurant shopping list was half-finished and poorly made.

It wasn't until she drove Baebin's car over the river that it registered: she was excited. Going into the lion's den alone was *possible*.

Go-Ri and Baebin made use of the crazy time difference. He was her early morning alarm clock, and they talked until he fell asleep with the video screen still on while she opened the restaurant. They grew together, even though they were a million miles apart.

Maybe this trip happened at the right time—they could learn more about each other and be comfortable together before they were actually... together. Still, as busy as her new life was becoming, time seemed to drag, and it felt like Baebin would never return.

B: Philadelphia tonight. Show #9
G: Did you get to sightsee?
B: No
G: ☹
B: You interested in seeing the show?

At seven o'clock, his time, Baebin passed his video call off to Chu Kwan and took the stage. Kwan found a good, safe spot to set up a camera stand, and Go-Ri watched. She was tickled when each of the guys waved and gave her "hand-hearts." When Baebin blew her a kiss, a group of girls near the phone screamed loudly.

When Go-Ri wasn't at the restaurant or on campus, she was in the apartment. Baebin's phone chimed at each visit, and usually, just knowing she was there sated his hunger for her. But sometimes, he would sneak a peek at her through the camera system. He dreamed of pulling the pencils from her hair and letting the mass fall down her back as she sat at the piano. *God, I just want to hold her again.*

The American tour schedule was tiring. This was more of a promotional tour for them, since IN7 was not well-known in the States yet. Besides the concerts and making videos for both their new American fans and their Asian fans back home, each location required several interviews, primarily for local stations.

In the New York City area, they appeared on a few of the popular morning shows that played across America. The morning interviews were especially challenging after being up late at night for the concerts, and they were very different than those at home. They were shorter, consisting only of a few questions and a quick dance piece to one of their songs. Asian audiences liked longer, full-length shows that included them playing a game or two. Mostly, the guys waited, catching a few minutes of sleep in the green rooms before their ten minutes on camera.

> B: KWAN AND I WENT TO AN ART GALLERY. SENDING SOMETHING HOME. I THINK IT WOULD LOOK NICE IN THE PIANO ROOM. LET ME KNOW WHAT YOU THINK.
> G: OK. I'LL BE READY FOR IT. HOW WAS NEW YORK?
> B: TIMES SQUARE WAS COOL

Just as Daeho did in Japan, it was Jaemin's turn to be their main interpreter, on and off the stage. The other guys knew basic phrases and could make-do, but Jaemin took the responsibility to lead them. Doing his best not to use the official translators that traveled with them, his headaches grew, and he started popping pain killers like candy.

An accident in Miami caused a slight panic during rehearsal when Daeho tripped over unsecured cables and landed hard on his side against the rugged crates that littered the backstage area. He made it through that night's performance with his ribs in a tight bandage. Dancing was painful, and Yejoon, who sounded the closest to him, sang his parts. The fans in the audience, unaware of the accident, were disappointed that he kept his shirt on and didn't show off his famous abs and dragon tattoo.

> B: DAEHO'S HURT
> G: GIVE ME HIS NUMBER
> G: DAEHO? YOU OK? B SAID YOU GOT HURT.
> D: GONGJUNIM! HELLO! I'M JUST BRUISED. MY PRIDE IS HURT MORE THAN ANYTHING. I WAS RUNNING AND DIDN'T SEE THE

Despite the minor hiccups, the tour ran smoothly. The stage and backstage crews flowed like magic, and there were no major issues.

Baebin, having a great time with his friends and teammates, was constantly busy, but every chance he could, he attended more upper-level meetings than usual. Management was a logical next step from being team leader. The behind-the-scenes production to keep the team on the charts took a lot of scheduling, planning, and people skills outside of what was already required of him. He soaked up everything he could, becoming a fixture in the conference calls back to South Korea and SKEC headquarters.

As Manager Kim guided him through the promotional tour process, he started designing and planning the release of "SuperStars" and their next album, *Galaxy*, which would drop in the next six months.

The analytical side and complexity of arranging everything was more interesting than he thought. He'd always liked detailed control, but now he was learning *how* to make the details on his own.

G: MISS YOU. YOU ARE HALFWAY DONE, RIGHT?
B: YES. CHICAGO. I HAVE TIME OFF TOMORROW.

As Chicago was their midpoint, they had a few extra days to unwind around their two shows. It was fun being just a tourist after a month of working twenty-four-seven. Sometimes, it paid to be a foreign star, visiting local landmarks.

A camera crew followed them for footage to be posted and possibly used in an upcoming, supplementary music video. They shut down the Skyline Observatory for an hour, met fans at the Bean in Millennium Park, and enjoyed a sunset dinner on a riverboat under the Chicago skyscrapers. Eating their way through Chicago, whisked from one bucket list item to another, the seven guys enjoyed the break, even though they all desperately needed sleep.

Backstage at their second show in Chicago, the usual chaos reigned. Most people sat around, doing nothing until it was their turn for a burst of panicked action. Used to the activity around them, the guys drifted from one station to the next, getting physically and mentally prepared. Yejoon's and Chinmae's mic pouches ripped again in Cincinnati and needed to be sewn. Kyong and Jaemin sat in chairs, getting their hair and makeup fixed while they played on their phones.

It wasn't until a name was mentioned that they picked up on the conversation swirling between the stylists. Kyong and Jaemin's gazes locked in the mirror. They quickly turned back to their phones.

K: DID YOU HEAR THAT?
J: IS IT TRUE?
K: DUNNO. PROBABLY.
K: WOULD MAKE SENSE THO. SONG-YE'S BEEN GONE A YEAR AT LEAST.
J: BUT WHAT ABOUT GONGJUNIM????? 😟
K: 😟

They glanced at Baebin, who sat on the couch in the middle of a video chat with their princess in South Korea. Baebin was on another planet right now, and all his *chingu* loved it. Every one of them fed off each other's energy—both good and bad. But the news of Song-Ye's return—if the stylists could be believed—was going to hurt their *hyung* most of all. Baebin needed to know from them before he heard it from someone else.

K: WHO'S TELLING HIM?
J: NOT ME
K: ROCK PAPER SCISSORS

Kyong and Jaemin stuck their hands out.

That night, the show went off perfectly. Daeho was almost back up to full strength with his ribs, and he convinced the medical team to unwrap him for the one song where he always unbuttoned his shirt.

The large shipping containers were on their way to Denver for their next show when Yejoon answered the knock on the hotel door. His apprehension rose swiftly upon seeing Jaemin and Kyong's uneasy looks.

Kyong spoke up. "We need hyung."

The three guys scattered about the room, waiting for Baebin to come out of the shower.

When he appeared, scrubbing his wet hair with a towel draped around his neck, Kyong nervously cleared his throat. "Hyung... umm... Nam Song-Ye is coming back to the Campus in about six weeks."

In shock, Baebin stared at his friends like they had punched him. "Wha—?"

"He's finished his Music Exchange Program contract in Japan, and SKEC is bringing him back. Most likely for a solo album or something on the acting side of the company, since they won't renew the Xscape contract."

Kyong squirmed in his seat on the nearest bed, staring at his toes as he rubbed them on the carpet. "Jaemin and I overheard it tonight backstage. We... thought you should know."

Baebin couldn't process the news. *Six weeks? That's only two weeks after we return. What about Go-Ri?* Blankly, he looked back and forth from friend to friend, and then, without a word, he turned back to the bathroom and shut the door.

After Kyong and Jaemin left for a group talk with the others, Yejoon came in and quietly sat next to him on the edge of the tub.

It was a travel day, so for the most part, easy. One thing the guys loved about being overseas was how rarely they were recognized. Even though their Asian looks made them stand out, along with their large contingent of bodyguards and staff who walked with them, they were mostly ignored and moved through the airports faster.

On the plane, Baebin knelt down and drew Chu Kwan in close. "I need to ask a favor. Talk to the guards you know who protected Nam Song-Ye. I want to know if he's done anything horrible in the past. If something's being covered up."

Kwan looked sharply at his friend. Guards knew a lot of juicy stories that could make headlines and fill the pages of international best-selling books, but they were tight-lipped for a reason. If they tattled, they would never be able to work in the industry again. "Wha—? Baebin, you know I can't."

"Look, I appreciate your discretion, and I don't want my secrets spilled either—"

"Berlin night club."

Baebin gave Kwan a dry look. *Dude. That was almost three years ago, and I was drunk. She kissed me first, and how was I supposed to know she had a boyfriend? Not my finest moment.* "Look. I wouldn't ask if it wasn't important. I'm not looking for gossipy dirt, just anything that... feels wrong." Baebin looked at his hand where it clutched the arm rest. "Particularly against women."

Kwan sat back again and searched Baebin's downturned face. It was such an odd request. The worry and intensity in his friend's face startled him. *This is unlike him. And it's so... vaguely specific. Of all people, Song-Ye? He's practically a nobody....* "Okay. Let me put out some feelers. No guarantees though."

As Baebin returned to his seat, Kwan started prepping the messages to his friends at home to be sent as soon as they landed.

Heads bowed together, Baebin and Chinmae whispered in their seats the rest of the flight, wondering whether Go-Ri should be told now and risk sending her into a fit of anxiety, or after Kwan has a chance to learn anything. It was an impossible decision, but they finally agreed that Baebin should tell her on his next phone call.

On the drive to the new arena, Manager Kim pulled Baebin out of the pack and had him ride with him in a private car.

Yejoon's request that morning was strange, but Manager Kim had contacted the central business office about it anyway. As the car started to move, he stared at Baebin, noting the dark circles under his eyes and the droop in his shoulders. He asked, "Why do you and Yejoon care about Nam Song-Ye? What is going on? Talk to me."

Not only was the elderly man his manager and mentor, but he was also a trusted advisor. The two had become close since Baebin was a trainee, and he looked up to and respected the man like a father. Baebin looked out his window at the rugged, snowcapped mountains in the distance beyond the Denver skyscrapers as they sped away from the airport.

Reasonably sure the American driver couldn't speak Korean, he finally opened up and told Manager Kim everything he knew. Through the reflection in the glass, he could see Manager Kim pale and go slack.

Puzzle pieces fell together, explaining Baebin's erratic behavior and strange requests over the last few months. "I had no idea."

"Choi Go-Ri is working at the Campus now, and if Song-Ye is coming back, I want to know what she's up against. He was shifty when we were trainees, and I don't trust him." Baebin turned to his manager. "If I remember right, you weren't exactly crying when that group left our team."

"Mmm. You were better off for it. They weren't right for you."

"Song-Ye could be different now, or he could start harassing Go-Ri again. And if he was violent with *her*, was he with anyone *else*? I don't want IN7 to get blowback just because we're in the same company. I want to know if there is more he is hiding. I've asked Chu Kwan to help."

Trying to keep his composure, Manager Kim rubbed his eyes, thinking about what he could do to help the girl he met once, just weeks earlier. "The guards don't talk, you know that. But I'll look into it, too. Let me think." He was one of the leading managers at SKEC due to the boys' success, but his overall power was limited. They finished the rest of the drive, silently staring out their windows.

Seven guys meant three doubles and a single room. The single, usually the larger one always had the most late-night visitors, along with food and drink, as the adrenaline wore off from a show. But tonight, *hyung's* room was quiet. Baebin stayed up until the early morning on a video chat with Go-Ri, gently breaking the news to her.

Nam Song-Ye being back in Korea was bad enough, but Go-Ri's work at the Campus was an unlit firecracker waiting for a match. This was something they should have expected, but they never wanted to consider it.

As the sun rose in Seoul, she huddled on his couch, wrapped in his childhood blanket. They both agreed it was too early to worry and tried to convince each other that they would be okay. Neither wanted to agonize about something that may not happen, but it was impossible to stop their minds from wandering down the dark path. That night, she stayed in his bed, wearing his pajamas.

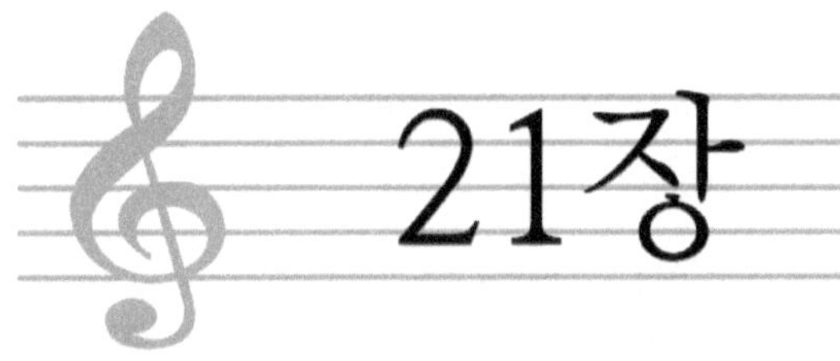

Within a week of her opening the little studio on the third floor, word spread throughout the music building, and her student list grew.

Between her scheduled lessons, musicians of all types and skill levels started knocking at her door with small pieces that troubled them.

No matter the instrument or style of music, Go-Ri willingly helped anyone who visited. The random drop-ins only stayed for a few minutes of help and a brief chat before running off. The people she met were all charming, and she was surprised by how much she enjoyed the unplanned visits.

It didn't take long for her to swing from a deep resistance to any association with the industry to enjoying every minute and every person she met while working at the Campus.

Now, she was happy to have as much company as possible. For the next week, she made a point to never be alone in the halls, and if she ate in the cafeteria, she found someone to sit with. After years of craving privacy, it felt strange to suddenly want to be surrounded by people—musicians—at all times.

Song-Ye wasn't even back yet, but she could feel the empty black pit growing, waiting to swallow her up again. With the looming threat of his return, she wondered if she had a choice. Would she stay? *Could I go?*

The IN7 American tour was almost over. Two weeks, and Baebin would be home.

The note from Mr. Kae's secretary left in Go-Ri's office mailbox seemed to prickle in her hand as she read it, and she soon stood in Mr. Kae's outer office, answering his unexpected summons. She had never met SKEC's CEO of Music before and couldn't fathom why she needed to now.

Was it about her, an outsider, working at the Campus? *Did I overstep a boundary without knowing? Did I make a mistake?* Surely, it wasn't about Song-Ye. Baebin hadn't told anyone but Chinmae. *Should I pack my things?* she wondered.

Ushered into the sizeable, plush office, replete with a long table overflowing with music files at one end, she approached a massive oak desk on the far side that was just as cluttered. Go-Ri bowed low and stood between the two wingback chairs in front of the desk, waiting for Mr. Kae to acknowledge her.

Packing the paper away, he looked up and pointed to a chair. He removed his thick, black-framed glasses and squinted at her in a quick appraisal before getting straight to the point. "I hear you've been granted a room in my building." She nodded her head in agreement, unsure what to say. "What exactly do you do here?"

Clearing her throat, she answered his question just as directly. "I give music lessons to ten adult students, who are your employees. I also teach five other students, who are children. Their parents work here at the Campus in different positions—mostly dancers. Your staff thought it would be easier for everyone to have the lessons here versus traveling to my place, where I also teach."

Wait, not my place. Baebin's place. Unwittingly, her mind conjured up images of Baebin next to her in the apartment. Pushing it aside, she focused on the distinguished, influential man in front of her.

"That makes fifteen. Who are all the others?" The tighter he squinted, the smaller his eyes became in his round, pudgy face.

Wha—? she blinked in surprise. *That's what this was about? He knew? Of course, he knew. This was his building.* "A few people have come looking for help with a piece of music," she answered honestly. "I don't consider them students since they stay with me for a few minutes and only need a little guidance. I'm sorry if I have overstepped—"

His pen started up a staccato rhythm, cutting her off as he continued to squint at her. "What do you play? What is your specialty?"

She started ticking off the twenty-two she could play well, both traditional Korean and other orchestral instruments, before beginning another long series of those she could only play moderately but felt confident enough to teach to beginners. She finished with, "I also compose my own music—jazz, classical, and traditional."

His tapping had stopped at some point, but his expression remained unreadable. "Pop?"

"No."

The tapping started back up. Her soft but emphatic answer brokered no discussion. Her stiff back tightened further. *Interesting.*

"You didn't say trumpet or French horn, but I've personally seen some go to your room."

Go-Ri's steady gaze remained neutral. "Yes. They needed help with a rhythm section. I try to help where I can. I am planning on learning how to play the trumpet next." She paused for a beat, then added. "I will stop the drop-ins if you insist, but I would like to stay to teach my students. It is easier for everyone if I travel here instead of your employees coming to me."

His tapping was now intense, and he stayed on beat as he waved her comment away with the other hand. "Continue exactly as you were. You may leave."

As she left the room, Mr. Kae opened her file again to compare notes. She confirmed most of what was written and filled in several of the blanks he'd wondered about. Her file was way too thin. *Why haven't we hired her?* How had such talent escaped his notice for so long? Where had she been hiding?

Mildly peeved that she found him instead of the other way around, he was insanely curious. And afraid he was slipping.

He buzzed Mrs. Jung. "Schedule that girl for another meeting next week. Come get her file and tell Mr. Wi he needs to work on it more. I want to know if she's played anywhere in public or has any recordings out. Oh, and there is a piece of music I need you to find by her next appointment." He hung up before his secretary could reply.

Putting his glasses back on, he stuffed the pen in his mouth and pulled a fresh stack of music within arm's reach.

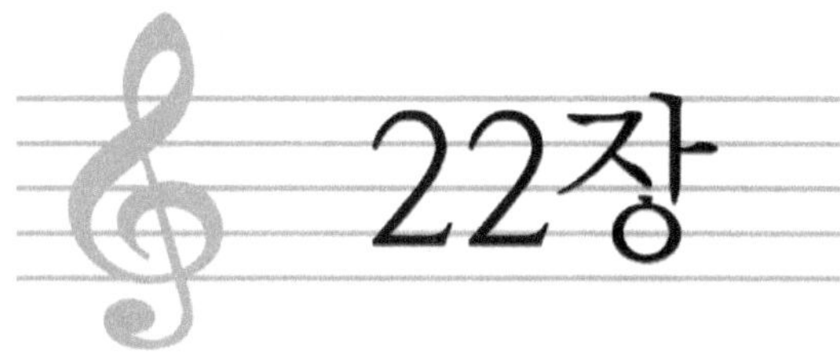

One week before Baebin came home, Go-Ri and Binna met at the apartment. Bringing a toolbox from home, Go-Ri was ready to finish his surprise. She found the exact bench they were looking for to go along the wall, and it would arrive in two days. So, to complete the finishing touches, tonight, the girls were going to hang the art.

They started in the main rooms where Baebin scattered pieces around, but what troubled her most was the last room. She swore Binna to secrecy and opened the door to Baebin's inner sanctum.

The girls worked around the room, hanging the floating shelves for the trophies and the new artwork Go-Ri created at a photo shop. She chose what she hoped were his favorite pictures from the stack and had them turned into large canvas prints. The thin, massive, floor-to-ceiling glass case she had custom-built for one wall was delivered several days ago and only needed to be filled with the rest of the pictures and memorabilia. A new reading nook and her favorite picture of Baebin in a small frame sat in one corner of the sound side.

Once they finished, they cleaned and dusted their way out of the room and shut the door. Go-Ri's stomach knotted. *I hope this was a good idea. Too late now; it's done.*

At the last minute, Go-Ri decided to spend the night. She missed him so much and wanted to be near him. Dressed in the pajamas she wore the first night there, she crawled into his bed. The scent of his cologne barely penetrated the air. *He needs to come home soon. I miss his smell.*

I miss him.

The sun wasn't up in Seoul when he called her from LA. She knew she looked a fright, but she took a picture of herself with her arm far outstretched. A minute later, the muffled groan she heard on his end of the phone shot tingles through her belly. Soon, there wouldn't be a need for pictures or phone calls. He would be here again. With her.

She was in his bed, in his pajamas, her hair splayed out over his pillow, looking gorgeous. *Amazing.* He wanted to be next to her, not in a hotel room in LA with Daeho. Savoring her picture, he was counting the hours until he could be next to her. He took a selfie and sent it to her.

An hour later, shampoo streamed down his back as he scrubbed cleanser across his forehead. Daeho slipped a hand inside the curtain and cranked the water to freezing. Baebin screeched and banged against the back wall as Daeho penguin-walked out of the bathroom, cackling.

Kyong and Yejoon, in the next room, just rolled their eyes at the sounds coming through the adjoining wall.

They had four days left in the States. One more concert in LA, and then they were doing a studio tour for a possible music video in a backstage lot. As in Chicago, the group took another whirlwind sightseeing tour of the beaches, Hollywood, the Observatory, and Rodeo Drive, recording several pieces with a camera crew.

After that, one last—and most prestigious—interview of the entire tour on *Jimmy Kimmel Live!* Then, a night-long wrap-up party for the entire three-hundred-person crew in the hotel ballroom, and they were finished.

Go-Ri received another summons to Mr. Kae's office.

Now what? Back straight, she sucked in her cheek, worrying the flesh between her teeth; she refused to let her knees shake. Once again, she bowed and sat in the same chair, waiting for him to speak.

He studied her, his thick glasses pushed high on the bridge of his nose, making his eyes look like two beads in a dimpled orange. "Why aren't you working for us?"

His tapping pen and the unexpected question took her aback. She blinked.

She thought of her buried, youthful, naïve dream and, again, settled for honesty. She would gain nothing by telling this powerful, intimidating man anything but the truth. "For a long time, I wanted to. But a few years ago, I was... I decided I would rather teach and compose my own music my way. I don't care for crowds, and I'm very selective about who I'm around and what music I play." Well, it was *mostly* the truth.

Mr. Kae stopped tapping, and for the first time, she could almost read something in his impassive expression. It flickered away as he opened a file on his desk and handed her several pages of music. "Tell me what you think."

She accepted the pages hesitantly and started reviewing them. Now, she was the one tapping. He watched as her eyes wavered across the page and her finger beat on her leg. When she finished, she closed her eyes to think.

Mr. Kae sat waiting, observing, noting, until she opened her eyes and handed the music back.

He waved the pages off and asked, "Well?"

"I'm not sure what you are asking of me. But if you want my opinion… the melody is pretty enough and almost set. Still…." *What kind of test is this?* Should she tell the truth or soften her comments? *Honesty couldn't hurt now,* she thought. *We're well past that.*

"The accompaniment is too complicated and overpowers the main line. There are too many instruments; it would sound better with a smaller set. Also, the trumpet is too high-pitched. It would sound better two steps lower. And the drum rhythm doesn't match the style of music. It's too…disorganized." Go-Ri's pulse hammered throughout every blood vessel, but she felt confident in her appraisal. She hoped she didn't overdo it.

"Mmm. Interesting." He examined her until, eventually, he started tapping again.

She bit the inside of her cheek, the metallic taste of blood faint on her tongue. Go-Ri wasn't sure what bothered her the most—his scrutiny or his tapping.

"Take that home and come back to see me in one week. I want to see what you can do with it."

Her eyes popped open, and her mouth dropped. "Wha—? I'm sorry, I don't understand."

"We will now pay for your lessons and drop-in visits for our staff, and you may continue with the children here, as well. Depending on what you do with that," waving his pen at the music in her hand, "and if you would like to work for me, I will also make room for you to work part-time, around your schedule, in one of our composition departments. I have a small, quiet group that does mostly background music for films that would suit you well. You can work in their office or in your studio. As long as you have reasonable enough output, you can work at your own pace on whatever suits you."

He pulled a new stack of files in front of him, clearly indicating the interview was over.

It took her a second to snap her mouth shut and remember to stand. She looked at the music and back at him, bowed, and almost walked the wrong way to the door.

Mr. Kae smiled as he peeked up, watching her leave. He hadn't been surprised by talent or unassuming charisma in a long time, and this lady shocked him. He couldn't wait to see her again next week and punched the intercom to tell Mrs. Jung to schedule it.

He pulled out his own copy of "Heaven's Lover," a song he wrote years ago, and reviewed it, assessing it with her blunt, bruising critique. His baby never felt right, and *dang it*, if this girl hadn't figured out why in a matter of minutes.

23장

Go-Ri canceled the rest of her appointments for the day and sat in Baebin's car, barely able to blink. *What just happened?*

She didn't know how many more twists and turns she could take. Making her way home on autopilot, she worked at MinGo until she burned the third order, and Mom sent her upstairs to get her out from underfoot.

The sets were in shipping containers, most of the crew was already home, and Baebin was five hours away from landing at Incheon.

Menial tasks finished, Go-Ri sat at the piano, staring blankly at Mr. Kae's music, her mind wandering in a thousand directions. The only sound in the apartment was the thumping of her heartbeat and the drumming of her fingers on the shiny black wood.

When the doorbell chimed, she squeaked, ripped from her reverie. Binna, Ji-U, and Kimh-So pressed their faces into the video lens, making goofy expressions as they waited for her to let them in. Laughter and friendship displaced the quiet anxiety as the three friends came in with groceries and drinks. They had all taken the day off work to be with her during the final countdown.

Soon, the kitchen was a disaster, as every pot was used and every inch of counter space, destroyed. Everyone pitched in, making any dish they could think of.

Despite the many hours they had to wait for Baebin to return, her friends only allowed Go-Ri two beers and a few shots of soju. Her friends would not want to face Baebin if he came home to a drunk girlfriend after being gone for two months.

They, on the other hand, would need a taxi. Go-Ri was so grateful for her wonderful friends and, for the thousandth time, appreciated them for sticking with her these last few years.

> B: JUST LANDED. STILL ON THE PLANE
> G: 😊 I'M GLAD

Cheers went up, and they allowed her one more shot to celebrate, along with a bowl of soup and some water. She wouldn't let her friends leave until they restored order to the kitchen and Baebin was in his car, headed for home.

Go-Ri was not a nail-biter, but she thought about picking up the habit. Two hours later, the next message arrived.

> B: CAR

Her friends gave her giant hugs and ran out the door.

Finally, heaven chimed, and the door opened. Go-Ri had wanted this moment for so long, and now, she didn't know what to do.

Baebin dropped his carry-on, kicked off his shoes, and frantically searched the room. *She promised to be here. Please tell me she is!* He refused to check the security cameras, afraid of what he wouldn't find.

He found her. His eyes swept over her as she stood in the living room. "Hi," he whispered.

"You're home," she whispered back.

"Mmm."

Slowly, she moved closer. Three steps away, she launched herself into his arms. He caught her up, holding her tightly. With a whimper, they clung to each other. Go-Ri kissed him first, and Baebin almost lost his grip as his knees buckled in relief.

All he could think about for the last few days was whether she would accept him or still be timid. Phone calls and video chats were nothing compared to face-to-face, and he was afraid she would build pieces of the wall again, separating them now that he was home. Baebin respected and understood her fears, but he wanted to kiss her, hold her. He wasn't looking to attack her, like some monster. He loved her and just wanted to show it more.

Threading his fingers through the long hair down her back, he gripped her head tight, holding her lips to his. Bumping noses, he swirled his tongue with hers when she let him inside. The shaky, urgent kiss deepened and grew as they explored each other again. It was like their first kiss. Only better. It was more intense, more intimate, more... *perfect*.

With a ragged sigh of contentment, Go-Ri rested her head on his shoulder. Through the layers of hotel soaps and traveling odors, Go-Ri found Baebin's woodsy scent as she burrowed into his neck.

Inhaling deeply, she lightly kissed the spot where his pulse fluttered before reluctantly untangling herself. "I know you're tired. I'm so glad you're home, but you must shower and sleep. Tomorrow is another day for us. I'll come back first thing tomorrow." Go-Ri held his cheek, brushing her palm over the tiny two-day stubble. She wanted to stay but didn't want to overwhelm him the second he returned.

"Okay. But if you leave, you'll have to explain to your mom and brother why I'm in your bed at their house," Baebin threatened with a cheeky grin. Her eyes grew wide and dark as her jaw dropped a fraction.

Baebin put a finger to her chin, closing her mouth, and begged softly, "Please don't leave. I couldn't stand it. I've waited so long to be here with you; I can't bear another moment alone."

Her color grew as her insides quivered with excitement.

By the time he came out of the shower with a towel around his neck and his hair still damp, she was ladling two bowls of *sulguk* with sides of rice. After the long journey, the mild seaweed soup settled well in his stomach. They ate quietly at the table, thinking about what was to come, and left their bowls to soak after dinner.

He held her hand and walked through the apartment, turning off lights, when he stopped short, sending her careening into his back with a small grunt.

He was a little too preoccupied to notice earlier, but now, he saw the finished rooms. Not a box was in sight. A beautiful bench sat along the wall, the pictures were hung, and all the little details, like rugs, plants, and decorations that he was sure weren't there when he left, completed the space. It was amazing—exactly what he dreamed of.

"You did all this?" He was in awe and highly touched.

"Mmm." Unsure if this was the right time, she hesitated to show him the changes in the studio. Gathering her courage, she decided to deal with the consequences now rather than waiting. "There's more. I hope it's okay." Unlocking the studio door, she pulled him inside and stood back to see his reaction.

His speechless amazement was more than she'd hoped for. "I talked to several recording technicians, and they promised none of this would affect the room's sound quality. The fabric prints and upholstered chair balance out the glass, and will be unnoticeable through the microphones." Go-Ri watched carefully as he took it all in.

Everywhere he looked, he could see the tender care and thoughtfulness she put into the décor. The new storage units under the desk, the large canvas photos, the massive honey oak cabinet that matched the overstuffed chair—everything was perfect. His home was complete. Every room was his safe haven. This was the place he wanted to escape to, recharge in, relax in.

She did this, and he couldn't imagine her not being there to share it with him. Pulling her in close, he wrapped himself around her and gawked over her shoulder at her work.

Tucking his chin into her neck, he sniffled, refusing to let the tears interrupt him. "I'm a little overwhelmed. Thank you, aein, for such a wonderful gift. I love you so much. Not just for all of this, but for being strong and for being with me."

She loved being his girlfriend, but to hear him call her "sweetheart" in such a tender way thrilled her. Go-Ri ducked down to get him to look at her, and when he finally did, she smiled so gently, so warmly, so happily. "It's *You*. You make me feel alive again. I love you, too."

He sagged against her, wanting to cry all over again. Pulling her close, he held her, and she, without any reservation, held him tighter.

For weeks, Baebin dreamed of holding her in his arms. Lying in bed next to her. Seeing her head on his pillow. Talking to her until the early hours of dawn.

Quickly changing, Go-Ri rushed to the bedroom, impatient to be with him again. Would tonight be as delicious as her memories from before his tour? He was back, and he said he loved her…

He was asleep.

Sitting on the bed, she stretched out a finger, brushing away his hair as he lay facing her. Go-Ri gazed down at him in the dim light, poring over every nook and cranny of exposed skin, his long fingers, every swirl of his ear with their empty piercing holes, the bluish tint of exhaustion under his eyes, the rounded nose over his full, defined lips.

Gently lifting his arm, she crawled underneath and molded herself to his warm body. She fell asleep, wrapped in his heavy weight, listening to the rhythmic beat of his heart.

Baebin hardly moved for over ten hours. The sky was still gray when Go-Ri snuck out of bed and made a breakfast of rice and porridge, covered both with towels to keep them warm, and prepared the coffee. Slipping back into bed, she wrapped her arms around his middle, and, holding him close, fell back to sleep.

The bright sunlight peeked through cracks in the curtains when he finally stirred. Disoriented, he couldn't remember what time zone or hotel he was in. The heavy, striped curtains confused him.

The breasts pressing against him and the tangle of hair around his arm reminded him that he made it back to Seoul. Back to his apartment. Back to Go-Ri. *I'm home.*

He rolled and pulled her against his chest, trapping her leg between his. Even though he desperately wanted more, and she felt glorious in his arms, he fell back to sleep in seconds.

She woke again an hour later and found herself sprawled across his chest with a hand under his shirt. Go-Ri froze. She listened and felt for any telltale movement from Baebin, praying he was still asleep.

He dashed her hopes when he growled lightly, "Oh, thank God, you're awake. You're killing me. Do you know how much you move in your sleep? And I think you drooled again." He drew his free leg up and tried to politely adjust himself.

She pinched him hard on the stomach and buried her face in his armpit after risking a glance at his shirt, checking for a wet spot.

His throaty laugh made her pulse flutter when he rolled her over onto her back and started kissing her ear and jaw. The wet, smacking, playful pecks slowly morphed into light caresses as he nibbled his way down her collarbone. Baebin threaded his fingers through hers while kissing every millimeter around her hairline and collar.

Head thrown back, she gave him access, the freedom to continue. She mewed softly but did not pull away.

Arching back, he waited until her eyes focused on his. His husky voice, raw with sleep and desire, matched his hopeful gaze. "I would like to touch you—nothing more. Will you let me?" Go-Ri gave an almost imperceptible nod. "Do you need to...?" He gave a slight jerk of the head to the bathroom. After a moment, she nodded again. "Okay. I'll use the hall bathroom. See you in a moment?" Baebin let her go, and she scooted out from under him and raced on wobbly legs to the bathroom.

Not only did she use the time to relieve herself, but also to think—make sure this was what she truly wanted. She had wanted this badly for weeks, but now that the moment had come, it was overwhelming. Staring at herself in the mirror, she lightly slapped her cheeks and squared her shoulders.

Sometimes, it's okay to have what you want, Choi Go-Ri.

She found him perched on the side of the bed, like a nervous cat waiting for her response. Unsure if she would flee or come back to him, he held still. Watching. Waiting.

One foot in front of the other, tall and composed, Go-Ri stopped just close enough to let their knees touch and offered a hand. He accepted it, drawing his thumb across a knuckle. "You sure?" he asked.

She fixated on his incredibly deep black eyes and bravely answered. "Yes. I'm not scared of you or of… us. I love you. I can't imagine being with anyone but you. I've missed you so much. I don't want to hold your pillow anymore."

"Mmm. I don't want to rush us. And I don't want to be with you just because I'm finally home. You are amazing, and I love you too much to push us further than we should."

Heat rose up her neck, but she refused to be afraid. "I like kissing you. And I want to do more than that. But I don't know if I can handle everything all at once. Can we just take it slow?"

Drawing her onto his lap, he pecked her nose. "All I want right now is to touch you." Murmuring near the outer crease of her eye, he let his breath stroke her temple. "I want to feel your skin." He swiped at the swirl of her ear. Tracing the outer ridge. "I want to learn what you like." At the corner of her mouth, he laid a kiss. "I want to be the first one—the only one—to make your heart race."

Then, his lips fully met hers, brushing lightly, "We have forever to do everything else." When she opened her mouth, accepting and returning the stroke of his tongue, his blood surged in every cell of his body.

God, he's a fantastic kisser, Go-Ri thought. It melted her bones. Any remaining doubt fled, and in its wake, an ache of arousal formed low in her belly. Her breasts tingled, egged on by the soft fabric of her borrowed top and the soft pressure of his firm chest. Needing to ease the swelling torment, her hands spread over his shoulders, drawing him closer.

When he shifted slightly and pulled the T-shirt over his head, she had to bite her lip to not purr at the sight. She knew he was toned because of his work, but he was hot. *Obscenely* hot. She pushed him back and leaned over him. She desperately wanted to look. Wanted to touch.

Ducking her head, she hid her face from his as her eyes and fingers roamed over his naked chest. His honey-colored skin stretched tight over ropy muscles. She didn't like tattoos, but changed her opinion when she saw his. These were sexy, especially the one that rimmed his collarbone, and she wondered, fleetingly, at its meaning.

Her fingers and lips explored him while he held a fistful of her shirt and the sheet beside him. Her legs cradled his waist, and the further her nails snaked down his abdomen, the more his arousal pulsed and stiffened. When she scooted down for more access, he felt his erection rise in the crease of her bottom as her mouth grazed his nipple. He let out a pinched groan. He couldn't take it anymore. Before she could think, she was pinned below him in the middle of the bed.

Months ago, he couldn't get her to even notice him. Had he known she was capable of such a carnal, lewd appraisal of him, he would have run naked in the streets long ago. His level of horniness shot up as he gave thanks to his coaches and trainers for just one moment of her appreciation.

He lingered in the curve of her neck, fitting his cheek against the arch, letting his lips skim her skin. Nudging her thighs apart, he rested his leg between them, and smoothing a hand over the curve of her rear, he drew her free leg over his, settling their bodies even closer together. Instinctively, she curled her toes around his knee, trapping him in place.

He needed more. His fingers wandered across her cheek. Traveling along a strand of hair, tucking it behind her ear, he fingered his way down its length, stopping at the top button. Not wanting to overestimate by going off her sighs alone, he snuck a peek.

She screwed her eyes shut, but her aroused, lost expression seemed willing for more.

Pausing for a heartbeat, he undid the button before his finger traced down to the next one, and two heartbeats later, it, too, was undone. The third button sat between her breasts. He felt the rounded globes through her shirt and slipped his fingers inside the fabric for just a moment before moving on. The moan that escaped her was a lovable mix between an *eek* and a groan. His eyes drifted closed, supremely satisfied.

She could feel his fingertips graze her skin—his mouth and tongue tracing where a button used to be. Slowly, he exposed her to the cool air and his hot breath. He continued the path to the last button. She thought she would die before he finished and vowed to never wear a button-down top to bed again.

Her nerves couldn't take it. Go-Ri was a quivering mess, her thighs clenched his leg between hers, keeping him pressed against her. She clutched at his hair when he cupped her breast; his tongue skimmed across her nipple before he sucked on the swollen tip. The feeling was like no other she had ever dreamed of. First one breast and then the other, he left warm trails across her chest.

His hand moved south in slow, roaming circles around her ribs and navel as he licked at the hollow of her neck where her heartbeat pulsed madly. Baebin loved the rapid tempo. *Her skin is even softer and warmer than in my dreams.* He enjoyed the simple smell of Go-Ri that couldn't come in a bottle.

Go-Ri let her hands drift down his body to find the same places on him that excited her. *If I like it, so must he*. The tips of her fingers danced over his skin. Exploring. Massaging. Inspecting. His chiseled back and butt rippled under her palms at each movement of his body. Skimming the tattoo on his side, she felt him flinch as her light touch tickled a rib. Repeating the pattern over and over, she tormented him.

For each moan she gave, she received one in return. Each gasp. Each shudder. She wanted to find his favorite spot and remember it forever. She had nothing to be afraid of. *Why did I ever fear Baebin? He's a good man, and not just here in bed.* His every thought and action promised love and security. She'd fallen for him long ago.

Her fingers skimmed the front waistline of his pants against his bare flesh, back and forth, hip to hip. He almost leapt out of his skin when she brushed across his tip during a pass. *She won't need to go any further if she keeps that up…!* Unconsciously, he shifted up a millimeter, signaling her to move lower.

Go-Ri didn't even touch him, exactly, but hovered near his groin where his stiff hard-on bulged relentlessly under his clothes. She could feel his heart hammering through his entire body. She kept her hand there, not sure what to do. She wasn't a nun—she knew *what to do*, but actually *doing it* was a different story.

Baebin propped further up on his shaking elbow and slowly laced his fingers with hers, guiding her, helping her wrap her hand around him through his pants. Nerves snapped all over, and his belly cramped up through his ribcage when her soft hand made contact. His thigh pressed roughly against her sensitive junction, and with each flinch of his hip, she moaned, wrapping herself tighter around his leg.

She wanted to thrash and scrub against the strange new frustration, to relieve the itch flaring inside.

He knew what *he* wanted for today but didn't know if this was the right time for Go-Ri. She seemed to be enjoying his touch, but he vowed to stick to his rule. Baebin didn't want to push her too far and regret it later.

They hadn't defined the parameters of what they would touch, how, how long, to what degree... anything. And it wasn't fair—*she* was doing most of the touching. Her hands continually played over him, shattering his control. He held her hand. Teaching. Coaching. As the initial surge subsided, he sagged against her, kissing the valley between her breasts. She started moving on her own, and he was able to release his own fingers to start exploring her body again.

For months, he thought about being with her just like this—touching her, kissing her. It was embarrassing, waking up to a wet dream with a teammate in the next bed. But more than once, he dreamed of her hand wrapped around his cock, like she was doing now. Maybe next time, he'd feel the heat of her palm on him without fabric in the way, her callused fingers stroking him. He could wait, and Baebin shivered in anticipation.

He didn't want to cum first, but he was so close, and she felt so good. He couldn't help himself. He hated himself for being weak. Digging into her hip, he tensed. Every muscle in his body contracted as his sac tightened fiercely, and he lost control, spilling out all over the inside of his pajamas. For a long moment, he curled over her, stunned and shaking, as lights danced in his eyes.

Witnessing his release was exhilarating. Intoxicating. She had done that. She glowed with newfound power and confidence—the confidence you get when you please someone thoroughly and realize you are worthy of giving that pleasure.

Slowly, he stretched out, and his bare chest slid against hers; Go-Ri whimpered softly as the smooth hardness made her already puckered nipples throb. Focusing on him had given her a moment's reprieve from her own sensations. But it was short-lived when he reclaimed a breast and its tight peak. The tip of his tongue and his teeth rasping over the tip was a seductive companion to his roving fingers that skimmed across her waist.

He loved her soft, curvy body and her reactions. Her chest arched in offering as her belly sucked in, trying to escape his touch. Soon, she also raised her hips an unconscious millimeter, signaling she wanted more. He lay alongside her and kissed her gently, his tongue pressing against her lips to enter her mouth.

Thoroughly distracted, she didn't notice his free hand dip slowly inside her pajama bottoms.

Running his fingers through the crinkly curls at her apex, he parted her swollen folds, which were already wet. Sliding one finger, then two, along the creases, he spread her moisture and found her clit, rubbing it in small circles, slowly increasing the pressure. Back and forth between the folds and her sensitive nub, he moved, loving the feel of her dampness, her groans, her slight humping movements. He was getting hard again, but he firmly shoved his own desires away.

In a panic, Go-Ri clutched his wrist, stilling him. It was too much. Too dangerous. Too scary. She couldn't breathe. She needed to stop but didn't want to.

Holding on to him as a lifeline, she felt the sinews in his arm and the fingers on her core twitch. A small, minuscule movement. She gasped and sighed against his mouth. She raised and lowered herself, using the hand on his arm as an anchor. She held on. She didn't want him to continue. She didn't want him to leave. Ever so slowly, he shifted a tiny bit more. Just a graze at first. Again, a gentle stroke.

His horse whisper warmed her ear, caressing her hair. "Hold onto me, aein. Don't be afraid." His calm encouragement was all she needed. Her hands let go and flew around his neck. She latched on, gripping him fiercely.

His long, slim fingers parted slightly, holding her open. When they came together again, his knuckles squeezed and pulled her sensitive spot while his fingers filled her slit. The more he touched, the more her senses frayed. Her whole body felt… *something*.

Was this how he felt when he came a minute ago? She remembered him almost turning into one giant cramp when he cried out. That is how she felt now. Every muscle in her body tightened. But this cramp didn't hurt. It was… delicious.

Another flick. She arched up against him, one moment taut like a bow string, then the next, she curled in a ball, trapping him between her legs. The tremors engulfed her as she contorted. She felt her wetness wash over his hand and soak into her panties. She ripped her mouth away from his and bit her lip, surrendering to the strange explosion inside of her.

The primal cockiness he felt with each shudder that rippled through her, feeling her slick moisture on his fingers, charged through him. Watching her climax was magnificent. He wanted to possess her bliss. He never wanted another man to see how passionate she was.

As her breath slowed, he gently adjusted her clothing and pulled the covers around them, drawing her close to him.

Resting his temple on one fist, he held her hand with the other, kissing the knuckles. Baebin asked quietly, "You okay, aien?"

Her shy, languid smile filled his heart. "Mmm. Definitely."

He grinned back, pleased he had made her happy. He continued to kiss her knuckles. Go-Ri reached up and pulled him back down for a long kiss.

His stomach rumbled, interrupting them at an inopportune time. Giggling, she broke free. "I think we are well past breakfast. And lunch. I made food for us earlier, though, and have coffee ready. Would you like to eat?" His stomach growled loudly in response.

He pulled her shirt away, nibbling on her collarbone like a corncob. Laughing harder, she batted him back and shoved a pillow in his face. He yanked it down far enough to uncover his eyes and muttered a muffled, "Yes."

It was well past noon when they crawled out of bed. They used separate facilities to make themselves presentable, and Go-Ri turned on the coffee as Baebin entered the kitchen. "Well, do you want breakfast?" She pointed to the food she made hours earlier. "Or dinner?" She pointed to the fridge.

Baebin chose a light breakfast with only one egg and sat on a bar stool. He stood up immediately and looked at the chair questioningly. It—and the rest of the matching set—hadn't been there two months ago, he was sure. While he had coffee, she warmed up their bowls, adding honey to his, and fried their eggs. He kept swiveling around in his chair, picking out everything else he had missed last night.

His eclectic art somehow fit with the pillows, knickknacks, and plants. She'd finished unpacking his books and memorabilia from his childhood and arranged them on the bookcase that could be seen from both the living room and piano room.

A long bench with most of her instruments tucked underneath was covered in beautiful fabric that looked great with the shiny black piano and the art he'd sent home from New York City. The shape and design of the wooden bench was everything that he wanted but couldn't describe.

She hadn't used his card while he was overseas, yet there were several new pieces in this area of the apartment alone. He remembered the improvements in the studio, as well, and wondered if there were more surprises in the bedrooms.

The cold November breeze on the balcony required blankets and more hot coffee as they watched the shadows grow over the city and lights turn on.

Go-Ri looked out at the view. *Before things go too far, we need to talk.* Baebin just got back, and while this might not be quite the right time, she wanted a fresh start. A new beginning. She wanted it now before she got too comfortable in their old ways.

The last few months had changed her, and she was ready to take on more. "Can I... I'd like to talk to you." She cleared her throat and pulled the blanket around her tighter.

"What is it? What's wrong?" He sat up, brows knitted together as he looked at her.

She waved her hand to settle him down. "Nothing serious. But I would like you to do me a favor. I know you're holding back. I see you question yourself every time you come near. You always ask me if I'm okay. It means a lot, honestly. But I want you to be you. Not someone you think you have to be. Today is a good day to start fresh. Almost like starting over. I may still get scared or startled, but I need to work through it, and I can't do that if I'm always protected. I don't want you to be afraid of me or for me."

Baebin tucked one leg under him and set his cooling coffee down on the little table, wrapping his blanket tighter around him. He sat for a long time, looking out at the city, mulling over all that she said.

"I'll do my best to stop. I can't promise to be good at it, but I will try. Just please tell me if I do something wrong or if something happens. I would like to work on it together with you."

She nodded before sucking in a big breath of air. "And... about Song-Ye. I've decided I like working at the Campus. I don't want to run away if he comes back, but I don't know if I can stay if he does. I don't know what to do."

Baebin saw red just thinking of him. He hesitated to broach the topic of his own history with Nam Song-Ye. He focused on a tour boat passing under the Banpo Bridge before it turned right at the bend of the river.

"Our group started with eighteen guys. Several dropped out, and then the others splintered off into a new group. We were all glad when Song-Ye and his gang left. They were bad news and caused us a lot of trouble. If they hadn't left, we probably would have lost our chance to debut. Honestly, I forgot about him since he moved to Japan last year."

With the boat too far out of sight, Baebin turned to look at her. "Of course, I want you to stay at the Campus, but I can't imagine how painful it would be for you to see him. I would never ask you to torture yourself like that. Let's see what your options are when that time comes, okay?"

Go-Ri rested her head on her knees, letting thoughts flow gently in her mind. She extended her hand to him and let his lean palm warm hers. She tried not to let thoughts of Nam Song-Ye and Baebin enter her mind at the same time. The former wasn't worthy of space with the latter.

She liked the Campus and wondered what it would be like to work near Baebin. But could she handle it if *he* was there, too? *And what about Mr. Kae and his—*

Go-Ri suddenly jolted upright and crushed Baebin's hand. *Hard.*

He let out a startled yowl, trying to pull free from her death grip. "Wha—?!"

She eased her strength and pecked his boo-boo, her eyes glowing in excitement. "I completely forgot! I have crazy news!" She told him about the most recent meeting with Mr. Kae. He had given her a week, and she had only four days left.

Baebin couldn't believe her luck. He had met the formidable Mr. Kae once when he was a trainee. Some people feared him, and some revered him. He was a global powerhouse in the industry.

Baebin grabbed her in a big hug and smacked a wet kiss on her cheek. Cheering her on, he threatened not to touch her until her project was done. "Well, you can start tomorrow." He grinned at her, wiggling his eyebrows suggestively.

She blushed, reading his dirty mind. She had apparently awakened a sleeping tiger.

They sat shoulder-to-shoulder on the bench as she played the composite line of the conductor's score for "Heaven's Lover." He liked her assessment of the piece and thought she was even better at picking it apart than he was. Baebin could see her mind already plucking at strings and fiddling with ideas as she improvised minor variations of key parts.

She didn't share anything more, and he let her play with it. Creativity needed time to simmer alone in its own pot.

The following morning, Baebin woke up first. Go-Ri had drifted to the far pillow and lay on her stomach with an arm hanging off her side of the bed. Last night was sheer bliss. They had second-time jitters and didn't go any further than the first time, but it was still one-hundred percent magical.

She was captivating, all sex tousled. It was a good look on her.

As he scrutinized her gorgeous appearance, he paused, only slightly miffed. Her eyes, behind their lids, flicked back and forth. He had a feeling she was dreaming of music and not him. He stuck out his foot and gently nudged her off the bed.

Landing with a thunk, she sat up, looking disheveled. Her wide, dazed eyes were puffy with sleep; her hair, a rat's nest. He took one look at her bare shoulders, visible just above the mattress, and rolled away, trying to cover his laughter. "Go to work. I want you back here as soon as possible."

She jumped on top of him and started tickling his ribs. They tumbled on the bed until the cover tangled horribly around and between them. Freeing her legs from the covers and almost losing a sock in the process, she wrapped herself around him, the beginning of his erection obvious to them both, even through the blanket. They kissed slowly and leisurely until she pinched his bare butt and shoved him off.

All business a short while later, she walked into the kitchen, cleaned, dressed, and with her hair in a ponytail. Baebin handed her coffee and set her breakfast in front of her. Soon, they moved several of her instruments next to his electric keyboard in his private studio. They rearranged the workspace for her to write, and he took the laptop stand to call his parents. He had been home for almost two days and felt guilty for forgetting them. Go-Ri kissed him and shut the door.

The next two days were the strangest he had ever experienced. He and Go-Ri had only been together for a little over thirty hours after the long tour, and now, a locked door separated them. But positions like the one she'd been offered at SKEC were rare and highly coveted.

She *had* changed, like she said. Her willingness to even think about the opportunity made Baebin tingle with pleasure. He hadn't been this anxious or excited since his first concert.

But anxiety turned to boredom as the day dragged on. In the middle of the night, he woke to her warm body next to his. Sweeping her hair back, he buried his nose in her neck and fell back to sleep, inhaling the faint scent of vanilla and eucalyptus lotion. At five o'clock in the morning, Baebin's alarm went off for the basketball game he scheduled with Ji-U and Kimh-so. The bed next to him was already cold.

He came back sweaty and wiped out. Both guys kicked his butt. By three o'clock, the sandwich he made for her was still untouched. He picked up the plate and a large glass of water and rapped lightly on the door before entering the code.

He found Go-Ri in the stuffed chair with the lamp on beside her. Both legs were thrown over the arm, her head was tossed back, and she was snoring softly. Baebin frowned at the dark smudges under her eyes. Her chest and the floor were littered with sheets and sheets of music.

He set the food down quietly and sat on the floor near her hip to peek at her progress. He was amazed at her work. There were pages and pages devoted to multiple instruments and various styles of music. All of it was extraordinary.

She did all this in a remarkably short amount of time. *She only has one more day. Would sheet music alone be enough to impress Mr. Kae?* A few minutes later, he padded softly out the door, deciding to let her sleep.

He came up with a plan—and Tae-Si was the key.

Then, gathering his courage, Baebin walked to MinGo.

Go-Ri's mom welcomed him home graciously but did not hide her displeasure at her missing daughter. It took a lot—explaining that Go-Ri was working (currently) and apologizing for his behavior with her (if she only knew!)—but he convinced her to close early tomorrow night and bring food for the army.

Well after midnight, Go-Ri tried to slip into bed unnoticed. Baebin softly rubbed a finger across her blue eyelids. "This is too much. I'm worried."

She yawned deeply, already half asleep. "It's my fault. I waited too long to start. I think I'm done now, anyway."

"I distracted you."

"Yes, you did."

It was still early when they heard her moving about. Tae-Si had arrived as promised and commandeered the couch and a game controller as they waited for her to emerge. She looked better than last night, but her dark and weary eyes were still bloodshot as she trudged in, finishing the braid that hung over her shoulder.

Go-Ri was shamefaced to see Tae-Si, who had to know she slept and showered at his friend's house. She wanted to hide, but she just told Baebin she was done hiding. *Ugh. I always have lousy timing.* Instead, she smiled bravely at the visitor and sank into a chair, intentionally choosing the one closest to Tae-Si.

Baebin noticed and smiled inside. He handed her the bowl of warmed porridge. "I hope you don't mind, but I asked Tae-Si to help you record your music. He's really good at it. I thought it might help with your presentation tomorrow with Mr. Kae."

She had only recorded a few times before, and anxiety didn't mix well with the porridge. Besides, Tae-Si was a professional who specialized in rap; why did he want to help *her?* Sure, he offered it before, but she didn't really take him seriously.

She mulled it over. *A recording would be better than notes on a page.* While everything was written, recording it would take a while, and she'd need help to finish on time.

Filling two travel mugs with hot coffee, she led the way. When she unlocked the door and Tae-Si saw the studio for the first time, he exclaimed, "Wha—! This is heaven! You didn't tell me you had all this!"

Baebin hollered back, "If I told you, you'd never leave!"

The door closed behind them, cutting off Tae-Si's smart-alec retort. For several hours, his friend and girlfriend were alone in the locked room.

He was getting fidgety when the three of the other guys arrived late in the afternoon. Baebin appreciated their willingness to cut into their long-needed vacation for tonight's surprise. No matter how hard they begged, he wouldn't spill the secret just yet, promising only that it was a good one.

Finally, when Baebin didn't think he could take much more, Tae-Si danced out of the room, brandishing a thumb drive, and slid his way to the kitchen for a beer.

Go-Ri followed him much more sedately but smiled from ear to ear. Her braid was frayed, and pencils stuck out of her hair. Disconcerted at the new company but pleased with her time spent with Tae-Si, she had no more doubts about Bebin's friends. Plus, she was too tired to care.

Daeho lost it at seeing the two walk in together from the hallway. "You two have been here the whole time?" Snorting and cackling outrageously, he pounded the pillow, laughing at *hyung*. "You let them be alone? Together? Or did she get smart and dump you already?"

Baebin snagged her arm as she tried to pass by, and she tumbled into his lap. Pulling the pencils out from her hair before she poked his eye out, he smooched her neck in full view of his friends, much to their delight and her dismay. "I trust her completely. Besides, she's too smart to dump me, and Tae-Si isn't good enough for her."

Grinning, Baebin threw a chip at Daeho. Go-Ri smacked Baebin on the shoulder. Tae-Si threw an apple slice at Baebin. Chinmae and Kyong sat back, out of the line of fire.

Embarrassed but oddly delighted, Go-Ri snuggled deeper into Baebin's shoulder and, after a second's hesitation, kissed him back.

Tae-Si, completely senseless of boundaries, told the others about the hidden studio. They raced to the door, shoving each other in their eagerness to be the first to see it. Baebin gave in and yelled the code. They all clucked their tongues in understanding. Each of them used their joining day for codes, too. Daeho even had it tattooed on his thigh in Roman numerals.

Baebin's private room was no longer private, but he realized it didn't bother him anymore. He could hear "oohs," shouts, and laughter coming through the open door. Baebin was proud of Go-Ri's work finishing the room and making it extra special.

The doorbell rang, waking Go-Ri, who had fallen asleep in Baebin's lap. He whispered in her ear, "That's the rest of your surprise. You'd better get up."

She climbed off him and took over the chair, warm with his body heat and filled with his scent, while he went to open the door. She was tucking the blanket around her feet when she jumped, recognizing the voices of her mom, Min-Jun, and Mr. Bak.

The guys left the studio and crowded in the entry to help bring in all the food from the hotel cart and load the island to capacity.

The group recognized the man from the lobby, and Go-Ri introduced them to her mother and brother. Min-Jun stayed silent but polite, keeping an eye on Baebin. *Omma*, her mother, just started nattering along and finally shooed them out of the kitchen, away from her food.

Before everyone could attack the dishes, Baebin raised his hands and called for attention. Time for his reveal. He glanced at Go-Ri. *I hope this is okay. Too late to ask for permission.* After relating an abbreviated version of her project and its story, his eyes slid to her once more.

"I snuck in yesterday and peeked at her music. It's good. *Really* good. I think we should have a concert before eating."

Tae-Si nodded in agreement and Go-Ri colored, pleased to show off her work. Baebin had seen her mess? That explained the mysterious sandwich. She thought she had been so tired that she couldn't remember making it.

They all filed into the piano room and sat in a row on the long bench. Tae-Si started dancing around again as he fired up the laptop. Go-Ri went to get the sheet music from the studio to follow along.

This will be good practice for my delivery to Mr. Kae tomorrow, she thought. *One last run-through. One last check before my presentation.*

"The title is 'Heaven's Lover.' We'll start with an excerpt of the original score as it was given to me. It is only missing a few of the instruments." She gestured to Tae-Si, who dramatically hit the play button.

The song finished, and she took a deep breath to control the tremble in her voice. "He didn't tell me which direction to go. I couldn't decide, so I did four. I play most of the parts you'll hear, but Han Tae-Si added the ones I couldn't, like the trumpet and drums, using the keyboard synthesizer. He helped put it all together for me."

Tae-Si hit play. One after the other, four different variations of the same melody filled the room. During the third staccato—and rather harrowing—piece, Go-Ri closed her eyes, her fingers moving along to a different rhythm. Lightly tugging Tae-Si's sleeve, she pulled him near and started whispering. Their heads and shoulders touched as they bent over the pages.

In a single-minded search, she combed the room for her required cases, pushing legs aside as they blocked her way under the bench. Sucking on three reeds at once, she reloaded the pencils in her hair before rejoining Tae-Si. As the music continued, the two began writing, using the piano as their table.

By the end of the fourth version, which had a more funereal style, everyone in the room wore amazed expressions as her creations played over the speakers. The room was quiet as they listened to the last, crying note.

Baebin watched in awe from his position near the window. He had seen her play and compose before, but not like this. Not with someone else. He hadn't seen her this comfortable with someone other than family and her three friends before.

The music was great, but *she* was amazing. She was a stranger in a familiar body. Dominant. Confident. Focused. Alive.

She looked up shyly, unsure of their silent reaction. "Mmm... that's it." They erupted in cheers.

Before they could move, Tae-Si waved and called out over the din. "Sorry, we are doing it again." He looked at Go-Ri for confirmation. "We'll skip the original version." He pulled a face that sent Go-Ri giggling. "You gotta hear what *gongjunim* just thought of." Tae-Si bounced lightly, humming with energy, as he found the starting point on the track before joining her to follow along with the pages.

Go-Ri began by playing along to the recording with the *danso*, adding its high flute sound as a romantic accompaniment to the first melody and giving it the bright playfulness of young love. Then, she switched to the oboe on the second upbeat piece, making it more of a quiet lover's ballad. She used the *haegeum* for the third, but instead of the usual long notes created by drawing the bow, she flicked it rapidly between the strings. It created an unusual percussive effect perfectly suited to the staccato variation—a background for what instantly became a lover's quarrel.

Tae-Si made notations as she played to help them edit later and beat out the conductor's rhythm for her during tricky passages.

Lastly, fitting the reed onto her bass clarinet, Go-Ri explained, "This one is supposed to be with a bassoon. I don't have one, but they do at the Campus. Try to hear this lower." She nodded to Tae-Si to hit play, and while the tone added was slightly off, the strain was right. They all could imagine the rich, low, crying notes the bassoon would make as it hummed under the funeral song.

The guys who lived with music every day of their lives couldn't believe what they were hearing. In minutes, she added one part in four unique but similar styles. The speed, quality, and ability to compose the way she did astounded them.

Before Go-Ri could unhook the neck strap, Tae-Si grabbed her in a tight hug and swung her around in a circle. Soon, she was yanked out of his arms and spun from person to person.

She stiffened slightly but swiftly let herself soak in the feeling. The love, security, acceptance—and the appreciation for not just her music but for herself, as well.

Baebin watched as one emotion flicked to another, speeding across Go-Ri's face as she relented and accepted their embrace.

The party finally migrated back to the kitchen for food while they discussed the mini-concert. Mom and Mr. Bak went to warm the food that had cooled during the performance while everyone else set the table and portioned out the side dishes.

Go-Ri welcomed the separation from the crowd to ease her thundering heart. Somewhere during her impromptu concert, she had forgotten to be nervous. But the rush of adrenaline, now that it was all over, hit her. Baebin helped her disassemble the instruments and store them back in their cases.

Finished, he drew her in his arms. He rested his head against hers and whispered over and over, "I'm so proud of you. I love you." His warm breath tickled her cheek; the fluttering air passed over her ear and warmed her deep in her heart.

Min-Jun scowled as he watched them together, where they hid behind the piano. He could see Go-Ri was happy, but he was afraid for her. He had to admit she wasn't a walking zombie anymore, but he was too pessimistic to pin his hopes on a good outcome.

"Be careful with the dagger eyes. You may hit the wrong target and cause pain you didn't intend."

Min-Jun glared up at the man who had caught him staring.

Chinmae turned to watch the couple as well. "It's hard, isn't it? I was worried, too, at first. No one is good enough for hyung. He deserves only the best." The boy stiffened, ready with a retort until Chinmae fixed his eyes on him. "But your noona *is* the best, by far. Kim Baebin knows it. We all do." Gently patting the boy on his shoulder, he guided him away to help in the kitchen and give the couple privacy.

Baebin and Go-Ri walked hand in hand to the table as everyone claimed their seats. This was Baebin's dream since he first looked at the apartment with the realtor: friends and family sitting around his own table. He was sure he was the happiest man in Korea at this moment.

Go-Ri and Tae-Si tucked sheet music between them on the table as they worked to finish the pages. Somehow, Go-Ri's hand held a pencil, chopsticks, and a spoon. Baebin sat on her other side, ensuring her bowl was always filled with meat.

After trying to pick up rice with her pencil for the third time, he took the spoon and chopsticks out of her hand and started feeding her, himself. Baebin grinned and could only shake his head as she just opened her mouth when she was ready for more, without even looking at him. Tae-Si was having a hard time, too, but Baebin figured he was on his own to feed himself.

Mom flitted around the table, treating them all like she would at her restaurant. As she passed by again, Mr. Bak finally grabbed her hand and made her sit. These were grown boys who could take care of themselves. She huffed and tsked at him, slapping his arm lightly, but she stayed seated, and the two settled into friendly conversation.

Sometime through the evening, Mom became *Omma* to five grown men. She loved, scolded, and cared for them as her own. *Omma* and Mr. Bak worked in the kitchen alone together after dinner—unless she called out, "You!" with a flick of her hand, and one of the boys would come running to take a tray of desserts or move a clean platter out of the way.

She never got their names right but knew instantly who needed an extra pat on the head or a kick to the rear—or, in Kyong's case, a wet cloth between the eyes after his drink spilled.

Baebin and Go-Ri were back in their usual chair. Thoroughly exhausted but glowing, she sat on the floor, surrounded by the love of family and friends, and the one she loved the most was sitting behind her. His finger secretly brushed her neck under her braid, and his knee provided gentle support as she rested against it. She was in a beautiful bubble.

She was happy to see her brother's scowl slowly disappear, too. He really had no choice with Daeho's antics, and those two looked like they were becoming fast friends. All the guys seemed to like her mom, brother, and Mr. Bak. *Omma* was undoubtedly smitten with them.

The more Go-Ri watched the elderly couple, *Omma* seemed to be smitten with Mr. Bak, as well. She glanced up at Baebin with a head jerk. He just grinned, winked, and shrugged his shoulders.

Baebin learned of Mr. Bak's crush long ago during their meals together and was pleased with himself for arranging the little tête-à-tête for the two. It was a noisy, interesting first date, but he was confident the elderly man would now have the courage to court her. Alone.

Baebin and Go-Ri were thrilled when the group started packing up to leave. *Omma* patted her cheek goodbye and whispered, "I'm proud of you." Still, she raised an eyebrow in warning, glancing between her daughter and the handsome man beside her, before kissing Go-Ri's cheek again.

Go-Ri wanted to raise a brow in return, taking note of Mr. Bak standing suspiciously close to her mother, but she wasn't brave enough to try it.

Again, Baebin had to call for several taxis. The guys really needed to stop driving here because they never drove home. With Go-Ri now in his life, Baebin wasn't about to let them stay over and hamper his growing relationship, at least for the near—possibly *very long*—future... even if he did finally have beds for them.

Baebin stood at the entry with his hands stuffed in his pockets and watched as each of his friends gave Go-Ri a gentle hug goodbye. They wished her luck in the morning and promised to be waiting for her in the practice room for details, even though they were technically on break.

The door finally shut before eleven, and the room fell quiet. Baebin and Go-Ri felt like little kids again, unsure of what to do. He held out his hand, and they slowly walked to the back, turning the lights off.

Relaxing alone in the shower, squirting body wash onto a puff, Go-Ri squeaked in surprise when the door opened. Quickly curling one foot over the other to hide her feet, she couldn't help but notice the hungry, feral gleam in Baebin's eye and his growing arousal as he joined her in the shower.

The bright lights of the bathroom, hazy with steam, set a stage she was unprepared for. The first rivulets of water that dripped down his honed muscles when he stood under the showerhead captivated her as much as the arms that encircled her, drawing her close.

They let the water flow over them, getting used to each other and enjoying these extremely private moments. He stood in front of her; strong fingers massaged her neck and shoulders, as he washed her from the waist up, letting the rivers of soap take care of the rest.

She didn't need to worry about her toes—he was preoccupied with other parts of her body. The solid thickness that pressed against her belly heated her as much as the water from the shower head. The stimulation of being naked together without explicit foreplay was erotic enough, portending the night to come.

As they lay in bed together that night, Baebin worked his way down her body from eyes to socks, kissing and massaging every square millimeter. She wanted to return the favor, but he wouldn't let her tonight.

He cradled her from behind and gave himself free rein. She could feel his entire muscular torso behind her back, and his manhood twitching between her thighs. His hands and fingers caressed, grazed, and cupped everything he could reach.

Trapping her legs, he kept one secured over his raised knee, keeping her open and spread to his touch. As he fingered her swollen, damp folds, she felt heavenly, writhing against his straining erection that pressed against the cleft of her bottom.

Arching back against him, she threaded her fingers through his soft hair as he licked and nibbled the sensitive spot below her ear. What felt overwhelmingly better was the palm that had captured her breast, rubbing and rolling the nipple until it stood firm and tender.

Sensation overload. His breath on her neck, his palm toying with her breast, and his unrelenting fingers on her clit brought her to the precipice. Reaching down, she gripped him, grinding and gyrating against his cock where it split her.

As she cried out her release, he massaged her clit and pumped himself into her hand, never stopping until he'd wrung every last drop from her. The cum that leaked from her coated his rod, sending him over the edge. Biting her shoulder, he spilled himself on the bed in front of her.

Her spasms slowed, and Baebin could feel her heart return to its base rhythm as she fell asleep. Stretching back without breaking contact, he fumbled for the towel he had brought from the shower. Wiping them clean, he pulled the covers over them before snuggling into her neck.

At five o'clock in the morning the following day, both Baebin and Go-Ri were up and moving about. *Omma* had brought Go-Ri's nicest dress over the night before, as well as her favorite chestnut-brown jacket and matching ankle boots. Go-Ri dressed in the spare room.

The light-blue florals and creamy white wood of the girly bedroom was in stark contrast to the rest of the apartment. This morning, the muted colors did nothing to ease her stomach. Sitting at the makeup table, which was now littered with lotions and supplies—almost all of it gifts from Baebin—she stared at her reflection.

What do others see in me? I'm a coward; no one special. Do I really even want to work for the company? Her rounded eyes that tipped at the corners screamed at her, "Go back to hiding. That's all you are good at. You really don't want to do this."

Yanking her gaze away, she brushed her hair until it crackled with static and pulled half of it up, jamming decorative pins in the back-swept updo. Without a further glance, she stalked out of the room.

Baebin had breakfast ready, but didn't scold her when she only drank half a cup of coffee. He left her to her thoughts, knowing she needed to do this alone for her own sake. Playing for and receiving approval from Mr. Kae was important. But accepting a job wasn't as high on the list.

Choosing to work at SKEC meant shelving her dream of her own teaching studio. She already had so many changes in her life lately, and her dream studio was a lifeline he wasn't sure she was quite ready to let go of. Whatever her choice, Baebin knew she would make it with a clear mind, and it would be the right fit for her at this moment.

By six-thirty, they were crossing the Han River, still lit in the orange glow of the streetlights. Her appointment with Mr. Kae wasn't until eleven, but she had a lot of work to do. That is, only if the CEO of Sound would agree to change the venue. She was asking for a lot. Instead of simply handing over her music file in his office, she was, in essence, interrupting his busy schedule with a full-blown concert.

Go-Ri went first to the production department of Building A, thumb drive in hand, to locate a room and a willing sound technician to accommodate her. Then, she begged Mr. Kae's secretary to help move the meeting location.

Mrs. Jung huffed and put her on hold, but it was only for effect. Secretly, she smiled and knew Mr. Kae would go to the ends of the earth to meet Ms. Choi today. She hadn't seen Mr. Kae this excited in a long time. Two minutes later, he approved the request.

Baebin went to his dorm room to air out the place, which hadn't been used in months. He dusted and emptied the suitcases delivered from the airport, and then, feeling frisky, hid Daeho's luggage in the closet under a pile of coats.

Kyong was already in the practice room, slowly going through the movements to an old song. Baebin knew he was hiding knee and hip pain. They all did. But when it came to dancing and performing, Kyong refused to show any weakness. It was a blessing and a curse that Baebin feared would one day bite him. His friend was a master choreographer in his own right and had his future set for him—if he didn't continue to get hurt.

Ten o'clock, and she was behind schedule. Go-Ri had her instruments in the rented production room and two copies of her composer's score waiting on music stands. She neatly arranged the four songs in files and in order. She kept the thumb drive in her pocket, unwilling to part with it until necessary.

Now, she had less than an hour to find the last, key element. One of her recent drop-ins played the bassoon, and he owed her a favor. Thirty minutes later, he carried it to the room and set it up for her. She stuck all the reeds in her mouth to soften the thin canes and did her best not to chew on them and snap the fragile sticks. Everything was ready; she just had to lose the nerves.

At ten forty-five, all seven members of IN7 texted her heart emojis. Baebin sent her a follow-up message:

> B: BE YOURSELF AND PLAY FOR YOU, NOT HIM. BE PROUD OF
> WHAT YOU HAVE CREATED. I LOVE YOU.

At ten fifty-five, Mr. Kae walked into production room 115A.

At ten fifty-eight, Baebin received a text from Manager Kim.

> MK: COME TO THE BUSINESS BUILDING AT 1:30PM. BRING CHOI
> GO-RI.

With the introductory speech over, Go-Ri nodded to the technician who sat behind the glass wall to play the recording. Mr. Kae and his second-in-command stood at a stand in the corner of the sound booth, reading the score and listening intently as she played the line she and Tae-Si had worked on the night before.

Earlier, she had perversely hidden all the pens and pencils in the room and hoped Mr. Kae didn't bring his own. If he started tapping again, she would lose her mind. Luckily, he stayed where she put him, quiet, impassive, and expressionless, barely looking at her.

Twenty minutes later, it was all over. Resting the bassoon on its case, she stood, hands folded. Just like last night, she had lost herself in the music, but now, the rush of suspense returned. The two powerful men stood quietly for several minutes, reviewing the pages before excusing the sound tech.

The ponytailed, spineless jerk, outfitted in hippy garb, sprinted from the room, abandoning Go-Ri.

Both men were unreadable. Only the sound of pages slowly turning whispered in the still room. Finally, number two spoke. "Expect a contract soon. We can discuss terms then." The forever-expressionless Mr. Kae bowed low to her and left with a huge smile, supremely satisfied at snatching up the best talent he had seen in ages. Once she had the room to herself, Go-Ri dropped cross-legged onto the floor, taking her first big breath since she had woken up that morning. *Oh. My. God.*

After returning the bassoon to its owner, Go-Ri headed to the dance building. The guys were still on break, so only Baebin and the four from last night were inside, shuffling through a song without music, one of them snapping out the beat. Completing a turn, Kyong spotted her through the glass and called a halt, waving her madly inside.

Five men stood frozen, staring at her, hopeful and excited. Several had their fingers crossed as they closed their eyes and prayed.

After a long, dramatic award-show pause, Go-Ri nodded, letting a euphoric, shameless grin sweep over her.

Baebin snatched her up and spun her around. The room, quiet only a moment ago, echoed with shouts and cheers loud enough to cause passersby to look in.

Red-faced, Go-Ri threw her head back, squealing with every turn as the others cheered and danced around. Eventually, she begged to be put down before she threw up, and the first thing she did, once released, was give Tae-Si a hug and a kiss on the cheek. "Thank you for all your help. I couldn't have done it without you."

Tae-Si gave Baebin a wink before bending Go-Ri backward and planting a huge smacking kiss on her surprised lips. Then, he swept her upright and took off running around the room before Baebin could catch him. Go-Ri put her hands to her flaming cheeks and started laughing hysterically again.

They put Yejoon and Jaemin on speaker so everyone could hear as she gave them a blow-by-blow account of last week's interview and today's presentation. Admitting that she truly wanted the job, she felt willing to settle for anything, but Yejoon, the most experienced at contracts, promised to review the proposal with her when he returned to guarantee the best outcome for her.

At twenty minutes to one, Baebin looked at the clock and paled. He had forgotten about Manager Kim's text. He was worried about it all morning, but hearing of Go-Ri's success, it slipped his mind. Waving the discussion closed, he called for an end to the day. With one last hug, four guys went one way, and Baebin and Go-Ri went the other.

Hand-in-hand, they walked out. When they passed their car, she looked up at him, puzzled. His sudden prickliness and sour mood worried her. "Where are we going? The car's back there."

Baebin snapped out of his dark thoughts and focused on the present. He scrubbed at his scalp, trying to calm down. "Sorry. We need to go to the Business Building. Manager Kim wants to talk to us."

"Why?" Go-Ri asked slowly. She couldn't help raising her first layer of defense.

"I don't know. This morning, Manager Kim asked me to bring you to a meeting. It could be about Song-Ye or about us dating. Or something silly, like parking spots. I am worried, but it could be nothing. I should have said something earlier, but I got sidetracked hearing how today went. I'm sorry."

"They couldn't make us break up, could they? Because of who you are?" The idea of it angered her.

"They won't. Trust me. I won't let them." Firm, Baebin pushed back on the idea of having his personal life controlled. *I'm not a trainee anymore.*

Wait. He said Song-Ye... Go-Ri wavered, not listening to Baebin. Her eyes glazed over as her pupils grew. "You think it's about *him*?" The ground rolled as if she was on a ship in the middle of a storm. *What do they know about him?*

Baebin dragged her to a bench and pressed her head between her knees before she fainted. Fanning her neck, he leaned in close. "Breathe with me. In... out... I'm sorry. I messed up. I really don't know what it's about. Whatever it is, we will find out together. Okay? Breathe, aein."

Gray, she sucked in air and forced herself to stand. Go-Ri and Baebin were led into a conference room with minutes to spare. She paced the room, shaking. "No.... No. No. No! It's not about *him,* is it? God, I hate him! You don't think he's here, do you? I can't see him again! I can't! He ruined my life!" She whirled on Baebin. "But what if it is about *us*? Will the company really not let us date? Are they going to control that, too?" She spun away to continue her pacing but quickly fell into a chair, crying. "Not today! Today was so good. Why?!"

Go-Ri worked her way again from marginal terror to a full panic attack within seconds. The room spun until Baebin again shoved her face down and blew on her neck again. From between her knees, she continued to babble incoherently. She jerked away and stood to run.

She needed to snap out of it. This wouldn't do. He didn't want her to be seen this way by others. Out of ideas, he yanked her back to him and clutched her face tightly. With their foreheads pressed together, he all but shouted at her, jerking her head. "Look at me! You're not breathing! Go-Ri! Aein!"

It was an eternity before she stopped looking through him and *at* him.

He wiped the tears from her cheeks. "I told you I don't know, but we are together. I'm scared, too, and I need you to be with me. I'll help you, if you help me."

He brushed aside the strand on her forehead that always laid down the middle, refusing to go to the left or right with her parted bangs. Forcing his body to unwind, he held her close, measuring the rate of her breath on his throat. He murmured into her hair as one of her jeweled hair picks poked him.

"It could be something as silly as a vacation or my dorm room assignment. We don't know. No matter what happens, we'll find out together, and *we will* decide what to do when we have information. Okay?"

Manager Kim walked in on them and waited patiently until they sat at the conference table. Setting a file down, he avoided her tear-stained face and pretended not to notice their hands as they clutched each other.

I do NOT want to be the one doing this! I am way out of my element! But if the company was going to get any information, maybe she would talk to him. She already looked like she could drop dead at any moment, and he revised his original plan to make Baebin leave the room.

Mr. Kim looked from Go-Ri to Baebin and back. His face was stern, but his eyes were soft. He pulled out his phone, set it to record, and laid it in the middle of the table. "Ms. Choi, we were introduced once before, a few months ago. I am Manager Kim Jae-un. I work with SKEC and IN7. Do you remember me?" She nodded. Kim said gently, "I need you to answer me with words. I'm sorry for the recording, but it's important."

Weakly, she nodded again and said, "Yes."

"Ms. Choi, I have been told you know Nam Song-Ye."

So, this *was* about him. She couldn't turn any whiter but brought her shaking hands together on the table, clenching them in a death grip. Her knuckles turned gray, and red half-moons shined where her nails dug in. She sat with a steel rod for a spine. All she wanted was to get through whatever this was and go home. "Yes. I know him."

"How do you know him?"

"School. Same grade but different rooms. We barely knew each other—and only through music class."

"Okay." Manager Kim responded kindly. "I was told you two had... a history in school. And that there was an... incident a few years ago."

Incident? That's one way to describe it. "Yes. He... ummm. He always followed me and showed up everywhere I went. The last time I saw him was almost two years ago in January when he beat me… and tried to rape me."

"Forgive me for asking, but can you tell me about it?"

Go-Ri wanted to run. But something about Manager Kim's calm, soft voice and grandfatherly concern made her glance up at him and cave.

"It was only supposed to be one date. Dinner and a concert." Go-Ri coughed hoarsely, her throat already hurting. "I didn't want to go. I didn't like or trust him… I thought we would stay around our neighborhood or someplace close for dinner, but he kept driving and driving. I don't know where we ended up, but it was one of those classic American-style diners way past the Lotte World Tower…"

Halting at first, Go-Ri's flood gates opened.

"By the time we got our food, he was drunk and annoying the other tables. All he wanted to talk about was himself and his music. I started tuning him out… I went outside to the bathroom… I didn't know he followed me until he dragged me deeper into the alley by my throat and slammed me against the wall. That's when he started hitting me…"

Go-Ri looked only at Manager Kim's silver tie tack with the South Korean flag on it. She had to stop a few times to breathe and clear the floating black spots from her vision, but she kept going. The insults, the beating, the pain, and the long, cold walk home.

She told him every single detail, like it had all happened yesterday—details only she and Nam Song-Ye knew. Details even Baebin was unaware of.

Go-Ri saw spots again. The paper origami box folded in around her, pinching in tighter. She looked Manager Kim in the eyes for the first time and politely asked, "Excuse me. I need a moment."

He opened his mouth to answer, but she stumbled to her feet first and found the trash can by the door. Baebin jumped after her and held her hair back as she dry-heaved. Tears streamed down his face as he looked over at his mentor and manager, who was also gray and trying to hold back his own sobs.

Go-Ri swayed as she sat back in her chair and took a tissue from the box on the table to wipe her mouth. "I'm sorry." Refusing to look anywhere else in the room, she let her eyes hunt for scratches on the table in front of her.

For two years, she hid the truth from everyone. No one knew everything. For some strange reason, it took Manager Kim, someone she didn't know, to finally let it out. Everything. Hiding and scarcely living was exhausting. She couldn't do it anymore. Baebin had helped break down the wall she was hiding behind, and now, she let it all go.

She was free but mortified at herself for allowing it to happen. She hated that others knew how foolish she had been for putting herself in that situation. She could handle the pain. It was the shame that upset her the most.

"Thank you, Ms. Choi. I can't imagine how hard it was for you to talk to me. I'm so sorry you had to do that. But you have helped us. Thank you." Manager Kim slowly reached for his phone, hit the stop record button, and left the room.

Go-Ri finally, completely, and utterly collapsed. "I'm so scared, Baebin! What do I do if Nam Song-Ye comes back? I can't stay! I can't do this anymore! I can't take it anymore!"

She was hyperventilating—gagging, like she was being choked again. Punched again with every heaving gasp. Baebin held her, wiping her tears as his own flowed down, until she passed out.

Baebin knew she hadn't told him everything that night at the *sansjang*. He was surprised at how much she had left out. How much of a difference a small word change here or there made to her story. And the story kept going. It was more violent than he could stand.

He had pictured something horrible, like a few slaps. But her reality was a beating—a beating that had left her with broken ribs and a busted face. Nam Song-Ye's egotistical bragging about his position in K-pop and his vitriol of blame and derision for their ruined evening would have made anyone reject everything about the industry, like she had done. She said she hated the cold. He would, too—walking home for hours, barefoot in freezing temperatures through snow. He could only imagine the damage her feet must have suffered.

Everything made sense. From her sock fetish, to the day Baebin came home angry, to her fear of people. It was worse than she had led him to believe. He pinged from anger to grief and back again.

In the next room, a group of men watched a monitor, its feed still recording via the camera inside the ornate, gold-framed mirror hanging over the fireplace. Everything from the moment the couple walked into the room was on film. The three top leaders of SKEC, along with Nam Song-Ye's manager, waited for Manager Kim to join them.

Everyone waited for Mr. Jong to speak first. Anger vibrated through the CEO and founder of SKEC. The room echoed with it as he rubbed a finger on the soft leather of his chair. He sat, thinking, staring at the employee files spread on the table in front of him.

"Why am I just now hearing about this?" Pinning Song-Ye's manager with a sharp glare, he asked, "Have you heard of any complaints against him? Is there anything you kept from his file?" Seeing Manager Ha squirm was all he needed. "I want a *real* report—*detailed*—on my desk by tomorrow morning."

He turned to Manager Kim. "And you? Wasn't Nam Song-Ye under you at one point? Did you know anything?"

Manager Kim stared back coldly, refusing to take the blame. "Check the file. I was only with him when he was a trainee and wasn't allowed to leave the Campus. He was a handful back then, and I recommended that he be let go. But he was moved to a new group under *his* care." He turned his furious glare on Mr. Ha. The wimpy man should never have been the manager for such a crude group of rejects. "I passed my file to him and lost touch. When my boys brought this to my attention, I did some digging while I was overseas, and it was easy to find that several important notes were missing."

"Mr. Park? Did you know?" Mr. Jong eyed his oldest friend and the CEO of Dance, who sat opposite him, watching for his tell. "You're the head of the dance division, and you sent him to Japan. Did you know of any issues? Please tell me you did a thorough check before we sent a veritable grenade over there."

The tall, thin, retired dancer looked affronted, but Mr. Jong saw the minute twitch in his shoulders. He wanted to wrap his hands around his friend's scrawny neck. All he cared about was the next dance star, the fame—not people or the company. Friend or no, he was tired of cleaning up Park's messes.

Pacing in front of the windows, Mr. Jong looked out over the complex he had built. The scandal—for the industry *and* his company—weighed heavily on his mind but not as much as the damage his employee did to an innocent woman.

Baebin carried Go-Ri all the way to the bed in their apartment and changed her into pajamas. For the first time, he took a good, hard look at her feet that, somehow, he never noticed all this time.

Honestly, she had cute feet. They didn't look horrible... until you looked closely. Three nails were very short, like they were growing back in, and some of the toes were an odd mixture of colors. Off-white skin surrounded splotches of pale blue and pastel violet. Waves of sorrow crashed over him at the suffering they must have caused her this entire time.

He caressed the ball of one foot. Reflexively, several toes curled under. He gently pulled one down that hadn't moved but was met with stiff resistance. Curious, he tested the other foot and found the same. *She must have been so cold that night to have gotten such bad frostbite*, he thought. After dressing her in the warmest, fluffiest socks he could find, he unlocked Go-Ri's phone and called Binna.

The clock in the living room ticked loudly in the quiet apartment when Binna rushed in, shooing him away. She was still there hours later when Baebin answered another knock at the door.

Chinmae stood outside, eyeing his friend. "Manager Kim sent me here to check on you two. Said that... something happened." The look on *hyung's* face was enough. He pulled Baebin close and felt his heavy weight sag against him.

The two sat on the floor of the studio for hours, talking until Baebin finally fell asleep, slumped over against his friend. Chinmae wondered if he should call a Code 6 again. *No, that's just gossip. This doesn't change how we feel about gongjunim and hyung.* He would wait to see what SKEC would do next before telling the others.

A soft tapping interrupted his roaming thoughts. Wiggling out from under Baebin, Chinmae cracked open the studio door and looked out at Go-Ri's friend. Judging by the circles under her eyes and her wild hair, she'd had as much sleep as he had.

Binna's eyes widened at who answered her knock. She pointed down the hall. "I got her out of bed. She wants him."

Chinmae opened the door wider and went to wake his friend. Refusing to let Baebin leave the room until he washed away the dried tears in the adjoining bathroom, Chinmae rummaged through the closet and found a new shirt. It would have to do until he could take a shower.

Binna reached out, snagging Chinmae's arm and casting a glance at the bathroom as she listened to the running water. "What happened? Didn't she have her presentation yesterday?" The cryptic phone call hours ago that sent her racing here was slim on details.

Scrubbing the heels of his palms into his dry eyes, Chinmae whispered back. "She was offered the job, but then they were called into the business office. The company found out about Nam Song-Ye and questioned her. She told them everything."

The pit of Binna's stomach twisted. "*Everything?*" Her friend's worst fears were coming true. Go-Ri never wanted this. Binna studied the man standing with her. Not the idol, but the man. "You know, too? About... what happened?"

He could only nod in reply. Keeping his eyes on the open door, he added, "Mmm. I've known some of it for a while. But while we were in America, we found out that Song-Ye will be coming back to Campus soon. So, they wanted to question Go-Ri about... it." Scrubbing his neck, he let out a sigh of frustration. "I don't know what SKEC will do. Our manager told me to stay here. They plan on another meeting with the police tomorrow." He glanced at the clock. "Today," he amended. "Soon."

Baebin flicked off the light, ending their discussion. Passing inspection, he was finally allowed to join Go-Ri on the couch, where she sat holding a mug and inhaling the steam from the chamomile-mint tea that was double-bagged for strength. Baebin's black, oversized hoodie created a sharp contrast to her pale and drawn face. She looked wiped out but was awake and functioning.

The four of them scattered about. Baebin sat next to Go-Ri, and the two friends wandered into the kitchen, where Binna prepped more mugs of tea and a pot of coffee. If what Chinmae said was true, it was going to be another long day.

When Binna finished cooking a batch of porridge, Baebin managed to get Go-Ri to eat a few bites before she shoved it away like an irritable child.

Warmed and cocooned, listening to the small shreds of whispered conversation around her, Go-Ri started to nod off against Baebin's shoulder when a thought came to her—something she didn't piece together until talking to Manager Kim.

"Binna. That night... how did I get to your place?" Go-Ri swore she remembered her gate and avoiding the creaking porch step.

Binna's hand froze, the spoon midway to her mouth. "Your brother found you and called me." So much had happened in those few days, and she had always been fairly sure Go-Ri didn't remember any of it. *Wasn't it better to forget?* Setting her spoon down, she sat on a chair near her friend.

"You must have come home after Mom had already left for the meat market. Min-Jun was going to school early to study and found you on the porch. He didn't know what to do and called me. You were barely with it, going in and out of consciousness. We wanted to take you to the hospital, but you kept screaming 'no.'" Binna kept her eyes glued on her friend, not looking at the men. "You swore you weren't raped and didn't want anyone to know what happened."

The horrible bruising and swelling had scared her, and she wasn't sure how to care for her friend. "So, we hid you at my place, since my mom was on a business trip. I washed you up and was going to take pictures of… everything… in case you changed your mind later and wanted to go to the police, but you wouldn't let me." She shivered, remembering that awful morning. How broken her lively, pretty friend was. "You were so out of it for days; I should have taken the pictures anyway. You wouldn't have known. But I was afraid you would find them and get upset."

"Mmm. I would never want to see them." Go-Ri shuddered in revulsion.

The room grew quiet as the girls thought about those awful days and nights. Go-Ri remembered trying to scream from the nightmares, but the pain from her cracked ribs hampered most of the loudest cries. She fingered a spot on her cheek that had taken weeks to have any feeling in it again.

Her fists clenched tight as mortification overtook her. "Wait, so Min-Jun knew the whole time but didn't say anything?" Upset, Go-Ri turned on Baebin next. "And how did Manager Kim know? Did you tell him? It's bad enough you told *him!*" She angrily pointed a finger at Chinmae.

She was working herself into a state, lashing out at everyone close to her but mostly at herself. She wanted to forget it all happened, but the more her pitiful story got out, the worse her embarrassment grew.

Chinmae cut in before Baebin could defend himself. "He didn't want to tell me, trust me. But he wasn't himself, and it was affecting his work and the group. I made him. I thought it was something to do with the prank he pulled on you and the usual dating BS we have to deal with because of who we are. I had no idea. And I had to tell the others…"

"They know, too?!" She was well past crying, but hot tears rimmed her eyes as shame bloomed in her cheeks.

"Yes. We weren't trying to be nosey, but he is our *hyung,* and something was wrong. We wanted to help him… We only talked to Manager Kim when we heard Song-Ye was coming back. We wanted to see if there was a way to stop it. Some way to help you."

She hung her head, unable and unwilling to look at him. "I didn't want anyone to know how stupid I was to let this happen to me. I was such a fool."

Appalled, Baebin knelt at her feet, clutching the sweatshirt that puddled around her waist. He wanted to throttle her for such a ridiculous feeling. "Why in the world would *you* be a fool?!"

"I let it happen! I should have fought harder, yelled louder. I didn't even want to go out that night! I knew better! I only did it, thinking he would get bored of me and finally leave me alone! But all the times he stalked me and groped me, I should have known! I shouldn't have been so stupid! It's my fault!"

"Oh, aein! You are not stupid. I never once thought that. None of us think that. We never have. That jerk is the fool. Only him." Baebin buried his head in her lap. He tried not to cry again in front of her, but when he felt her fingers grip his hair, he couldn't hold back.

30장

Go-Ri wasn't ready. She didn't want to face Manager Kim again or talk to the police. She was one heartbeat away from running. She remembered a cartoon where an animal slammed a door shut and used multiple different locks to block the door. That was her right now. She wanted to go home and be left alone. For the rest of her life.

She gripped Baebin's hand under the blanket, her nails digging into his skin, as one face and then another popped up on the screen for the video call. Each new and surprising addition meant one more person added to her list of shame.

She smothered a groan when Mr. Kae logged in, and she didn't like hearing Baebin and Chinmae's surprise murmurs at seeing a man labeled "Mr. Jong" appear. He was the last and, apparently, the most important. He was all business, and with minimal introduction, he passed off the meeting to Inspector Goe, the only man in a uniform, not a suit.

"Miss Choi, I listened to your recording from yesterday, and I have to say I have some concerns. You know it's not an official statement, right?" Go-Ri already disliked the condescension in Inspector Goe's voice. "If you decide to press charges, you will have to come in and file a report." The officer sat back in his chair, interweaving his fingers over his slight paunch. "Are you planning on doing that?" He obviously didn't care one way or the other if she did. But most likely, he wished she wouldn't.

"I-I don't know."

"Well, Mr. Nam is a high-profile figure. If all you want is money, then I would suggest suing him instead. You can try asking for an apology, too."

Go-Ri's hackles rose. She knew which way this farce was going. "If I wanted money, I would have sued him two years ago."

"Well, Miss Choi, this minor incident happened so long ago that it is probably the best outcome for you. After all, you willingly dated him."

"I didn't date him; I agreed to one dinner. There is a difference. And I wouldn't say I went altogether willingly, but you are correct, I wasn't kidnapped. Being beaten half to death and almost raped may be minor to you but not to me."

"So, you weren't raped?"

"No. I never said I was. I said I *almost* was. Something startled him, and he suddenly got off me and ran away. Otherwise, I might have been."

"How do you know something startled him? Did you hear anything? Maybe he wasn't going to do anything anyway."

"Well, my skirt was up and he was taking off his belt. So, I'd say that was his plan. Why he stopped, I'm not sure."

"Hmph. Any proof of the beating?" he asked. "Witnesses? Hospital records? Photos? Without that, it's just hearsay. You are trying to damage this man's good reputation without evidence."

Go-Ri shrank inside. Binna was right. There was no proof.

Waving his hand, Inspector Goe continued. "Your recording said you'd known him for years and that he had been stalking you. So, why did you date him, if not for money?" He wouldn't let her answer. "He's the famous one. Why would he stalk you? It would seem to be the other way around, and you're just upset the date didn't go like you wanted."

The air sizzled in the apartment as the inspector's voice carried over the TV. In his office, Mr. Kae threw down his pen.

Baebin lost it. "Why are you accusing the victim?! You have no idea—"

"I am speaking to Miss Choi. I don't need comments from her boyfriend. You are here out of courtesy."

"You aren't listening!" Baebin shot back.

"I am. I heard her recording. But she also has no proof, and Mr. Nam is a public figure who has no history of acts like those she is accusing him of. Am I just supposed to believe her and ruin his good life with baseless claims?" The inspector sat back again and raised an eyebrow.

Manager Kim coughed in the dead air and glared into the camera. "Manager Ha," he said, "don't you have something to say?"

A small, nervous man, sweating through his collar, gulped audibly. "Umm. Well. I do know of a small number of incidents Mr. Nam had with a few fans. Umm. Women. But I handled them personally, and everything is fine now."

The inspector rolled his eyes in disgust at the man's stupidity. "Fine. Give me a list. I'll see if there is anything worth looking into. But for you, Miss Choi, all I can do is take your statement. You have no evidence of stalking and no pictures or hospital reports. I don't know what I can do to help you. There is nothing I can investigate." He seemed pleased to toss up his hands and end the inquiry before he had to do any work.

Binna ground out from her stool in the kitchen, "You could do your *job*."

"Who's that? You have something to say?" Inspector Goe looked around the screen as if trying to peek around the corner, peeved at the sarcastic remark.

Binna stomped into view behind Go-Ri and Baebin on the couch, clutching her friend's shoulder. "I'm Ms. Choi's friend." She spat out. "I was the one who helped her recover from her 'minor incident.'" She wagged her fingers in air quotes. "Her brother and I both saw how badly she was beaten. Can't you look into the restaurant they went to? See if there are any cameras in the area?"

Her angry glare shifted to the box with Mr. Ha's face. "And it's shameful of you, *sir*, to have buried other incidents to let him continue hurting people like Choi Go-Ri. *No one deserves to suffer because of him!*"

Go-Ri put her hand on Binna's, where it rested on her shoulder, stopping her tirade before she spewed even more. Once on fire, Binna could be uncontrollable. "I wouldn't know how to find the restaurant," Go-Ri admitted. "I only remember being on the other side of Seoul, past the Lotte World Tower and the movie theater across the street."

Binna huffed. *Seoul was big, but how hard was it to find one restaurant?*

The inspector groaned. "I know how to do my job, miss. I'll look into it. But I won't promise anything." He clicked off as fast as possible.

Before anyone else had a chance, Baebin spoke up. "Mr. Jong? Will Nam Song-Ye really be returning to Campus? Ms. Choi was supposed to start working there under Mr. Kae. I don't want her signing a contract without knowing if he's coming back."

"We will have a discussion on our end and get back to you," Mr. Jong said. "Mr. Kae, send her the contract, but be sure to include the clause that it 'can be cancelled at any time without penalty.' Will that be sufficient for you for the moment, Ms. Choi?" When she nodded, he abruptly ended his feed.

The apartment was deadly silent.

"Hmph. The inspector was an ass," Binna grumbled.

Go-Ri didn't feel the need to correct her language. "I expected it. Why would he believe me? It's because of people like him that I didn't want everyone to know."

"God, that was straight out of a melodrama! I didn't know people actually spouted crap like that! And he is a cop!" No one could argue with Binna. It was an affront to hear Go-Ri not only be distrusted but also *blamed*. The call went just how Go-Ri had predicted.

Go-Ri sat huddled against Baebin's side as Binna slammed pots and dishes from breakfast in the sink, then busied herself by starting an early lunch for the group. Shoving a cutting board and vegetables at Chinmae, Binna ordered him to help as she continued to mumble curse words under her breath.

The racket in the next room sliced through her skin and reminded Go-Ri of another busy kitchen. *The lunch rush will be starting soon, and Omma's been working alone for a week.* She needed to move, to stop thinking. To escape for just a while.

"I'm going to MinGo. I need to help Omma. I just need to go." Her firm declaration and sudden motivation startled everyone. Refusing to be swayed, she kissed Baebin soundly before waving bye to Binna and Chinmae. She was out the door before anyone could stop her.

Baebin joined the pair working in his kitchen. Resting on his elbows, he rocked back and forth in thought. "That inspector... I don't trust he'll do much. We may not find proof of the past, but what about when Song-Ye comes back?" Binna and Chinmae stopped and looked at him, puzzled. "He may try again. Where's he gonna go first to find her?"

Binna supplied the obvious. "The restaurant. He doesn't know about the apartment or her work at the Campus yet. But we can't watch the place forever, and Omma doesn't have cameras."

"What if Song-Ye is finally tired of her and doesn't bother her anymore? Then we have nothing to catch him with. What if he moves on to someone else?" Chinmae hated even saying that out loud.

Baebin answered, unsure how he felt about either outcome. "I would love it if he did leave her alone, but if he doesn't, shouldn't we be prepared? We may not be able to help others, but we can at least do something about Go-Ri."

The trio worked through dozens of game plans, improving some ideas and tossing others.

31장

The bed shifted behind him, and cold air brushed Baebin's shoulder. An arm, cold to the touch, wiggled under his as Go-Ri's hand found the spot where his heart beat. She pulled the blanket back around his shoulder, trapping them both inside.

"Mmm, *aein*. You're back," his groggy voice croaked. Linking his fingers with hers, he pulled her closer behind him and settled in tighter.

"You don't mind, do you? I didn't want to be alone tonight." She kissed his shoulder before resting her cheek on it.

"I'll never mind. I missed you."

He should go back to sleep. But he was awake now. All of him. He should be a good boy. At least for today. But the feel of her breasts pressing against his back through her thin shirt felt good. The way her hips curled around his butt felt good. Her hand on his chest felt good. Her thumb feathering a barest whisper of a touch across his skin felt... *good*.

Every nerve in his body stopped working—except for the space no wider than a button. *Go left. Just a little more left,* he silently begged. Pleaded. She had to feel his heart pounding.

Her thumb twitched and brushed wider. His breath hitched as his nipple pebbled instantly at her touch, shooting pleasure from his chest to his groin. He couldn't hold back the moan.

She jerked her hand free. "I—sorry."

"Please don't stop. Touch me." His hand curled around hers, and he drew it back to his chest. Baebin shifted slightly back, tucking his shoulder under her chin and bringing her face closer to his. "Can you touch me?" He couldn't reach her lips but settled on brushing his mouth across her brow. Her hand, as it splayed across his chest, felt glorious.

I should focus on her, he thought. *She needs loving, not me...*

She let him stroke his body with her hand. Her calloused fingertips explored his hard, smooth skin.

She had only come to him to be held. She needed to be in his arms tonight. To erase every bad thing that had happened lately. But feeling his shudders and his warm breath in her hair filled the hollow pit inside her. He was incredibly sexy. Mesmerizing. And he wanted her. *Her*. The power he gave her was intoxicating.

She couldn't see what she was touching, but she let her fingers draw the map. Her bottom lip ran across the ball of his shoulder as she skimmed her hand further down, bringing his along with it. She knew what she sought and felt the woosh of air escape him as she found it inside his briefs.

He quivered and thickened as she encircled his flesh with their joined hands. Sliding her palm up and down, she felt the drops of moisture at his tip and spread it around with the pad of her thumb. He was warm and silky. Hard.

He fisted the pillow under his cheek and groaned. The feel of her soft palm on him as they stroked together was too much, too soon. He didn't want to cum yet.

Pulling away, he rolled her over and settled his body on hers. Sucking in ragged, sharp breaths, he rested his nose in the crook of her neck, breathing in the scent of Go-Ri.

The pressure against her chest, his stiffness below that pulsed against her, pushing her panties into her swollen center, wetting them with her own desire, felt heavenly. Wrapping her arms around his neck, Go-Ri threaded her fingers through his hair. She drew up her foot and rested it behind his knee, tipping her pelvis and letting herself slide against his length.

Finally, he kissed her. Mind-numbing. Sizzling. Carnal.

This wasn't why she came back to him tonight. She hadn't planned on this. But *God*, he felt good. *No.* This *was* what she wanted. She *wanted* to be in his arms. She *wanted* Baebin.

Baebin sat back on his haunches long enough to divest her of every stitch of clothing. His greedy eyes raked over each newly exposed inch of skin as the fabric came off. He flopped down heavy and hard, pressing her into the mattress. His lips fastened on her nipple, sucking, as his hands molded and reshaped her breasts. Lightning shot across and down her body as he arched and shifted, his bulge stroking against her nub.

Only his briefs separated them. The wet cotton parted her folds and chafed against her overly sensitive skin. She felt the storm coming. Lightning continued, each second growing closer and closer, until one flash exploded over her. *In* her. Blinding her.

He was almost there with her. It took every ounce of willpower to hold back. He loved watching her lose control, feeling every muscle in her body clench. He wanted to see her happy under him.

Slowly, she relaxed, and he gently thrust against her, ready for his turn.

When she recoiled, pushing his cheek away, he froze.

"No." Already flushed, her nerves a jumbled mess, she could only blink. *How do you ask for... it?* She wanted *everything*. Nothing else would be enough. If tonight, after all that had happened, wasn't the right time, then when would it ever be?

"Bae, I..." her eyes skidded around his taut face, glistening with perspiration and hunger, "I want more... I want... *you*."

Already close to exploding, his skin tightened, and his belly cramped. "Aien? I don't think tonight is right... I don't want you to regret your first time—"

She brought his face to hers and whispered against his mouth, "How could I regret being with you? When I think of today, I only want to remember this. To remember being with you. Right now. So, please, Bae, no more waiting."

She drugged him with a kiss.

Resting on a shaking elbow, he peeled away the last remaining obstruction.

Keeping his mouth fused to hers, he stood proud at her entrance. Heavy. Throbbing. Prodding. Slowly, he nudged inside. She whimpered at the new sensation, and he almost came just at the feeling of his tip being engulfed in her warmth. Gripping her hip, he pushed in. He felt her flinch as he broke her barrier.

The shock melted away as she felt him stretch her to capacity. His hot length fueled her fire, inside and out, hotter than before. Her small whimper became a sigh and then a moan as he rocked against her. Retreating, then filling her again. She was already there; the storm hadn't left. It swirled around her, stronger. And *crashed*. The violent waves of dark and light clouds danced over her.

Baebin couldn't hold out any longer. The feeling of her squeezing around his cock threw him into the vortex. Crying out her name, he shuddered, one fist balling the sheets and the other tangled in her hair.

Their thundering hearts slowly settled into a pattering beat as he gently pulled out. After gathering himself, Baebin padded to the bathroom for a towel. He cleaned himself off there, wiping away their juices and the smattering of her blood before returning to the bed.

It felt strange being empty. Lonely. Go-Ri was barely awake as he cleaned her. He had done it before, but tonight it felt even more intimate. Tender. She didn't remember him pulling her into his arms and drawing the covers over them.

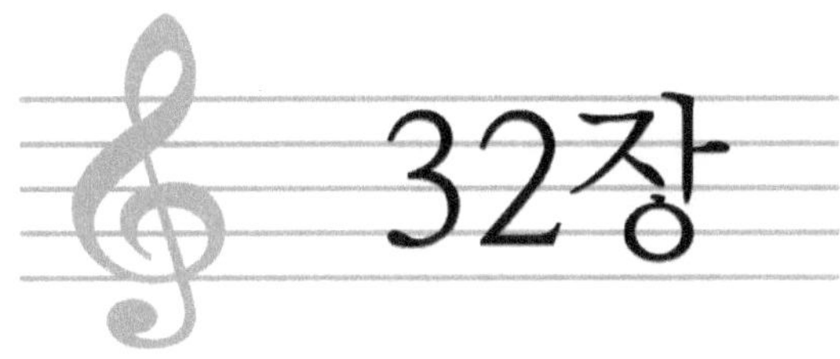

The sun cracked through the curtains when Baebin felt a tongue lick the tattoo on his side. Then it moved to that little space where his ribs met his belly. He jerked when it swirled around his nipple.

"Good, you're awake." The vibration of Go-Ri's voice filtered through his skin. She snaked a hand down his stomach, sliding lower, fingers teasing the fur of his groin.

His morning wood ached, for multiple reasons. He had a slight problem.

He grabbed Go-Ri's hand and hoarsely protested, covering his eyes. She watched, confused, as he stumbled out of bed. Hearing the sound of water, then the toilet flushing, she started giggling. She was still biting her lip when he finally came back.

His ears flushed pink. He lay down, not entirely on his stomach, and buried his head under a pillow. "Don't laugh! Do you know how hard it is to pee with *that*?" he cried.

A burst of laughter escaped her before she bit her lip again. "I'm very, very sorry. Can I make it up to you?" She lightly rubbed her hand over his back, outlining each crease of muscle as she traced her way down to his fantastic butt.

She leaned over and placed a peck on the ticklish spot on his ribs. He jerked and swatted her away. She ducked. She kissed higher up his side and ducked again. Giving one more kiss to the tattoo on his shoulder blade, she pressed him flat on his stomach and climbed on top.

He grunted and wiggled slightly to adjust his body parts underneath. His movement sent the best-looking ripples up his back and tremors through her center, where she felt him move between her tender legs.

In the soft morning light that poked through the curtains, Go-Ri paused a moment to study the tattoo on his shoulder.

Larger than the palm of her hand, the ornate pocket watch, with its long chain hanging down below the bottom of his shoulder blade, lay on a wrinkled piece of paper that appeared to be a piece of a calendar. A little dial for the seconds at the bottom of the watch's face stopped at 13. The hands of the watch would have read 3:50 on any other clock, but what confused her was that each of the numbers around the dial were all the number seven.

Tracing the chain down his back, she watched him shiver. "What does this mean? Tell me about it."

"Hmm?" Both the pillow and his bloodless brain muffled Baebin's response. He could feel her center as she sat on his lower back, and just a moment ago, she had been teasing him. *Now she wants to talk?* He couldn't catch up fast enough to her to think.

"Your tattoo." Go-Ri's nail trailed back up the chain to circle the pocket watch. "What's it about? Why are all the numbers a seven?"

I'll tell you if you stop doing that, he thought. The muscles in his back flinched involuntarily as she continued to trace the art on his shoulder. It took all his focus to force himself to form a sentence. "It's a date. The same one I use for the studio lock. The hands are the day I joined IN7. March 10, 2013. The daily calendar page is the day we debuted."

"Ah! And the sevens are for the seven of you! Clever!" Go-Ri traced it one more time before leaning down to give it a kiss.

He gave a guttural groan and gripped the pillow over his head when her tongue licked the chain. With every slight move she made, the tips of her breasts shifted against his ribs. "Are we done talking now?!"

"Mmm." She liked to tease him, but she was done. There were better things to do at the moment. It was enough to watch his flesh break out in goosebumps and see him shiver where she touched.

She lay down on top of him and held his hands where they clutched the pillow. Her breasts and tongue caressed everywhere her hands had until he couldn't take it anymore and flipped her off, sending her flying onto her back with a surprised shriek.

They lay crooked on the bed, with one of her legs hanging off an edge, and he kissed his way up her leg and belly. One hand reached up to gently squeeze a breast, flicking her swollen tip. "Are you sore? We can just touch."

She pulled him up for a kiss, ignoring their mild, musky morning breath, and wrapped her legs around him.

A few minutes later, he was entering her again, and they both groaned in bliss.

Memories of yesterday's storm still flashed lightly around them. Their first time together was beyond words, but this was even better. There was no more worry or anxiety or wondering. Just pure togetherness from the beginning.

They ended hot and sticky, with only their feet under the sheet. Her stomach rumbled first, and he followed right after in agreement. Go-Ri sat up and sighed. "I don't think I ate yesterday." *How long had it been?* Her days jumbled together.

He sat up and took her hand. "Shower first, then food." Looking at her bare body, he amended, "Shower, *clothes,* then food. Or I'll be the only one eating," he said, wagging his eyebrows.

Cleaned and dressed, they sat at the table across from each other with bowls between them. This was the first chance they'd had for a serious private discussion since she fled after the conference call. Both had a lot of thoughts and questions floating in their minds and didn't know what to land on first.

Baebin started, asking the most basic and challenging question, "What do you want to do now?"

She sat thinking about that, chewing slowly. "Honestly, I don't know. Everything happened all at once; I'm overwhelmed. I feel like I'm in a maze. Ten ways to start, and I don't know what or where the prize is."

"Mmm. Okay. So, you have multiple paths to choose from. What's path number one?"

Raising her eyebrows at the approach, she set her chopsticks down and crossed her arms on the table. She held up a finger. "One. I go back to my mom's place, work at her restaurant, and quit music altogether." Seeing his brow furrow, she waved her hand. "It's safe and decent but not what I want to do. I don't think I can ever go back to the way I was.

"Two." Another finger rose to join the first. "I stop working at the Campus and go back to my original plan of running my own studio." Shrugging, she added, "A better option and one I'll keep open, but I'll probably lose students, and now I think I'll get bored fast. I don't want to wait for you to come home. I want to be busy."

Baebin loved that she thought of the apartment as her home and the idea of her waiting for him.

"Three." She held up a third finger. "I stay just the way I am now. Teach at the Campus and help the walk-ins. Mr. Kae said I could. I like my room, and I've met some wonderful people—don't tell Chinmae that." She grinned and paused in her visual count to wag a finger at him. Baebin just waved his hands, agreeing.

"Four. Depending on what they offer me, I work in the composition department. I really like that idea. I'm not afraid of that anymore. Even going into the presentation, I was unsure what I wanted, but Mr. Kae's reaction was better than anything I've ever gotten. Depending on the contract and how much say I have over my music, I see it being challenging and rewarding."

She picked up a piece of meat with her fingers and chewed slowly. On cue, her thoughts returned to *him*. "Three and four depend on Song-Ye. I want to work at SKEC, but I can't handle running into him all the time. I'm okay now to try another company. I know now that I can do it and be fine. I don't want to work anywhere else, but if I can play and write in peace, then it's worth the sacrifice."

She looked at her bowl. "I don't know if I want to file a report. I probably should. I should have years ago. But the way Inspector Geo reacted... that will keep happening, and I don't know if I can handle it. Now, I also have to consider the media and the company."

Baebin understood her fear, but he didn't agree with it. He wished she would file with the police, but it was her choice. How the inspector or anyone else felt didn't matter. The report would expose Nam Song-Ye's evil nature and boost Go-Ri's ability to heal.

"Five." Back on track, she held up her hand, wiggling all her fingers as she smiled. "I quit and become a groupie. I can kick out the leader of *Echos* to run your fan club." Baebin snorted so hard, he had to clear his nose, and both collapsed in a fit of giggles.

"Ok, fine. Five is off the table, too." She sighed. "So, I guess I have three viable doors. They are the same three I had before, even if you count applying for new companies. I have new information, but I still don't have enough to decide."

Go-Ri looked down at the table and started wiping the sides of her glass with her fingers. "I still feel like I'm waiting on someone else to move their chess piece so I can move mine. It makes my skin crawl."

Baebin sat back and drew his knee up. "That's exactly how I felt all the years I was a trainee. No matter how hard I worked, I was always at someone else's whim. They could send me home at any minute. Someone else controlled my life."

He sighed and added sadly, "I thought I was done with that, but I think they still do. Now it's not the company, it's the *fans*—the fame. It only takes one, maybe two bad albums to lose our base, and it all crumbles away."

Her former anger against the company and the industry echoed in his mind. "I didn't believe you when you said it, but it's true. *Everyone* controls me. I don't think I fully realized until now how much of my life is on the edge. I work so hard for just one more day. One more performance. I never know when it will be my last."

He hesitated, not wanting to burden her. "I've got a maze of my own. I've been trying to figure out what to do when IN7 is all over. It's inevitable. I want to stay in the industry, but what do I do next? I can go solo—I'm creating my first solo album now—but I've also been training with Manager Kim to learn more about his job. The behind-the-scenes work is interesting—the planning, the scheduling, the details. It fits my personality. I hate to think of a life without IN7, but I have to be realistic. I don't know what path to choose either."

She nodded sorrowfully, understanding the difficult situation he faced.

Go-Ri and Baebin sat thinking about how much both of their lives straddled a thin line. It made them shudder.

She asked him a question even though she knew his answer. "If you were me, which path would you take?"

He looked at her sadly. "You know I won't answer that. Just like I won't ask you to pick for me. It wouldn't be fair to push you in a direction you may not want. I'm sorry. I can't help you decide, but I will always support whatever you choose." He grinned. "Just not number one… or five. The *Echos* president is cool."

She threw a piece of meat at his head, and it sailed past his ear as he ducked out of the way.

Baebin might still be learning the subtleties of Go-Ri's little quirks, but he could see her growing a steel spine. This was what first drew him to her. Go-Ri always had guts, even when she was hiding, and she wouldn't back down from anything. She always had courage, strength, and wit.

She squared her shoulders, straightened her back, and looked at him with calm, collected eyes. "I need more information to decide. Like Chinmae said, I'm trying to decide without knowing everything. So, right now, I choose door number three—stay the course and keep teaching at the Campus—only until I get a satisfactory contract. And I'm going through that door tomorrow."

Her voice dropped, but she was still firm with determination. "Depending on Song-Ye, I will consider looking into other music companies. I can always teach on the side, but I won't quit music again because of him. I love the work. It's thrilling to be around others who love music like I do. I don't want to lose that."

Baebin waited for any small change or indecision, but she was unwavering. "You sure? Tomorrow?"

"Yes. Absolutely. I have to. But I want to ask for one thing from the head man… Mr. Jong? I want to know if and when Song-ye returns. I don't want him sneaking up on me. I hope I deserve that much."

Baebin drew in a steady, sure breath. Then he unplugged his phone from the charger and turned it on. It buzzed like crazy from all the missed messages, but he ignored everything and dialed Manager Kim, putting it on speaker. When Mr. Kim answered, Baebin spoke, never taking his eyes off Go-Ri.

"Hi. It's me. Choi Go-Ri and I will return to work tomorrow morning on three conditions. First, we will be notified by Mr. Jong at least one day before Song-Ye returns to Campus. Second, I want cameras installed in her room and the hallway outside it. They must be recording, not just watching. Third, we get his daily schedule and know where he is at all times." Baebin added, "If the conditions aren't met, we both will leave immediately. Forever." He hung up without waiting for a response or rebuttal from Manager Kim.

Go-Ri's mouth was agape. He simply shrugged. "I agree with your decision. Good plan." Standing up, he smiled. "I'll do the dishes; you put away the food."

Twenty minutes later, they sat outside on the cold balcony. The wind coming off the river and swooping up the tall building tugged at the blanket wrapped around them, blowing her hair against his cheek. Baebin tucked the folds securely around her feet and rested a hand over them. Lights on the arches of the Banpo Bridge flicked on, one girder at a time. Go-Ri rested her head on his shoulder and gazed at the city lights across the river. "I love you."

He kissed her temple and rested his cheek on her head. "I love you more."

As he waited for Go-Ri to come out of the shower, Baebin sat cross-legged on the bed and checked his phone for the first time in days. He scrolled, reviewing all the texts he ignored since rushing home to Go-Ri after her breakdown with Manager Kim.

Several messages reminded him that group work was starting soon, and the recording studio needed his personal schedule to fit in sessions for his solo album. Daeho and Jaemin each had one out, and Baebin thought now was a good time to try it himself, to see if it was the direction he wanted for the future.

One message was from his *noona*.

> N: I THINK I'M PREGNANT!! DON'T KNOW FOR SURE YET. SHHHHH.

He was thrilled for his sister, who had a hard time conceiving his niece and then lost a second baby last year. His mom had a difficult time with the loss of the grandbaby and cried for days. Baebin sat up with a start.

Oh, crap.

He hadn't even thought about that with Go-Ri. *Ohhhh, God.* He grimaced, and his insides clenched. *Crap!* They hadn't used protection. It'd been ages since he bought condoms, but that would be priority number one now... if it wasn't too late already. He scrubbed his hair, wondering what to do.

Go-Ri came into the room, wearing nothing but purple knee socks covered in cat faces and his Eiffel Tower T-shirt. Without pants or a bra, she was even sexier. He quickly averted his eyes and was grateful for the pillow on his lap. Would it be too obvious if he ran to the store right now?

She saw the phone in his hands and the creases along his brow. Sitting across from him, she waited. Without looking up, he said, "I got my work schedule."

That was true, he thought. *Mostly.* It was easier than saying, "'Hey, I think I knocked you up.'"

"Mmm. Well. I guess we both knew it was coming. Fun time over." She patted his knee and tried to stay bright for him. He had been home a week, and it had been a rollercoaster. Maybe the normalcy of his un-normal, crazy work life would be for the best right now.

She went to get the big calendar they started using long ago, when she first gave lessons here—back when they promised not to be in the apartment at the same time.

Sprawling on the bed, they began pulling all their data from various schedules to fill one calendar. He was going to be very busy. Besides the usual routines of rehearsals, vocal recordings, and fan meets, he had two video productions on the enormous soundstage, a TV comedy show, and even a short trip to India next month. Not to mention his new solo projects.

Baebin was trying to find dates to spend time with her. She didn't know how he would even have time to *sleep*, let alone come home.

They added in her lessons, both at the studio and with the students she still taught at the apartment. If they figured in her potential schedule for the Composition Department, she was stretched thin, as well.

I need to help Omma at the restaurant, too. Her mother really needed to hire staff now. *She's put it off for too long. Min-Jun and I can't help like we used to.* Go-Ri ran down a mental list of tasks, from scoping out job websites to researching how to quickly find part-timers.

They scoured the calendar for the days when their schedules would allow them to ride in to work together or meet for lunch. While he was on tour, she had use of his car, but now, they realized that wasn't going to work with both of them home. Go-Ri insisted on taking the bus, but he privately had other plans that would guarantee to completely infuriate her. It came in several shiny colors and with cool features.

They both wanted to have more gatherings where they could host large group dinners with family and friends. They figured there would be around sixteen guests; supposedly, their table could fit that... except the guys were rather large. It would be a tight squeeze.

"Looks like you have a trip or event coming up, too. Let's add it." Baebin turned her phone towards her so she could get the information to write down the few days she had blocked off with dots.

Puzzled, she looked over his shoulder to see her phone. She had nothing planned outside of work... Baebin pointed to a row of days on the calendar. "Ack! Umm, no. That's nothing." She snatched the phone from his hand, completely mortified as she tried to scroll to the next month. It also showed a few days with colored dots.

"Mmm. Romantic getaway with another guy?" Baebin teased. "You'll have to start clearing those with me now. We can use the red pen to mark them here. Drawn in hearts." He grinned, tapping the large wall calendar spread on the bed.

Go-Ri groaned. He really needed to shut up.

Baebin hesitated, baffled. *My jokes aren't* that *bad. What was* the *big deal?* He thought they didn't hide anything anymore… especially after last night. "Sorry. I didn't know it was private. I kinda thought…"

Go-Ri groaned louder this time and buried her face in a pillow. *Shut up! Ugh.* He was going to have to know eventually, but not like this! She's a girl, he's a boy, they are… together. She groaned again. "Yes, it's private!" she yelled through the pillow.

When she flung it down onto her lap, her face shone scarlet, and her hair crackled in the dry air. He would have thought she was adorable if he wasn't so confused and upset. She rolled her eyes. "That's my… *girl* calendar."

"Wha—? What is that? How many calendars do you…" Suddenly, it clicked, and his eyes popped open. He turned as red as she was.

She could tell the second he figured it out and flopped back down on the pillow.

He closed his eyes briefly to compose himself. If he laughed now, she would definitely kill him. He hauled her back up and held her hands. "Hey. Look at me." He waited until he finally had to use his finger to push her chin up. She scrunched her eyes shut to avoid his gaze.

He couldn't help the snort that escaped. It wasn't his fault. She was too funny with her eyes screwed shut like a little child. "Hey. It's okay. I understand. Remember, I do have a mother and a sister. Do you think I'm an ancient guy who hides from that sort of thing?"

"Every time we…" Go-Ri fanned her hand around the bed and started over. "When I…" Now, she fanned herself.

"You were always gone when..." She rolled her eyes and crashed her head into his chest, huffing loudly.

He held her head against him and swept her hair to the side, giving a silent chuckle. She felt the vibration, sat up, and glared. He laughed until he remembered the text from his sister. Sobering up, he said, "I truly am not bothered by it. I understand. But we may have a problem. I, uh... we... uh..."

Now, it was his turn to be embarrassed and wave at the bed. "I wasn't prepared for, umm, *us* yet. We didn't use anything. Protection."

Go-Ri's mouth opened in surprise, her fit disappearing in a flash. *Ohhhh. He's right.*

She waved him off and flushed once more. *We are really getting all the cards on the table at once, aren't we?* "Well... I've got that covered. I've been on medication for years because my monthlies are bad."

Oh, boy, she realized in dread, *except for the last few days!* With everything that happened, she hadn't even thought of *eating,* let alone taking her medication. She gave a big mental smack to her forehead.

Baebin paled. "Bad? How bad? Have you gotten checked out? What happens?" He thought of his sister and all her difficulties as he peppered Go-Ri with questions.

Slapping a hand over his mouth to stop him, she gave him a droll look. "Duh, I've been checked out. I have medication, you idiot. I'm usually fine. It's just the normal stuff now. I would have told you at some point, but it was need-to-know, and you... *didn't.* And then I forgot. I got... preoccupied."

"Can you please let me know when you are in pain? My sister has a lot of problems, and I'm just worried about you." Grinning, he added, "If you get as crabby and mean as she does, we'll definitely need to add it to the calendar so I know when to duck and stay at the dorm!" He laughed as the first pillow-missile launched in his direction.

He loved seeing the flash of butt in pink panties as she scrambled for another pillow, and he smacked it before dashing out of the room. Her offended squeal behind him was a huge turn-on and her pounding footsteps made him sprint harder. He called over his shoulder, "I'm going to hide the knives now!"

Baebin caught the stuffed animal she snagged off the bookcase and threw it at him as he rounded the island. Ten feet of white marble separated them. Palms smacked the counter as they grinned at each other, trying to gauge which direction the other would move.

The evil, calculating glint in her eye made him pause as she slowly dragged a pot on the counter closer. Baebin held up his hands in surrender, one fist still clutching his childhood bunny.

Never breaking eye contact, she took the lid off and swirled a finger inside, loosening a clump of the cold sticky rice.

"Hey, wait a minute. You sure you haven't started your period already? You're getting cranky." He ducked in time, but the poor bunny took a direct hit to the face.

Armed with couch pillows, fruit, and anything soft they could find, they chased each other around the apartment, laughing like teenagers.

Go-Ri managed to corner him against the pillar, poking him in the ribs. He found his moment and caught her around the waist, pinning her arms to her sides. Turning, he pressed her against the side of the bookcase, knocking books into both the piano and living room, where they thudded loudly to the ground, before he swooped in for his winning kiss.

His seductive voice and tongue tickled her ear. "If you want to play with food, we have better-tasting things than rice." He dragged her shirt off over her head and fondled her breasts. "I think strawberries would taste wonderful here." He toyed with a nipple before tugging lightly. "We don't have chocolate syrup, but honey would work, too."

Go-Ri froze for a moment—just a slight pause before letting the heat of his breath warm her cheek and drag her sweetly back to the present. She wrapped her arms around him and greedily hunted for his mouth to taste the honey he spoke of.

Baebin was wonderful. Perfect. Not *him*. She was fine. She *most definitely* wanted more.

But he felt her hesitation. It was enough to douse his hot desire to take her hard against the bookcase as he remembered the image she had painted of Song-Ye. How he had assaulted her against the wall in a cold alley.

Shit! He was a monster just like him. Selfish. Arrogant. Stupid. *How could I do this?*

He jerked out of her arms, appalled at himself. He could only watch as she stumbled. "God, I'm sorry." His erection poked stiffly against his shorts, and he belatedly realized he had left her naked and exposed. Snatching up her shirt, he held it out, averting his face.

The swift change from laughter to passion to the sudden emptiness of her arms left Go-Ri feeling muddled. She reached for him, looking for the missing kiss, not the clothing in his hand.

Baebin swatted her away and stepped further back, almost toppling over a chair in the living room; his erection starting to droop. "No, aien. I can't. Not like this. I can't. I can't be like him."

Blinking away her mental clouds, she saw lust and desire still in his eyes. Also fear and... regret?

What did he say? ... *can't be like...*? Flashes of jumbled emotions hit her all at once, crushing her like a boulder slamming into her chest. Furious, her palm cracked against his cheek.

Her passion-fueled fog turned into uncontrollable anger. Forgetting her nakedness, she launched at him.

"No! No! You do not get to do this! How dare you!" She hit him over and over with clenched fists, her voice louder than her sobs. "Do you think of *him* when you see me? He does not get the right to come between us! Not like this!"

Baebin stumbled as she shifted from pushing him away to yanking him closer. Grabbing a fistful of his hair, she brutally brought his mouth to hers, dragging him close to her up against the shelves.

When he tried to pull away, she bit his lip hard and dug in her heels. She was punishing him but didn't care. She would make him do what she wanted. Make him kiss her where she wanted. She shifted his mouth from her cheek to the corner of her jaw to the base of her neck, forcing his movements.

It made him sick. He didn't want to play a part in her nightmare, but with a gut-punch, he knew he must. It would be easy to push her away, but he knew if he did, it would destroy her. The moment he started loving her, he became a part of what happened in her past.

If this was what she wanted, then he would give it to her. He would make himself relive that horrible night with her and overwrite what happened. He didn't need to think too hard to remember how she described her night in the alley. It was already ingrained in his memory. But whatever she made him do, he would only go as far as her release. No way would he take her. Not like this.

He just prayed he could stop if she needed him to. He prayed their love for each other would survive.

Seizing her shoulders, he slammed her back against the bookcase. The massive, sturdy piece shuddered, and books and nickknacks dropped to the floor in the room beyond. Dragging her to the front of the case, he perched her hip on a shelf, letting her foot dangle off the ground.

First her neck. *That's where she said he started.*

Squeezing for a millisecond, he tilted her head back and gently caressed her throat, rubbing her pulse points with his thumbs and lips. Massaging her spine, Baebin erased all the traces of *his* strangle-hold. The toy car behind her head rolled and broke on the ground, sending Lego shrapnel everywhere around the piano.

Gently crushing her breast, he took note of where his fingers lay before lightly nipping and sucking each spot in turn, covering Song-Ye's marks with his own. *That pitiful excuse of a human didn't have the right to desecrate such a beautiful body.* Baebin loved how her nipples puckered tightly in his mouth and her moans grew with each tug.

His fist, which he gently pressed inward against her belly—a reminder of the punches—slowly flattened, roaming to her dark, trimmed bush and back again. He lightly tickled her ribs with his fingertips, guessing which ones had broken.

He worshipped her body. She was amazing. Sensual. Desirable. His and *only* his. *Does she understand how much I crave her? Need her?*

His fingers stroked her skin, and his tongue lapped everywhere his hands didn't cover before he clamped his lips over hers. Punishing. Taking. Treasuring. His tongue plundered the tender interior of her mouth until she returned in kind, giving as good as she got. He could spend a lifetime and never get tired of kissing her, loving her.

This is all my fault. The thought pounded in her head as he pressed her backwards into the bookshelf. *I pushed him too far. I didn't mean for... But... I... I need this.* Clutching his shoulders, she held on and drained her mind of everything but the kind, loving man standing in front of her right now. The *only* man she wanted.

Baebin's desire still hovered on the sidelines. Caught between loathing and lust, he growled in frustration as his body reacted independently. Her supple, lean body, combined with her feminine musk, overruled his reasoning.

He tugged sharply at the flimsy seams of her underwear, leaving them hanging in shreds around her waist. Forcing her to wrap both legs around him, he caressed her hips, moving upward to her soft bottom and then inward to her very center. One finger, then two, drilled inside her.

She wasn't ready yet for the invasion, and the harsh thrusting made her groan in protest until she felt his thumb gyrate against her button. With each stroke, inside and out, she leaked and spilled onto his fingers as he tormented her sensitive core. Her mewing cries reached a fevered pitch as she drew closer to the finale, but her release always seemed to skip away, just out of reach.

"More! Almost... there!" Go-Ri was so close. "I need...!" She scrambled to reach down for him, where he pressed again against her hip, while still maintaining her grip on his shoulders.

"Only this and no more." He told her, his voice ragged and harsh with his own desire. He vowed to keep the promise he made to himself.

"No! Please! I need you!"

Her wail of frustration gnawed at him. Every touch of her skin against his fanned the flames he tried to keep at bay. Her wetness, her passionate response, her fingers as they clawed his back, holding him tighter... Her begging tipped the balance.

Giving up and giving in, he reached between them and yanked down his shorts just far enough to free his aching cock before clutching her hips and adjusting himself at her entrance. In one thrust, he drove deeply inside her.

He stretched her to maximum fullness. Go-Ri arched back in shock; he was deeper than ever before, and it overwhelmed her. The vase she bought months ago for her roses tumbled to the ground in the other room, exploding into a million pieces as Go-Ri crashed with it.

The instantaneous orgasm surprised them both, but Baebin continued to drive into her and push her farther and farther past the edge.

Losing control and almost out of strength, he found her hands and pinned them behind her. Kicking books out of the way, he dropped them both to the floor with her legs still locked around him. Rocking slowly inside, grinding gently against her, he waited for her convulsions to slow, kissing her once-broken cheek and then-swollen jaw. He captured her lips once more before leaning back on his haunches.

She came once, but it wasn't enough. He would never get enough of feeling her writhing in ecstasy under him. And tonight, Baebin needed to destroy any last, remaining traces of the man that lingered between them.

Pressing her onto the floor and keeping her hands trapped underneath, he pushed slowly into her. Stroking. Tormenting. Propelling them both to the next and final cliff. Each thrust was harder than the one before, until they crashed painfully over the farthest boundary, leaving them both shaking and in tears.

He felt her leg slide off his hip as she passed out from the sheer force of her second intense orgasm. Somehow, he gathered enough strength to pull out and commando crawled to the couch for a blanket. Fixing her twisted sock and adjusting her arms, he tucked the blanket around her and sat propped against a nearby chair.

He hated himself.

He had effectively done what Song-Ye couldn't, even though she'd given her permission—practically forced him to do it. *How could a man do that to a woman, especially someone he loved?* This was the worst thing he had ever done. And he would never forgive himself for having such a mind-blowing release.

After brushing away the silly strand of bangs that never stayed with the others on her forehead, he got to his feet and stumbled to the shower. The piano room was destroyed. He remembered the sounds of books and other things falling and belatedly thought of the neighbor below, who must have heard everything.

The path to the hall was clear of shrapnel, but he was pretty sure it would take a while to find all the Lego and glass pieces scattered across the floor and under the piano. That, however, was a problem for another day.

He sat in the shower for the longest time with his back against the wall, resting his arms on his bent knees. He let the hot water run over him and wash the angry tears off his face.

The door opened, and she stood, wavering. Her thighs and the curly hair at her apex were coated, growing crusty with their drying fluid; fresh rivers dripped down her legs from her walk to the bathroom.

Silently, she asked permission to join him. He didn't give it, but neither did he push her away. Curled between his knees, she rested her cheek on his chest and wrapped an arm around his waist.

As Baebin fried their eggs, Go-Ri pulled the broom and dustpan out of the pantry.

"Leave it," Baebin snapped, before easing his temper. "I'll be back in a few days and will clean it up. I'm the one who made the mess."

She wanted to disagree on who the responsible party was, but his tone left no room for argument.

In their Campus parking spot at six o'clock, Go-Ri hesitantly pressed a kiss to his cheek before walking alone to her building. They hadn't said a word since the kitchen and wouldn't be seeing each other for a few days. It was a horrible way to part, but last night wasn't something a simple five-minute conversation could fix.

Baebin scrubbed his face and went to the gym to blow off steam. He wanted to sweat away his troubles, but the fitness center was already packed.

He hadn't seen anyone since before his tour, and everyone waylaid him, welcoming him back with a thousand questions. Since most of those inquiring were still up-and-coming in the industry, he felt obligated to talk and share his experiences of the tour that now seemed a lifetime ago.

He just wanted to be alone.

He was happy to be back at work. As much as he loved Go-Ri, he needed time and space. To think. To re-focus. He very firmly locked his memories away and refused to even think about anything that had transpired since he was here last. He would have a good few days before the rest of his friends returned, even if it hurt.

Now, he needed to work on his solo project. The tour pushed back his recording schedule, and without the others, he could make up for lost time. He still had to work on the managerial projects he started in America for the release and promotion of "SuperStars" and *Galaxy*—his first attempt at learning upper management.

Go-Ri had three regular appointments and several make-up sessions for those students she canceled when she was working on her music at home. Now that she was back, the steady stream of drop-ins filled her open time, and the morning flew by.

She was surprised to receive a large envelope, hand delivered with her name in bold black letters. *Mr. Kae works fast.* She sat staring at it, refusing to open the clasp. He was on the video call and knew her shame. *Why did he still want to hire me?* She wouldn't stand for it if it was only out of pity.

She pulled out the sheets of paper but didn't get far before realizing she couldn't do this alone.

> G: YEJOON? HELLO. YOU OFFERED TO REVIEW MY CONTRACT…
>   DO YOU MIND? I WOULD LIKE HELP.
> Y: HELLO GONGJUNIM! YEP. COME SEE ME. I'LL SEND U THE
>   ADDRESS.

Go-Ri found Yejoon two hours later off-site, folded up and scooched down in a chair, getting prepped for a photo shoot for a high-end fashion designer.

While his tall body and perfect proportions made for a great model, it wreaked havoc on the shorter makeup artists tasked with making him even more handsome.

In the chair next to him sat Manager Kim. Go-Ri was unprepared to face any of the men from the video call, especially Manager Kim, who saw her get sick at the initial interview.

Turning around, she was halfway down the hall when Mr. Kim called out from the doorway.

Tears clouded her eyes, and she gripped the satchel across her chest with both hands. She hauled herself back, praying to get this over with quickly. He had a different tie tack on today.

Jerking his head inside, he said, "Hello, Ms. Choi. Yejoon asked me to help go over a contract with you. He's good with them, but I've got more experience."

Her eyes skittered to Yejoon, who smiled broadly and waved at her through the mirror. Yejoon looked the same as usual—aside from the heavy makeup.

Belatedly, she remembered he knew about her past, too. He always had, along with the rest of them. But he had never given her any indication of pity or disgust. "I didn't know you would be here. I'm sorry he bothered you." She spoke through frozen lips. "He shouldn't have done that."

Manager Kim gave her a shrug and a calming smile. "My boys are more than a job, they are my children. I'd do anything for them."

He paused for the briefest of moments. "I'm happy to have a new daughter, and I'll do anything to protect her, too." Manager Kim poked his head into the makeup room. "Let's look at your contract."

Go-Ri nodded slightly and slowly returned to the room. Yejoon called her over to the empty chair next to him, completely unaware of the discussion that had happened just meters away.

Thirty minutes later, Manager Kim and Yejoon had reviewed every line of her new contract, made minor revisions, and identified which terms to bargain on later. All in all, they both agreed the original was fair, and they were thrilled for her new position.

She returned the contract with its written changes to Mr. Kae's office, then drove home.

Go-Ri kicked her brother out of the restaurant to go study and worked the rest of the day. She and *Omma* finished for the evening and prepped for tomorrow. Taking two drinks from the cooler, she called for her mother to sit down and rest.

She worried about this moment for two years, and still, she didn't know where to start. "Omma, I need to talk to you."

Go-Ri finally told *Omma* about what happened two years ago and how she hid at Binna's until she recovered; she wasn't on a beach trip like they had said.

Then, Go-Ri told *Omma* about Baebin. Everything. How they met, how he lied, and how she hurt him. But mostly, how much Go-Ri loved him. She opened her heart and told *Omma* all her fears. Mostly, she was afraid of losing him.

Omma sat quietly and listened. She wanted to weep but knew Go-Ri didn't want that right now. If her eyes said anything, Go-Ri had already suffered enough and just needed a comforting ear.

She wished her baby had told her the truth all those times she'd asked what was wrong, but she knew sometimes torment must be dealt with privately. *I hid my tears, too, when my husband died.* Only after working through her own sadness was she able to let go of the past and move on with her life.

"My baby, my ae-gi. Kim Baebin is a nice man. If he truly cares for you, you won't lose him. Your father and I found apologies and patience helped us through the difficult times. Maybe it will for you, too. You should talk to him." *Omma* patted her daughter's hand as the two sat across the table in the darkened restaurant.

Go-Ri worked the next two days at the restaurant, open to close, primarily by herself, to give Mom and Min-Jun a break. While they were gone, she sent out advertisements for two positions. Omma *can yell at me later. With Min-Jun needing to study and my new work, she needs the help.* MinGo was always popular, but in the last few years, the small family struggled to handle its staggering growth. Now, hiring outside the family was unavoidable.

Mr. Kae sent a driver to her with the contract. Go-Ri fed him lunch while reviewing the changes privately in the small, cluttered back office. She was happy that he accepted most of her requests, and she could handle those he didn't. It was an excellent deal for her, which she thought would never be attainable, especially during these last few years.

She signed, made a copy, and sent the driver back to Mr. Kae with the contract.

> G: HELLO. DONE AND SIGNED. ☺ THX FOR YOUR HELP!
> Y: ☺ YEA! CONGRATS!

Two hours later, she received a bouquet of flowers from Yejoon.

It wasn't until the following day that she screwed up the courage to return to the apartment. Go-Ri stood in the *hyeongwan* until the automatic light turned off. She looked around like a stranger in a new space. The dim light filtering in through the sheer curtains glinted off the broken glass and damaged knickknacks, the destruction a cruel reminder of how badly she may have ruined her chance at love with Baebin. *I'm not surprised he hasn't cleaned. It took me this long to face it myself.*

Slowly, methodically, she restored the apartment to order—she reshelved books, swept glass, returned pillows and fruit to their spots. She gathered the salvageable knickknacks into a pile to be glued later and boxed the rest for Baebin to decide what to do with. Finally, she closed the door behind her and went back to the restaurant.

Baebin watched her from his phone. *I should've cleaned up the mess. It's been three days. I can't keep hiding like this.* Seeing her cry as she tidied their apartment made him ache for her.

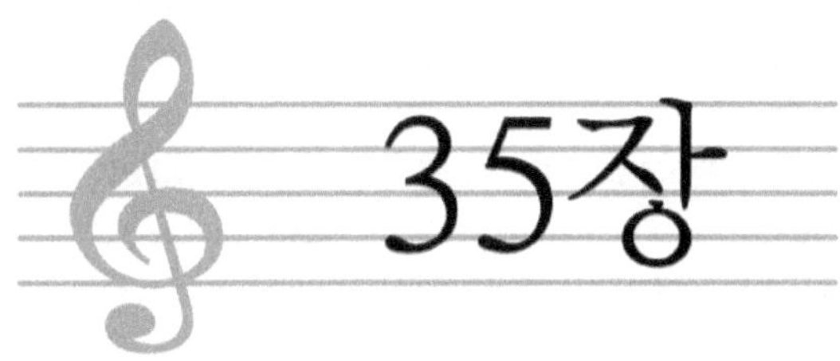

Go-Ri pulled into Campus and received her permanent employee badge from the gate guard. The regular morning attendant in the shack smiled and bowed to her, congratulating her on the new position.

She spent the morning getting acquainted with her new department. Upon meeting her new boss, Mr. Yoon, she learned more about her duties and received a stack of files and thumb drives. He showed her to a desk and introduced her to the other people in the department. They were quiet and studious—more fit to be in a science lab than a creative music department. She liked them all instantly.

Her contract stated she could work anywhere she pleased. She was given access to any instruments and rooms she needed, and a list of musicians who would play her work during the creative process. Several of the names she recognized as her drop-ins. Her teaching schedule would continue, but now, she had set hours for drop-ins to better regulate the flow of people visiting her. As predicted, her schedule was full.

By lunch, she was back in her studio, rubbing her temples as a slight headache grew from all the information thrown at her. Woo-Ge would be coming today at two o'clock for his lesson, so she had some time to relax and play her own music, which would help calm her.

A soft knock at the door startled her, and she peered through the small window with its shade pulled halfway down. It was Baebin. She couldn't remember when she told him where her room was. They hadn't spoken or texted since the morning they parted at the car a few days ago.

She got her period this morning and spitefully wondered if she could blame her crankiness on it, as he had teased *that* night. But Go-Ri knew she was just embarrassed to see him so soon. Her flow was a reminder to take her medication seriously now that she was intimate with Baebin. His visit added stress to her day that she didn't need, but she waved him in with a smile she didn't really feel.

Setting a bag on her desk, he said, "I bring food and well wishes. I figured you wouldn't remember to eat today." He could see the strain creasing around her eyes and knew that the morning, no matter how good, was taxing for her. Baebin moved to stand behind her and lightly rubbed her temples and forehead. "Yejoon told me about your contract. I'm proud of you, but I wish you would have told me yourself."

Sinking back into his strong fingers, she instantly felt the tension ooze away. "Mmm. I know I should have. But I was embarrassed to talk to you so soon after... I'm sorry."

"Me, too." He wished he knew what else to say. He looked around the room, appreciating the layout. She had a little desk in the corner with a filing cabinet, an impressive array of instruments lined up under the wall of windows, and a large upright piano near the middle of the room, positioned perfectly to catch the light without blinding the player.

Music rooms always have that odd smell, Baebin thought. *Like... old wood, oil, and dusty papers.* The smell brought back memories of his old school days before joining SKEC and the times spent in the chorus room where he got his first taste of music. Afraid to get too comfortable, he walked to the far corner for two stools.

Taking his cue, she turned on the stereo. His brow jutted upward when K-pop came out on low. Blushing, she refused to look at him. "I'm trying. I want to learn your music. You shouldn't always have to listen to mine."

He joined her at the stereo and hunted through the stack of music. He found her Bill Evans' CD and swapped it out. "I like this one. What he does on piano, and his improv is amazing. You don't have to like my music. Only me."

Giving her one *dosirak* lunch box from the commissary and a set of chopsticks, he sat down with his own. His voice was barely a whisper. "I miss you."

"I miss you, too." She stared at the container in her hand. "Baebin, I'm sorry. You were only trying to be considerate, and I shouldn't have taken my anger out on you. I shouldn't have pushed you to do... that. It's my fault. I hate that I can't control when I lose it. Please don't hate me."

He couldn't be more surprised if she'd hit him again. "Why would I hate you? You didn't do anything wrong. I hate *myself*, not you. I never want to hurt you and be like that with you. You are too special to be treated like that. It makes me no better than Song-Ye."

"You are *not* like him. You never could be, and I've always known that, even from the beginning."

They ate and talked until Woo-Ge dashed into the room, carrying his music bag. He jumped at Baebin, who had to shift quickly to avoid a direct hit with the bulky sack. Woo-Ge squished Baebin's face and gave him a big wet kiss before slithering down and getting a hug from Go-Ri. His mom came running in after him. "Dang it, he's fast!"

Woo-Ge began his scales on the piano, starting with C major. A quick learner, he was already mastering two-handed E scales with their four sharps. Go-Ri promised to deliver the little student back to the dance building after all her lessons today, and Mrs. Sun and Baebin left together.

After his lesson, Woo-Ge played at her desk, with the writing lessons she had given him and his coloring book, while she taught her following two students. She walked Woo-Ge to his mom afterward and sat in the hall, waiting for Baebin to finish.

With a duffle bag over his shoulder and his cap in hand, he strolled out of the practice room an hour later, surprised to see her sitting on the floor. "Aien? I thought you left. You could have come in."

"I didn't want to bother you." She finally looked at him. "I… can I ask a favor?"

"Always." Baebin crouched down in front of her drawn-up knees. "What do you need?"

"I want to go to the police station. I want to file a report." She was apprehensive but firm and steady. Unwavering. "It may not do any good, but I want it official. It's time. Would you go with me?" His hands warmed her skin where they rested in the gap between her socks and capri pants. His mere presence was a comfort.

"Mmm. Let's go now." He pulled her to her feet before donning a heavy coat over his sweatshirt, trapping in body heat so he didn't cool off too quickly in the chilly outside air. Swiping back his damp hair, he put on his cap as they walked to his car.

Inspector Goe was not pleased to see them so close to the end of his shift. Go-Ri had hoped to have better luck with a new officer but had to settle with the rude man. She let every barb he threw bounce off. She was here for one thing: to get her story on record. The inspector didn't need to believe her; he just had to type.

Baebin was more furious than she was when they got back into the car. He slammed the stick into drive and squealed out of the lot.

"It's okay. Don't get a ticket." Go-Ri rested her hand on his lap. "I don't care about him. He doesn't matter to me."

Baebin squeezed her hand before letting out a big whoosh of air. "I know. But still. He doesn't have to be such a jerk." Kissing her fingers, he glanced over at her. "I'm proud of you. You did great. I have two more days off. Will you come home with me? It'll be freezing, but we can go to the beach tomorrow."

"No. I'm sorry. I promised Omma to train her new employees tonight. And I've missed so much work lately, I have make-up lessons tomorrow."

They rode to the apartment together, and he walked her up the hill, their gloved hands holding tight and their breath leaving white puffs in the air.

As Go-Ri changed into work clothes, Mom packed him dinner to go. He had been to MinGo many times, but today, he scanned the place, identifying lines of sight and hidden areas, inspecting the ceiling, and noting where he thought cameras should be. He needed to talk to Mom alone about changes he wanted to make to her restaurant.

As Go-Ri walked in a few minutes later, Baebin was clearing tables and delivering water to a waiting customer before taking a selfie with a fan. Go-Ri grinned. How quickly she had forgotten who he was to everyone else. How quickly it didn't matter to her anymore.

Catching his eye, she jerked her head to the kitchen. Behind the wall, away from prying eyes, she planted one on him before slapping his butt and sending him off with his bag of food. "Go away. Don't flirt with our customers. You're gonna cause a riot."

Her playfulness caught him off guard, but he grinned and kissed her back. "I only have eyes for you, aein. Text me later. Love you."

She tsked at him, secretly pleased. As he left the kitchen, the two new hires passed him and turned to ogle, instantly recognizing the singer.

Raising an eyebrow at the teens, she warned them. "Yes, it's Yong-ee. He comes often. Will it be a problem? You can leave now if it is." Satisfied with their contrite expressions, she started their training. She forgot the new girls would recognize him. *If they go all googly-eyed every time he comes in, I'll have to look for replacements.*

It was eerie being alone. The last night he'd been home, it started great but ended badly. He wanted to erase that night from his memory. All he could hope for was to put it behind them; get through it. It was something they would've had to face at some point; he just wished it didn't have to happen the way it did.

Baebin had known for a while that he truly loved Go-Ri and wanted to be with her. They couldn't continue to simply play house. For one thing, he didn't want to upset her mom, who would soon learn what they were doing if she didn't know already.

Would Go-Ri be willing to take their relationship a step further? She was going through so much in her life right now, he didn't know if she could handle another change.

He liked the quiet apartment and the chance to be alone, but he wanted her next to him, not just for tonight, but for always.

Baebin hit the remote before tossing a set of keys to Go-Ri. The red sporty Kia next to his white SUV beeped, and its lights flashed. "You're driving that." His mouth twitched at her surprised look.

"What did you do?" She almost dropped her music satchel as her hands fisted on her hips.

"When we have to drive separately, this will be easier." He climbed into his car, shutting off her complaints. He was waiting for her at the Campus when she pulled into a new spot near his a few minutes later. "Well?"

She screwed up her face and stuck her tongue out at him. It was awesome, but she wasn't going to give him the satisfaction. "It doesn't smell like your gym socks, at least."

Baebin threw back his head and laughed.

They walked together, hand-in-hand, to the sound building, parting ways in the courtyard. He was recording in the B side today, and she had a new soundtrack for a historical drama she was working on with a co-worker in the Composition office.

IN7 was back. There was no easing into their schedule. *Chasing You,* their ninth mini-album and the second of the year, was out, which meant rounds of promotional events and polishing routines before new songs got rotated into their concert set. Their song, "Summer Crush", was already nominated for the Melon Music Awards and the Hanteo

Award, and everyone had high hopes it would be good enough for a MAMA nomination.

Prepping for the India tour, the boys started a crash course in Hindi, memorizing necessary phrases. Beyond what normal tourists learned—"thank you," "hello," "good morning,"—they also changed key lines to their music to please the foreign audience. Particularly racy dance moves needed to be altered to conform to the culturally conservative mandates before the Indian government would allow them to perform in their country, as well.

The changes needed to become automatic quickly, so no mistakes happened on stage.

The second week home from America, Baebin finally had an afternoon off. In fact, every Tuesday for the next month was an early day for the guys. He and Go-Ri jumped at the free evening and invited everyone to dinner. Not just for one night, but a standing invitation for every Tuesday for anyone interested in coming.

The *sinbaljang* was overflowing with shoes, and the apartment was full. They celebrated the new album and Go-Ri's first few weeks officially on the job.

Omma was thrilled to see her new babies again. She studied up on the group and finally learned their names. Yejoon and Jaemin, who missed the first dinner, were quickly added to her flock... like they really had a choice.

Meeting Baebin's parents, officially, for the first time in person, was a bit daunting but not as nerve-racking as Go-Ri expected. The two *Ommas* hit it off, plating all the food from MinGo, while Mr. Bak and Baebin's father sat at the table and poured whiskey and soju for each other.

It was a work night, so the large group didn't stay long. After the door closed behind their last guest, Go-Ri and Baebin looked at each other. It was like they were a new couple all over again. They only saw each other a few times since her first day at work, and that was mainly at the Campus.

He held out his hand to her, and they walked quietly back to the bedroom, turning off lights as they went.

Laying on his bare shoulder, she traced the writing on his collarbone. The odd angle almost made her cross-eyed as she tried to read it, but his warm, silky skin begged to be touched. "I've been meaning to ask you, what does this say? It's Latin, right?"

He looked down at his chest like he hadn't experienced the torture of getting the tattoo and didn't know it was there. Her fingers on his body and her breath in his armpit were maddening. "Mmm. Yes, Latin. It says, 'Let your light shine.' It was my first one."

"Mmm. Fitting. Perfect for you." Go-Ri gave it a peck and shifted slightly. His chest was a velvet boulder under her cheek. Running her finger up his side, she traced the tattoo that ran the length of his ribcage. "What about this one?"

He snatched at her hand, flinching violently. The hand that was playing in her hair subconsciously jerked, almost taking a clump of long strands with it. The sudden jerk stopped her from blowing on his nipple, but her howl of protest and the ticklish jolt to his rib made him giggle uncontrollably. "Knock it off! You know I'm ticklish!"

She scrubbed at her scalp laughing with him. "If you're ticklish, why did you get one there? Didn't it hurt?"

"It hurt like crazy. But pain trumped funny. At least, at the time." He pressed her back into the bed, rubbing at her damaged scalp before kissing it. He savored the glossy tousled strands that smelled of vanilla and almonds. Leaning on his elbows, he looked down into her eyes, greedily eating her with his gaze. "Aein," his voice was husky and deep, "can I kiss you? I swear, it won't be like—"

She rose up and kissed him. Her light, chaste kiss dissolved into a slow, simmering caress that stole his mind. She was the best drug in the universe.

Baebin dropped a spoon covered in *kimchi* sauce, splattering red goo all over the white cabinets and floor. While trying to wipe it up, he knocked the pot on the stove, and a huge puddle ran across the counter and dribbled over the edge. "Oi! No!"

Go-Ri rolled her eyes, groaning. "Aiech, you are a disaster in the kitchen! I spend more time cleaning up after you than anything!" Snapping his butt with a towel, she hip-bumped him away and helped clean up the floor.

He stepped around her, intentionally knocking her over and poking her ticklish spot under her shoulder blade.

She yanked his pants down and snuck open a cabinet door. Two seconds later, he whacked his knee on it.

Go-Ri answered her ringing phone, giggling as Baebin tried to pull his pants back up with the one finger that wasn't covered in sauce. Plopping to the ground, she leaned her head back against the refrigerator door, the laughter a fading memory.

She put it on speaker, and Mr. Jong's voice carried through the now-silent kitchen. "—know that on Monday, Nam Song-Ye will be returning to Seoul. He will have a week off before returning to the Campus."

Baebin hurled the towel he had used to clean his hands into the sink. "Sir, can I ask why you are allowing him to come back? You know what he did to her!"

"I do. And please know, Ms. Choi, we do believe you." Go-Ri could hear the sincerity in his voice. "We feel it's best to bring him in where we can watch him until the investigation is finished, and he is charged. Unfortunately, we legally cannot break his contract without an official reason. So, at the moment, our hands are tied until we hear from the police. We will limit his activities and keep him in the dance building as much as possible, and we'll let you know of any changes to his schedule."

Baebin knelt between her upturned knees, wiping the tears that silently streamed down her cheeks. "And what of Go-Ri? What is she supposed to do?"

"We are hoping she stays. She has the option to work from home. I also checked her contract before I called; with or without the escape clause, I will not hold it against her in any way if she chooses to leave." They could hear the struggle in his voice. "I'm sorry, Ms. Choi. Even though we believe you, we need verifiable, concrete evidence, and that must come from the investigators."

Baebin clicked off and tossed the phone aside. Pulling her between his thighs, he wrapped his arms tight around her, wishing he could fuse her body to his. Suck her inside him. Swallow her whole until the mess disappeared. He could feel her nose squish against his sternum as her tears soaked his shirt.

Song-Ye was coming back. Baebin needed to put his plan into action, and number one on the list was talking to *Omma*. He had to do it *soon*.

The next morning, Baebin dressed for a run and set off up the hill while Go-Ri slept. He was huddled in the doorway of MinGo, out of the cold wind, when *Omma* came to open up.

She was surprised to see Baebin alone and could tell something was on his mind. Patting him on the cheek, she welcomed him inside and started a kettle of water. Setting two mugs of tea on the office desk, which was cluttered with financial records, delivery bills, and old receipts, Baebin perched on boxes of disposable chopsticks while she took the rickety, antique office chair.

Winding and unwinding the string of the tea bag around his finger, he finally broke the silence. "Go-Ri says she told you about… umm… Nam Song-Ye." *Gad, what if she really didn't?* He certainly didn't want to be the one to break the news to *Omma*.

"Mmm. Yes, she did. It broke my heart."

He drew in a steadying breath. "He's coming back next week. I'm worried about what he will do. Will you allow me to have cameras installed in MinGo? I'm worried for you, Go-Ri, and the new girls. I don't trust him."

"Okay. I like the idea of cameras." It made sense. She had been considering it for years anyway.

Baebin heaved a sigh of relief, letting go of the strain he had been holding for weeks. But *that* was child's play. He crossed his fingers and toes and prayed to every god in the universe. "I would also like Go-Ri to move in with me."

For that, *Omma* sat back and blinked. Rapidly. "Wha…?"

"Song-Ye knows where you live, right? He's from this neighborhood? He's coming here first before returning to work. If you prefer, I can also add cameras to your home— on the outside only; I don't want to invade your privacy. But he doesn't know where I live, and I already have a tight security system." Selfishly, he silently begged for option A.

Absolutely not! No mother would give that permission. Did he think she was born yesterday? She already had an idea of what the couple were doing alone but refused to dwell on it.

She openly studied the young man. He was always polite and thoughtful, and just recently, her *ae-gi* said how much she loved him. This man was every mother's dream for her daughter.

Omma already knew his answer, but she wanted to hear it. To *see* it. "Do you love my daughter?"

"Absolutely!"

His sudden, startled, fierce look and lightning-fast response was all she needed. His love and desire to protect and support Go-Ri were written on his face. "I cannot give you permission."

Baebin sagged. He knew it was too much to ask.

"You need to ask her. She is an adult. If my Go-Ri is willing, I won't say no." She tempered his euphoric delight with a raised finger, calmly warning him. "But! I will poison your food if you play with her feelings. Make a decision soon on your future."

He fell to his knees in front of her, bowing low in respect and appreciation, before gripping her thin but strong, calloused hands. Thirty minutes later, after they made plans, he all but skipped down the hill to Go-Ri.

"You did *what?!*"

"I talked to Omma." Baebin tried to come up with a million excuses and reasons to ask her to move in with him. After his first two subtle attempts, hinting at the idea, crashed and burned, he had no choice but to tell her. Besides, if she found out he tried to trick her again, he feared no baby would ever come from his loins.

Go-Ri's head smacked on the table. Several times. "What did she say?" The question floated out under her veil of hair.

"I gave her sound reasons, and she said it was up to you."

Go-Ri lifted her head and pierced him with a soul-stripping glare.

"And... tomorrow night, I'm going back to monitor workers installing cameras inside MinGo. It will be the same system I have here. I want everyone protected." He held up a hand, forbidding any complaints. "That's not up for discussion. Omma already agreed, so don't argue."

She huffed quietly and stared out the window at the icy rain pinging off the glass banister. *Actually, cameras aren't a bad idea. But living together?* She pinked at the idea. *How would she face Omma? Or Min-Jun?* Her head thudded on the table again.

At midnight, the lights were on at MinGo. After the usual ritual of closing shop, Go-Ri and Baebin ran around, covering every surface with towels and sheets to prepare for the workers, who would drop dust as they fished wires through the ceiling.

The installers were pros and knew exactly the best places and angles needed to protect the space. They attached a secondary keypad close to the door for arming and disarming the system. As a test dummy, Baebin walked throughout the dining area and kitchen, while Go-Ri watched the monitor from the main panel in the office, checking the resolution and camera angles. Lastly, he stood outside, pretending to look in through the windows and doors. A patrol car pulled up behind him.

Go-Ri watched as Baebin's hands shot up in alarm as he turned to face the cops. She debated how long to make him suffer. Laughing wouldn't help his situation, but it was too hard not to. Officers Kong and Kim were regulars, and Mom often had containers of leftover food ready for them.

Go-Ri joined them at the curb with canned coffee she'd snagged from the cooler on the way.

"Hello, officers! These are for you." She handed over the cans before linking arms with Baebin, reassuring the officers and stealing Baebin's warmth in the chilly night air. "Sorry for worrying you. He's harmless. We're installing cameras."

The officers relaxed upon seeing her and stored their retractable batons before pulling their thick coats back down over their duty belts. Eyeing the couple, the taller of the two officers tilted his head, searching for a memory. "I know you…" Snapping his fingers, he found it. "My daughter has posters of your group. Sorry, I don't remember your name."

That was her cue to go. Go-Ri patted him on the arm, and with a wave to the cops, she headed back inside.

Glancing over his shoulder to ensure she was gone, Baebin signed a page from the man's patrol book and asked the closest officer, "Mind if I ask what your shift is?"

The officer answered. "We're in the neighborhood, eight to eight. Twelve-hour night shifts." He peeked inside the restaurant at the workers. "We haven't heard of any troubles here. Any reason in particular for the cameras?"

Baebin sized up the two officers and decided to test them. "What if I said there is a group that has been known to harass the owners for years? The ringleader is coming back to town, and I don't trust that he will leave the family alone."

Both men stiffened and crossed their arms. "That's very disturbing. MinGo is always one of our favorite places on the route. We've only been here for a little less than a year, but we can ask around for any known troublemakers we aren't aware of."

Baebin crossed his arms, as well, pleased at their response. "How difficult would it be to add a few extra passes? Especially just after they close or before they open. At least for a little while."

"That's easy. Won't be hard to adjust our route."

Taking another risk, he had to ask. "How well do you know Inspector Goe?" The officers looked at each other before grunting. Their eye roll was louder than an earthquake. "Mmm. You interested in picking up some work from me? Off the books?"

The cameras went live, and sixteen hours later, Nam Song-Ye returned to Seoul.

Baebin continued to rotate between the dorm and the apartment. The late nights and early mornings were just too hard on him to go back and forth every day. He hated being apart from Go-Ri, but if she followed the plan, she would be safe.

Number one: stay away from MinGo.

Number two: don't be alone outside of her locked studio.

The day after returning to the Campus, Nam Song-Ye strolled into the large cafeteria with his teammates from Xscape as the conquering hero.

Miffed at the muted response, he scanned the room. Newer groups he didn't know or remember filled most of the tables. But he was their *sunbae*, a senior in age and experience, who was supposed to be revered, not ignored. They were supposed to know *him*, not the other way around.

Kyong tapped the table for attention as his eyes narrowed over Jaemin's shoulder. No one moved. Those on his side of the rectangular table, with a view of the door, watched Song-Ye and the rest of Xscape closely. They groaned in unison when the group spotted them.

Seven men kept to their seats, playing with their food as Song-Ye swaggered across the room. It was all Baebin could do not to beat him to a pulp right there.

Nam Song-Ye quickly realized that to regain his popularity at SKEC and rise even higher in the ranks, he needed recognition from the current alpha pack. It irritated him to no end that it was his former group, IN7. Today, he would bow and scrape just enough to get what he needed.

Tomorrow, *everyone* would know their place.

Reaching his former trainee teammates, Song-Ye slapped the table and leaned down. His overt cheerfulness contrasted with the calculating gleam in his eyes. "Hey! I'm back! Sorry, I was too busy to stay in touch. I did so many commercials and concerts in Japan, it was crazy! The recording sessions were insane!"

Song-Ye made sure to brag just loudly enough for the neighboring tables to hear. The newbies around them needed to learn *he* was the cool one. "I was so busy; they couldn't get enough of me over there."

No one at the table stood to greet him or offer a chair. "Mmm. Glad you had a good time. We were busy, too," Jaemin responded.

Winning the MAMA, all of them thought. *Bite that one, pipsqueak.*

"Speaking of, we should go." Yejoon tossed down his napkin, and as one, they all stood. Carrying their trays, they filed past Song-Ye without a single look, leaving the man fuming in their wake.

Daeho glanced over his shoulder at everyone. "I'm *not* going to be the one to tell *Gongjunim*. I don't want to see her cry." Everyone agreed. "Dang it, I'm hungry!" he added. "I didn't get to eat anything!" Everyone agreed on that, too.

Song-Ye watched as the smug assholes walked away from him. He hated the snobs years ago, which is why he took a chance with a different group geared more toward rap and harder music. It burned him when IN7 debuted faster and climbed the charts higher.

Going to Japan was supposed to be his breakout season, but he hated it there. His manager at JA wasn't a pushover like Mr. Ha. Constantly shuttled from one event to another, barely understanding the language, he had no freedom to party.

The only chicks he met were from the company. All were skinny, flat-chested, and not worth his time. He liked meat—like Choi Go-Ri. She was trim without being scrawny and had plenty enough boobs and butt to grab and squeeze. The perfect hourglass.

He stripped her in his mind again. Remembering the night he almost had her. She was half naked and felt prime. If only they hadn't been in that dirty alley. And if only she hadn't opened her mouth. Next time would be better, and she couldn't stop him.

Now that he was back, he was *going* to top the charts, no matter what. Either with his group or solo, if he had to. And he was *going* to finish that date. *I know she must have missed me while I was gone.* She hadn't been at the restaurant last week, but he would find her. Soon.

Go-Ri chafed at the new confinement, but it was better than running into Song-Ye. Every moment she stepped outside, she felt afraid.

Once again, she kept her head down and blended in with the crowd. When she did screw up the courage to eat in the smaller dining hall closest to her building, it was always in the company of one or more of the IN7 boys or with a group of musicians. She missed visiting the dance hall. Missed sitting outside in the sun. Missed being able to breathe.

Each week, she printed out Nam Song-Ye's schedule supplied by Mr. Jong's secretary. She had it taped on the wall next to her desk. She knew Song-Ye's movements better than he did.

If any changes arose, Go-Ri received a phone call, and she added it to the page. If he was even remotely close to her building, she locked herself in her room with the shades pulled down. Her walks to and from the car were in the company of security guards or the guys and only took place when he was guaranteed to be busy elsewhere.

Gongjunim was only alive on Tuesday nights. Dinners continued as planned. Sometimes, it was only a handful of people; other weeks, it was elbow-to-elbow.

What Go-Ri loved more than the eclectic mix that ranged from dancers to accountants was blending friends and family. She loved the children who ran through her home, and she secretly dreamed of having her own.

They'd purchased a second and then a third portable table, but *still*, people had to find room on the bench or the floor.

Song-Ye grinned, looking around the old, familiar recording studio. *God, it's sweet being back in the booth. The Japanese studios were high-tech but cramped, and the staff was rude. They didn't even try to speak Korean.* Dancing was nice, and he loved seeing his fans in person, but the recording studio was where the magic happened. Mr. Ha took forever arranging sessions for him in the sound building, and he was only granted a few hours at a time to record his first solo album.

What he really needed was a few modeling and commercial jobs to raise his brand recognition within Korea. If he was going to beat Baebin and his group, he needed more popularity. *That's what I need to do. Solos and modeling. I've got the looks, and modeling is a snap. I'll be the alpha around here again in no time.*

Song-Ye stopped by the main office that filled the bottom-center floor and served both wings of the U-shaped sound building. He nodded to the frumpy, plain secretaries working behind the counter as he made his way to the hundreds of mail cubbies that lined one wall. He hadn't checked his box since coming back and hoped he had a few new song ideas in it.

"Hello, Ms. Han! You are looking beautiful today!" a voice behind him called out jovially.

Song-Ye peeked over his shoulder at the musician with a twisted neck strap who leaned against the counter. A pudgy secretary perked up and joined him, slapping his hand playfully.

Well, she's decent enough… if she'd lose thirty kilos and dump the outdated sweater. He pulled everything out of his box. Most of his mail was a year old; only the top three or four memos were new and still worthless.

Everything was headed for the trash bin when his ears pricked up.

"I can't find Choi Go-Ri. Can I leave a note in her box?"

Song-Ye sidled closer and studiously opened every bit of mail while listening to the gossipers chatter away without paying him any attention.

"Oi! I haven't seen her in days. Her neighbor swears she's here, though, and hiding in her office. Maybe she's working on some new piece." Ms. Han leaned in for a conspiratorial whisper. "Even Mr. Kae told us not to bother her, and her drop-ins are canceled until further notice. What do you think she's working on?"

She took the musician's pink sticky note from the memo pad and stuffed it into a box that was already overflowing before returning to her spot at the counter. They weighed all the options of Ms. Choi's secretive work until they ran out of ideas.

Song-Ye gathered up his papers and hunted for a trash can, casually strolling past the bank of cubbies. He read the label.

Choi G - Rm #329

He stood in the spacious, three-story foyer, unsure of what to do. He was going to be late for a fitting, but this was something he couldn't let go. *If it's really her, I can't miss this chance.* How many Go-Ri's were there who wrote music?

Mr. Ha was a pushover, and Song-Ye could do what he wanted, but since Japan, everything had been strange— like he was being monitored. He'd gone to MinGo a few times but hadn't seen her. His old buddies from school hadn't seen her lately either.

Taking the nearest set of stairs, he bounded lightly up three flights. His heart was racing, not from exertion but with anticipation. Along both sides of the hall, light spilled through the half-glass doors in an almost rhythmical pattern, but a shade pulled down on the right disrupted the beat:

Left light, right light, space, space. Left light, right light, space, space. Left light, *right shade*, space, space.

He squinted around the edges of the lowered shade but couldn't see anything aside from a piano and a dirty whiteboard. A door down the hall opened, and a small man shuffled papers to his other hand, hunting in his pockets for his keys. Song-Ye promptly knelt and tied his shoelace.

The man hurried past, clutching his files. "She's not taking visitors and doesn't like notes under her door." He was gone before Song-Ye looked up.

Song-Ye scanned the hall again and took another peek around the shade. The bottom, up just a millimeter, gave a better view. It was *his* Go-Ri. Just as in high school, she sat cross-legged at her desk with pencils stuck in twists of hair. But the short school skirt and knee socks that she wore back then were much sexier than her long skirt today.

He scrubbed at his crotch, remembering how soft her thighs felt in the alley. The pants she wore at her mom's restaurant defined her shapely butt and were still a joy to touch every time she passed by his table, but his favorite would always be the school mini skirt.

Another neighboring door opened, and conversation filled the hall. Now that he knew where she was, he would come back. He could wait to restart his relationship with Choi Go-Ri.

Go-Ri compared the printout on the wall to her watch. Yesterday, she was notified that Song-Ye had access to the B wing from one o'clock to four o'clock. It was half past four now.

Changing to a Miles Davis CD, one with his second quintet and Herbie Hancock on piano, she sat back and cleared her mind. Listening to Miles play was the main reason she wanted to learn the trumpet next. She focused on the music and the waves of notes that sighed and flowed until she heard seven taps on her door.

Yejoon stood in the hallway, grinning down at her. She could get used to an escort as hot as he was—that is, when Baebin was unavailable. "Coast is clear, *Gongjunim*. I saw him go into the design building on my way here."

She packed up her satchel as he took a moment to listen to the trumpet before turning off her stereo. Locking the door behind them, she looked at her knight in shining armor, smiling for the first time this afternoon.

Holding out an elbow, Yejoon bowed. "Shall we, m'lady?"

Laughing, she took his proffered arm and rested her head on his shoulder for a moment. "You are my favorite visitor today."

Yejoon sniffed in mock dismay. "I'm sure you'll say the same thing to Jaemin tomorrow."

"Mmm. Probably," she agreed, chuckling. "But thanks for being today's bodyguard." Ruefully, she added. "I'll be glad when this is all over. You're sweet. I'll never forget what you all are doing to help me."

He ruffled her hair lightly as they set off down the hall and out to their cars. They talked the whole way and parted at the gate. He turned left to his next gig, and she turned right to go home.

It was painful to watch Go-Ri withdraw and hide again. Day after day, everyone could see her wearing down. The nervous, scared girl they'd first met returned in full force. Each of them wanted to smother her with love and protect what was theirs—and *only* theirs.

Baebin wept at the loss of all her effort to come back out of her shell.

Once again, multiple personalities seemed to split from the one she'd worked so hard to reclaim. As they drove over the bridge to the Campus, she seemed to withdraw into her old insecurities. On the drive home, he never knew which girlfriend would return. Most of the time, she was funny and loving. But other times, he wondered if he'd gotten into the car with the devil himself.

He took it in stride. She had every right to be moody. But once or twice, he locked himself in the studio with headphones on.

Thanks to Manager Kim, Baebin played with his schedule as much as he could. He hadn't been home this many nights in a work week since… *ever*.

For a distraction, they grew braver and started going out together around Seoul to see the Christmas lights along the Cheonggyecheon stream and shop for presents. Their neighborhood didn't feel safe any longer, but as they ventured further out to more populated tourist spots, they were noticed.

As they feared, pictures started cropping up. News of the mystery couple hit the top five Korean internet search results. Baebin dyed his hair back to dark brown, but he was still noticeable. Even bundled up in long, thick coats and swaddled in scarves, he couldn't avoid the super sleuths wondering at the identity of the woman who always accompanied him.

Most of *Echos* loved that he had a girl and cheered for him. Others were furious that a stranger had stolen him away.

The angry posts on the *Echos* page bothered Go-Ri the most. She loved all the guys, but she wasn't worth ruining all they had worked for. One particularly nasty anti-fan post threatening harm to several IN7 members pushed Go-Ri over the edge, and she called for a private Tuesday Dinner.

"I've never wanted to interfere with what you do," she told the group, doing her best to hold back the tears. "I don't know what I would do if any one of you got hurt because of me. I couldn't live with myself if I were the reason for trouble with *Echos* and IN7. You guys come first. I should leave." She glanced at Baebin. "We should... stop all this."

Seven men stared at her like she had sprouted three heads. Then her ears throbbed with their deafening chorus of rebuttals.

"You don't want us to get hurt? What do you think your leaving would do to us? To *me*? That would be worse than anything some dumb 'anti' could do!" Baebin exclaimed. His friends fully supported him. "I told you long ago, who I am and what I do are two separate things. And *you* are a part of my real life. If you ever break up with me, it better be over something I did, not because of some idiotic, lame weirdo I've probably never met!"

Daeho threw a radish at her. "If you leave him, then you leave all of us, and we won't stand for it." The rest joined in, pelting her with food until she promised to never say something like that again.

In the bathroom that night, she picked sticky rice out of her hair and found grains that fell into her shirt. Baebin lay in bed with his back turned to her. Just before Go-Ri's alarm went off she felt him curl around her.

"Please don't say anything like that again. Do you have any idea how much that hurt me?"

His deep husky voice, laden with emotion, made her want to weep. Rolling over, she buried her nose in his collarbone. "I'm sorry. I only meant to protect you and everyone else."

"I know you meant well. But don't worry. Let us handle it." Baebin swiped at his nose and rested his cheek on her head, pulling her closer.

Two days later, Manager Kim, Baebin, and Go-Ri were summoned to the publicity office to handle the growing PR problem. They both knew it would happen, eventually. Like other celebrities, who often had it rough, trying to have a private life in the public eye, it was time for them to face it, too. Baebin would go live with the truth while the company battled the threats.

The next day, Baebin hosted a vlive from their couch to address his fans. Go-Ri sat behind the phone stand, watching him. The other six chimed in throughout the rest of the day with their own videos, confirming that Baebin was dating, and they supported the couple whole-heartedly, which dispelled any rumors that they were against the relationship.

Within a week, the top spot at the best celebrity interview show changed, and IN7 was on set. The guys snuck Go-Ri in as a makeup artist for the group.

The initial questions for the group touched on their latest album, but Baebin quickly became the focus. One by one, he answered the questions, using the scripted lines the PR department helped him craft.

The host had one specific question to ask at the end. "When you sing now, are you singing to her or the fans?"

He'd memorized his answer down to how and when to pause and every inflection in between. But he spoke truly from his heart and only looked at Go-Ri off-camera.

"I love my fans deeply. I'll always sing to and for you. But having this amazing girl in my life has also given me a new understanding of what I have been singing about all along. I knew what I *wanted* love to be like, and I now understand what it really *feels* like. I hope to share what I'm learning with you and that you feel it, too. I hope you like how she has helped me grow."

Then, the show went off the rails.

The host asked the others, "When they talk privately, is it boring, 'how was your day?' or is it mushy stuff? Who's mushier, him or her?"

Daeho took over. Of course, he would.

Finger phones held to both ears, he imitated the couple, making kissy faces and coos to each side in turn. Then, as the rest of the members watched, he ran around the set, stuffing tissues in his ears and rolling around on the ground, pretending to hold a pillow over his head while gagging. Finally, running offstage, he yanked off a cameraman's headset, placed it on his own head, and returned to his chair to face away from the group, pouting.

The entire set dissolved in hysteria. Baebin's unstoppable laughter rang out over all the others' as he doubled over, clutching Daeho's turned back.

Go-Ri and the rest of the real makeup crew snorted painfully, trying to muffle their giggles. Even Manager Kim couldn't hold back his laughter. He was known in the industry for many things, but his sense of humor was not one of them. Yet, if anyone could get him, it was Daeho.

At the end, the host grabbed Baebin's arms and slyly jerked his head off-set. "She's cute. I'm happy for you," he whispered. Baebin's eyes widened and flitted automatically to Go-Ri. The host hooted in laughter—he took a chance and guessed right. Winking at Baebin, he added, "Your secret's safe with me. Just give me the exclusive when you propose." He walked offset, wishing he knew how to click his heels.

In January, just before their India trip, Go-Ri texted Tae-Si.

G: ROOM 103A @ 10.
T: K! CAN'T WAIT!

Her first project was complete. Nine musicians sat crammed into a recording studio as three of the songs Tae-Si had helped her record all those weeks ago became official. Mr. Kae's original love ballad became a soundtrack for a new historical film, due out next year.

Go-Ri and Tae-Si huddled in the corner, holding each other tightly as they listened. Neither could stand still, and Tae-Si secretly recorded the music on his phone.

The entire IN7 dance room listened to the playback. A few hours later, Go-Ri's tiny studio overflowed with flowers.

The tour in India was going great. Even with all the stage, costume, and dance changes, it was smooth sailing.

They were three days from returning home when it was Baebin and Chinmae's turn to room together in Mumbai. Both guys were looking forward to a quiet night. They were always together, but it was hard finding time to just unwind alone and do their manly version of girly talk.

Baebin felt guilty for the past few months, focusing on his own problems. It was his turn to give back and be a friend again. They lay in their beds and talked all night.

Just before nodding off, Chinmae asked, "When are you going to propose?"

"Very soon. I can't wait much longer. I'm really glad you like her."

Go-Ri checked her watch. *Where is the security guard? I need to leave now if I'm going to make it home for my six o'clock lesson.* Verifying Song-Ye's schedule with what she memorized, Go-Ri fumed. *He's in a practice session. I can't wait any longer, or I'll be stuck for another hour.*

With her phone and music bag in one hand and keys in the other, she trotted quickly through the crowded parking lot, keeping her eyes focused on her shiny red car. She knew just how far away she had to be to hit the remote button and start the engine.

A hand closed over hers as she touched the handle.

"Oh, aein. Here you are." His hot breath sent white steam flooding around her neck in the cold air. The wispy tendrils nearly knocked the wind out of her. *Right words. Wrong* person. The one person she never wanted to see or hear from again. The dissonant sound of "aein" on his lips screeched in her ears.

Her entire body seized as her stomach curdled and her mind rebelled.

"I have been looking everywhere for you; didn't you know that? Imagine, you've been here, waiting for me! You're so sweet." Song-Ye caressed her knuckles before kissing the tender spot under her ear.

From his vantage point, he enjoyed the fluttering pulse in her throat and the view down the modest V of her shirt, barely visible inside the gap of her long, wool trench coat. He remembered touching, squeezing, holding those soft breasts. He grew stiff with desire to touch her again and pressed himself closer to her backside.

Don't vomit. Don't faint. Breathe.

Go-Ri clutched the lapels of her coat together with one hand, shielding herself from his gaze and breath. Her world folded in on itself like an origami finger box. Tighter and tighter, it pinched in, blocking all light and sound around him. His rancid breath, his sweaty body pressing into her, the disgusting wet spot he left on her neck.

Breathe. Don't faint. Run. the quiet voice whispered in her brain again. The small sliver of her mind that still functioned hunted for purchase as she reeled. Instead of his fishy lunch breath, she found the faint smell of gas fumes and clung to it. The car, already running and warm from the bright sun, purred nicely under her fingers. The monster behind her in the reflection had dyed his hair a weird, pineapple-yellow. Small curls of steam spiraled off his sweaty, smelly body. His eyes were gray—not red, like in her nightmares. The demon was just a man.

She inspected herself in the window as if she were judging a stranger. She wasn't hurt. She wasn't bleeding.

Get in the car. Move. Go.

With every ounce of strength she had left, Go-Ri pushed back, jerked the handle, and threw herself inside, almost catching his fingers as she yanked the door shut. Slamming the gear into drive, she blew out of her parking spot, narrowly missing Song-Ye's toes in the process.

That bitch! Song-Ye smashed a hand on the trunk as she sped away. *What just happened?* She must have just been surprised. *She'll be crawling back for forgiveness soon.*

She barely gave the guard time to open the gate before flying through. The seatbelt buzzer droned on for three blocks before she realized she was in the clear. She pulled over to puke.

Go-Ri desperately searched her phone for someone, *anyone*, who could help her, but she vetoed each of them. They were all either working or out of the country. Hysteria threatened to consume her as she finally broke down.

Panicked and stuck, she had no choice but to go through it alone. Sucking in air through snot-filled nostrils and pushing it out of her mouth, she focused on the beat of her heart and imagined Baebin whispering in her ear.

Breathe in, aien. Breathe out.

The supremely satisfying new-car smell gently seeped into her brain. *The new car that Baebin bought for me.* The seat heater was warm and comforting. Prying an eye open, she counted the pages of her music that fell out of her bag onto the floorboard. *Her music.* The new piece she was creating. She fixed both eyes on the silly kitty-cat bobblehead Baebin stuck on her dash just before he left for India.

She flicked its head, which careened in every direction before settling into a gentle, nodding rhythm. Up and down. Up and down. The cross-eyed, goofy, plastic cat nodded and eyed her as she eyed it back.

Go-Ri watched the metal pendulum swing at sixty-two beats per minute, back and forth across the pyramid base with a gentle, persistent *tick* that droned alongside the beautiful melody from the Steinway. Thankfully, her student didn't need any detailed instruction—only a few reminders to watch key phrases or correct her fingering through an arpeggio.

The girl's college scholarship piece had to be perfect, down to the note. Chopin's "Nocturne" required precision, and she was almost ready. Chopin was good for the soul. By the end of the lesson, Go-Ri could smile again.

Calm and in control, Go-Ri gave herself only two tasks before crawling into bed.

Sitting in Baebin's office chair in the studio, she composed a short but detailed email to Mr. Jong and Mr. Kae, spelling out exactly what happened in the parking lot. At the last minute, she added Inspector Goe. He was a jerk, but his harping about the lack of evidence was true. *Nothing can be done about the past, but going forward, things will change.*

She debated adding Manager Kim to the email, as well, but nixed the idea. He was overseas and would probably blab to Baebin, who would freak and be on the first plane home, tour or no. *I'll tell him later.*

Right now, she was safe and unhurt. She hadn't done a stellar job of handling it, *but pretty freaking good,* she thought to herself. She'd count it as a win.

The second task was easier and just as important. Go-Ri doused Baebin's pillow in the cologne he had forgotten and held it tight until she fell asleep. Two days, and she'd have the real thing back next to her.

All the work they did leading up to the short India tour was worth it. No one made mistakes, and the trip went perfectly. Even with all the changes and the stress that went with it, the small tour was easier than the two months in America.

Baebin loved seeing new countries and being on stage. He loved the welcome-home sex even more. Nothing beat Go-Ri jumping on him the minute he walked in the door.

The euphoria of the homecoming melted soon after he arrived, and Baebin quickly grew anxious. Nothing seemed to be going right. He was getting tired of hearing "I'm fine" from Go-Ri when she obviously wasn't. Whenever he asked about her time alone, she would turn the tables and pepper him with questions about his trip.

Song-Ye didn't help. A week after returning from India, his overly fake friendliness grew cold and watchful. The guy was getting under his skin. They never had a good relationship, but now, Song-Ye felt… *different*. Calculating. Baebin never had a stalker before and now understood how creepy it felt.

The free evenings Baebin arranged to spend with Go-Ri slowly disappeared as work piled up. IN7 cycled through TV, radio, and internet shows, hyping their song and rallying their fan base for the upcoming February award shows.

The schedule Baebin created with Manager Kim for the *Galaxy* launch was almost finished. Next, he needed to work on transportation and accommodations for the in-country promo tour. So far, Manager Kim liked his work.

They were already finalizing the song list for the album that would release after *Galaxy*, due out the following year.

Baebin became an official SKEC mentor to a new class of trainees and spent more time in their meetings than in his own. He was best suited to teach and guide the smaller group of wannabe leaders for the new teams, who would become the next generation of K-pop stars. One of them would top IN7 one day. It was interesting being a part of it and watching them grow.

Mr. Park, the CEO of the dance division, who had discovered him and put together IN7, had changed. Or maybe Baebin now noticed who he really was. He liked creating stars and wasn't interested in the minutiae. Meetings he attended were tense and unproductive. Baebin sensed he was a king who wanted the glory, while making the peons do the work.

The cold rain was irritating. It drizzled nonstop for two days, and even under the awning where Song-Ye stood, it splashed in puddles, soaking his ankles.

Go-Ri had been hiding. She still hadn't come to apologize and welcome him home. Each day that passed, he grew angrier. It hadn't taken long to figure out her habits. She was never alone, and if she was in her room on the third floor, she always had the shade pulled down. He left notes under the door, but she never responded.

Every night around five o'clock, someone walked her to her car. It wasn't the random security guard that pissed him off, *but why was she always hanging out with Baebin and his crew?* His blood boiled on the days she drove away with that scum.

Since that time two months ago, when she almost ran over his foot, he had no chance to talk to her again. To touch her. To hold her. *What the hell was her problem? When was she going to learn she could only be with him?*

A quarter after five, two figures walked along the sidewalk under one umbrella. Song-Ye easily recognized her long legs and shapely butt that bubbled below her waist-length peacoat. She was clinging to the guy, laughing as he swung her up and over the larger puddles. She had a beautiful, throaty laugh. It made him horny as hell. And *furious.*

A minute later, the same black umbrella and gray sweats appeared out of the rain. Baebin snapped the umbrella closed, shaking it free of excess water before turning to go inside.

Song-Ye spoke over the patter of rain and the waterfall that fell from the awning. "Stay away from Choi Go-Ri."

Baebin jumped. So intent on the rain and returning to practice, he hadn't noticed Song-Ye standing there.

Everything Baebin researched in the last four months said not to antagonize or respond to guys like Song-Ye. It didn't say don't punch the daylights out of them, which was what he wanted to do, but he wouldn't give Song-Ye the satisfaction of stooping to his level. He wasn't about to be the one arrested for assault.

Ignoring him, Baebin took a step inside. Before the door could close behind him, Song-Ye grabbed him by the wrist, spinning him around.

"I said, stay away from Choi Go-Ri. She's mine." He squeezed Baebin's wrist. A muscle ticked in his jaw.

He really is a psycho, Baebin thought. *Screw the research.* He stepped closer, toe to toe, letting his eyes drag across his enemy. Weird Orangey-yellow spiky hair, receding hairline, gray eyes that should be attractive but were small and lopsided. *Hmm, decent physique… but a bit thin. I could take him in a fight if it came to it.*

Patting Song-Ye on the shoulder, he leaned in close. "You really should get over yourself. You aren't that special. She was never yours to begin with."

Stepping back, he looked around the ceiling for a camera before holding up his wrist that Song-Ye still held. "You don't have to beat someone smaller than you to be charged for assault. This is enough. Let. Go. *Now.*"

Song-Ye hesitated before releasing him. Fury still lit his eyes, and Baebin could feel him vibrate.

As Baebin walked through the lobby, leaving a trail of water from the umbrella, he called back over his shoulder, "And brush your freaking teeth. Your breath stinks."

The first thing Baebin did upon rounding the corner was call security and request a copy of the lobby footage. Then he stalked into the bathroom and slammed the door to a stall. He stood, hiding and shaking with rage and fear.

For multiple Tuesday Dinners in a row, a long string of others' announcements and celebrations thwarted Baebin's plan. At the first one, his sister, now in her second trimester, announced her pregnancy. At the next, Min-Jun was accepted into University to study engineering. Then

Omma and Mr. Bak beat him to the punch and got engaged first.

Baebin couldn't handle it anymore. He told them all in a private message—somewhat jokingly—that they better shut up and show up next Tuesday or never attend again. It was *his* turn.

The apartment was packed like never before. Go-Ri had lost count of the guests around an hour ago, and she called MinGo for more food. Baebin's parents and siblings sat next to hers. Go-Ri's childhood friends, her students, a few co-workers, the group, managers, bodyguards, dancers, and all their spouses… everyone was there.

In the middle of a conversation with Tae-Si about a soundtrack she was working on, Go-Ri felt a peculiar hush in the room that contrasted jarringly with the usual din of the Dinners. Prickles shot up her arms. She glanced at Tae-Si, who winked at her and looked pointedly over her shoulder.

Behind her, Baebin knelt on one knee—with a ring in his hand.

She only had eyes for him. It had been her wish for months. Since before India. Maybe, since before America. Their lives were unique, and that's what made them special. Together. They had accepted each other for who they were.

All those months ago, when she had stopped running and hiding, he was in front of her. Waiting to be seen. To be noticed. She wanted him. To *be* with him for the rest of her life.

Go-Ri flew at Baebin, tackling him to the ground, covering him with kisses. She kissed the man she loved. Laughter and shouts rang out around them.

He thumbed away a tear, and his voice whispered in her ear, just for her, making every nerve ending tingle. "Aein. Please marry me. Please say yes. You are my everything."

Pressing her forehead to his, she whispered back. "Yes. I'm always yours. Always have been. You are my everything, too."

He found her hand and slipped the ring on, but they were both holding each other's gaze too intently to watch the momentous event.

Bodily lifted off Baebin, she was spun from one friend to the next, lastly receiving kisses from six of the country's hottest men. Go-Ri hunted the room for the hottest. Her eyes narrowed into slits when she found Baebin tossing back a shot of soju with his father and Mr. Bak. She would never forgive the elders if they got him drunk. She had plans for later.

He caught her stare and quirked an eyebrow. Slowly, he licked his lip, swiping away a drop at the corner of his mouth. *I'll be licking you tonight.* His laughter rang out loud and clear above everyone else's as she read his mind and fled to the kitchen, blushing.

The two moms inspected the ring and huffed in disapproval. But Go-Ri loved it. The thin silver band split into two rows of diamonds on each side, twisting together in the middle to form a small knot. It was a mirror image of them and would be perfect for her lifestyle. She would never have to take it off, no matter what instrument she was playing.

The moms went to the kitchen to cry and finish the wedding plans they had started the day they met.

It was an insanely perfect, fabulous, fantastic Tuesday— that would seemingly *never end.* Go-Ri dearly loved everyone and was glad they were there for this beautiful moment—but they had to leave. Now. She and Baebin later swore that some friends were staying, just to annoy them.

When the last person finally left, and they slammed the door behind him, Baebin and Go-Ri dashed to the bedroom and flopped down on the bed, devouring each other from head to toe.

It was IN7's turn on the giant sound stage. They were filming two large performance videos and portions of music videos that involved massive sets and several cameras that flew overhead on cranes.

One by one, the members rotated on set for their cameos as they finished hair and makeup. The group shots and short dance segments, filmed by crews using shoulder cameras for close-ups, took the longest to complete, and it all led up to the grand finale, when the wide-range shots began. The buildup charged the sound stage with palpable excitement.

Go-Ri snuck in and spent several hours watching the chaos, amazed by all of it. She could see now what Mrs. Sun had told her months ago when she first watched them record their practice video for "SuperStars."

Seeing this now—along with "Flame," their second song—against the backdrops of stars, moons, and other space props, was surreal.

Near the end of production, action slammed to a halt. Yejoon, in the middle of a jump-spin, slipped and fell. Medics were called as everyone huddled around him, and Go-Ri cried alone for him at the back of the set. They were used to injuries, but this was different. Worse. He continued as long as he could, but the filming ended shortly after. They were done. It would have to be enough.

That night, Go-Ri drove Baebin home. For days, strain and worry for his friend kept him on edge, and he couldn't wait to return to see the group—and Yejoon.

His friend was out of commission. Yejoon was forced to back out of a runway walk, and during their next few concerts, he sat on a stool, unable to dance.

Staring out the massive windows, watching morning workers shuffle in before dawn, Baebin started his third mile and altered the speed to match the EXO song playing through his headphones. He sang along to the music, working on his breath control. He had to admit, EXO— always their stiffest competition at award shows—made fantastic music.

A shrill ringing interrupted the song, making his heart leap. The caller ID caused him to punch the down-speed button and jump onto the side rails until the treadmill slowed to a manageable pace. He answered Officer Kong's call as he started walking, wobbling slightly as he adjusted to the new speed.

Which one was Kong? Was he the taller man with the teenage daughter or his partner with the glasses? "Hello, officer. How are things this morning?"

"Sorry to bother you. You said I could call any time."

"Yep. I'm already up. No worries. You have any news for me?" Baebin grabbed the towel he used to cover the readout screen and mopped his face. Next to him, Chinmae snuck a peek at his screen to compare stats, but Baebin slapped him away with the towel.

"I think I have good news."

"Great. Go for it."

"I've spoken to my friends across the city, and I think I found the diner you were asking about."

"Really? That's great!"

"You said to look for an old-style, classic American diner across from a theater with red lights east of the Lotte World Tower, right?"

"Yes. With movie posters inside between each of the windows."

"Well, we found two. The one that fits best is way over in Ogeum-dong, but the theater doesn't have red lights."

There were over four hundred dong's in Seoul. He had no idea where this neighborhood was located. And Go-Ri was adamant about the theater having red lights. He switched over to a map on his phone to start searching. "Help me out, where is that?"

"At the foothills of the eastern mountains, just before you leave the city. Almost an hour drive from your place."

Dang. It fits what she said about the long drive there and the longer walk back. "Okay. Can you check if there are any cameras in the area? Or if the owner remembers anything unusual? I'm looking two years back—mid-January. I doubt there is any footage left, but I need whatever you can find."

"Okay. I can—mmm. Hold on a moment, sir." Baebin could hear the two officers chatter but couldn't make out what they were saying.

Baebin tuned out the officers as they talked quietly. They were still on duty and had real work to do.

"You still there?" Officer Kong came back on the line. "We just passed MinGo, and we think the yellow car you warned us about just pulled away. We couldn't get the plate number."

It was a gut punch to the stomach, and Baebin tripped as he suddenly grew lightheaded.

"The lights are off, and everything seems okay, but we are going to check it out."

Baebin let out a violent string of curse words as he slammed his hand on the emergency-stop button.

Chinmae, running next to him, jumped in fright, stumbled, and almost fell off his machine. Seconds later, *hyung* was sprinting outside, past the bank of windows, toward the parking lot.

Song-Ye's pretentious yellow Porsche was not in the Campus lot, and the gate guard had him leaving three hours ago. Baebin sent *Omma* a text to inspect the restaurant for anything unusual, then called Go-Ri to find out her location, but her phone went to voicemail. Swearing, he called again with the same result. He contacted the security company and walked in circles, waiting for a backup recording to be sent to him.

His leg shook up and down as he sat on a bench and watched the footage. At the top of the screen, he could make out the yellow car at the curb, and a few moments later, Nam Song-Ye's face pressed against the glass of MinGo as he peered inside. The feed ended with Officer Kong shining his flashlight through the restaurant windows and checking the lock.

Baebin was furious. *Somehow, Song-Ye always manages to slip away.*

Twenty minutes later, a yellow Porsche drove into the Campus lot and parked. Its owner nearly sprinted to the dorm after scanning the parking lot.

Baebin hit redial on his phone again. *If she doesn't answer, I'm calling Officer Kong.* Go-Ri pulled into her spot to find Baebin sitting on the parking block in front of her space.

She opened the door a crack before he could block it. "Damn it! You need to answer when I call you! Go home and stay there. Don't go to the restaurant either."

She blinked at him, confused. "Why? I just got here. I can't go home; I have a meeting for my TV show project and three students today. Did you call me? Let me out." She pushed open the door and crawled out through the tiny gap of space he gave her while she tried to find her phone and the key fob.

Baebin growled in frustration, wishing she would just do as he said. Gripping her elbow, he force-marched her the entire way to her room. She barely had time to hit the remote lock before she got out of range.

She scooped up the note from under her door and stuffed it in a drawer. She would date it and forward it to Mr. Kae to send to the inspector. The first one she opened freaked her out so badly that she refused to open any since. Not everything slipped under her door came from him, but she didn't care; she passed everything on.

Go-Ri meant to tell Baebin about the notes and the incident in the parking lot, but it would only scare him. She was handling it as Inspector Geo wanted and didn't want to cause Baebin undue alarm—particularly when he was so busy with the new album and Yejoon's injury. He was already upset this morning, so she decided to push it off. Again. *I'll tell him another time.*

Tossing her bag onto the desk, she crossed her arms and turned to face Baebin. "What's going on? What happened?"

"Song-Ye was at MinGo this morning. You didn't answer and I thought he may have found you."

She blanched, and her mouth drooped in shock. "What time? Was Omma—or the staff—there?"

"No, the place was still closed. The cops saw him, and I have the footage." He paced around before sitting on the piano bench. He and the guys had agreed not to say anything, but she needed to know.

Measuring his words carefully while flexing his fingers, he looked at her. "We see him all the time on our side of the Campus. I think he is getting… unstable. He disappears, he's acting weird, and he threatened me the other day. He knows you are here, and he doesn't like you being near us. Near me. I don't think it's safe for you here."

Other than his creepy notes, Go-Ri hadn't seen or heard from him since the encounter at the car almost two months ago. She thought the schedule system was working pretty well. It wasn't an ideal long-term solution, but temporarily, it was fine. "I'm scared, too, but I was fine when he found me…" Baebin's shocked expression made her scalp tingle. Her brain slammed to a stop a moment too late.

"He *found* you? When? How?"

"You were in India. He cornered me at my car." Baebin jumped to his feet, shaking off her hands as she tried to still his agitation. "I didn't tell you because I was fine. He didn't hurt me, and I got away without passing out or anything. I told Mr. Kae and Inspector Goe. They have the parking lot footage."

Baebin stretched to his full height and pinned her with narrowed eyes. "This is *exactly* why you shouldn't be here anymore!" He marched toward her until the corner of her desk pressed into her hip, and she had nowhere to go. "So you *know* he's crazy and that he's stalking you again, but you're staying anyway. You're an idiot! You're putting yourself in harm's way, just like—"

They both froze. A fresh new swirl of emotions flooded the room.

"Say it," she snapped. "Don't stop now. Just like *what?*"

He took a step back, hating himself. "No. I didn't mean it."

"Yes, you did. I'm an idiot. Just like *last time*. I'm stupid for letting myself get hurt."

"No. I don't think that."

"Yes, you do. You just said it! It's all my fault. At least Inspector Goe is obvious with his feelings. But you lied to me." She pointed to the door and hissed, "Get out."

He held the knob for a long minute before he murmured over his shoulder. "For the record, I've never thought that. Just because he was a creep, you wouldn't have known he could be so brutal. I've always believed that, Go-Ri. I spoke badly, and I'm sorry."

Halfway down the hall, he heard her door slam and the lock catch.

At five o'clock, Daeho came to escort her. He may as well have told the brick wall all the funny dad jokes he'd heard lately, given her silence. She even drove away without saying goodbye. *Sheesh. Those two seriously need to be locked in a room together until they make up*, he thought as he returned to the other grouchy toad.

It was after eleven o'clock before Baebin crept into the apartment. He wasn't sure what to expect.

The lamp next to the couch illuminated his bed for the night. His lip twitched. She was mad but still had spread out a pillow and blanket for him. His toothbrush and lotion were on the coffee table.

As he walked to the bedroom, the light underneath the door clicked off. "I'm home, aein. I love you." For the first time ever, he showered in the hall bathroom.

He woke, smothered and hot. The feeling of her breasts pressed on him, and her position between his legs made his cock squirm on its own against her belly.

"Stop it. I'm still mad at you." She pinched his rib and flipped her head the other direction sending hair over his shoulder and arm.

"I'm trying. Sorry." He craned his neck down and kissed her head. "He's hard to control when you're around."

She half-snorted, half-harrumphed.

He completed the alphabet and was working his way through the national anthem when he heard her whisper, "I'm sorry. I love you."

He kissed the top of her head again, inhaling her clean-scented hair. "I love you more. I'm sorry. I was just scared. I didn't mean it."

"I was going to tell you, but I didn't want you to worry about it with all you have going on. I'm handling it as the inspector told me to."

"We agreed, no more secrets. Please don't do that again."

She nodded and fell asleep. It was completely unfair. Baebin rubbed her back lightly, staring at the ceiling and the shadows caused by the muted city glow. He started singing the national anthem in his head again.

The next morning, Baebin and Go-Ri sat in Mr. Jong's office, waiting for the spur-of-the-moment meeting he called.

It took over an hour, but when all the parties were on the screen, Mr. Jong got right to the point. "Inspector Goe, you go first. I know you warned us this investigation would take time, but we've sent you Song-Ye's notes to her and a lot of videos, yet I've barely heard a word back from you. It's been five months now. Where do we stand? Any progress on the previous attack or the other incidents that Manager Ha finally brought to our attention?"

Notes? Baebin wrote on the notepad offered them. Sliding it closer to Go-Ri, he tapped the page.

Crap. She had promised no more secrets—but forgot about the notes. Now wasn't the time to tell him. But he couldn't yell at her in front of witnesses.... *He leaves notes under my door, she wrote. I give them to Mr. Kae and the inspector.*

Go-Ri could see the muscle twitch in his jaw as he read it. The glare he flashed her warned of a repeat discussion on secrets. She turned back to the screen, avoiding Baebin's cold look.

The Inspector set the file down in front of him. "I can't tell you about the other investigations, but I had a chance to review the latest video when I was called into work extra early this morning." No one cared that he had lost sleep. "We can bring in Mr. Nam and question him. He will be given a written warning to stop his behavior. Since all these incidents are fairly new, that should be enough for him to back off."

Baebin cut in. "If a warning doesn't stop him, what next? If the time he spent in Japan didn't change him, nothing will."

"If he continues, then the case would be escalated. He will be prohibited from being within one hundred meters of Miss Choi, and he will not be allowed to contact her in any way. Or, at your request, we can automatically escalate the case now. If he were a violent stalker, he could be detained, but because he's not, the prosecutors will decide as they review the file whether there is enough evidence for a trial."

Go-Ri wanted to laugh. The inspector still didn't get it, still didn't believe her. Besides, a warning would do nothing but make him angry.

"I will say, though, once that happens, the investigation would end more quickly, and based on the facts we currently have, any sentence Mr. Nam may receive would be light—maybe a year. And it will be next to impossible to keep it out of the media."

Go-Ri paled at that. A year was nothing, and she didn't want it in the media. She looked across the table at Mr. Jong. Go-Ri had realized months ago that the company hadn't created the monster—he already was one. Song-Ye may have liked and used the fame he'd gotten since working with SKEC, but it only fed who he really was.

She liked the company and didn't want them to suffer. It would only hurt the others, like her co-workers and IN7, who would be wrapped up in the scandal.

But she was tired of being scared.

As if reading her mind, Mr. Jong reached out and patted her hand. "You need to do what's best for you and only you. Don't think about anything else. Only think of what will bring you peace."

With a glance at Baebin, Go-Ri spoke for the first time. "He *is* a violent stalker. I told you what happened. I want to be left alone. He's not going to stop until he is forced to. I want the restraining order."

With a simple nod of his head to Go-Ri, Mr. Jong turned to the monitor. "That's settled. Mr. Ha, you will take Mr. Nam to the station before noon. Contact my office when you are finished." His stare burned through the screen at the visibly shaking manager. "Don't screw it up."

Mr. Jong turned to Mr. Kae. "I am putting Choi Go-Ri on home assignment until the matter is resolved." He continued speaking over Go-Ri's sputtering objections. "Arrange her files and a delivery service, and make sure she has access to video meetings with her department and any musicians she works with."

His orders continued to fly as plans went into motion. Baebin and Go-Ri could only watch the adeptness with which he arranged everything. Everyone, including the inspector, jumped at his bidding.

Mr. Jong stood and buttoned his jacket—a reflexive action honed by living in a suit for thirty years. "We are done here. Everyone can go but Mr. Park. *We are definitely not finished.*" He hit the mute button on the remote console and turned his back on his friend and partner, who had let him down.

"Mr. Kim, you are leaving next week for Australia, correct?" Mr. Jong asked. Baebin nodded. "Okay. I'll speak to your manager and try to get as much time off for you as possible until then. I'm sorry you have to go right now, but we can't have you backing out of the trip."

Bowing low to Go-Ri, he apologized. "Ms. Choi, I am truly sorry for everything that happened. If I could change time for you, I would."

Mr. Jong watched the couple leave before returning to the screen. Hitting unmute, he glared at his friend. "I've been reviewing all the files from your department. You have a lot of explaining to do."

Four o'clock came much too soon. Baebin quietly untangled himself from Go-Ri's sleeping body and padded to the bathroom for a shower. Standing under the hot jets, he relived each delicious moment of their last night together.

He tiptoed back to the bed, gently kissed her forehead, and wiped away a bead of water that had dripped from his wet hair before returning with his travel clothes, makeup kit, and the jewelry he had left on his suitcase last night.

He knew well enough that fans and cameras would be watching the group arrive at Incheon airport for the start of the Australian-South Asian tour.

It was the beginning of a long three weeks, and Go-Ri said her goodbyes last night. She could hear him tiptoe around the apartment before the front door closed behind him.

She was truly alone now. Her heart thudded in her chest as tears burned in her eyes. She wasn't terrified—she was *angry*. This jerk had upset her whole life years earlier, and he still had a grip on her. She wanted Song-Ye to pay. Song-Ye was at the Campus. *Her* Campus. She missed being there already.

Her thoughts spiraled in circles but always returned to what she truly wanted in the deepest part of herself. Love. Music. Respect. All three in equal amounts. All three needed and depended on one another. All three, Baebin, his friends, and the Campus gave back to her.

Months ago, she prevented anything but the smallest sliver of life from entering her little bubble. If Tae-Si wrote her story as a song, he'd say her bubble had shattered into the universe, creating stars that watched her grow... or something goofy like that. Now that she had life in her grasp again, she refused to let go. She could *do* this.

The black May sky was just starting to fade into a weird mix of pre-dawn gray and fluorescent streetlights when Baebin returned to the Campus and loaded his suitcase with all the other bags. The day would be full of hurrying up, waiting, smiling, and waving. For over six years, his favorite part of being a member of IN7 was always the tours.

Baebin loved being on stage, showing off all their hard work over the last few months, creating new songs and routines, and hearing how much the audience loved it. He enjoyed meeting the fans and got a real kick out of some of them. If they only knew how silly they looked as they fawned over the group and waved their banners.

He lived, worked, and breathed for these trips. For the fans. This trip, he was introducing his first solo and the duet with Jaemin. Both were coming out on the next album, and they liked giving the fans a taste of what was to come.

But the US trip, the India tour, and now the Australian-South Asian tour weren't as exciting as usual. He couldn't wait to go—but he wanted to be home with Go-Ri. He'd mentioned it last night, and she threw a fit. She was right; music was his life, and it included trips. He wouldn't be gone forever. Besides, he reminded himself, the welcome-home sex was worth it.

Pushing his confused thoughts away, he climbed in the van and focused on the job ahead.

The ride was mostly quiet, except for Jaemin and Kyong, who said goodbye to *Echos* on a vlive and started recording their first episode for a trip montage blog they had planned. Baebin chatted along and waved to the camera, smiling and giving hand hearts, but soon, he ducked into the corner to be alone.

Pulling into a small parking area near Incheon's commuter lot, they picked up Daeho.

If anyone had a reason to stay behind, it was him. His grandmother, the matriarch of the Chun family, and Daeho's biggest supporter, had passed without warning several days prior to the flight. It wasn't right that he had to leave before the traditional three days of mourning ended.

The guys argued that he should be allowed to take a later flight, but the company denied their request. All of IN7 rode the rest of the way to the departure gates and proceeded to climb out of the van to a flurry of snapping cameras.

Fourteen hours later, they had passed through the second camera mob, ridden another van to their hotel, and argued over who needed the shower first. That evening, Yejoon stayed behind on the floor with his heating pad, eating from a bag of seaweed rice crips he brought with him, while the rest joined the entire stage crew in the banquet hall for the kickoff party.

After two hours of celebrating, Baebein managed to text Go-Ri before he fell asleep on top of the covers, still wearing his contacts and makeup.

B: MISS U ♥

G: HURRY HOME ♥

This was their third trip to Australia, and while two cities were new, this tour wasn't as long or stressful as the debut

American tour or as tense as the India tour with its many required changes. They had much more down time, giving them the flexibility to take in the sights and relax between their scheduled events.

Unfortunately, Chinmae spiced things up in Perth. Touring the Fremantle Market with Kyong and Jaemin for their blog, he slipped off a curb and severely twisted his ankle. Now, during every show, both he and Yejoon performed secretly wrapped and heavily bandaged. Onstage, they acted as if they were at their peak physical condition.

Go-Ri rejected the offer of a personal bodyguard and kept her trips outside to a minimum. There wasn't much for her to do anyway, since she couldn't go to the Campus or MinGo.

It wasn't just Song-Ye they were worried about, but his slimy band of high school friends who still did his bidding. Song-Ye may be under guard, but they weren't. For now, it was safer for everyone if she stayed away. The less information he received about her, the better.

Even if she visited Binna, she first called Song-Ye's bodyguard to check his whereabouts before texting Baebin and *Omma* where she was going. But with Song-Ye sequestered and under strict guard at the Campus, thanks to the restraining order, she was getting itchy from her seemingly overcautious inactivity.

It had been ten days since Baebin left and almost three weeks since the restraining order was issued. Song-Ye hadn't made a move since then, and her relief was tremendous.

Omma put Go-Ri on speaker as she sat at the cluttered office desk with a cup of hot tea and the daily receipts. Since they couldn't be together in person, they spent every chance they had talking on the phone.

"You need to have the new girl open tomorrow, Omma. Your cough isn't getting better. You taught her how to turn on the gas, right?"

"She knows how and is better than Mr. Bak, yes, but she has another part-time job in the mornings."

Go-Ri giggled. Mr. Bak almost blew up the restaurant two weeks ago and singed his eyebrows in the process. For a widower who lived alone for years, he had no idea how to work a gas stove. He was now banned from touching it.

"When are you going to stop calling him Mr. Bak? You're married now. Even I call him Oppa! He's a great guy. You deserve to be happy again, Omma. I'm glad you've moved on."

She could hear her mother's blush in her nervous laughter. The couple quietly married a month ago after a very short engagement. They had been friends for years and didn't see the need to drag it out. Still, they were like giggling teenagers that Go-Ri both loved and ran from. *Eww.* Mom didn't need to know her private life, and she *certainly* didn't want to know theirs.

"I would love to sleep in, but until Min-Jun gets back from his beach trip, I'm all alone until noon. Any chance you could help me tomorrow? Just to turn things on and get started? I can be here for opening time with the customers."

"I wish I could. You know how hard it is for me just to go outside for five minutes."

"I know, ae-gi. Sorry I asked."

Go-Ri sat on the couch after the call, letting a movie drone on in the background. *Why can't I?* Under strict guidelines, it should be safe. She called Song-Ye's bodyguard before checking her watch and texting Baebin.

An hour and a half later, Baebin finally called back. They were finishing up in Brisbane, and the backstage area was in chaos. Baebin held the phone up, and everyone crowded behind him to wave and say hi.

Sweat caked their makeup and made their hair poke out in weird directions. "You guys look gross!" Go-Ri teased fondly. "I miss you!" She spent ten minutes checking in with them as if she hadn't spoken to them yesterday.

Baebin knew his friends were in regular contact with her privately. Each had a special connection with her. Other men might feel concerned or jealous, but he loved it. The bond between everyone around him was precious. He hoped for the same relationship with their girlfriends, as well.

Baebin finally shooed everyone away and had the video to himself. "Aein, I miss you. I wish I was home."

"Aw. You're sweet. But I know you're lying. You're off with your friends, making the world happy with your music. Besides, there is nothing to do here but boring work." Baebin looked so happy. Every time he finished a show, he had a satisfied shine about him. She was the happiest when he was happy.

"Soo... I'm going to help Omma tomorrow morning for a few hours. Her cold is getting worse." Go-Ri couldn't keep putting off the reason for her call. She braced herself for his lecture.

"Absolutely not! I forbid it!"

"First of all, I'm not your slave or your underling, so don't say 'forbid.' And second, I've already checked. Song-Ye is going to be in the gym and then the recording studio from six to eleven tomorrow. Why can't I go help Mom? She needs a break, and no one else can help."

"What if he sneaks out? Or what about his local friends?"

"The guard will text me his whereabouts in the morning. The officers will come around, too, and I can call the guard before I walk home. I'm only going to be there to start up, so I won't have to worry about people."

Baebin hated that it was a reasonable plan. "I don't like it."

"I know. Tell me what you don't like, and let's see what we can change."

"Mmm. Have Binna swing past on the way to work. And keep the doors locked and most of the lights off. No sneaking students in."

"Okay. Done. What else?"

"Keep the cameras on, stay in the back, and text me when you leave." He *loathed* that he couldn't think of anything else.

"Done."

"I really hate this."

"I know. But I'll be fine. I love you."

"I love you more."

For the first time in months, Go-Ri unlocked the door to MinGo as the sun rose over the eastern mountains. The low glare through the windows caught in the still air and shimmered off the wall near the door, making the warm moss-green paint painfully bright.

She hadn't realized how much she missed the spicy, pungent smells of *buldak* and *kimchi* stew that seeped into every pore of the restaurant. It hung thick in the air and warmed her as much as the sun shining in the strangely bright, clear sky. She grew up in the restaurant. The food, the smells, the regular customers—all were a comfort when she needed it most.

Finding a scrap of paper and a marker, she drew a big heart with an arrow and a B & G in the middle. She propped it up on the counter in view of a camera before starting the large vats of rice and soups for the day. When everything was ready, Go-Ri hid in the office and finished last night's billing Mom had left behind. As promised, she kept the door locked and lights off. She waved to the officers when they knocked, and then to Binna when she passed by.

Mom arrived just before opening. She looked exhausted, even with the extra sleep. The dry cough had settled high in her chest and caused a strangled barking sound. "Omma, you need to go to the hospital."

"No. I'm on medicine; I just need honey tea. Go home now before your fiancé calls off the wedding. Thank you for helping me." Pulling on an apron, Mom turned on the lights and the outside sign.

"Things were fine this morning, so I'll work tomorrow, too. Don't stay all day. And leave me the receipts." Go-Ri grabbed her bag and blew Mom a kiss before heading out. She walked down the street and texted Baebin.

G: All finished. Going home now. Love U
B: Love U 2. Be safe.

He included a screenshot of her sign.

He really did check on her. She didn't feel overprotected—she felt *safe*. Cared for. She would never tire of the feeling.

The next morning was a repeat of the first. Go-Ri felt useful for the first time in ages. Finishing her chores, she waited in the office for Baebin's call.

It was barely light in Melbourne when their video came on.

"Aw, Poor Tae-Si!" Go-Ri snickered at her friend, who trembled miserably in the background.

Everyone but Tae-Si was excited about the private jet that would take them to a nature preserve in the outback for the last day of filming for their music video. The entire album was a play on words—'a galaxy of emotions'. Australia had great locations that didn't need much CGI for the desired concept of an "alien" landscape.

Baebin pulled him in for the camera. Tae-Si was green and huddled in a down coat. "He already puked once. He'll be fine."

She giggled. "Hey, Tae-Si, if you're a good boy, I'll make you cookies when you get back!"

He scrunched up his nose at her. "Not funny. I hate flying! This thing is TINY!"

The rest of the guys came into view, tackling the two. "Time to go! Hey, Gongjunim! We'll send you pictures when we get back!"

Baebin blew her a kiss. "I won't have cell service until tomorrow afternoon. We are staying out there for night shots. The stars are supposed to be insane! Be careful, just like yesterday, okay?"

"I've already checked in with his guard, and it's all good here. I'm staying with Binna tonight, so just have a great time with your friends." She waved off and started working on tomorrow's shopping list.

Binna came home to find Go-Ri working magic in her kitchen. "*I should marry you. A home-cooked meal when I walk in the door! Smells delicious!*"

"You're crazy! Go clean up. I'm almost done here. Let's eat so we can drink!"

Omma's cry came through the phone multiple glasses later, piercing her ear. "I gave Mr. Bak my cold! Is there any way you can open again tomorrow? I swear it will be the last time."

"Omma! Baebin is gonna *kill* me!" Go-Ri wished she could clear the alcoholic fuzz from her brain to remember his schedule. Today, he was in the outback; tomorrow, he was back to civilization. *Did he say morning or afternoon?*

"Just stay for the meat delivery. You don't even have to turn anything on."

Ugh. Give her an inch, and she takes a mile. "Fine. I'll call the Campus now. But if I don't like his morning schedule, I'm canceling on you."

"Omma needs you again?" Binna giggled when her friend face-planted on the coffee table. "I see why Baebin would be worried, but Song-Ye is heavily guarded now."

"Mmm. Yeah. But I still don't trust him. Ugh. I need to quit drinking, or I'm gonna hurt tomorrow."

Ever since Mr. Ha dragged him to the police station, Song-Ye wanted to punch something. *Stalking? Me? I'm the famous one—shouldn't she be in the wrong? It's not my fault she's ignoring my letters and hiding from me!* A hundred meters' distance was ridiculous. *How am I supposed to talk to her? To be with her?*

When given the choice, he returned to the Campus. She hadn't been back to MinGo, and it would be easier to get to her in that dinky studio.

They needed to talk. She needed to learn a lesson. *I'm not going to tolerate this irrational behavior from her any longer.* Both she and Baebin needed to be put in their place. But her car was never there, and he hadn't seen her in weeks.

Baebin and his crew were gone, too. That was the only bright spot in all this stupidity. *How could he be on another tour? How was their silly sing-songy hip-hop so popular?* Too much high melody, not enough punchy rhythm. His own solo album was going to blow them away. Put them where they belong—in his rearview mirror.

If she wasn't here, she *had* to be at MinGo. His old buddies said she hadn't been there either, but he couldn't believe she wasn't at the family restaurant. He had to find a way to get there and see for himself. Maybe he could find something out from the mother.

His new leech of a bodyguard barely let him pee without supervision, let alone leave the Campus on his own. They moved his roommate, In-Su, and Mr. Ro took over his bed. The guy was annoying and snored. *Why do I need a bodyguard if I'm not allowed to leave the grounds?*

Song-Ye stood in the bathroom with an ear pressed to the door. *That moron is always talking to someone.* If he wasn't eating, he was talking. The one-sided conversation was dull. The fat toad was discussing his morning schedule again.

"He doesn't leave the Campus until three in the afternoon for a group event with fans. You'll be fine to go to the restaurant in the morning, Ms. Choi," the guard said. "If plans change, I'll let you know right away."

Song-Ye jerked back and stared at the closed door. His anger morphed into delight, and a small burble of laughter escaped him. She couldn't hide from him anymore. Now, he needed a way out of the Campus by morning.

Song-Ye left the bathroom and searched for his wallet. "Hey! If we can't leave, how about I get us a pizza and some beer? Or whisky? You call the desk downstairs, and they'll get the delivery." Song-Ye held out his credit card to Mr. Ro and worked to appear pleasantly normal. Inside, his heart raced.

This is my chance.

Go-Ri's head hurt. Binna always added too much soju to the beer when she made *somaeks*. The light shining in the window was painful. She only had to be here for a few hours to sign for the meat delivery, and then she planned on crawling home on all fours to hide under the covers.

Last night, the guard said Song-Ye would be in the gym at six o'clock, then breakfast, then dance. She had the entire morning free until he left for some group thing in the afternoon. Go-Ri laid her head on the cool counter, waiting for the painkillers and coffee to kick in.

The knock on the glass roused her. Shielding her eyes from the glare, she reached for the lock to let in the delivery guy. She froze. Petrified.

Through the glass door, Song-Ye and Go-Ri stared at each other.

Time stopped.

The face that pressed against the glass outside was angry. As angry as when he was beating her. Her body shook, and her legs refused to move.

He wasn't supposed to be here! He had... what was his schedule this morning? Go-Ri couldn't think. She didn't know what to do.

Alarm. Code. Run.

The pounding on the door frame started again, and the shuddering wood finally drove her toward the alarm pad. Go-Ri's fingers shook as she struggled to punch in a series of buttons—just as Nam Song-Ye broke the lock and pushed inside.

Song-Ye snatched at her as she turned to run, catching a fistful of hair and slamming her head against the wall. "Where are you going? Don't you owe me an apology? It's really hard to talk to you when you always run away."

Not again! I'm sure I got the alarm right. Didn't I? I have to get away. I can't let Baebin down. I... I... I have to... Refusing to look at the monster, her eyes rolled around the space, trying to sort through the floating spots and the pain in her skull.

Move. Breathe. Hide.

He was not a normal human. Terrifying and hideous, the monster towered over her, filling the air around her. Go-Ri couldn't keep track of his hands as they roamed. Clawed. Hit. Hurt. Did he have only two hands, or were there more? She felt the buttons pop on her favorite coral blouse as he yanked down one side, trapping her arm in the sleeve.

His tongue slithered over her skin before his teeth sank into her neck. Slime dripped from his mouth, leaving wet trails on her cheek and down her chest. Each snarling word he uttered grated and tumbled inside her blank head, unrecognizable and greased with the stench of his breath.

Push away. Breathe. Run.

Wiggling an elbow between them, she pushed with all her strength. Her boost of energy spurred her, and she fought harder—any sliver of space between them was a monumental gain. Getting a leg free, Go-Ri drew up her knee, *hard*.

Her aim was off and only dealt a small blow to his groin. Still, the painful jab was enough to escape his grasp.

His squeal thrilled her. Running, stumbling, she almost made it to her phone on the counter when what felt like a dozen tentacles wrapped around her waist and squeezed. Then a hand gripped her neck.

Go-Ri clawed at the hand wrapped around her throat and tried to pull away from the hot breath that growled incoherently in her ear as the monster chewed on her earlobe.

A hand reached around in front of her, grabbing her phone before she could, and she wept hot, frustrated tears when he smashed it to the ground and stomped on it.

On the verge of fainting and giving up, Go-Ri felt a hand fumble at the button and zipper of her jeans. It was his arousal, which he jabbed into her back, that terrified her the most.

No! He could hit her all he wanted, but Go-Ri would *not* let him touch her like that! Only Baebin—only with love!

With one last shrill shriek, she aimed. Using everything she had left, she prayed and flung her head back.

Whatever she connected with behind her elicited a thundering howl from the monster that pierced her ear before he shoved her away, slamming her into a table with its overturned chairs on top. She toppled to the ground amidst the pile of debris.

Get up! Run! Now!

Scrambling to her feet, she looked over her shoulder as she ran behind the counter. His feral, animalistic eyes were as red as the blood dripping from his nose. Song-Ye wavered side-to-side for a moment, then picked up the chase.

Go-Ri slammed the office door behind her and locked the deadbolt that Baebin had installed. She punched the panic button on the alarm, then grabbed the old landline off the desk. She crawled underneath the desk and dialed 112, screaming before the emergency line was connected. "Help! He's here!" Over and over and over. Her screaming and the pounding of her heartbeat sounded off-rhythm with Song-Ye's echoing thumps at the solid, old door.

You're okay! You did good! You're safe now! Breathe!

"Help me!"

Song-Ye gave up trying to get through the thick door. His face hurt, and he was dripping blood everywhere. *Damn it! That bitch!* Out of options, he knew he missed his chance. He'd try again another time.

Rounding the counter back to the dining area, he came face-to-face with two officers. Song-Ye bellowed with fury as they threw him to the ground. He felt a knee press into his back as handcuffs clapped around his wrists.

Binna, hungover and late for work, but keeping her promise to check on MinGo on her way to the bus stop, screamed when she rounded the corner and saw the blue-and-white police car with its flashing lights parked haphazardly on the curb. Running through the broken door, she cried out for her friend, afraid of what she would find.

Officers Kong and Kim, struggling with their captive, could not stop her as she sprinted through the dining room, screaming for Go-Ri. Her friend wasn't in the front, the kitchen was empty, and the cramped hall to the back alley looked normal. Running back to the front, Binna spied the wet blood on the office door.

Binna cried out for help, praying her friend was okay. Wailing, she could only wait and watch as a third officer rushed in and used every tool he could find to smash the door off its hinges.

The toe of one shoe stuck out from under the desk. Hidden behind the rickety, wooden office chair, Go-Ri lay unconscious with the phone still in her hand.

Binna sat beside Go-Ri's hospital bed, watching her sleep. Somehow, she had to find the courage to contact Baebin before he realized Go-Ri's phone was out of service or before someone like that horrible inspector reached him first.

Taking a gulp of air and drawing on her friend's survival instinct, she called Kim Baebin.

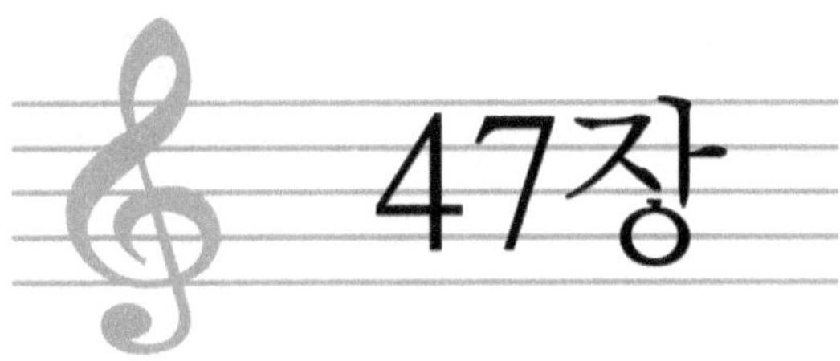

Mungo National Park was the coolest place Baebin had ever seen. With the compacted sand shifting colors from red to white and back and the low scrub brush, the landscape created the perfect backdrop for their music video.

The winter evening in the southern hemisphere at the glampsite under the stars was freezing, but they had more than enough wood for a huge bonfire for the seven guys to share. They celebrated their friendship, an awesome new memory for their travel books, and the completion of one more music video.

Everyone but Tae-Si rode in helicopters the next morning as the sun crested the farthest reaches, highlighting deep gouges left by wind and water in the compressed sandplains. Tae-Si chose to keep his feet on the ground and take pictures of the kangaroos and emus that roamed the area until they forced him back into the "tin-can" airplane for the return trip to Melbourne.

By the time they arrived at the hotel, the staff already had the banquet hall bordering the swimming pool decorated with string lights glowing in the trees, set up for the IN7 "Goodbye to Australia" party. Tomorrow, they would be heading to Singapore for the South Asia portion of the tour.

The guys were caked in sand and dust and hadn't showered in two days, but the crew party came first.

Checking his phone for the third time, he finally had enough battery to call home. There were two old messages from Go-Ri, a voice message from *Omma*, and from Binna... there were *over a dozen* phone calls and texts from her, asking him to call her ASAP.

His skin tingled as the hair on his neck prickled. Yanking the phone off the cord, he retreated to the farthest corner to call, a thousand fears flooding through him.

Manager Kim rushed in from the adjoining room where he had been planning for tomorrow with his staff. He needed to find the boys—needed to find Baebin before he called home.

"Binna? I just got your messages—" Scrubbing his forehead in worry, his hand came back red and dirty.

"Baebin, I... I need to tell you... she's okay, but—"

"Put her on!"

"No. I can't. She's sleeping."

"Binna! What happened?!" Two-hundred heads turned as one at his roaring yell. Six men dropped their forks and ran to surround him, blocking him from the others. "Binna! Put her on!"

"No. Please listen."

"I'm switching to video! Let me see her!"

"No! Baebin. I won't. She'll be okay, but I won't let you see her. Not right now." She could hear his anguished cries, and it ripped her heart out, but she would not accept the video call until Go-Ri woke up. "Please listen to me."

Chinmae picked up the phone *hyung* had dropped. "Binna?"

"Chinmae?" Binna almost sighed in relief. "Please help me. Go-Ri is in the hospital, but she'll be okay. Song-Ye found her this morning at MinGo. Omma is with the police, and I'm here with her. Tomorrow, after she wakes up, Go-Ri will call him. I know Baebin doesn't understand, but I didn't want him to see her like this."

"Mmm, okay." Chinmae replied. "Stay with her. Thanks for letting us know. We'll wait to hear from you again."

Baebin paced furiously in the tight corner. His friends stood nearby, arms outstreatched, either to cage the wild boar or hug their distraught *hyung*.

Baebin had never hyperventilated before and now understood the overwhelming panic and sheer struggle it took to breathe and keep his vision from swirling.

Before Chinmae could relay Binna's message, Manager Kim pushed his way through the huddle.

He looked at each of them before settling his pained gaze on Baebin. He gripped his favorite boy's chin until their eyes met and gently broke the news. "Somehow Song-Ye found out Go-Ri would be at the restaurant this morning. He got his bodyguard drunk and snuck out of the Campus. He left his car behind, so they didn't know where he was until the officers responded to the alarm. He's been arrested. She's hurt, but not as bad as... the first time."

He gripped Baebin's chin harder and shook it as the young man started to wail again. "She's okay. It's all over. It's *over*."

Baebin yanked free of the tight hold and paced in the confined corner before shoving through the barricade of bodies. Grabbing the nearest chair, he sent it whirling and ran out of the room. He ripped the door open, and it swung wide on its hinges, banging loudly as it bounced off the wall.

The entire room went ghostly silent. Never ever had the two-hundred-person crew seen such a wild outburst from the calm, composed leader, who usually laughed and, at worst, gave muted reprimands.

The rest of the friends stared in horror at each other until a tremendous crash sounded from the room next door. The sound was followed by several smaller thumps and loud screeching. Chu Kwan was first out the door, with the other team members and their bodyguards hot on his heels.

Kwan flew through the neighboring door and was shocked to see how much damage Baebin had caused in such a short amount of time. In the middle of the wreckage, between the overturned drink cart and the flipped coffee table, Baebin stood with the second flower vase in his hand. He sent it soaring toward the wall to join its twin. He trembled in a white-hot rage, blinded by tears and screeching between sobbing breaths.

Chu Kwan, Jaemin, and Daeho tackled Baebin to the ground. His fury was so great, he almost managed to buck them all off. He started pounding Jaemin anywhere he could reach before holding him and sobbing into his neck and chest. Chu Kwan clambered off Baebin when he felt his rage subside and blocked the door from all outsiders—including Manager Kim. Jaemin and Daeho held Baebin close. The rest of the guys wrapped their arms around the three, and they all huddled together in shock and grief.

For a lifetime, Baebin screamed and sobbed before being reduced to a whimpering, hiccuping mess. "She's going to run again! She'll hide! What if he really broke her this time? I'm going to lose her!" On and on, he rambled his fears. The others held the same worries as they quietly eyed each other over *hyung's* head.

Kyong and Chinmae kissed Baebin's hot, sweaty head and slipped out of the room to bring back cleaning supplies. All of the guys were gathering the broken bottles and the plaster shards from what used to be a lamp when Baebin spoke quietly from where he still sat huddled on the floor. "Please leave. Let me do it. I made the mess, I should clean it up."

He sat still for a long time, utterly drained, his mind completely blank, until he had enough strength to gather his legs under him. He stood woodenly and started sweeping up the glass. For the rest of the night, he slowly and methodically went around the entire room, returning everything he could to rights.

Finding his phone, Baebin sat back down on the ground and texted Manager Kim.

> B: PLEASE SET UP A MEETING WITH THE HOTEL CLEANING STAFF AND MANAGEMENT FOR THE MORNING. I WILL APOLOGIZE FOR MY MESS.

He sat until his eyes grew heavy and sticky. He wished for his contact case but didn't dare leave the room yet.

A tapping at the door woke Baebin where he lay on the floor in front of the still-damp couch; he was freezing and downright gross. Manager Kim stood outside with his shower kit, a fresh set of clothes, and his glasses. He had forty-five minutes before the requested meeting was to start.

Baebin didn't leave the hotel locker room shower until long after the river flowing down the drain changed from red mud to clear water.

Dressed in slacks, a white shirt, and tennis shoes, Baebin waited inside last night's banquet room, ten minutes early for the meeting. Behind him stood Chu Kwan, Manager Kim, and the translator.

His face was still blotchy but free of dirt and tears; there was no saving the contacts he wore the night before. His eyes were so swollen that it would be a few days before he could put a new pair in again.

With his head bowed and hands clasped before him, he was extremely aware of the staff filing into the room with their curious glances toward the Korean delegation. Everyone huddled around the small stage on one end and watched as Baebin took a deep, shaky breath and walked forward.

Feeling like a school kid about to get scolded, he dropped to his knees with his hands on his thighs. The onlookers were surprised but kept quiet. In a clear, emotionless voice, he began to introduce himself. "I am Kim Baebin. I've been a guest here for a few nights." He paused to let out his breath, giving the translator a chance to speak. "I behaved poorly and damaged one of your rooms."

The translator spoke slowly, repeating his words. Bits of Go-Ri's story had already gotten around, and he wished

Baebin would give him something better to tell the waiting audience. An excuse. A reason.

Instead, Baebin simply pointed to the room next door and apologized again, and with a deep, low bow, bringing his forehead to the floor, before standing up. "I will pay for the damages myself, but I know that does not absolve my guilt. I hope you let IN7 return to your beautiful hotel again next year."

There were small shuffling sounds before the hotel executive spoke from the back of the room. "We appreciate and accept your apology. We'll look into what needs to be repaired and contact you shortly. Thank you for being honest and forthright."

As the room emptied, the staff whispered to each other and glanced his way. The translator leaned in toward Baebin. "They are saying no one has admitted to breaking anything before, and they are betting on how bad the damage will be."

Baebin closed his eyes and tuned out the translator.

After the room cleared, Manager Kim turned to him and said, "I know you didn't mean to do it. I probably would've done it, too. It's good that you apologized quickly. I'll do my best to minimize the repercussions from SKEC." He softly added, "I'm very sorry, and I hope Ms. Choi is okay. Please let her know I'm thinking about her."

The cleaning crew stood wide-eyed in the room that was supposed to be destroyed. Wet pillows were stacked by the door ready to be laundered, towels lay over wet spots on the carpet, the empty drink cabinet listed just slightly to the side, and a few small items, like vases and a lamp, were missing.

They were done tidying in ten minutes and took the bags of trash Baebin collected throughout the night on their way out the door. This was the fastest and easiest cleaning job ever.

Baebin was in the van before the rest of the guys came downstairs. He hid in the far back corner with his knees drawn up to his chin and his coat thrown over his head, dozing fitfully.

One by one, the rest of the members quietly piled in. Yejoon squeezed in next to Baebin in the back seat, stretching his long legs down the center aisle, ready to comfort his friend if needed. Tae-Si came last, bringing Baebin's suitcase from their shared room.

Baebin stayed in hiding, clutching his phone to his chest, agonizing over whether—or when—he would get a call from either Go-Ri or Binna. Not knowing was the worst. He was so far away and had no idea what was going on or the extent of Go-Ri's injuries.

They were almost at the airport when the group heard a soft buzzing and Baebin's muffled response.

Everyone kept their eyes forward—and their ears open. Nothing understandable came from under the coat, and the conversation was short and mostly one-sided. Yejoon could feel the tense shoulder next to him relax before Baebin's head swiveled to rest against him.

Soon, the call was over, and the coat was dragged away a few minutes later. Baebin's hair was disheveled, and his face was sweaty. Saying nothing, Yejoon pulled out his small travel makeup kit and handed him tissues and a mirrored compact.

By the time they reached the airport, Baebin was collected and unreadable. He wore his glasses, a ball cap, and a mask. Daeho was also wearing his mask because of his cold, and the two walked side by side, waving to the throng.

"Aien. I love you. Can we do this on video?"

"I'd rather not. I haven't had a shower." It was a lame excuse, but she couldn't think of anything else.

He had a million things to say, to ask. But he couldn't pick one to start with.

"I'm doing great. Truly. I'm taking a mini vacation here with breakfast in bed." Go-Ri worked to keep her voice upbeat and normal, but her swollen jaw and the remnants of the medication made her tongue thick. "Inspector Goe came by earlier. He believes me now. Isn't that funny?"

Her laughter was unusual. Short and pinched. It made Baebin want to weep. "Mmm. Better late than never, I guess. He always was a fool."

"I don't remember much of what happened, but your camera did the trick. Inspector Goe says Song-Ye was yelling at me the whole time. That he even talked about... the alley. Now, they have proof. So, basically, I'm free."

"I'm coming home tomorrow. There is no way I can finish the tour."

"No, you're not. I forbid it. If you do, I'll divorce you."

"You forbid? I'm not your slave or underling." His lips quirked as he parroted her words back to her. "And we aren't married yet."

"Semantics."

"You'll still marry me?"

"Why wouldn't I? You are the reason I breathe. I know this sounds weird... but I felt you next to me. You were beside me the entire time. Talking to me. I am okay because of you. Now, finish your job, and *then* you can come home."

Binna tiptoed in with a basin of water and a towel. "I have to go. My ugly nurse is here for my spa treatment. Love you."

"Love you more."

Binna stuck her tongue out at her best friend and hesitated before setting the bowl down. "Sorry. I didn't mean to interrupt your call."

"Good timing. I couldn't stall him any longer." Go-Ri raised the cast on her left arm a bit higher for her friend to change the ice resting on her chest and ribs.

Binna washed away the old ointment on her face before adding a fresh layer and an ice pack.

Tomorrow would be a good day. She could change the ice for heat and bury herself in its warmth.

She hated being cold.

"Binna. Thank you. ...For everything." Crying hurt. The pain in her face pulsed through and around her skull. The sudden, hiccupping breath shot bullets through her stomach. "I don't know why you've stuck with me. I don't know if I've ever said how much I love you. You are more than my best friend."

"Shut up. If you make my mascara run, I'll add another bruise right here." Binna pinched her just above the cast. She huffed and swiped at her eyes. "Dang it. I told you." She flashed a forefinger covered with black makeup before giving a peck to the broken arm.

Come hell or high water, Go-Ri was leaving the hospital. Being stuck there was worse than the apartment. She couldn't sleep with all the visits from family, friends, and police. The only upside was that she didn't have to feed herself. The bruising and pain were almost gone, but the fresh nightmares would take a little more time.

Baebin was coming home tomorrow, and she vowed to be anywhere else but the VIP hospital room the company moved her to.

Baebin stood at the closed door and watched her through the little window. Go-Ri sat on the floor, playing the *gayageum* with her eyes closed and a pencil stuck in her hair bun. She was creating an accompaniment to the music playing on a CD.

Her right hand flowed easily, plucking at strings, but her left, hampered by the cast, moved slower. He noticed the tiny, unusual, offbeat mistakes she never made before and saw her frown of disapproval as she flexed her fingers and started again.

This was one of her latest projects, and it was good.

Quietly, he shut the door behind him, and she opened her eyes. Gently pushing the long, old instrument off her lap, she clambered gingerly to her feet and hurried to his arms. Their kiss held deep passion and longing.

"Aein, I'm scared. I don't want to hurt you."

"I can take it. Just don't squeeze." She whispered.

He reached behind for the door lock, and after pulling the shade down, he walked her backwards to the piano bench. They worked together just enough to free him from his zipper, and she shimmied out of her panties. She sat on him with her legs gripping his thighs. His back banged the keys until she reached behind him and slammed the lid shut.

They rode it out, crying into each other's mouths, doing their best to keep any sounds inside the room. Both finished quickly in tremoring waves that caused toes to curl and spots to float before their eyes.

Go-Ri sat on him, panting against his shoulder as he finally softened enough to slip out. "You're early."

"I skipped the meeting."

Trying not to run, they made it to the apartment elevator. It moved too slow for them, and he held her lightly against the wall, kissing her until the door opened. He didn't care if there were cameras watching. *Let them.*

They kissed their way into the apartment, almost forgetting to shut off the alarm system. Baebin and Go-Ri stifled a quick sheepish giggle as she punched in the code with seconds to spare.

That would cause a bit of a pickle. Elevator cameras were one thing, but having officers appear would surely ruin the evening.

Clothing littered the hallway as they made their way to the bedroom. Go-Ri landed on the bed and sucked in a small hiss of pain, as Baebin stripped off his last article of clothing and knelt before her.

"Oi. Sorry. You okay?"

"Stop it. Are you going to ask me that every five seconds?"

He looked up between her splayed legs at her grinning wolfishly. "Okay. I'll stop. But I knew it—you bounced!"

Go-Ri couldn't follow his train of thought until... "Seriously!" She let out a gurgle of laughter, remembering their shopping trip to the furniture store a year ago. His naughty wink made her groan in embarrassment. "You're awful! You can make me bounce next week. Just stick with kissing for today."

"Mmm. Just kissing? But you didn't say where..."

Her groan rapidly evolved to a moan as he moved from her knees up her body. As he did, so did her skirt. He gripped the folds at the waistband, ran his tongue in and out of her center, and sucked on her button. She grabbed his hair and yanked at him until he kissed his way up to her mouth.

He pecked and licked at every mustard yellow bruise he could find before claiming her lips.

She loved the taste of herself on his mouth and loved the feel of him inside her even more.

Baebin was home and back in her arms.

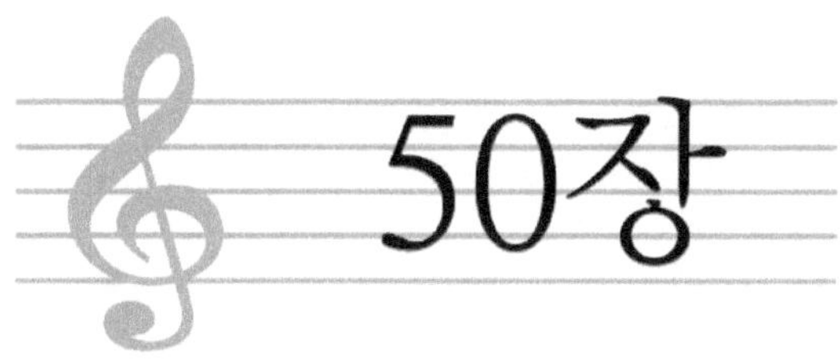

"The trial for Victim A is complete, leading to the conviction of singer Nam Song-Ye. Trials for Victims B and C will begin in a few months. Nam was a member of the K-pop group, Xscape, that had a few..." The reporter droned on as they showed footage of the criminal being led away in handcuffs to a waiting detention van.

Baebin's car pulled out of the private underground garage. As he drove away, Go-Ri held his hand. "Take me to the restaurant."

"Okay. Call Omma and order."

"No," Go-Ri said. "The diner. I still don't even know where it is. I just... need to see it."

Baebin knew where it was. For some twisted reason, he went there once a few months ago. He didn't like this idea, but he would do anything she asked if it would bring her closure. He turned left and drove to the eastern foothills where he parked outside the restaurant across from the alley.

She was quiet the entire ride and made no move to get out—only sat looking.

People were milling around outside the theater, and the new neon blue lights glowed brightly against the restaurant windows. The alley had lights now, and she could see a CCTV camera at the entrance. The owner of the diner bustled around his tables. She didn't remember him having glasses that night three years ago.

Swiping at a tear, Go-Ri squeezed Baebin's hand and laid her head back.

Go-Ri took one of the longest private showers he could remember. Baebin didn't know what to expect, but he had dinner on the coffee table covered in towels. He was halfway through a bottle of wine when she came to the living room.

His heart sang when he saw her dressed in his pajamas instead of her own. She wrapped her long, beautiful hair in a towel. He would never tire of seeing her like this.

Keith Jerrett's piano played over the speakers, and Baebin insisted she eat a few bites as he dried and brushed her hair. Go-Ri ate a little before snuggling into his side, like she did for the very first time over a year ago.

Go-Ri took a self-imposed break from the Campus to organize her jumbled thoughts.

The trial had been painful. Photos of her body at the hospital and copies of the disgusting notes Song-Ye wrote to her were nothing compared to a video clip Officer Kong found of her stumbling out of the alley years earlier and the video evidence of the assault in MinGo.

None of her supporters could bear to watch, but the sound was unavoidable. His voice. Her screams. The sickening sounds of contact with every hit. She felt detached. Mind and body separated. Numb.

A week later, she still didn't feel whole. Her friends and family always believed her, but to physically see it for themselves... to relive it with her, was excruciating.

She brought files home and planned on working at the piano or in the private studio, but mostly, she slept or read. She insisted that Baebin continue his schedule as usual and always had food and a warm bed ready when he could come home.

If she worked on anything, it was her own music. Go-Ri had yet to confide in Baebin, but she was considering trying to create a solo album. She liked the process and the idea that her own songs would be recorded.

Soon, she needed to decide on her future. The mini "vacation" reminded her how much she enjoyed her work in the Composition Department and with her students at the Campus, but she wasn't sure if she should stay. Maybe a new recording company, away from the memories, would be better.

Mr. Jong made the first move.

Leaning back in his leather armchair, he studied her over the rim of his glasses. "We want you back. What will it take?"

He was always direct and to the point. She liked how he politely commanded attention and calmly controlled the room. *No wonder he and Mr. Kae were such good friends.*

"Why? I've caused so much damage to your company."

"*You* didn't. *He* did. We want *you* back."

Setting her cup aside, she faced him. "Mr. Jong, I do want to return to work. I am truthfully surprised by how much I love it here."

Go-Ri drew in a breath and looked at her tea for strength. "While everything wasn't your fault, it bothers me how he was able to sneak away from everyone who was supposed to be watching him. Not just this last time, but all the times before, as well. How can I trust you?"

Mr. Jong surveyed her for a long moment as she sat perfectly still on the couch opposite him. "My company let you down. I didn't know until it was too late what kind of person Mr. Nam was, but I still hold myself accountable. I have fired Mr. Ha and CEO Park. They had a duty to recognize his behavior from the beginning and correct it. They failed the company, and they failed you."

Go-Ri did her best to control her features, but she was dumbfounded. It was her turn to stare. She sat back on the sofa and tried not to let her jaw hang open.

"Will you stay with us?" Mr. Jong asked again.

For ages, she gazed over his shoulder at the picture of the snowcapped Korean mountains soaring majestically above a carpet of purple flowers. Finally returning her eyes to his, she answered, "I have one request."

Two hours later, Go-Ri left the Business Building with documents in her bag. Not waiting for a break in the music, Go-Ri walked into the practice room and sat next to Manager Kim on the bench. Her lips quirked at their startled looks. Baebin was dumbfounded. She hadn't mentioned coming here this morning at breakfast.

Handing her stapled and signed contract to Manager Kim, she giggled as she watched him scan it with wide eyes.

The guys abandoned their choreographer and snatched it from him, reading over each other's shoulders.

"I'm coming back to work tomorrow. And my first job is to knock you all off the number-one position on the charts."

She let out a joyful laugh. "Okay, that will never happen, but I'm going to try!"

Go-Ri looked around the room, beaming at her fiancé and her friends, along with the other dancers and workers, who had all rescued her from the edge and brought her back to life—back to an even better present.

The guys couldn't believe what they were reading.

Go-Ri had a signed contract for four solo albums of her own music. One hundred percent of the proceeds would go to a new foundation that would help survivors of stalking and abuse receive support for their emotional needs, court costs, and push for better regulations in the laws to protect victims. On top of that, the company would contribute thirty percent for every album sold. The foundation would be established and advertised by SKEC, but she would be the lead chair and decision maker.

The contract allowed for additional albums of outside artists, if she covered any potential artist and production costs.

"I asked for two albums at 100%, but Mr. Jong did the rest. I get to record my own music how I want." She grinned sheepishly. "I'll never be as famous as you, but... I get to make my music my way."

She giggled and pressed her fingers to her mouth to hold back tears. Baebin grabbed her and pulled her in for a giant hug. He planted a hard, long kiss on her lips as the rest of the group, including Manager Kim, squished around them, dancing in a circle. The second Baebin let go, they swung her from person to person.

Within weeks, she had a full signup sheet in her mailbox—bands, musicians, sound techs, recording artists, and even video production crews—all wanting to donate anything she needed.

IN7 was the first to sign up, and Tae-Si was already creating a song especially for her.

Several of Go-Ri's students and fellow musicians played as Baebin waited nervously on stage.

Towering displays of pale pink and white roses covered the banquet hall, and their heavy scent filled the air. Bak U-Jin was blushing with the honor of escorting Go-Ri to her waiting groom. Having two boys himself, he never thought he would have the chance to fill this role.

Baebin could only gape at how gorgeous Go-Ri looked when she appeared from around the crowd. Her long, flowing hair was piled on top of her head with tendrils flowing down her neck and shoulders. Countless pearls and beads studded her long white dress. She was strong. Amazing. And *his*.

A pair of wooden ducks sat nose-to-nose on the podium, their beaks wrapped in red-and-blue silk thread, as Go-Ri and Baebin exchanged rings. Their chaste kiss in front of hundreds of guests caused thunderous applause.

Returning to his feet after the customary bow to both their parents, Baebin kissed Go-Ri on the cheek and whispered, "Stay still. I've got something for you." Surprised, she watched as he abandoned her where she stood in the middle of the raised dais.

Running over to his friends, he took the microphone Chinmae was holding, and music played over the sound system. Together, the group created a unique, one-of-a-kind song for the Bridal Serenade. They would only ever perform "Our Love for You" for the ladies of IN7.

Seven of the hottest men in Korea sang to Go-Ri alone, and she couldn't hold back the tears. These men were the love of her life.

The best one of all was now her husband.

THE END – FOR NOW

A SOUNDLESS LOVE

A FUTURE BOOK IN THE IN7 SERIES

Yoo Chinmae slipped out of the Campus's main gates to jog on the streets, skipping his usual morning workout with the guys. His bodyguard, Lee So-Hyun, ran just behind him, keeping watch while still giving him space to be alone—as alone as is possible in downtown Seoul. Winding through the smaller avenues and alleyways in the sweet hour between late-night cleaning staff and early-morning office workers, Chinmae could almost breathe, almost think.

The Campus—a mini music complex built in Seoul by the South Korean Entertainment Corporation—was always loud and crowded. It teemed with artists and staff of all kinds, some coming and going daily and others living onsite in the dorms, like he did, rarely escaping its grind. For just a moment, Chinmae needed an escape from the overwhelming claustrophobia of the place.

Step by step, pounding through the miles, Chinmae kept an eye on his watch as he clocked himself and over his shoulder to see if So-Hyun was keeping up. He knew he ran a grueling pace, but wasn't ready to slow down.

He was desperate for privacy. Desperate for just five minutes of normalcy. Desperate for a break. Jogging around the glow of each streetlight to stay in the fading shadows of the skyscrapers, he managed to maintain his usual tempo until he reached the main thoroughfare of Hakdong-ro.

He looked at his watch again and did the math in his head, calculating how much time he had left before he needed to return to campus for practice. *If I keep running straight ahead, I could leave Seoul and all of this behind. Anywhere would be preferable to here.* He sighed. *What I wouldn't give for a new, different life.*

Acting, singing, and being one of the lead dancers of Insatiable 7, or IN7, SKEC's top K-pop group, was something he was good at, but it wasn't his passion; it wasn't his choice. Whether he was on the set or onstage, he was just pretending.

My entire life is fake.

It was frustrating and exhausting being isolated in a sea of people who didn't know the real him. Even after seven years of living and working with his friends and fellow group members, he still felt like an outsider. He simply… *existed* in their boisterous and lively shadow.

The street grew crowded as the hot summer sun rose, forcing Chinmae to slow his pace. Seoul was a massive city, and the area around the Campus was one of the most significant and busiest sections. Dozens of cars and scores of people moved in every direction, even at this early hour.

So-Hyun, his ever-present and crucial shadow, drew closer, his eyes shifting over the thickening crowd. At the next light, he called for a halt. "Chinmae-ssi, how about we take a break? Let's get off the street for a moment and let this wave of people pass."

It had been weeks since Chinmae last walked outside alone. Even then, he only escaped to the nearest library on their day off and sat reading in the corner, enjoying the quiet. After being cooped up at work for so long, he forgot that his clothes and hair—neither out of the ordinary on campus—were conspicuous and obvious identifiers for the public. Now, he was drawing attention, and encountering strangers face-to-face made his heart race.

Chinmae was about to suggest another, quieter alleyway, but So-Hyun looked like he was going to drop. The short, burly guard was a better wrestler than a sprinter. He never complained, though, and the pair became something akin to friends over the last four years as IN7's popularity grew—as did the need for Chinmae's protection.

He dreaded returning early, but So-Hyun was right: he needed to get off the street. "Mmm, sure. We're done. Let's stop and rest at the coffee shop until it's time to go back. We can get drinks for everyone, too."

He re-tucked his sweaty purple hair inside his ball cap, and they crossed Hakdong-ro to duck into the nearest shop. They found seats by the second-floor windows and killed time on their phones, waiting to leave for dance practice, which started in a few hours.

Tradition dictated that the elder members, or *hyungs*, took care of those younger than them. But Chinmae, as the *maknae*, or youngest of the group and the entire production crew, hated receiving handouts. He felt embarrassed at being babied, at being "less than" or indebted to the others. Any chance he had, he tried to even the score.

Carefully, he bananced two large take-out trays, bearing over a dozen drinks for his friends and the dance crew. He hit the button for the crosswalk at the double-wide intersection with his elbow. Lee So-Hyun stood close behind, blocking the jostling crowd and carrying his own container of drinks for the other guards.

Chinmae kept his head down, and as he tried to work a straw around into his mouth from one of the cups, first one car and then another obnoxiously blared their horns. He looked around, trying to find the reason for the commotion, and spotted a wounded, frightened dog struggling to stand in the middle of the intersection.

A strangled cry nearby was his only warning before a tiny girl ran past him toward the street. Impulsively, Chinmae dropped an entire container of drinks to catch her around the waist. He picked her up awkwardly in his arms and spun in a circle, narrowly avoiding a car in the turn lane. Somehow, he managed to keep his grip on the other box and still hold on to the girl as he wobbled on the curb.

"Chinmae-ssi! Watch out!" So-Hyun yelled as he grabbed his charge's shirt and pulled him and the girl back onto the sidewalk and away from traffic.

Chinmae held her off the ground, trying not to spill the remaining drinks as she fought him like a banshee, hitting and kicking him while moaning guttural cries.

"Stop! Are you crazy?! Stop kicking me! Wait for the light!" he told her, still refusing to let go and risk her running into traffic again. When the timer changed and the intersection was clear, he set her down, and they both rushed to the injured dog, So-Hyun hot on their heels.

It looked like a large terrier—starved and flea-ridden, with at least one broken leg. It was terrified and couldn't move well, but it still tried to shy away as they drew near.

Thrusting his remaining box of drinks at the girl, who still hadn't said a word, Chinmae lifted the animal, careful not to add to its injuries. The trio ran the rest of the way to the other corner, out of the way of traffic.

"Ahh!" She pointed, wide-eyed, to a vet's office half a block down the street.

The poor animal may have been skin and bones, but it was cumbersome. Flinging open the door to the clinic, she shoved Chinmae's drinks at a staff member before dragging him down a hall on the left by his sleeve. She threw open doors as they passed until she found one she liked and smacked her palm on the empty table. Expertly, she started hitting buttons on a large rolling monitor, firing it up before picking up the leads and sorting them out.

Thoroughly confused, Chinmae did as she directed, glancing at his guard, who shrugged and lingered in the doorway. Chinmae turned and focused on the girl—*lady*.

She was small but definitely *not* a little girl. She hadn't said a word yet, but she commanded attention, acting like she owned the place. As she turned on other equipment, a staff member handed her an odd stethoscope that Chinmae had never seen before. The monitor beeped to life, and she snapped to a girl running past, asking for more tools—in sign language.

Wha—? He couldn't help but blink in astonishment. *I haven't seen sign language since visiting Grandfather before the Australia tour. So, she's a woman. A veterinarian. And she's deaf?*

She checked the injured animal from nose to tail. After attaching the leads, she turned on the handheld device on her stethoscope, not bothering to lift the earpieces from where they hung around her neck. She read the vitals on the device and the rolling monitor closely.

One hand roamed around, using the chest piece on her stethoscope, and the other moved over the dog's legs and back, feeling for more injuries. Her hands and eyes filled in what her ears couldn't grasp before focusing on the broken leg.

When her staff brought her tools, she remembered he was there. Glancing up, she waved him away like a gnat and returned to her work.

Not ready to be dismissed, Chinmae smacked the table within her vision and answered her in Korean Sign Language. "No. I'm staying."

About The Author

Raised in Southern Indiana, Gretchen has lived all over the country and recently settled in the Western Carolinas. Married to a hard-working husband, they have two wonderful adult children, and an aging furry mutt who keeps her up all night.

Gretchen is a night owl, and several years ago got caught up on recorded shows, so she started channel surfing for something new. She became captivated by a historical Korean drama series which led her down a rabbit hole of all things Asian. Now, she's become hooked on Thai B-Love, Korean dramas and K-pop music. Much to her kids' delight, she is currently juggling over 50 manga books, not so patiently waiting each week for a new chapter to load!

FIND GRETCHEN REDD AT HER WEBSITE:
https://www.gretchenredd.com/
FOLLOW GRETCHEN REDD ON FACEBOOK:
https://www.facebook.com/gretchenredd.author
FOLLOW GRETCHEN REDD ON INSTAGRAM:
@Gretchen1Redd